CLASSICS OF BRITISH SHORT FICTION
(VOLUME I)

英国短篇小说经典
（上卷）

朱 源　徐华东 / 主编

图书在版编目(CIP)数据

英国短篇小说经典.上卷/朱源，徐华东主编. —北京：北京大学出版社，2019.6
ISBN 978-7-301-30460-0

Ⅰ.①英…　Ⅱ.①朱…②徐…　Ⅲ.①短篇小说–小说集–英国　Ⅳ.①I561.4

中国版本图书馆CIP数据核字(2019)第084279号

书　　　名	英国短篇小说经典（上卷） YINGGUO DUANPIAN XIAOSHUO JINGDIAN (SHANGJUAN)	
著作责任者	朱　源　徐华东　主编	
责 任 编 辑	朱丽娜	
标 准 书 号	ISBN 978-7-301-30460-0	
出 版 发 行	北京大学出版社	
地　　　址	北京市海淀区成府路205号　100871	
网　　　址	http://www.pup.cn　　新浪微博:@北京大学出版社	
电子信箱	zln0120@163.com	
电　　　话	邮购部010-62752015　发行部010-62750672　编辑部010-62759634	
印 刷 者	天津中印联印务有限公司	
经 销 者	新华书店	
	787毫米×1092毫米　16开本　19印张　350千字	
	2019年6月第1版　2019年6月第1次印刷	
定　　　价	58.00元	

未经许可，不得以任何方式复制或抄袭本书之部分或全部内容。
版权所有，侵权必究
举报电话: 010-62752024　电子信箱: fd@pup.pku.edu.cn
图书如有印装质量问题，请与出版部联系，电话: 010-62756370

《英国短篇小说经典》（上卷）

主　编　朱　源　徐华东
副主编　常少华　傅　琼　李远征　罗卫华
译　者　朱　源　徐华东　常少华　傅　琼　李远征
　　　　　罗卫华　石晓杰　刘晓晖　杜洪峰　王　丹
　　　　　邵　林　张　伟　韩亚元　杨　芳　陈　莺
　　　　　周小琴　刘丹翎

代序

好的短篇小说集就是一座精品博物馆

——呼唤英汉对照版英美短篇小说经典问世

2016年7月,华东师大校园美丽的丽娃湖畔风景宜人,高朋满座,迎来了来自世界近20个国家两百多位知名作家和学者参加的盛会。这是第十四届世界短篇小说大会,也是首次在亚洲召开的、以"短篇小说中的影响与汇合:西方与东方"为主题的大会。这次大会是由世界英语短篇小说研究会组织的,每两年召开一次。中国作家、学者、翻译家更是积极贡献,打破语言障碍,中外交流,其乐融融;华东师大是东道主,上海文化界、文学界做了全面的部署和多方面的配合,会议开得十分成功,也产生了持久的影响。

及至今日,这使我们应然有了一个直接的积极的理由,来谈论一下英美短篇小说在中国的译介。其中由北京大学出版社即将推出的《英国短篇小说经典》和《美国短篇小说经典》,恰好给了我们一个实体文本,让我们有所依凭地讨论一下这个话题。当然啦,这也给了我一点勇气,让我能够借题发挥,不拘一格,坦露一下自己的观点,开启这两部书的序言——犹如拉开一道无形中被遮掩了的序幕。

一

提起短篇小说(short story/fiction, novelette),许多读者可能不以为然,何必小题大做?时下人们都在务长篇,谁还看短篇,写短篇?更何况是外国短篇小说。花花草草、莺莺燕燕,美则美矣,要不是余闲多多,谁还顾得上?其实,短篇小说不像人们所想象的那样"小",更不是小事一桩,不值一提,要是推介一本短篇小说集,也不至于需要特殊的理由吧?

只要说起短篇小说,人们就会以短小精悍作为其审美特征。可篇幅短小也不是短篇小说存在的充足理由,虽然可以说是必要条件。就文学作品的篇幅而言,可以说,长有长的好处,短有短的理由。在中国长篇小说大行其道的今天,许多人只知道长,不知道短,还要说长道短,就不能不令人担忧了。可我既不是击长护短,也不是主张不长不短,而是主张大家了解短,知道长。这就不得不从长说起,从长计议。

其实,长篇小说(novel),在国外往往等同于通俗小说(popular fiction)或消遣小说(light fiction)。走进一家书店或图书馆,最高的一层就是长篇小说的专库,堆满了顶到天花板的书架,排满了大部头的长篇小说。貌似庞然大物,其实光顾者寥寥无几。而靠近底层的短篇小说集、诗集和散文集,当然也有立于经典而不倒的长篇巨著,倒是读者络绎不绝、流连忘返之地。在大饱眼福之后,出来时也要买上一本,免得空手而归。国内的书店正相反,大部分把长篇小说摆在一层显赫的位置,甚至等同于世界名著。其实许多人看也不看,就直接上楼了,寻找他想要的"其他"书籍去了。这难道不发人深思?

这是什么原因呢?

这是因为,在国外许多有识之士看来,短篇小说才是精品,是艺术品,值得仔细挑选和阅读领会。而在国内,则把长篇小说当作文学经典和代表作,作为某一作家成功的象征和试金石,有的甚至作为获奖的必要条件。不错,据说鲁迅先生当年与诺贝尔文学奖失之交臂,就是因为没有长篇。而沈从文因《边城》获得提名,假若他再多活半年,诺贝尔文学奖的桂冠也许就会降临在他的头上。而《边城》,最多是个中篇。其实,许多中篇小说(novelette)和短篇小说可以等同视之,只是容量稍大,情节也不太复杂,写作上并没有太大的差异。英文本身以novelette兼指短篇和中篇,就是这个道理。而fiction,则是所有小说的统称(所谓"虚构性叙事作品",无论是韵体还是散体),或者狭义地指长篇小说。路遥的代表作诚然是长篇《平凡的世界》,但他的中篇《人生》却是成名作和代表作,较早地拍成电影,在作者生前就获得了承认。至今重读,发现其结构之严谨,人物之生动,主题之深刻,并不逊色于《平凡的世界》。人们也许会说,前者是单一线索,后者则是复线发展,不错,但这不是长篇与中短篇小说区分的关键。

也许按照中国的惯例,对于一个作家而言,短篇只是装饰和点缀——有了长篇而出了名,何愁不能出个人短篇小说集?但这是夹带策略,算不得正途。许多人连短篇也没写好,就写长篇,缺乏训练基础,反倒弄巧成拙。而中篇是成名的敲门砖,进了此门,真正瞄准的目标是长篇。可惜,中篇在中国也不发达,也许在国外也是个另类。几乎很少会有人光顾这个不短不长、"飞短流长"的折中领域。要不就是短篇写长了,长篇写短了。幸而这一"惯例",并非放之四海而皆准,也非举世所公认。

退一步而言,路遥当年病入膏肓,来日无多,却拒绝治疗,而拼命要一口气写完《平凡的世界》,其理由无非是认为,长篇作品在于贯气,若写作中止,则文气中断，再接续实为不可能。看来，路遥的选择是正确的，他的生命没有白费。相反，被路遥视为导师的柳青，作为关中作家的先辈，却因为"文化大革命"，被迫中断了《创业史》的写作。第一部的完成也略显仓促，待到他缓过劲来，重操旧业，全力投入第二部写作，已经晚矣，终于没有完成，留下了千古遗憾。再由此想到，柳青还计划写完互助组写合作社，写完初级社写高级社，再写人民公社，胃口很大，倘若不是好大喜功，也是为长篇所累，终于功败垂成。归根结底，以有限之人生，写无限之长篇，甚至"悠悠万事，唯此为大"，悖论一也。

可是话又说回来，古今中外，写长篇小说出名者多，反而是短篇小说，貌似容易，却难出精品，成功者寡。就世界范围而言，从古希腊的奴隶伊索口述的寓言算起，古阿拉伯的《一千零一夜》、意大利的《十日谈》，到了近代，以语言论，唯有英语中的欧·亨利，法语中的莫泊桑，德语中的茨威格，俄语中的契诃夫，独能以短篇名世。此外，斗转星移，虽然名家辈出，集子不断，但若考究起来，在短篇小说领域，至今称为圣手巧匠者，仍然百不一遇，除了天才与时代因素而外，文体、文类自身的因素，民族语言敏感之程度，难道不也应当考虑在内？

本来，语言问题就够复杂的。文体、文类，难道也成为问题？是的。就写作的难度而言，短篇小说不仅不比中长篇小说容易，甚至更难。且听知者言之：

> 短篇小说是一种极具挑战性的文体，不仅需要娴熟高超的叙事技巧、精巧严密的布局，还需要博大的心志和深邃的思想。真正优秀的短篇小说既不允许有叙述上的败笔，更不允许有思想上的平庸，它是技巧与思想完美结合的产物。（《世界上最精彩的小说》，华文出版社，2010年）

诚哉斯言！

这使我想起美国诗人、小说家爱伦·坡的诗论。爱伦·坡认为长诗之不可能，因为诗歌须让人一口气读完，反复回味，才是正品。诗歌之外，散文和短篇，也符合此原理。书画亦然。

我个人觉得，短篇小说犹如美术博物馆里的古典精品，凡·高绘画、罗丹雕塑、青藤花鸟、白石草虫，皆是小幅作品，方寸之间，显示乾坤气象，而一笔之弱败，导致整幅作品成为废品。哪个不是集终生之学养，得一时之观察，苦心经营，心有所悟，形诸笔墨，才能成功？篆刻较之绘画更甚！

长篇之奥妙，或者说其难处，看来首要的在于结构，因为语言与经验的缘故。短篇亦然。短篇之结构，旨在精巧，卒章显志，出人意料，但不宜过于复杂曲折。而长篇之结构，却是要大气浑成，不炫技巧，从头至尾，一气呵成，容不得拖沓、无聊。如此看来，长篇完全符合此原理者，实乃凤毛麟角。就连有些世界名著，例如《战争与和平》，也不是没有缺点，唯其皇皇巨著，山丘起伏，林壑茂盛，能遮丑而已。更有《红楼梦》，总体设计匠心独运，中间难免冗长拖沓，反复修改，年谱错落，细节照应不周，而续书的缘故，更难免有狗尾续貂之嫌。石涛的《搜尽奇峰打草稿》，顾名思义，更是草创之作，观其结构，虽然巨笔浓墨，气势有之，但缺乏小心收拾，不能说是上品。其原因就是，他是从局部起笔绘制全景，这样的画法并不适合长篇，只能用于小品。小说亦然。

观古人之长篇巨著，如《千里江山图》《富春山居图》《清明上河图》，乃是稀世珍品，而有作者如此心胸和丘壑者，如此精道之笔墨者，历代实为罕见。而如今的艺术馆，尤其是现代书画馆，动辄参天巨幅，除了吸引眼球之外，许多技巧未熟，笔墨未精，丘壑未成，却自命出手不凡，巍然高悬厅堂，夺人眼目，让人瞠目，旋即欲逃走。纽约现代艺术馆里，整座墙壁一幅巨画，或整个展示铺地而来，堆满了瓶瓶罐罐，也令人想起我们的长篇小说，一年据说出两千部，有的人几个月就写一部，可观者毕竟少数，多数艺术残缺，思想平庸，如时下的电视剧，摇头摆尾，重复拉长，捉襟见肘，不堪卒读者，不在少数。这不徒是创作态度轻率所致，与作者的艺术观、文学观，想必也有关系。

作为一种体裁，短篇小说古已有之，以中国文学史为例，最早的先秦寓言，可作为它的前身和雏形，只是因主题而设故事，目的在于道德教训或击败论敌，非纯文学之属；而明代冯梦龙书中的短篇，已具有规模和高度，与世俗生活市井文学相表里，有自然主义之风；到了蒲松龄，人鬼莫辨，狐媚成精，精于构思，文笔摇曳，文言短篇遂攀上了高峰。至于民国以降，乃至新文学运动中的白话短篇，也有不少成就，名家虽不为多，也绝非罕有。倒是后来逐渐衰落了，长篇急剧增长了。这二者之间虽无必然联系，但也不是一点关系没有。世风和心态，体制和褒奖，理论和评论，都有关系。

二

回到英美短篇小说的主题上，始觉得也有一些话要说。

英语世界，原是以叙事见长的，别的不论，就连英语诗歌，也是叙事成分较多，精品接连不断。现代长篇小说自笛福始，名家辈出。近世报业发达，狄更斯得以长篇连载；萨克雷之锋利，哈代之老辣，毛姆之博闻，康拉德之深刻，加上爱尔兰、威尔士，便有乔伊斯之意识流，再加上诗人写小说者，便有王尔德、迪伦·托马斯等。长篇小说叙事传统优厚，短篇与散文，也不例外。美国更是后来居上，华盛顿·欧文、霍桑开其端，海明威、莫里森断其后，作家是黑白并举，作品是长短并收，而欧·亨利，乃跻身世界级短篇小说大师之列，与法国之莫泊桑、奥地利之茨威格、俄国之契诃夫，并驾齐驱。不过，相比于英美的经验论和实用主义，法国审美之感观，德国哲思之神秘，在文史方面，尤见其长。近世以来，法国的小说理论，特别是叙事学和符号学，后来居上，独占鳌头，英语小说似乎有点难以招架，至少在理论上给人这种印象。好在西方世界的现代文学理论，从现代主义到后现代主义，乃是一整体现象，作为文学创作和理论批评，甚至艺术观点和潮流，则是交互的整体的影响。

这使得英语小说的选编和出版，独成别致的景观。

既然是英美短篇小说，自然是英美的资料要充足得多，因为那里是原产地。同样，出版的个人选集和综合选集也要多。个人的集子姑且不论，综合性的集子，以《诺顿短篇小说集》为最全，除了《诺顿文学选读》，还有《小说一百篇》，也是重要的选集。还有一些大学文学课教材，也有按国别分类的，基本上是英国短篇小说选，或美国短篇小说选，而一般通识性文学教材，则是按小说、诗歌、散文、戏剧分类，当然也包括短篇小说。其中大部分集子，既有总序也有作者介绍，还有必要的注释，可以说是应有尽有。这为我们国内的选编提供了原材料。另一部分，是专门供英美学生作教材用的，包括原作欣赏和写作手册，欣赏部分按主题、情节、人物、语言等方面分类，写作部分则有积累资料、选题写作、修改润色等分类，甚至发表推介都有，十分方便。

就我所见，国内的短篇小说选编，大多数直接取材于上述不同的集子，但也有不同的选编目的和方法。一类是原作鉴赏型的，其中多数不分国别，有原文和注释，有的还有思考题。作者介绍，有用英文写的，也有用汉语写的。这类教材，也有按国别分类的，或按写作技巧分类的，例如情节结构、人物性格、象征隐喻、语言风格等。重庆大学出版社出版的《英语短篇小说赏析》，就是这种类型的，全英文的不分国别。南京大学出版社出版的《英美短篇小说》，除了作品本身、阅读资料和思考题是英文的，其他部分都是中文的，这样便于中国学生接受和讨论，除按主题、情节、人物、视角、象征分类之外，还有实验小说，单列一章，附录则有批评术语解释；每一部分，不仅有作者及其创作概况，还有作品赏析与相关评论，是直接针对这篇作品的，甚至还有问题与思考，更有阅读链接，可以说是体制最完备的了。这套书是《英美小说》的修订版，实际上，原先所选内容也全是名副其实的短篇小说，这也可以看出选编者的学术底线。

外研社出版的《英美小说选读》，却是前英后美，长短不分，即有的是短篇小说，有的则是长篇小说的节录，这样混杂的编排，至少在概念上混淆了短篇小说和中长篇小说，应该说是不够严谨的。不过，这个集子除了与选文密切相关的其他内容之外，还有文学术语或文学知识（理论与批评），其中有的是西方文学理论流派观点介绍，有的是对具体作品的分析。可见这个本子的编选的实用目的和学术倾向。

还有一类是英汉双语编撰的英美短篇小说集，例如华文出版社出版的《世界上最精彩的小说》，甚至封面上有"影响一生，感动一生，珍藏一生"的宣传推介语，号称"最美的英文经典"。乍看起来是有点商业化倾向，但实际上却是严格的短篇小说选集，不仅收录的全是小说名家，而且其译文也流畅可读。

本书以中英文对照形式编排，译者均为文学界的知名翻译家和研究专家，不仅原汁原味地呈现了作品的风采，醇美的译文更能帮助我们深刻体会小说的荒诞、诙谐、幽默与真情，感受大师们的艺术功底和写作才华，是广大文学爱好者和英语学习爱好者的必备读物。（《世界上最精彩的小说》，华文出版社，2010年）

阅读这本书的译文，也有这样的感觉，此番说法感觉并不过分。不过，名家并非全是以短篇小说而著名，有的作品长达二三十页，是否仍然算作短篇小说，也值得思考。这好像又回到了何谓短篇小说，它的文体特征和审美特点是什么这样一些根本的问题上来了。

三

该回到我们手头的这两本书上了。

放在读者诸君手头的这两部书，一部是《英国短篇小说经典》，一部是《美国短篇小说经典》，都是英汉对照，而且分为上下卷，可见出编选者的雄心勃勃和内容的丰富全面。两位选编者一位是从事英语语言文学的教授，一位是立足出版界但从未丢弃学问的实业家。他们除了完成自己的本职工作以外，始终在学术研究和出版上谋求发展，而且取得了可喜的成绩。这四卷部头不小的书，就是他们多年心血和努力的见证。大约十二年前，他们就启动了这项浩大的工程，从三千多篇原文中选出一百篇左右，其中大部分是没有翻译的，大约用了三年时间，完成了翻译工作，又继续精选，淘汰掉不满意的，再加上反复的修改，觉得可以出版了，才准备付梓。结果就是现在的七八十篇了。但和同类书籍相比，已经是鸿篇巨制了。

代序　好的短篇小说集就是一座精品博物馆

他们的初衷，是按照《国家英语课程标准》，为大学生和青年人阅读英美文学经典提供食粮，所以这两个本子，只是按照时间顺序选编最好的英语短篇小说，并且提供上佳的译文，并没有其他的条件限制。原文之前有用英文写出的作者介绍和作品提示。原文之后，用英文提供了供讨论和思考的问题，以便于课堂讨论。最后还提供了参考译文。之所以是参考译文，因为短篇小说作家百人百姓，作品面貌各异，语言风格悬殊，是不可能统一的。且不说英国英语和美国英语差异明显，汉语译文也不可能一样。至于如何体现英美语言的差异，并且反映在汉译中，迄今还是一个没有得到充分讨论的问题，也有待于在实践中努力解决。而我在阅读的过程中，看到个别地方还有改动余地的，便不揣冒昧，顺手改了几处，希望能有助于译文质量的提高。

所选的短篇小说，我还是根据个人兴趣抽取看了几篇。英国的短篇小说，看了哈代写英法战争的《1804年的传说》，使我想起哈代的诗剧《列王》，属于重大题材；王尔德写的《没有秘密的斯芬克斯》（讽刺性很强），以及迪伦·托马斯的《真实的故事》（是写一个少女杀人案的，风格凄美）。因为他们三位同时都是诗人，而且代表了英格兰、爱尔兰和威尔士三个区域文化的创作风格和文化底蕴，可以说是有目的地选取。美国的短篇小说，我看了三个不太熟悉的作家，分别是安布罗斯·比尔斯的《枭河桥纪事》（印象深刻，堪称绝唱），斯蒂芬·文森特·波奈特的《巴比伦河畔》（被题材所吸引，但观感比较模糊），还有著名作家梅尔维尔的《小提琴手》，是天才无名声而快乐的主题（结构精巧，寓意深刻）。这几位作家固然是我所感兴趣的，有的是因为熟悉，有的则是因为陌生而感兴趣，多数作品也都是有兴味的，那些随手翻翻而没有阅读或者看了几行就进不去的作品，没有记录下来，也没有留下太深的印象。

我的一个总体印象是，惯于写长篇小说的，要么把短篇作为长篇来写，要么把不能写长篇的资料用来写短篇，而在写法上基本没有什么不同。而不太写长篇的，或者诗人等其他艺术家，他们写的短篇要好看得多，往往有一个特殊的题材和视觉，特别适合写短篇，或者给人以深刻而新颖的印象，令人过目难忘。而专门写短篇的作家，则有自己写短篇的经验和资料，写起来得心应手，令人叫绝，但他们的短篇小说集，也不是篇篇都是精品，写得多了，重复是难免的，所以，真正传世的，值得一看或反复阅读的，还是那几个短篇作品。这便引出了一个话题，也许最好看的短篇小说集子，是集最佳短篇作家的最佳作品的集子。

以下仅举这个集子中的一例，来验证一下自己的感觉。

在《美国短篇小说经典》（上卷）中有介绍安布罗斯·比尔斯的一篇《枭河桥纪事》，我以为可作为代表。安布罗斯·比尔斯（1842—1914）是美国记者、专栏作家、小说家,一生充满传奇色彩。他以苦涩辛辣的风格赢得了"辛辣比尔斯"的绰号。他的代表作是《魔鬼词典》,而战争中的骇人事件则是他写作短篇的焦点。南北战争中他参加了北方部队,战后,在旧金山做报刊编辑。1913年,他只身前往革命中的墨西哥,在那里失踪,死因不明。可以说,他的一生就是一段传奇,而他的《枭河桥纪事》,是其代表作。

《枭河桥纪事》被称为安布罗斯·比尔斯短篇小说中的佳作。故事的主人公佩顿·法科尔是一个南方种植园主,他因企图破坏北方部队在枭河桥上修建铁路而被处以绞刑。犯人临死前的心理活动描写堪称大家手笔,逼真细腻的描写背后又流露出事件的过程和起因,对人性的深刻洞察和战争的残酷的描写互为表里。一开头被吊在桥上的汉子,以及整个桥面的军方布置,被写得惊心动魄又真实可感,着实发人深思:

一个汉子站在北亚拉巴马一座铁路桥上,俯视着桥下20英尺处湍急的河水。他双手反扣,手腕上缚着绳子。另一根绳子紧紧地套在他的脖子上,系在他头顶上方一个结实的木头十字架上,绳头下垂及膝。几块松动的木板铺在支撑铁轨的枕木上,成为汉子和行刑人的落脚之处。行刑人是两个北方军列兵,由一位中士指挥。这位中士如果在地方上,很可能会成为一名负责治安的官员。不远处,在临时搭建的平台上,站着一位身着军阶制服、全副武装的军官。他是个上尉。桥两端各有一位哨兵,站立成"放哨"的姿势,也就是步枪位于左肩前方,枪机抵住横过胸前的前臂——这样的姿势迫使人身体笔直挺立,动作规范却很别扭。看来他们两个无须知道在桥中央发生的事情,只要封锁好横贯桥面直抵两端的木板通道就可以了。

这一段精彩的描写使人想起南斯拉夫电影《桥》的一个镜头,但比那个要震撼人心,因为有一个人即将被处死在桥上。这里的文字略有调整,因为翻译还是要语句松弛,描写从容些,才能阅读顺畅,有思考的余地。

结局可想而知,但仍然给人以思考:

佩顿·法科尔死了。他的尸身(脖子已经断掉),吊在枭河桥的横木下方,缓缓地荡来荡去。

最后,就自己的观察,谈几点短篇小说的写作特点或技术要求,以求教于方家:

1. 短篇的容量有限,要尽快进入主题,引起读者的兴趣。即使描述也要引人入胜，平淡中也要有趣味，有悬念，否则读者会丢弃不读。

2. 结尾要出人意料，或者在逼近必然的结局时，要么不可逆转，要么能做出新的或令人信服的解释，否则读者会有上当的感觉，甚至不再读这个作家的作品了。

3. 虽然短篇的结构也可以多姿多彩，但最好的结构，是简单而又引人入胜的，内涵无限丰富和寓意深刻的。不要把长篇的宏大题材用来写短篇。

4. 因为展开和铺垫的时间和篇幅有限，要流露足够的信息作为暗示和启示的线索，揭示和解释进程与结局的合理性和必然性，所以要惜墨如金。

5. 过分精巧的布置和细密的文笔，虽然称为"匠心独运"，但终会有不自然的感觉。这在长篇中是忌讳，在短篇中尚可容忍，但最好不要重复地犯这种错误。

6. 过于晦涩或深奥的短篇，如同绘画缺少鲜明的调子，灰掉了。这在长篇中可以说是隐藏很深的技巧，在短篇中却是缺乏鲜明的色彩和感觉，使人莫名其妙，失之朦胧。

7. 生活经验的局限，或者艺术观念的单一，表现手法的雷同，都可能限制一个人的短篇小说创作水平和成就。没有就不要写，不要变着法儿写，否则也会让人看出来。

8. 太像小说的短篇，终究不是上品。上品应是富于诗意或像散文的短篇小说，太像小说会流于精巧或耽于说教，虽然诗歌和散文也难免，但毕竟要好一些。戏剧性强也是太像小说的一类，有看点就行。

9. 无论何种艺术作品，大凡是过目难忘的，或有价值的，需有趣、细腻、深刻、博大、奇妙，但不必平分秋色，切忌过犹不及；一滑入精巧、烦琐、古奥、混沌、怪诞，就走入魔道了。短篇小说亦然。

无论如何，读短篇小说要有心情，今日之时代迸发，时间紧迫，长篇固然要潜下心来读，才有收获，即便要读短篇小说，也要平心静气，不可过于草率。心不定，则思不宁，难于入定，何谈收获与感受？

至于短篇小说的翻译，只能有一个大概的认识。首先是废除翻译腔和狭义的忠实观，使其在语言和语气上达到翻译文学的程度。其次，深谙作者的意图和文笔，竭力向译文靠近。再下来，就是一口气译完，不要半途而废。实在不行的，也要反复修改，使其气韵贯通，文采内敛，切忌浮躁和花哨。毕肖人物语言和精于描述，长于叙事，乃是常识性的说法了。

坦率地说，本来是短篇序言，却写得很长，实不足观。好在这两部英国和美国的短篇小说经典，都没有各自的绪论，以序言充绪论，固然难当重任，而序言本身杂糅中外，兼谈艺术，近乎东拉西扯，也非正途。倘若有可观处，倒是编译者和广大读者抬爱了。

  但愿大家能够喜欢汉英对照版的英美短篇小说经典，也不枉费了我在这里苦口婆心地发了一番议论。

王宏印（朱墨）
2018年12月22日星期六
于古城长安西外专家楼

前　　言

　　现代意义上的英语短篇小说形成于19世纪。美国作家埃德加·爱伦·坡既是该文学体裁的早期实践者也是理论家。他在1842年为霍桑的第一个短篇小说集《重述的故事》所写的书评中表明了对短篇小说的看法。他将短篇小说界定为"须要在半小时至一二个小时内读完的短篇散文体叙事作品"，这样才能保证读者在阅读过程中不受任何干扰，以获得总体效果。短篇小说家还必须有意识地安排每一个细节，以取得某种预设的独一无二的突出效果。其实短篇小说发展的实际情况要复杂得多。其篇幅从500个英语单词到20000个英语单词不等；其形式变化多样，可以聚焦于某个场景、一段经历、一次行动、对某个或几个人物内心的揭示，甚至还可以是离奇的幻想。但相对于长篇小说来讲，短篇小说无论在形式和内容上都保持了其简洁、经济、紧凑、完整的鲜明特征，基本上遵循了"一人一事""一线到底"的情节发展模式，因而才能产生爱伦·坡所谓的强烈的"单一效果"。一篇短篇小说是一件精心构思、精细雕琢的精美艺术品。19世纪前期的英语短篇小说大多还遗留着西方古代传奇故事的痕迹，同时也受当时西方浪漫主义文学思潮的影响，其中的人物、情节类似于中国古代传奇笔记小说中的"志怪""志人"，往往是现实生活与鬼怪等超自然力夹杂在一起，强调故事的趣味性与新奇性。19世纪后期至20世纪初的英美文学是以现实主义、自然主义为主流的时代，短篇小说也不例外，注重对人生、社会现实的细致描述与深刻揭露。20世纪以降的英美短篇小说侧重于用心理手法描写人物的内心世界，发掘故事内所暗含的对人性、社会以及自然的批判与思考。

　　早在18世纪，英国作家笛福、艾迪生、斯梯尔、哥尔德斯密斯就已经开始写短篇故事，刊登在当时开始盛行的期刊上，着重描绘环境气氛与刻画人物。1827年发表的《两个牲畜贩子》一般被英美评论界认为是现代英语短篇小说之祖，作者是苏格兰小说家、诗人瓦尔特·司各特。虽然这一时期的英国短篇小说还多与神秘和超自然元素纠葛在一起，但已经开始注意人物性格刻画和对人性与社会的揭示。狄更斯和哈代皆属于维多利亚时代老派的讲故事高手，前者诙谐幽默，后者阴郁悲怆。自史蒂文森开始，英国短篇小说的风格焕然一新，化陈腐平常为神奇新鲜，充分体现了奇妙构思与文字表述的功效。继而有吉卜林将传统叙事技巧推向了一个新的高度，显示出其故事的复杂性与多样性。威尔斯的短篇小说同他的长篇小说一样，同样显示出他的科幻色彩和对社会问题的忧虑。萨基的短篇小说擅长以别出心裁的情节和气氛讽刺社会的虚伪、冷酷和愚蠢。毛姆的短篇以简洁而富有悬念著称，描述了欧洲人在异域的冲突，也体现了他对人性的洞察。德·拉·梅尔的短篇充满了唯美、理想化的诗意幻象，其复杂程度与阅读难度极具挑战性。康拉德、乔伊斯、伍尔夫、劳伦斯皆为现代主义小说大师。康拉德突显了异域的叙事文体风格，从语言表述到叙事结构都有创新，同时反映了在英国殖民统治背景下人性、种族的冲突。伍尔夫的短篇小说创作于长篇小说写作的间歇，她探寻的是意识的心理本质，认为在生活表象之下才是超越时间的现实，描写当下的精神活动比描写外在行为更加重要。劳伦斯以精炼的措辞、微妙的节奏感，表现了对现代复杂人际关系的困惑。乔伊斯在短篇小说领域同样开一代新风，在独创的印象与象征的框架下，突出了"顿悟"这一现代小说的关键要素。凯瑟琳·曼斯菲尔德专注于短篇，她以敏锐的观察力和对人物心理冲突的描写见长，在内容和形式上对短篇小说作为独立的文学叙事体裁的发展做出了突出贡献。

现代短篇小说在美国的发展尤为迅猛，成绩斐然。其中早期华盛顿·欧文和霍桑的作品充满浪漫、神秘色彩。爱伦·坡只写短篇，其作品结构严谨、恐怖怪异。梅尔维尔的作品已经初显现代人的精神困惑。马克·吐温和布雷特·哈特展现出西部的幽默与写实风格。安布罗斯·比尔斯在其短篇中尝试了现实与梦幻的结合以及意识流叙事手法的运用。亨利·詹姆斯突出心理现实主义，其晦涩、繁复的文体同样体现在其短篇之中。欧·亨利也只写短篇小说，特点是通俗化、程式化、大众化。史蒂芬·克莱恩、西奥多·德莱赛、杰克·伦敦呈现出对现实更逼真、更无奈、不加道德评价的新闻报道式的自然主义风格。薇拉·凯瑟返回到更朴实、传统的叙事风格。司各特·菲茨杰拉德以浪漫理想化的视角观察浮夸、颓废的现实生活。舍伍德·安德森虽然非一流作家，但他对极端闭关狭隘的地方人物的描写影响了福克纳对于美国南方乡土生活的详尽描述，其简明的语言叙事风格也影响了海明威的写作风格。福克纳以揭示美国南方传统的解体与人类命运的主题而闻名，他常以创作短篇开始，继而将其拓展为长篇小说。他认为短篇小说集中的内在形式同长篇小说中的一样，都必须具有内容与结构上的统一性。海明威的经历极富传奇性，他以短篇与长篇小说创作并重，以描写"硬汉"形象与运用简洁、凝练的"冰山"写作原则而著名。以上三位作家虽然风格迥异，对英语现代叙述艺术形式多有创新，但在描述与揭示现代人面对快速发展的现代工业、商品社会所遭遇的困惑与异化感方面多有契合之处。凯瑟琳·波特的南方题材与福克纳相近，但在叙事风格上却保持了经典的传统英语小说形式。另一个美国南方女作家弗兰纳里·奥康纳既凸显了哥特式、怪异的描述风格又揭示出现代人道德沦丧、精神异化的主题。

前　言

短篇小说作为现代叙事艺术形式具有很强的国际性，欧美的长篇小说家几乎都涉足此领域，除了英美之外，成就最突出的还包括俄国的果戈理、屠格涅夫、契诃夫、托尔斯泰，法国的梅里美、福楼拜、都德、莫泊桑，德国的霍夫曼，奥地利的卡夫卡等。

本套英国经典短篇小说选编和翻译共分上下两卷，精选了从18世纪至20世纪中叶英国主要短篇小说家的重要作品。体例上包括四个部分：作家作品简介及所选作品简评、正文、思考问题、对正文及简介简评的全译。我们选编和翻译本套书的主要目的有四。其一，为英国短篇小说课以及英国文学课提供一种适宜的教材。短篇小说的完整性和凝练性有利于学生在有限的时间内有效掌握文学的基本特征，也便于教师的授课安排与要求。其二，本套书是严格意义上的全译，这有助于学生透彻理解原文，借鉴译文，进行文学翻译本身的练习。其三，通过阅读完整的原文，使学生亲历英语语言的历时与共时特点，不同的文体特征，丰富独特的表现力，帮助学生提高自己的英语表达能力。其四，帮助学生深层次地了解英美人士的生活习惯、思维方式、情感表现，以及民族心理特征。本套书适用于高年级英语专业本科生与研究生以及较高级阶段的英语学习者。

编选名家作品常留有遗憾。由于版权或是篇幅限制，我们只能割舍少数名家或名作。同时我们也尽量避免重复翻译，努力保证选材的代表性和译文的文学性。文学翻译往往是"费力不讨好"之事，但有志于文学翻译的人却乐在其中。我们虽然在选编与翻译过程中尽心尽力，但其中仍会存在各种问题，希望有关专家与读者批评指正，不吝赐教。

我们要衷心地感谢南开大学外语学院英语系博士生导师、中国文化典籍翻译研究会会长王宏印教授。先生学贯中西、博古通今、治学严谨、著作等身。能够在繁忙的教学和学术研究中，抽出时间为小书作序，令学生后辈感激之至。他的序言引文如小溪流水、娓娓道来、内涵丰富、沁人心脾……同时要特别感谢北京大学出版社的领导和外语编辑部的编辑对本书出版所给予的大力支持和帮助。

主编
2019年2月

目 录

Daniel Defoe (ca. 1660—1731) ·· 1
The Apparition of Mrs. Veal ·· 1
丹尼尔·笛福（约1660—1731）·· 10
维尔夫人的幽灵 ··· 10

Joseph Addison (1672—1719) ·· 17
A Story of an Heir ·· 17
约瑟夫·艾迪生（1672—1719）··· 22
一个继承人的故事 ··· 22

Richard Steele (1672—1729) ·· 26
Tom Varnish ·· 26
理查德·斯梯尔（1672—1729）··· 29
汤姆·万尼诗 ·· 29

Oliver Goldsmith (ca. 1730—1774) ··· 31
The Disabled Soldier ·· 31
奥利弗·哥尔德斯密斯（约1730—1774）···································· 37
伤残士兵苦难记 ·· 37

Walter Scott (1771—1832) ··· 41
The Tapestried Chamber or The Lady in the Sacque ················· 41
瓦尔特·司各特（1771—1832）··· 55
挂毯卧房（别名"长袍夫人"）··· 55

Elizabeth Gaskell (1810—1865) ·· 65
The Half-Brothers ··· 65
伊丽莎白·盖斯凯尔（1810—1865）··· 76

| 同母异父兄弟 | 76 |

William Makepeace Thackeray (1811—1863) ········ 84
Snobs and Marriage ········ 84
威廉·梅克比斯·萨克雷（1811—1863） ········ 89
势利鬼与婚姻 ········ 89

Charles Dickens (1812—1870) ········ 93
The Signalman ········ 93
查尔斯·狄更斯（1812—1870） ········ 106
信号工 ········ 106
The Boots at the Holly-Tree Inn ········ 116
冬青树旅馆的布茨先生 ········ 126

Thomas Hardy (1840—1928) ········ 134
Absent-Mindedness in a Parish Choir ········ 134
托马斯·哈代（1840—1928） ········ 138
心不在焉的教区乐队 ········ 138
A Tradition of Eighteen Hundred and Four ········ 141
1804年的传说 ········ 147

Robert Louis Stevenson (1850—1894) ········ 152
Markheim ········ 152
罗伯特·路易斯·史蒂文森（1850—1894） ········ 168
马克海姆 ········ 168

Oscar Wilde (1854—1900) ········ 182
The Sphinx without a Secret ········ 182
奥斯卡·王尔德（1854—1900） ········ 188
没有秘密的斯芬克斯 ········ 188

Joseph Rudyard Kipling (1865—1936) ········ 193
The Limitations of Pambé Serang ········ 193

约瑟夫·鲁德亚德·吉卜林（1865—1936） ········· 199
潘贝·赛朗的局限 ········· 199

John Galsworthy (1867—1933) ········· 203
Compensation ········· 203
约翰·高尔斯华绥（1867—1933） ········· 209
补偿 ········· 209

Hector Hugh Munro (Saki) (1870—1916) ········· 214
Sredni Vashtar ········· 214
赫克托·休·芒罗（萨基）（1870—1916） ········· 220
斯莱德尼·瓦什塔 ········· 220

Walter de la Mare (1873—1956) ········· 224
The Creatures ········· 224
瓦尔特·德·拉·梅尔（1873—1956） ········· 234
精灵 ········· 234

William Somerset Maugham (1874—1965) ········· 243
The Luncheon ········· 243
威廉·萨默塞特·毛姆（1874—1965） ········· 249
午餐 ········· 249

Theodore Francis Powys (1875—1953) ········· 253
The Bucket and the Rope ········· 253
西奥多·弗朗西斯·波伊斯（1875—1953） ········· 261
桶与绳 ········· 261

Alfred Edgar Coppard (1878—1957) ········· 267
Dusky Ruth ········· 267
阿尔弗雷德·埃德加·柯帕德（1878—1957） ········· 276
黑发露丝 ········· 276

Daniel Defoe
(ca. 1660—1731)

Daniel Defoe, English novelist, pamphleteer, and journalist, is often considered the founder of the English novel. Although his father intended him for the ministry, Defoe involved himself in politics, trade and journalism, travelling abroad extensively. He earned fame and royal favor with his satirical poems. He once worked for both the Tory and the Whig governments. He published the periodical *Review* and wrote for it all by himself. As a writer, he remained enterprising until his death.

Defoe was the pioneer writing about believable characters in realistic situations with simple prose. His literary masterpieces include *Robinson Crusoe* (1719) about living on the isolated island after the shipwreck, and *Moll Flanders* (1722) about the adventures of a woman who is compelled to make her own way. His other major works are: *A Journal of the Plague Year* (1722), *Captain Jack* (1722) and *Roxana* (1724). Despite the negative reactions till the late 19th century, Defoe received widespread and serious critical attention in the 20th century, and his works have been analyzed in modern critical approaches. In his last years, Defoe also produced works involving the supernatural.

The Apparition of Mrs. Veal

The following is a story of the apparition. As intimate friends from childhood, Mrs. Bargrave and Mrs. Veal share much of their spiritual and emotional misfortunes. When they meet, they always comfort each other. Absent from each other for a long time, one day Mrs. Veal suddenly appears at Mrs. Bargrave's place. Once again they talk just as before. Mrs. Veal's appearance is most shocking because she has been dead before she meets Mrs. Bargrave, and yet Mrs. Bargrave insists on having seen Mrs. Veal in person that day. Ghost stories are told both in the East and West, and this is Defoe's version with much exactness and vividness. In fact it somehow reveals the complexity and subtlety of human psyche in want of comfort and protection.

This thing is so rare in all its circumstances, and on so good authority, that my reading and conversation have not given me anything like it. It is fit to gratify the most ingenious and serious inquirer. Mrs. Bargrave is the person to whom Mrs. Veal appeared after her death; she is my intimate friend, and I can avouch for her reputation for these fifteen or sixteen years, on my own knowledge; and I can affirm the good character she had from her youth to the time of my acquaintance. Though, since this relation, she is calumniated by some people that are friends to the brother of Mrs. Veal who appeared to think the relation of this appearance to be a reflection, and endeavor what they can to blast Mrs. Bargrave's reputation and to laugh the story out of countenance. But by the circumstances thereof, and the cheerful disposition of Mrs. Bargrave, notwithstanding the ill usage of a very wicked husband, there is not yet the least sign of dejection in her face; nor did I ever hear her let fall a desponding or murmuring expression; nay, not when actually under her husband's barbarity, which I have been a witness to, and several other persons of undoubted reputation.

Now you must know Mrs. Veal was a maiden gentlewoman of about thirty years of age, and for some years past had been troubled with fits, which were perceived coming on her by her going off from her discourse very abruptly to some impertinence. She was maintained by an only brother, and kept his house in Dover. She was a very pious woman, and her brother a very sober man, to all appearance; but now he does all he can to null and quash the story. Mrs. Veal was intimately acquainted with Mrs. Bargrave from her childhood. Mrs. Veal's circumstances were then mean; her father did not take care of his children as he ought, so that they were exposed to hardships. And Mrs. Bargrave in those days had as unkind a father, though she wanted neither for food nor clothing; while Mrs. Veal wanted for both, insomuch that she would often say, "Mrs. Bargrave, you are not only the best, but the only friend I have in the world; and no circumstance of life shall ever dissolve my friendship." They would often condole each other's adverse fortunes, and read together *Drelincourt upon Death*, and other books; and so, like two Christian friends, they comforted each other under their sorrow.

Some time after, Mr. Veal's friends got him a place in the custom-house at Dover, which occasioned Mrs. Veal, by little and little, to fall off from her intimacy with Mrs. Bargrave, though there was never any such thing as a quarrel; but an indifferency came on by degrees, till at last Mrs. Bargrave had not seen her in two years and a half, though above a twelvemonth of the time Mrs. Bargrave hath been absent from Dover, and this last half-year has been in Canterbury about two months of the time, dwelling in a house of her own.

In this house, in the eighth of September, one thousand seven hundred and five, she was sitting alone in the forenoon, thinking over her unfortunate life, and arguing herself into a due resignation to Providence, though her condition seemed hard: "And," said she, "I have been provided for hitherto, and doubt not but I shall be still, and am well satisfied that my afflictions shall end when it is most fit for me." And then took up her sewing work, which she had no sooner done but she hears a knocking at the door; she went to see who was there, and this proved to be Mrs. Veal, her old friend, who was in a riding habit. At that moment of time the clock struck twelve at noon.

"Madam," says Mrs. Bargrave, "I am surprised to see you, you who have been so long a stranger"; but told her she was glad to see her, and offered to salute her, which Mrs. Veal complied with, till their lips almost touched, and then Mrs. Veal drew her hand across her own eyes, and said, "I am not very well," and so waived it. She told Mrs. Bargrave she was going a journey, and had a great mind to see her first. "But," says Mrs. Bargrave, "how can you take a journey alone? I am amazed at it, because I know you have a fond brother." "Oh," says Mrs. Veal, "I gave my brother the slip, and came away, because I had so great a desire to see you before I took my journey." So Mrs. Bargrave went in with her into another room within the first, and Mrs. Veal sat her down in an elbow-chair, in which Mrs. Bargrave was sitting when she heard Mrs. Veal knock. "Then," says Mrs. Veal, "my dear friend, I am come to renew our old friendship again, and beg your pardon for my breach of it; and if you can forgive me, you are the best of women." "Oh," says Mrs. Bargrave, "do not mention such a thing; I have not had an uneasy thought about it." "What did you think of me?" says Mrs. Veal. Says Mrs. Bargrave, "I thought you were like the rest of the world, and that prosperity had made you forget yourself and me." Then Mrs. Veal reminded Mrs. Bargrave of the many friendly offices she did her in former days, and much of the conversation they had with each other in the times of their adversity; what books they read, and what comfort in particular they received from Drelincourt's *Book of Death*, which was the best, she said, on the subject ever wrote. She also mentioned Doctor Sherlock, and two Dutch books, which were translated, wrote upon death, and several others. But Drelincourt, she said, had the clearest notions of death and of the future state of any who had handled that subject. Then she asked Mrs. Bargrave whether she had Drelincourt. She said, "Yes." Says Mrs. Veal, "Fetch it." And so Mrs. Bargrave goes upstairs and brings it down. Says Mrs. Veal, "Dear Mrs. Bargrave, if the eyes of our faith were as open as the eyes of our body, we should see numbers of angels about us for our guard. The notions we have of Heaven now are nothing like what it is, as Drelincourt says; therefore be comforted under your afflictions, and believe that the Almighty has a particular regard to you, and that your afflictions are marks of God's favor; and when they have done the business they are sent for, they shall be removed from you. And believe me, my dear friend, believe what I say to you, one minute of future happiness will infinitely reward you for all your sufferings. For I can never believe" (and claps her hand upon her knee with great earnestness, which, indeed, ran through most of her discourse) "that ever God will suffer you to spend all your days in this afflicted state. But be assured that your afflictions shall leave you, or you them, in a short time." She spake in that pathetical and heavenly manner that Mrs. Bargrave wept several times, she was so deeply affected with it.

Then Mrs. Veal mentioned Doctor Kendrick's *Ascetic*, at the end of which he gives an account of the lives of the primitive Christians. Their pattern she recommended to our imitation, and said, "Their conversation was not like this of our age. For now," says she, "there is nothing but vain, frothy discourse, which is far different from theirs. Theirs was to edification, and to build one another up in faith, so that they were not as we are, nor are we as they were. But," said she, "we ought to do as they did; there was a hearty friendship among them; but where is it now to be found?" Says Mrs. Bargrave, "It is hard indeed to find a true friend in these days." Says Mrs. Veal, "Mr. Norris has a fine copy of verses, called *Friendship in Perfection*, which I wonderfully admire. Have you seen the book?" says Mrs. Veal. "No," says Mrs. Bargrave, "but I have the verses of my own writing out." "Have you?" says Mrs. Veal; "then fetch them"; which she did from above stairs, and offered them to Mrs. Veal to read, who refused, and waived the thing, saying, "holding down her head would make it ache"; and then desiring Mrs. Bargrave to read them to her, which she did. As they were admiring *Friendship*, Mrs. Veal said, "Dear Mrs. Bargrave, I shall love you forever." In these verses there is twice used the word Elysian. "Ah!" says Mrs. Veal, "these poets have such names for heaven." She would often draw her hand across her own eyes, and say, "Mrs. Bargrave, do not you think I am mightily impaired by my fits?" "No," says Mrs. Bargrave; "I think you look as well as ever I knew you."

After this discourse, which the apparition put in much finer words than Mrs. Bargrave said she could pretend to, and as much more as she can remember—for it cannot be thought that an hour and three quarter's conversation could all be retained, though the main of it she thinks she does—she said to Mrs. Bargrave she would have her write a letter to her brother, and tell him she would have him give rings to such and such; and that there was a purse of gold in her cabinet, and that she would have two broad pieces given to her cousin Watson.

Talking at this rate, Mrs. Bargrave thought that a fit was coming upon her, and so placed herself on a chair just before her knees, to keep her from falling to the ground, if her fits should occasion it; for the elbow-chair, she thought, would keep her from falling on either side. And to divert Mrs. Veal, as she thought, took hold of her gown-sleeve several times, and commended it. Mrs. Veal told her it was a scoured silk, and newly made up. But, for all this, Mrs. Veal persisted in her request, and told Mrs. Bargrave she must not deny her. And she would have her tell her brother all their conversation when she had the opportunity. "Dear Mrs. Veal," says Mrs. Bargrave, "it is much better, me-thinks, to do it yourself." "No," says Mrs. Veal; "though it seems impertinent to you now, you will see more reasons for it hereafter." Mrs. Bargrave, then, to satisfy her importunity, was going to fetch a pen and ink, but Mrs. Veal said, "Let it alone now, but do it when I am gone; but you must be sure to do it"; which was one of the last things she enjoined her at parting, and so she promised her.

Then Mrs. Veal asked for Mrs. Bargrave's daughter. She said she was not at home. "But if you have a mind to see her," says Mrs. Bargrave, "I'll send for her." "Do," says Mrs. Veal; on which she left her, and went to a neighbor's to see her; and by the time Mrs. Bargrave was returning, Mrs. Veal was got without the door in the street, in the face of the beast-market, on a Saturday (which is market-day), and stood ready to part as soon as Mrs. Bargrave came to her. She asked her why she was in such haste. She said she must be going, though perhaps she might not go her journey till Monday; and told Mrs. Bargrave she hoped she should see her again at her cousin Watson's before she went whither she was going. Then she said she would take her leave of her, and walked from Mrs. Bargrave, in her view, till a turning interrupted the sight of her, which was three-quarters after one in the afternoon.

Mrs. Veal died the seventh of September, at twelve o'clock at noon, of her fits, and had not above four hours' senses before her death, in which time she received the sacrament. The next day after Mrs. Veal's appearance, being Sunday, Mrs. Bargrave was mightily indisposed with a cold and sore throat, that she could not go out that day; but on Monday morning she sends a person to Captain Watson's to know if Mrs. Veal was there. They wondered at Mrs. Bargrave's inquiry, and sent her word she was not there, nor was expected. At this answer, Mrs. Bargrave told the maid she had certainly mistook the name or made some blunder. And though she was ill, she put on her hood and went herself to Captain Watson's, though she knew none of the family, to see if Mrs. Veal was there or not. They said they wondered at her asking, for that she had not been in town; they were sure, if she had, she would have been there. Says Mr. Bargrave, "I am sure she was with me on Saturday almost two hours." They said it was impossible, for they must have seen her if she had. In comes Captain Watson, while they were in dispute, and said that Mrs. Veal was certainly dead, and the escutcheons were making. This strangely surprised Mrs. Bargrave, when she sent to the person immediately who had the care of them, and found it true. Then she related the whole story to Captain Watson's family; what gown she had on, and how striped; and that Mrs. Veal told her that it was scoured. Then Mrs. Watson cried out, "You have seen her indeed, for none knew but Mrs. Veal and myself that the gown was scoured." And Mrs. Watson owned that she described the gown exactly; "for," said she, "I helped her to make it up." This Mrs. Watson blazed all about the town, and avouched the demonstration of truth of Mrs. Bargrave's seeing Mrs. Veal's apparition. And Captain Watson carried two gentlemen immediately to Mrs. Bargrave's house to hear the relation from her own mouth. And when it spread so fast that gentlemen and persons of quality, the judicious and skeptical part of the world, flocked in upon her, it at last became such a task that she was forced to go out of the way; for they were in general extremely satisfied of the truth of the thing, and plainly saw that Mrs. Bargrave was no hypochondriac, for she always appears with such a cheerful air and pleasing mien that she has gained the favor and esteem of all the gentry, and it is thought a great favor if they can but get the relation from her own mouth. I should have told you before that Mrs. Veal told Mrs. Bargrave that her sister and brother-in-law were just come down from London to see her. Says Mrs. Bargrave, "How came you to order matters so strangely?" "It could not be helped," said Mrs. Veal. And her brother and sister did come to see her, and entered the town of Dover just as Mrs. Veal was expiring. Mrs. Bargrave asked her whether she would drink some tea. Says Mrs. Veal, "I do not care if I do; but I'll warrant you this mad fellow"—meaning Mrs. Bargrave's husband—"has broke all your trinkets." "But," says Mrs. Bargrave, "I'll get something to drink in for all that"; but Mrs. Veal waived it, and said, "It is no matter; let it alone"; and so it passed.

All the time I sat with Mrs. Bargrave, which was some hours, she recollected fresh saying of Mrs. Veal. And one material thing more she told Mrs. Bargrave, that old Mr. Bretton allowed Mrs. Veal ten pounds a year, which was a secret, and unknown to Mrs. Bargrave till Mrs. Veal told her.

Mrs. Bargrave never varies in her story, which puzzles those who doubt of the truth, or are unwilling to believe it. A servant in the neighbor's yard adjoining to Mrs. Bargrave's house heard her talking to somebody an hour of the time Mrs. Veal was with her. Mrs. Bargrave went out to her next neighbor's the very moment she parted with Mrs. Veal, and told her what ravishing conversation she had had with an old friend, and told the whole of it. Drelincourt's *Book of Death* is, since this happened, bought up strangely. And it is to be observed that, notwithstanding all the trouble and fatigue Mrs. Bargrave has undergone upon this account, she never took the value of a farthing, nor suffered her daughter to take anything of anybody, and therefore can have no interest in telling the story.

But Mr. Veal does what he can to stifle the matter, and said he would see Mrs. Bargrave; but yet it is certain matter of fact that he has been at Captain Watson's since the death of his sister, and yet never went near Mrs. Bargrave; and some of his friends report her to be a liar, and that she knew of Mr. Bretton's ten pounds a year. But the person who pretends to say so has the reputation to be a notorious liar among persons whom I know to be of undoubted credit. Now, Mr. Veal is more of a gentleman than to say she lies, but says a bad husband has crazed her; but she needs only present herself, and it will effectually confute that pretense. Mr. Veal says he asked his sister on her death-bed whether she had a mind to dispose of anything. And she said no. Now the things which Mrs. Veal's apparition would have disposed of were so trifling, and nothing of justice aimed at in her disposal, that the design of it appears to me to be only in order to make Mrs. Bargrave satisfy the world of the reality thereof as to what she had seen and heard, and to secure her reputation among the reasonable and understanding part of mankind. And then again, Mr. Veal owns that there was a purse of gold; but it was not found in her cabinet, but in a comb-box. This looks improbable; for that Mrs. Watson owned that Mrs. Veal was so very careful of the key of her cabinet that she would trust nobody with it; and if so, no doubt she would not trust her gold out of it. And Mrs. Veal's often drawing her hands over her eyes, and asking Mrs. Bargrave whether her fits had not impaired her, looks to me as if she did it on purpose to remind Mrs. Bargrave of her fits, to prepare her not to think it strange that she should put her upon writing to her brother, to dispose of rings and gold, which looks so much like a dying person's bequest; and it took accordingly with Mrs. Bargrave as the effect of her fits coming upon her, and was one of the many instances of her wonderful love to her and care of her, that she should not be affrighted, which, indeed, appears in her whole management, particularly in her coming to her in the daytime, waiving the salutation, and when she was alone; and then the manner of her parting, to prevent a second attempt to salute her.

Now, why Mr. Veal should think this relation a reflection—as it is plain he does, by his endeavoring to stifle it—I cannot imagine; because the generality believe her to be a good spirit, her discourse was so heavenly. Her two great errands were, to comfort Mrs. Bargrave in her affliction, and to ask her forgiveness for her breach of friendship, and with a pious discourse to encourage her. So that, after all, to suppose that Mrs. Bargrave could hatch such an invention as this, from Friday noon to Saturday noon—supposing that she knew of Mrs. Veal's death the very first moment—without jumbling circumstances, and without any interest, too, she must be more witty, fortunate, and wicked, too, than any indifferent person, I dare say, will allow. I asked Mrs. Bargrave several times if she was sure she felt the gown. She answered, modestly, "If my senses be to be relied on, I am sure of it." I asked her if she heard a sound when she clapped her hand upon her knee. She said she did not remember she did, but said she appeared to be as much a substance as I did who talked with her. "And I may," said she, "be as soon persuaded that your apparition is talking to me now as that I did not really see her; for I was under no manner of fear, and received her as a friend, and parted with her as such. I would not," says she, "give one farthing to make any one believe it; I have no interest in it; nothing but trouble is entailed upon me for a long time, for aught I know; and, had it not come to light by accident, it would never have been made public." But now she says she will make her own private use of it, and keep herself out of the way as much as she can; and so she has done since. She says she had a gentleman who came thirty miles to her to hear the relation; and that she had told it to a roomful of people at the time. Several particular gentlemen have had the story from Mrs. Bargrave's own mouth.

This thing has very much affected me, and I am as well satisfied as I am of the best-grounded matter of fact. And why we should dispute matter of fact, because we cannot solve things of which we can have no certain or demonstrative notions, seems strange to me; Mrs. Bargrave's authority and sincerity alone would have been undoubted in any other case.

Questions

1. What kind of woman was Mrs. Veal? And what relationship did Mrs. Bargrave have with Mrs. Veal? Why did they fall off from their intimacy?
2. Then how did Mrs. Veal suddenly appear at Mrs. Bargrave's house? What did they talk about and how did they interact with each other?
3. What meticulous details were provided to ensure the validity of Mrs. Bargrave's meeting with Mrs. Veal and was there any physical contact between them in the description of their meeting?
4. How could Mrs. Bargrave be so convincing in telling the tale about meeting Mrs. Veal when in fact Mrs. Veal was dead?
5. Why could ghost stories be popular and attractive across the boundaries of space and time?

丹尼尔·笛福
（约1660—1731）

英国小说家、政论家、报人丹尼尔·笛福常被看作英国小说之父。虽然其父有意培养他当牧师，笛福却投身于政治、贸易和办报，广泛地游历于世界各地。他写讽刺诗赢得了声誉和王室的青睐。他既为托利党又为辉格党政府效力。他出版《评论》期刊并完全由自己撰稿。作为作家，笛福笔耕不辍，直至去世。

笛福开创了以简朴的散文体描写真实情形中现实人物的风气。其文学杰作包括：《鲁滨逊漂流记》（1719）讲述海难后荒岛余生，《摩尔·弗兰德斯》（1722）讲述一位女子被迫独自闯荡的冒险经历。笛福的其他主要作品还有《瘟疫年记事》（1722）、《杰克船长》（1722）以及《罗克莎娜》（1724）。尽管19世纪后半期之前文坛对笛福多有负面评论，但在20世纪笛福受到评论界广泛关注，人们开始以种种现代文评方法分析他的作品。笛福晚年还出了一些有关超自然的作品。

维尔夫人的幽灵

下面是一个幽灵的故事。巴格雷夫夫人和维尔夫人自小就是密友，她们都有不幸的精神与情感生活。每当见面她们总是彼此安慰。俩人很久没见面之后的某一天，维尔夫人突然出现在巴格雷夫夫人家。她们又叙谈如故。维尔夫人的出现骇人听闻，因为她在见到巴格雷夫夫人之前就已经去世，然而巴格雷夫夫人却坚持声称那天她亲自见到了维尔夫人。鬼怪幽灵的故事东西方都已经司空见惯了，这个故事是笛福的幽灵版本，其中描写的精细度和生动性令人叫绝。其实故事从某种程度上揭示出人们的心灵需要安慰和保护时的复杂、微妙的心理。

这件事前后发生的经过实属罕见，其真实性又确凿无疑，无论是从我的阅读中还是与人交谈中，我都从未发现过类似的事情。这件事恰好可以满足最乐于和善于探究问题之人。巴格雷夫夫人就是维尔夫人死后现身的证人；她是我的老朋友，相识来往已有十五六年了，我可以担保她一贯以来的好人品；我也可以肯定她从青年时期直到认识我期间的好性格。讲了这件事之后，巴格雷夫夫人遭到维尔夫人兄弟的朋友们的诽谤，这些人似乎认为幽灵现身本身就是毁誉之事，他们竭力诋毁巴格雷夫夫人的名声，并嘲笑这件事纯属无稽之谈。但凭借该事情真相的原委，以及她本人的乐观性格，即使有其可恶的丈夫在其中使坏，巴格雷夫夫人的脸上并没有显出丝毫的沮丧；我也从未听她流露出任何消沉、抱怨之词；即使在其丈夫的恶行之下，她也从未流露过任何负面的情绪，这一点我和其他几位可信之人都亲眼看见过。

大家必须清楚，维尔夫人是一位三十岁左右的未婚淑女，在过去几年里遭受突发性错乱之苦，在其身上的具体表现就是说话间突然离题。她由唯一的兄弟供养，在多佛为兄弟照看家。维尔夫人生性虔诚，其兄弟给人的印象是性格沉稳；但现在他却竭力将这桩事儿大事化小，小事化了。维尔夫人从小就是巴格雷夫夫人的密友。维尔夫人当时处境艰难；其父并没有承担好父亲照顾子女的责任，结果是孩子们遭罪。而巴格雷夫夫人那些年也有个好不了多少的父亲，所不同的是她衣食无忧；维尔夫人则是衣食皆忧，她常说，"巴格雷夫夫人，您不仅是我最好的朋友，也是我在世上唯一的朋友；生活中无论何事都不会消除我对您的情谊。"俩人就各自的不幸常互相安慰，一起读德勒兰库尔的《论死亡》，以及其他书籍；就这样，她们像两位基督之友那样，在痛苦之中互相安慰。

维尔先生的朋友在多佛海关为他谋得一份差事之后，维尔夫人与巴格雷夫夫人的密切关系就一点一点减弱；她们彼此虽然从未争吵过，但互相在某种程度上疏远了，最后巴格雷夫夫人有两年半没有见过对方，其中有一年多巴格雷夫夫人不在多佛，最近半年中有两个月住在坎特伯雷自己的家中。

就在自己家中，在1705年9月8日这一天，巴格雷夫夫人午前独自坐着，想着自己不幸的身世，虽说处境艰难，她还是说服自己应该皈依上帝。"好了，"她说，"至今我生活都有着落，而且毫无疑问我的状况仍将如此；我也心满意足了，等时候到了，我的痛苦也就结束了。"于是她拾起针线活儿，但还没等开始做，就听见有人敲门。她起身去看谁敲门，结果是她的老闺蜜维尔夫人，一身女骑装打扮。此时钟正敲响中午十二点。

"夫人，"巴格雷夫夫人说，"见到您很吃惊，有好久没见到您了。"但巴格雷夫夫人还是告诉对方见到她很高兴，并主动以吻相迎，维尔夫人也同样回敬，可就在俩人的嘴唇几乎相碰之际，维尔夫人却用手挡在眼前说，"我不太舒服，"于是乎回避了这一礼节。她告诉巴格雷夫夫人她要出门旅行，很想先看望她一下。"可是，"巴格雷夫夫人说，"您怎能单独旅行呢？我真感到惊讶，我知道你有个很体贴人的兄弟。""哦，"维尔夫人说，"我给我兄弟留了个条，然后就离开了，我特别想在旅行之前看望你一下。"于是巴格雷夫夫人同她从第一间屋子里走进另一间，维尔夫人在一把扶手椅子里坐下来，那椅子正是巴格雷夫夫人听见维尔夫人敲门时坐的。"这不，"维尔夫人说，"我亲爱的朋友，我来是为了重新恢复咱们的老交情，请原谅我中断了咱们的友谊；如果您肯原谅我，您就太了不起了，堪称女中之杰。""嗨，"巴格雷夫夫人说，"别提那事了，我从未多想过。""您怎么看我？"维尔夫人问。巴格雷夫夫人说，"我以为您同世上其他人一样，富贵使您忘却了自己也忘却了我。"随后维尔夫人提起巴格雷夫夫人在过去的日子里如何提供种种友善的帮助，她们彼此在逆境中如何频繁交流，还有她们所读的书，特别是她们从德勒兰库尔的《论死亡》中所汲取的安慰。她说那本书是有关这一主题写得最好的。她还提到写死亡的舍洛克博士以及两本翻译过来的荷兰书，还有其他几本书。但是她说德勒兰库尔对死亡的看法最清晰，并认为德氏对探讨这一问题的其他人的未来处境也看得最准。之后她问巴格雷夫夫人有没有德勒兰库尔的书。巴格雷夫夫人说，"有啊。"维尔夫人说，"拿来。"于是巴格雷夫夫人上楼把书拿了下来。维尔夫人说，"亲爱的巴格雷夫夫人，假如我们的信念之眼就像我们的肉眼一样睁大着，我们就应该看到四周有天使保护我们。我们现在对天堂的概念绝对不像德勒兰库尔所说的；因而在自己的痛苦中解脱吧，相信全能的主对您有特殊的关怀，您的痛苦就是上帝恩宠的征象；这些痛苦完成赋予的任务之后，自然会离您而去。相信我，亲爱的朋友，相信我对您说的，未来每一分钟的幸福都将无限地由于您所遭受的痛苦而奖赏给您。我绝不相信（她虔诚地用手拍着膝盖，实际上在讲话的大部分时间里她一直如此）上帝会让您在这种痛苦状态下度日如年。但是，您放心，您的痛苦必将离您而去，或者说您将远离痛苦，这一天很快会到来。"维尔夫人悲悯而神圣地说着，巴格雷夫夫人多次哭泣起来，她被深深地打动了。

　　后来维尔夫人提及了肯德里克的《苦行僧》，作者在该书的结尾处记述了早期基督徒的生平。维尔夫人推荐他们的行为方式作为今人的榜样，并说，"他们的谈话不像我们这个时代的样子。现今，"她说，"一切交谈都只是虚夸、空洞，与他们的大相径庭。他们那时的交谈为的是启迪心灵，互相建立信念，因而不像咱们今天这样，咱们今天也不像他们从前了。但是，"她说，"我们必须像他们从前那样。他们之间有真诚的友谊，可是现在哪儿去找那样的友谊？"巴格雷夫夫人说，"现今确实难找真正的朋友。""诺里斯夫人有一本抄写精美的诗集，叫《完美的友谊》，我特别喜欢。您见过那本书吗？"维尔夫人问。"没见过，"巴格雷夫夫人说，"不过这些诗，我有自己的手抄本。""真的？"维尔夫人说，"那就拿来啊！"巴格雷夫夫人从楼上拿来了手抄本，递给维尔夫人读，可她却谢绝了，并没接过来，说"低头会使她头痛"。随后她请求巴格雷夫夫人为她朗读，巴格雷夫夫人照做了。俩人赞美着被称作《完美的友谊》的那些诗，这时维尔夫人说，"亲爱的巴格雷夫夫人，我将永远爱您。"在这些诗里，"乐土的"一词用了两次。"啊！"维尔夫人说，"这些诗人们用这类词形容天堂。"她常常用手挡住眼睛说话，"巴格雷夫夫人，您是不是觉得我一阵阵犯病,被折磨得不成样子?""没有,"巴格雷夫夫人说,"我觉得您看起来跟我从前认识您时一样。"

幽灵的这番话,据巴格雷夫夫人自己说,比她所能描摹的措辞更精雅,也更丰富——因为无法想象一个人能记住一个钟头加三刻钟的对话,而她自己认为只是记住了要点——这番话之后,维尔夫人对巴格雷夫夫人说,她要请对方给自己的兄弟写一封信,告诉他让她把戒指给某个人;还有,在她的柜子里有一小袋金子,她要让人把两块大一点的给其表弟沃森。

这样边说着,巴格雷夫夫人觉得维尔夫人又要犯病了,于是她自己就在维尔夫人膝盖前的椅子上坐下来,以防病来了会使维尔夫人倒在地上。与此同时她觉得扶手椅会防止维尔夫人向两边倒。她想转移维尔夫人的注意力,于是几次拿起她的长袍袖子大加赞赏。维尔夫人告诉她长袍的料是精炼丝绸的,而且是新的。但尽管如此,维尔夫人还是一再坚持她的请求,叮嘱巴格雷夫夫人一定不要拒绝她。她要巴格雷夫夫人有机会向其兄弟转达她们彼此交谈的内容。"亲爱的维尔夫人,"巴格雷夫夫人说,"我觉得还是您自己说为好。""不,"维尔夫人说,"虽然这件事现在似乎与您无关,之后您就会明白其中的道理。"于是巴格雷夫夫人为了满足她的一再请求,想去拿笔和墨,但是维尔夫人说,"现在别记,等我走了再记,但您一定要保证做到。"这是维尔夫人分别时嘱咐的最后几件事之一,巴格雷夫夫人一一应允。

后来维尔夫人问起巴格雷夫夫人的女儿。巴格雷夫夫人说女儿不在家。"不过如果您想见她,"巴格雷夫夫人说,"我去叫。""好啊,"维尔夫人说。说完,巴格雷夫夫人就离开去邻居家找女儿。可等她回来,维尔夫人已经出门来到街上,面对着牲畜市场。那天是礼拜六(正是集市日),她站在那儿,准备等巴格雷夫夫人回来就告别。巴格雷夫夫人问她为何那么着急。她说她得走了,不过也许周一才上路,并告诉巴格雷夫夫人,她希望上路之前能在表弟沃森家再见到她。之后她说要告辞了,便离开巴格雷夫夫人,巴格雷夫夫人目送她直到在拐弯处消失,当时是下午一点三刻。

维尔夫人由于旧病发作,死于九月七日正午十二点,死前的清醒时间不超过四小时,并在此期间接受了圣礼。维尔夫人出现的第二天,也就是礼拜天,巴格雷夫夫人患伤风,嗓子痛,很不舒服,那天出不了门;可是礼拜一早上她就派人去沃森上校家,想知道维尔夫人是否在那儿。沃森的家人对此感到很惊诧,叫人捎话说维尔夫人不在那儿,也没人等她去那儿。对于这个回答,巴格雷夫夫人对女仆说她一定是弄错了名字,或是没说清楚。于是她围上头巾,带病亲自前去沃森上校家。她虽然不认识这家的任何人,也要去弄个究竟,看维尔夫人是否在那儿。这家人说他们对她的询问感到不解,因为维尔夫人一直不在城里。他们肯定,如果她在城里,她会在他们家的。巴格雷夫夫人说,"我肯定她礼拜六有将近两个钟头和我在一起。"他们说那不可能,因为假如她在的话,他们一定会见到她。正当他们争执之际,沃森上校进来,他说维尔夫人的确死了,死者的纹章匾正在制作中。巴格雷夫夫人马上派人找到负责纹章匾的人,并查明情况属实,这使得巴格雷夫夫人大吃一惊。于是她就向沃森上校全家讲述了事情的全部经过,诸如她穿着什么样的长袍,长袍上有什么样的斑纹,还有维尔夫人告诉她长袍的料是精炼丝绸等。这时沃森夫人惊叫起来,"天哪,您的确见过她,因为除了维尔夫人和我之外,没人知道那长袍是精炼丝绸的。"沃森夫人还承认巴格雷夫夫人对长袍的描绘很精确,"因为,"沃森夫人说,"是我帮她制作的。"这位沃森夫人满城四处张扬,亲自证明巴格雷夫夫人见到了维尔夫人的幽灵,这确有其事。而且沃森上校立刻陪同两位绅士来到巴格雷夫夫人家,从她口中亲耳聆听此事。这件事迅速传开,绅士们和上层人士、明贤之人以及无神论者都纷至沓来,最后对于这件事的说明反倒成了巴格雷夫夫人义不容辞的任务。来者对事情的真实性大多极为满意,他们清楚地看到,巴格雷夫夫人并非患忧郁症,因为她出现时总是愉快、悦人,赢得了大家一致的赞许和尊重,人们都以能从她口中亲耳聆听到此事为荣。我事先该告诉您,维尔夫人还告诉过巴格雷夫夫人,她妹妹和妹夫才从伦敦来看她。巴格雷夫夫人说,"您安排事情怎么这么古怪?""也是迫不得已,"维尔夫人回答说。而她的妹夫和妹妹也的确来看她了,他们就在维尔夫人快要断气之际到了多佛城。巴格雷夫夫人问她喝不喝茶,维尔夫人说,"喝茶我倒不反对,不过我敢保证那个疯子"——指巴格雷夫夫人的丈夫——"打碎了你所有的茶具。""不过,"巴格雷夫夫人说,"我总会弄到喝茶的东西。"但是维尔夫人还是谢绝了,她说,"别管了,算了吧。"于是这事就过去了。

我一直与巴格雷夫夫人同坐,有个把钟头,这期间她回忆着维尔夫人新的言谈。她还告诉巴格雷夫夫人另外一件有关钱的事,老布雷顿先生每年给维尔夫人十英镑,这是一桩秘密,巴格雷夫夫人直到维尔夫人亲口告诉她才知道。

巴格雷夫夫人讲起这故事从不走样,这使怀疑故事的真实性或不愿意相信之人大为困惑。巴格雷夫夫人家隔壁邻居院子里的仆人听见巴格雷夫夫人同某人交谈有一个钟头,那是她正同维尔夫人在一起。巴格雷夫夫人同维尔夫人分手后,就去了隔壁邻居家,她告诉邻居同一位老友畅快地交谈了一会儿,并且叙述了谈话的全部内容。自从此事发生后,德勒兰库尔的《论死亡》一书奇怪地一销而光。据说,尽管巴格雷夫夫人讲述这件事经受了许多麻烦和疲惫,她却分文不取,也不让女儿收任何人的东西,因此她讲这件事并非有利可图。

但是维尔先生却竭力压制这件事,并说要见巴格雷夫夫人。而事实上自从他姐姐去世后，他就在沃森上校家，但却从未靠近巴格雷夫夫人。他的一些朋友说巴格雷夫夫人是个骗子，说她知道布雷顿先生每年给十英镑的事。我所认识的人大多可信，而出此言者却偏偏是个臭名昭著的骗子。眼下，维尔先生一派君子风度，他倒没说巴格雷夫夫人是个骗子，而只是说她的恶夫弄昏了她的头脑，但她只需出面对证，就会有效地驳倒这一伪称。维尔先生说他在姐姐临终前曾问过她是否有什么交代，但她却说没有。现在维尔夫人的幽灵托付要处理的东西微不足道，也不牵涉法律程序，所以这项澄清事实真相的计划对我来说，似乎只是为了让巴格雷夫夫人说明事件的真实性的需要，其中包括她的所见所闻，以确保她在通情达理之人心目中的名誉。与此同时，维尔先生承认有一小袋金子，但并非是在柜子里找到的，而是在梳妆盒里。这似乎不可能。针对这一点，沃森夫人证明维尔夫人对自己柜子的钥匙格外小心，她不可能将柜子托付给任何人。既然如此，毫无疑问，她不会将金子放在柜子外面。而维尔夫人常用手挡眼睛，并且问巴格雷夫夫人病痛是否毁了她，对我来说，这些似乎都是她有意要提醒巴格雷夫夫人她自己有病，使巴格雷夫夫人有心理准备，不要觉得托她给兄弟写信、处置戒指和金子这些行为有什么怪异，就好像一个临终人的遗嘱似的。接下来的一切让巴格雷夫夫人感觉她又要旧病复发，同时显示出她又一次对巴格雷夫夫人无限的爱和关怀，让她不感到害怕。这些的确都出现在她的掌控之中，特别是她选择白天巴格雷夫夫人独自在家时来访，免了见面相吻的礼节，还有她告别的方式，避免了第二次吻别的礼节。

那么，维尔先生为什么认为这件事影响很坏——他显然是这么认为的，这可以从他竭力压制这件事中看出来——我想象不出为什么，因为大多数人认为她人格高尚、言谈虔诚。维尔夫人有两件大事要完成，一是安慰痛苦之中的巴格雷夫夫人，二是原谅她中断友谊，而且期间充满了虔诚与鼓励的话语。因此，如果要说巴格雷夫夫人能炮制出从礼拜五到礼拜六这么一套故事——假如她从一开始就知道维尔夫人的死——而情节毫不混乱，也毫无个人私利，那她必然是一个聪明绝顶、幸运无比，也罪大恶极之人，我敢说，要完成以上诸多事宜，她必须超过任何一个旁观者的才能。我几次问过巴格雷夫夫人她是否真的摸过那件长袍，她谦逊地回答道："如果我的感官还可靠的话，我肯定摸过。"我问她拍维尔夫人的膝盖时是否听见声响。她说不记得听见什么了，但是说维尔夫人的存在似乎就像我现在和她谈话那样真实。巴格雷夫夫人说："假如你还不相信的话，那么我也许很快就会以为现在是您的幽灵在和我说话，这就像让我相信我并没有真的见到她一样；因为当时我全无恐惧，接待她像朋友，也像朋友一样告别。"巴格雷夫夫人接着说，"我不会花一个子儿去让别人相信这事。我对此无利可图，我自己知道，只有不断的麻烦。假如这件事不是由于偶然而真相大白，公众永远也不会知道。"但是现在她说她要将此事私存于心，尽量避开公众。之后她确实这么做了。她说曾有位绅士跋涉三十英里来听她讲这件事；她也曾对着满屋子的人讲过这件事。有几位特别的绅士也曾听巴格雷夫夫人亲口讲述过这件事。

　　这件事给我震动很大，我对此就像对相信一件有根有据的事实那样感到满意。我们为什么只是因为不能解决某些我们所不能确定或证明的事情，就要去争辩事实的本质呢？这使我疑惑不解。巴格雷夫夫人的可信和真诚本身在任何其他事情中都会是不可置疑的。

Joseph Addison
(1672—1719)

Joseph Addison was looked upon as one of the most prestigious editors and chief contributors to the English periodical literature of the early 18th century. His works were characterized by being natural, austere and succinct, full of civilization and persuasion, which influenced the development of the English literature dramatically and played a leading role in moralizing his fellowmen.

Joseph Addison, son of a clergyman, graduated from Oxford with a MA degree, where he became a good acquaintance with Richard Steele. In 1705 he wrote and published "The Campaign", a poem written in heroic couplets, to celebrate the victory at the battle of Blenheim. At this time, Addison renewed his friendship with Richard Steele and was a regular contributor to Steele's *The Tatler*, in which the essays he contributed exposed the luxuries enjoyed by those who were idling their lives in the bourgeois society. Later the two friends went on to found *The Spectator* which rose at its peak to a circulation of 14,000 copies. In the two periodicals, he wrote many essays satirizing those good-for-nothing for their vanity and extravagance by depicting the typical men, customs and lifestyles of all walks of life. What is suggested in the essays serves as a lasting reminder to the readers of all ages.

A Story of an Heir

The following story begins with an encounter with a young gentleman with a considerable estate but, good-for-nothing during the auther's walk with Sir Roger. Stirred up by Roger's description about that heir, Addison thought of a stroy about two friends. He told the story at length to illustrate that one's fortune and happy life can only be obtained by his own effort and hard work.

As I was yesterday taking the air with my friend Sir Roger, we were met by a fresh-coloured ruddy young man who rid by us full speed, with a couple of servants behind him. Upon my inquiry who he was, Sir Roger told me that he was a young gentleman of a considerable estate, who had been educated by a tender mother that lived not many miles from the place where we were. She is a very good lady, says my friend, but took so much care of her son's health that she has made him good for nothing. She quickly found that reading was bad for his eyes, and that writing made his head ache. He was let loose among the woods as soon as he was able to ride on horseback, or to carry a gun upon his shoulder. To be brief, I found, by my friend's account of him, that he had got a great stock of health, but nothing else; and that if it were a man's business only to live, there would not be a more accomplished young fellow in the whole country.

The truth of it is, since my residing in these parts I have seen and heard innumerable instances of young heirs and elder brothers who either from their own reflecting upon the estates they are born to, and therefore thinking all other accomplishments unnecessary, or from hearing these notions frequently inculcated to them by the flattery of their servants and domestics, or from the same foolish thought prevailing in those who have the care of their education, are of no manner of use but to keep up their families, and transmit their lands and houses in a line to posterity.

This makes me often think on a story I have heard of two friends, which I shall give my reader at large, under feigned names. The moral of it may, I hope, be useful, though there are some circumstances which make it rather appear like a novel, than a true story.

Eudoxus and Leontine began the world with small estates. They were both of them men of good sense and great virtue. They prosecuted their studies together in their earlier years, and entered into such a friendship as lasted to the end of their lives. Eudoxus, at his first setting out in the world, threw himself into a court, where by his natural endowments and his acquired abilities he made his way from one post to another, till at length he had raised a very considerable fortune. Leontine on the contrary sought all opportunities of improving his mind by study, conversation and travel. He was not only acquainted with all the sciences, but with the most eminent professors of them throughout Europe. He knew perfectly well the interests of its princes, with the customs and fashions of their courts, and could scarce meet with the name of an extraordinary person in the *Gazette* whom he had not either talked to or seen. In short, he had so well mixt and digested his knowledge of men and books, that he made one of the most accomplished persons of his age. During the whole course of his studies and travels he kept up a punctual correspondence with Eudoxus, who often made himself acceptable to the principal men about court by the intelligence which he received from Leontine. When they were both turned of forty (an age in which, according to Mr. Cowley, there is no dallying with life) they determined, pursuant to the resolution they had taken in the beginning of their lives, to retire, and pass the remainder of their days in the country. In order to this, they both of them married much about the same time. Leontine, with his own and his wife's fortune, bought a farm of three hundred a year, which lay within the neighbourhood of his friend Eudoxus, who had purchased an estate of as many thousands. They were both of them fathers about the same time, Eudoxus having a son born to him, and Leontine a daughter; but to the unspeakable grief of the latter, his young wife (in whom all his happiness was wrapt up) died in a few days after the birth of her daughter. His affliction would have been insupportable, had not he been comforted by the daily visits and conversations of his friend. As they were one day talking together with their usual intimacy, Leontine, considering how incapable he was of giving his daughter a proper education in his own house, and Eudoxus, reflecting on the ordinary behaviour of a son who knows himself to be the heir of a great estate, they both agreed upon an exchange of children, namely that the boy should be bred up with Leontine as his son, and that the girl should live with Eudoxus as his daughter, till they were each of them arrived at years of discretion. The wife of Eudoxus, knowing that her son could not be so advantageously brought up as under the care of Leontine, and considering at the same time that he would be perpetually under her own eye, was by degrees prevailed upon to fall in with the project. She therefore took Leonilla, for that was the name of the girl, and educated her as her own daughter. The two friends on each side had wrought themselves to such an habitual tenderness for the children who were under their direction, that each of them had the real passion of a father, where the title was but imaginary. Florio, the name of the young heir that lived with Leontine, though he had all the duty and affection imaginable for his supposed parent, was taught to rejoice at the sight of Eudoxus, who visited his friend very frequently, and was dictated by his natural affection, as well as by the rules of prudence, to make himself esteemed and beloved by Florio. The boy was now old enough to know his supposed father's circumstances, and that therefore he was to make his way in the world by his own industry. This consideration grew stronger in him every day, and produced so good an effect, that he applied himself with more than ordinary attention to the pursuit of every thing which Leontine recommended to him. His natural abilities, which were very good, assisted by the directions of so excellent a counsellor, enabled him to make a quicker progress than ordinary through all the parts of his education. Before he was twenty years of age, having finished his studies and exercises with great applause, he was removed from the university to the Inns of Court, where there are very few that make themselves considerable proficients in the studies of the place, who know they shall arrive at great estates without them. This was not Florio's case; he found that three hundred a year was but a poor estate for Leontine and himself to live upon, so that he studied without intermission till he gained a very good insight into the constitution and laws of his country.

I should have told my reader, that whilst Florio lived at the house of his foster-father he was always an acceptable guest in the family of Eudoxus, where he became acquainted with Leonilla from her infancy. His acquaintance with her by degrees grew into love, which in a mind trained up in all the sentiments of honour and virtue became a very uneasy passion. He despaired of gaining an heiress of so great a fortune, and would rather have died than attempted it by any indirect methods. Leonilla, who was a woman of the greatest beauty joined with the greatest modesty, entertained at the same time a secret passion for Florio, but conducted herself with so much prudence that she never gave him the least intimation of it. Florio was now engaged in all those arts and improvements that are proper to raise a man's private fortune, and give him a figure in his country, but secretly tormented with that passion which burns with the greatest fury in a virtuous and noble heart, when he received a sudden summons from Leontine to repair to him in the country the next day. For it seems Eudoxus was so filled with the report of his son's reputation, that he could no longer withhold making himself known to him. The morning after his arrival at the house of his supposed father, Leontine told him that Eudoxus had something of great importance to communicate to him; upon which the good man embraced him and wept. Florio was no sooner arrived at the great house that stood in his neighbourhood, but Eudoxus took him by the hand, after the first salutes were over, and conducted him into his closet. He there opened to him the whole secret of his parentage and education, concluding after this manner: *I have no other way left of acknowledging my gratitude to Leontine, than by marrying you to his daughter. He shall not lose the pleasure of being your father by the discovery I have made to you. Leonilla too shall be still my daughter; her filial piety, though misplaced, has been so exemplary that it deserves the greatest reward I can confer upon it. You shall have the pleasure of seeing a great estate fall to you, which you would have lost the relish of had you known yourself born to it. Continue only to deserve it in the same manner you did before you were possessed of it. I have left your mother in the next room. Her heart yearns towards you. She is making the same discoveries to Leonilla which I have made to yourself.* Florio was so overwhelmed with this profusion of happiness, that he was not able to make a reply, but threw himself down at his father's feet, and amidst a flood of tears, kissed and embraced his knees, asking his blessing, and expressing in dumb show those sentiments of love, duty, and gratitude that were too big for utterance. To conclude, the happy pair were married, and half Eudoxus's estate settled upon them. Leontine and Eudoxus passed the remainder of their lives together; and received in the dutiful and affectionate behaviour of Florio and Leonilla the just recompense, as well as the natural effects, of that care which they had bestowed upon them in their education.

Questions

1. Compare the two ways the two friends seek their fortunes and achieve their success.
2. Why did the two friends exchange their children for their upbringing?
3. Comment on the way of the upbringing of the two children in the two families.
4. What does the author try to induce readers to reflect upon by the last sentence at the end of the story?
5. What does the story teller try to convey to readers?

约瑟夫·艾迪生
（1672—1719）

约瑟夫·艾迪生是18世纪英国文学史上最有影响的编辑与期刊主要撰稿人之一。其写作风格清新简洁、朴实淡雅，作品的字里行间充满了倡导文明和劝人从善的内容。这些作品极大地影响了英国文学的发展，同时在教化其同胞方面也起到了主导作用。

艾迪生是一个乡村牧师的儿子，毕业于牛津大学，获文学硕士学位。他在牛津与理查德·斯蒂尔相识。1705年他用英雄双行体创作并出版《征战》一诗，庆祝布伦海姆一战大捷。就在此时，艾迪生与理查德·斯蒂尔重续友情，成为斯蒂尔《闲话报》的长期撰稿人。他的文章揭露了资产阶级社会阶层中虚度光阴者的奢靡生活。后来俩人又合作创办《旁观者》，其最高销量曾达到14,000份。在这两份杂志中，艾迪生撰写了大量文章，把社会不同阶层中的典型人物、他们的风俗和生活都写进自己的作品中，嘲讽那些一无是处者的虚荣与奢靡。他的作品警示后人，长久不衰。

一位继承人的故事

下面的故事讲述了作者与罗杰爵士在乡间散步时，偶遇当地一位腰缠万贯却一无是处的年轻财产继承人的经历。听了罗杰爵士对那位继承人的描述，作者深受触动，于是详细讲述了他所听过的有关两个朋友的故事，告诫人们只有靠自己发奋图强，生活才会富有美满、其乐融融。

昨天，我与朋友罗杰爵士在户外散步时，遇见一位面目光鲜、红润的年轻人。他骑马从我们身边疾驰而过，后面还跟着几个仆人。我问罗杰这位年轻人是谁，罗杰告诉我说他是这儿很有钱的一位绅士。他受教于一位温柔贤良的母亲，他母亲就住在离我们不远的地方。这位母亲很贤淑，对儿子照顾得无微不至，可是却把他惯得不像样子，什么都不会做。自打他小时候，她就发现念书会影响他的视力，写字又常常使他头疼。结果，他刚学会骑马扛枪就被允许在林中自由嬉戏玩耍了。总之，我发现用朋友的话来形容，他只拥有健康的体格，别的一无是处。如果说一个人活着就是为了生存，那么整个这个地方就没有比他更有出息的人了。

实际上，自打我搬到这儿一带居住以来，我看到和听到了许许多多有关年轻继承人和他们兄长的故事。他们要么整天老想着继承财产的事儿，觉得其他的努力都是徒劳无益的，要么就被仆人或家人哄着，一直被灌输着坐享其成的观念，更糟糕的是，教他们念书写字的人满脑子想的也都是这样的事儿。这些人只知道繁衍后代，把土地和房产传给他们的子孙，别的什么也干不来。

罗杰的这番话使我常常想起一段有关两个朋友的故事。故事的主人公都是化名的。虽然故事里的一些情节更像是一部小说而不是真事儿，可是我倒希望其寓意会给人以启迪和教益。

尤多克斯和莱安蒂纳俩人起家窘迫。他们俩都很正直、善良，而且对事物很有见地。早些年，他们在一起学习并建立了终生的友谊。尤多克斯一出道就全身心投入到宫廷的政务中。凭着天赋和后天的努力，他的仕途一帆风顺，不断得到升官晋级，最终积攒了大量的财富。莱安蒂纳正相反，他到处旅行学习，与人交流，寻找一切机会提升自己的智力。他不仅熟知了多方面的科学知识，而且结识了全欧洲大多数著名教授。他非常了解当地宫廷的风俗和时尚，熟知王公贵族们的兴趣之所在。当时报纸上提到的名人虽然他并没有与之交谈过或见过，但几乎没有他不知道的。总之，他把对人的了解和从书本中学到的知识融会贯通起来，成为当时同龄人中的佼佼者之一。在整个学习和旅行中，他和尤多克斯及时通信交流信息。而尤多克斯从莱安蒂纳那里也学了不少的知识，得到了宫廷的主要官员的赏识。当他们到了四十岁的时候（根据考利先生的说法，四十不可再蹉跎），他们决定按照人生之初的打算回归故里安度余生。为了此心愿，他们两个几乎同时娶妻。莱安蒂纳用他和妻子的钱在尤多克斯家旁边买了一个农场，每年能有三百英镑的收入。而尤多克斯早就购置了产业，年收入数万。他们又几乎同时当上了父亲。尤多克斯生了个儿子，莱安蒂纳有了一个女儿。令莱安蒂纳悲痛欲绝的是他年轻的妻子（她是莱安蒂纳幸福的来源）在生下孩子不久就去世了。要不是尤多克斯每天都来看他、和他聊天、安慰他，他可真是痛不欲生，整个人都会崩溃。有一天他们还像往常一样亲密地聊天，莱安蒂纳想到他没有能力给自己的女儿提供良好的教育环境，而尤多克斯也考虑到这样一个问题：他的儿子要是知道将来能继承一大笔财产就会不努力上进。于是两人决定对换抚养各自的孩子，也就是男孩归莱安蒂纳来抚养，女孩将和尤多克斯住在一起，直到这两个孩子长大成人，具有自主的判断能力。尤多克斯的妻子知道儿子在莱安蒂纳这样的家里长大是再有利不过了，同时她也总能看见自己儿子，就逐渐接受了这种安排。与此同时，她也收养了莱安蒂纳名叫莱奥尼拉的女儿，并把她视为自己的孩子一样教育她。这两个朋友彼此都在努力培养、苦心营造对膝下孩子们的亲情。尽管"父亲"这个称呼是虚的，他们二人都把孩子视如己出，倾注了好似亲生父亲的全部情感。弗洛里奥这位小继承人和莱安蒂纳生活在一起，他对莱安蒂纳充满了爱和责任感。莱安蒂纳也教育他爱尤多克斯，所以当尤多克斯来家串门时他也特别高兴和喜悦。尤多克斯抚养孩子细腻入微，充满亲情，又很审慎地关注孩子的成长，受到弗洛里奥的尊敬和喜爱。眼下，这孩子长大了，理解所认父亲的境况，他决定发奋图强立志走出一条自己的路。这个想法在他内心深处变得越来越强烈，并且效果显著，他付出了比常人都多得多的努力，认真地做好莱安蒂纳要他做的每一件事情。他天资聪颖好学，再加上有这么一个名师指点，很快在所接触到的知识领域中都取得了非常大的进步。不到20岁，他就完成了大学的课程和训练，获得一致好评，离开学校进入伦敦律师学院。在该学院，没有几个学生去深入学习法律知识，因为他们知道即使没有知识他们也能继承大笔财产。弗洛里奥却完全不同。他发现每年在农场赚300镑对于莱安蒂纳和他自己来讲只不过是一笔糊口的小钱而已。所以他坚持不懈、刻苦钻研，直到他精通国家的法律法规。

　　在这里，我想要告诉读者的是，当弗洛里奥住在养父家时，他总去尤多克斯家玩而且受到欢迎。在那里他和莱奥尼拉从幼年就开始相识，彼此慢慢地由相知变成相爱。然而，这种在各种各样的荣誉和美德等情感教育中培养起来的爱，却成了令人煎熬的激情。他并没指望娶一个能继承巨额财产的女人为妻，他宁可死也不愿意用迂回的办法来获得财富。莱奥尼拉小姐美丽绝伦，谦逊高雅，同时也暗恋着弗洛里奥，但是她小心翼翼，没有流露出对他一丝一毫的情感。弗洛里奥那时正忙于学习各种知识及先进技艺，这一切不仅能使他拥有财富，而且还能使他在当地出人头地。同时，他心中却默默地受到感情的折磨，他那颗善良高尚之心燃起炙热的烈火。此时他突然收到莱安蒂纳的召唤：让他第二天去他们常见面的地方。原来尤多克斯被儿子杰出的表现而感动，他再也忍不住了，想把真相告诉自己的儿子。第二天早晨弗洛里奥回到了寄父家，莱安蒂纳热泪盈眶地拥抱了他，说尤多克斯有很重要的事情要告诉他。弗洛里奥很快就来到了附近的豪华别墅前，刚一见面打招呼，尤多克斯就把他拉进密室。他向儿子挑明了其身世和受教育等秘密，最后他说：我没有其他方法来表达我对莱安蒂纳的感激之情，只有让你娶他的女儿为妻。尽管我告诉了你的身世，他仍然还是你的父亲，依然该享受为父的快乐。莱奥尼拉也还是我的女儿，她的孝心虽然未给予亲生父母，仍堪称是人世间的楷模，这一切值得倾我所有去回报她。看到一大笔财产从天而降你肯定会感到很快乐吧，如果你一生下来就知道自己拥有这些财产，你就没有现在这样开心了。今后对待这些财产依然要像你以前没有拥有过它那样去看待。你母亲就在隔壁，她心里日日思念着你。她现在向莱奥尼拉透露同一个秘密，就像我刚刚告诉你的一样。此刻，弗洛里奥沉浸在无比幸福之中，他有点不知所措，一句话也说不出来。他匍匐在父亲的脚下，泪如泉涌，亲吻拥抱着父亲的膝盖，祈求父亲的祝福，默默地表达内心难以言状的爱意、责任、感恩。最后，有情人终成眷属，尤多克斯把一半的财产分给了他们。莱安蒂纳和尤多克斯在一起共度余生，享受着弗洛里奥和莱奥尼拉孝顺和深情的照顾所带来的天伦之乐。这也是他们在培养教育孩子过程中由于付出关爱而得到的自然结果。

Richard Steele
(1672—1729)

Sir Richard Steele, English essayist and playwright, was born in Dublin. He was educated at Charterhouse and Merton College, Oxford. Steele entered the army in 1694 and rose to the rank of captain by 1700. During these years of military service in London, Steele became acquainted with a circle of literary and artistic figures, and he began to write. Steele's fame rests on his founding of *The Tatler* (1709—1711) and *The Spectator* (1711—1712), forerunners of modern journalism, the writing of which was joined by his close friend Joseph Addison. In 1714 he became governor of Drury Lane Theatre, where he produced *The Conscious Lovers* (1723), one of the century's most popular plays and perhaps the best example of English sentimental comedy. Steele's first play, a moral tract, *The Christian Hero* (1701) was followed by three comedies *The Funeral* (1701), *The Lying Lover* (1703), and *The Tender Husband* (1705). Politically, he was a zealous Whig, and his fortunes varied with the fortunes of his party. He was knighted in 1715. Steele retired in ill health to his estate in Wales and died in Carmarthenshire.

Tom Varnish

Steele's writing reflects his charm, spontaneity, wit, and imagination. The following is a humorous story about a vain and foolish young man who tries to seduce a lady, only to get himself tricked. Concise as it is, the story is very subtle in description and unforgettable. The image of this bold, arrogant and cocksure young man will cling to the readers' mind.

Because I have a professed aversion to long beginnings of stories, I will go into this at once, by telling you, that there dwells near the Royal Exchange as happy a couple as ever entered into wedlock. These live in that mutual confidence of each other, which renders the satisfaction of marriage even greater than those of friendship, and makes wife and husband the dearest appellations of human life. Mr. Balance is a merchant of good consideration, and understands the world, not from speculation, but practice. His wife is the daughter of an honest house, ever bred in a family-way; and has, from a natural good understanding and great innocence, a freedom which men of sense know to be the certain sign of virtue, and fools take to be an encouragement to vice.

Tom Varnish, a young gentleman of the Middle Temple, by the bounty of a good father, who was so obliging as to die, and leave him, in his twenty-fourth year, besides a good estate, a large sum which lay in the hands of Mr. Balance, had by this means an intimacy at his house; and being one of those hard students who read plays for the improvement of the law, took his rules of life from thence. Upon mature deliberation, he conceived it very proper, that he, as a man of wit and pleasure of the town, should have an intrigue with his merchant's wife. He no sooner thought of this adventure, but he began it by an amorous epistle to the lady and a faithful promise to wait upon her at a certain hour the next evening, when he knew her husband was to be absent.

The letter was no sooner received, but it was communicated to the husband, and produced no other effect in him, than that he joined with his wife to raise all the mirth they could out of this fantastical piece of gallantry. They were so little concerned at this dangerous man of mode, that they plotted ways to perplex him without hurting him. Varnish comes exactly at this hour; and the lady's well-acted confusion at his entrance gave him opportunity to repeat some couplets very fit for the occasion with very much grace and spirit. His theatrical manner of making love was interrupted by an alarm of the husband's coming; and the wife, in a personated terror, beseeched him, "if he had any value for the honour of a woman that loved him, he would jump out of the window." He did so, and fell upon featherbeds placed there on purpose to receive him.

It is not to be conceived how great the joy of an amorous man is, when he has suffered for his mistress, and is never the worse for it. Varnish the next day writ a most elegant billet, wherein he said all that imagination could form upon the occasion. He violently protested, "going out of the window was no way terrible, but as it was going from her"; with several other kind expressions, which procured him a second assignation. Upon his second visit, he was conveyed by a faithful maid into her bed chamber, and left there to expect the arrival of her mistress. But the wench, according to her instructions, ran in again to him, and locked the door after her to keep out her master. She had just time enough to convey the lover into a chest before she admitted the husband and his wife into the room.

You may be sure that trunk was absolutely necessary to be opened; but upon her husband's ordering it, she assured him, "she had taken all the care imaginable in packing up the things with her own hands, and he might send the trunk abroad as soon as he thought fit." The easy husband believed his wife, and the good couple went to bed; Varnish having the happiness to pass the night in the mistress's bedchamber without molestation. The morning arose, but our lover was not well situated to observe her blushes; so all we know of his sentiments on this occasion is, that he heard Balance ask for the key, and say, "he would himself go with this chest, and have it opened before the captain of the ship, for the greater safety of so valuable a lading."

The goods were hoisted away; and Mr. Balance, marching by his chest with great care and diligency, omitting nothing that might give his passenger perplexity. But, to consummate all, he delivered the chest, with strict charge, "in case they were in danger of being taken, to throw it overboard, for there were letters in it, the matter of which might be of great service to the enemy."

Questions

1. How do you describe the tone of the author?
2. What is your attitude toward Tom Varnish?
3. Does Tom Varnish deserve the tricks played on him? Why or why not?
4. How could Tom Varnish come up with the idea of seducing the merchant's wife?
5. What do you think is the most distinctive feature of this story?

理查德·斯梯尔
(1672—1729)

理查德·斯梯尔爵士是英国散文家、剧作家。他生于都柏林,曾先后就读于卡特公学和牛津大学默顿学院。他于1694年入伍,1700年被提拔为上尉。在伦敦服兵役的岁月里,斯梯尔广交文学艺术界人士,并开始笔墨生涯。他创办的《闲话报》(1709—1711)和《旁观者》(1711—1712)使他名声大噪,并成为现代新闻杂志业的先驱。后来其密友约瑟夫·艾迪生加入其中,成为主要撰稿人。1714年他开始掌管皇家竹瑞街剧院,在那里他把自己的《自觉的情人》(1723)搬上舞台。该剧非常成功,是18世纪最著名的戏剧之一,也是英国伤感喜剧的代表剧目。斯梯尔的首部作品是一出道德剧《基督教徒英雄》(1701),后来他发表了三部喜剧:《葬礼》(1701)、《说谎的情人》(1703)和《温柔的丈夫》(1705)。在政治上,他一直都是热心的辉格党员,他一生的荣辱沉浮也与他的政治派别息息相关。斯梯尔于1715年被授予爵位。他晚年因身体原因退休后住在自己的威尔士宅地,死于卡马丹郡。

汤姆·万尼诗

斯梯尔的作品充满了魅力,自然流畅,机智风趣,想象力丰富。下面的这则幽默故事讲的是一个自负愚蠢的年轻人试图勾引一位淑女,结果却被好一番愚弄。故事尽管用词简练,但是描写细腻,让人难忘。这个年轻人鲁莽、傲慢、自大的形象会印在读者的脑海里。

本人向来讨厌故事开头冗长,还是干脆直入主题来告诉大家,在伦敦交易所附近住着一对已步入婚姻殿堂的非常幸福的夫妇。他们互相信任,认为婚姻比友谊更让人满足。这也使夫妻之名成为人生中最亲近的称谓。白伦斯先生是位事业有成的商人。他颇谙世事,这倒并非源于勤于思考,而是由于见多识广。其妻乃良家之女,家教开明,通情达理,纯真无邪,自由自在。聪明人会把这当作美德看待,而傻瓜却认为她软弱可欺。

汤姆·万尼诗是中殿律师学院的一位年轻绅士。在他二十四岁那年,他的好父亲因太急于让他受益而撒手而去,留给他一处豪宅和一大笔钱。钱由白伦斯先生掌管,于是汤姆·万尼诗便有理由经常出入白伦斯的家。汤姆是个难以调教的学生，他把阅读剧本当作提高法律知识的办法，把戏剧当作生活指南。经过深思熟虑，他得出结论，像他这样一位风趣又风流的男子与商人之妻发生一段奸情是合情合理的。一有这样的想法，他便给夫人写了一封情书，信誓旦旦要在次日晚上某个时间等她约会。他知道那时候她丈夫会外出。

信件一送达就到了商人手里。商人并没有什么特别的反应，不过决定要和夫人一起对这小子荒唐的豪勇行为尽情揶揄一番。他们在不伤害他的前提下，毫不顾及这位危险的时尚达人的感受，想出些法子要耍耍他。万尼诗按他定的时间准时赴约。夫人精准到位地演绎出见他进门时惊慌狼狈之情，他则应时应景，优雅又勇敢地重复了几句双行体诗句。正在他充满诗情画意地诉衷肠时，有人来报，说商人丈夫到了。夫人佯装害怕，恳求道："如果郎君真的想配得上对他有爱慕之情的女人，那就应该从窗户跳出去。"他跳了，落在事先特意为他放好的羽毛褥垫上。

这位情种为自己的情人遭受了痛苦，心里却美的无法用语言形容。这事儿一点都没有破坏他的心境。第二天万尼诗写了封优美万分的短信，为了这件事他在信中动用了全部想象力倾诉衷肠。他郑重声明："从窗户逃出去并没什么大不了的，但是从夫人身边逃离真让人受不了。"他还写了几句悦耳动听的词句，这为他赢得了第二次约会的机会。他第二次赴约的时候，忠诚的女仆把他带到夫人的卧室，让他在那里等待夫人的到来。但是女仆按照夫人先前的布置又跑进来，把门插好，以便把主人挡在门外。她刚把这位爱慕者藏到箱子里，就赶紧把门打开迎进先生和夫人。

您也许会认为箱子一定会被打开的；但是当先生要求打开箱子的时候，夫人的一番话使他打消了念头："人家好不容易亲自把东西都已经打包好了，先生可以在认为合适的时候把它发往国外。"随和的丈夫相信了妻子的话，于是恩爱夫妇上床就寝；万尼诗有幸在夫人的寝室过了一夜，不被惊扰。第二天黎明来临，但我们这位爱慕者无缘欣赏到夫人羞红的脸庞；那天早上有关这位多情种子的感受，我们唯一所知道的是，他只听到白伦斯先生要钥匙，并说道："既然货物如此贵重，为确保安全我要亲自把柜子送去，当着船长的面，把柜子打开。"

货抬走了，白伦斯先生一丝不苟地走在箱子旁，不错过任何一个折磨这位"乘客"的机会。更登峰造极的是，他在交付箱子的时候下了严格的指示："一旦货物遇到危险，有可能被非法取走，就将箱子抛下船，因为箱内有书信，信中的内容如果被敌人得知将会对其极为有利。"

Oliver Goldsmith
(ca.1730—1774)

Oliver Goldsmith, Anglo-Irish playwright, novelist, poet, and essayist, was born in Pallas, Ireland, where his father was an Anglican curate. Goldsmith earned his Bachelor of Arts in 1749 at Trinity College, Dublin, studying theology and law. He later studied medicine at the University of Edinburgh and the University of Leiden, and then toured Europe, supporting himself by playing the flute and by begging. On his return, he settled in London, where he worked as an apothecary's assistant. Perennially in debt and addicted to gambling, Goldsmith had a massive output as a hack writer for the publishers of London, but his few painstaking works earned him the company of Samuel Johnson, and became a member of his circle. Near the end of his life, Goldsmith made an ample income, but, through extravagance and open-handedness toward needy friends, spent far more than he earned. He died in London.

Goldsmith's works include the novel *The Vicar of Wakefield* (1766), a social and political satire, in which rural honesty, kindness, and patience triumph over urban values. Other works include "The Traveler" (1674), a philosophic poem that established him as an important writer and the poem "The Deserted Village" (1770), which marked the transition in English literature from neoclassicism to romanticism. Goldsmith also produced dramatic works. *She Stoops to Conquer* (1773) achieved an immediate success. It remains one of the best-known comedies of the British drama.

The Disabled Soldier

The following story tells about the misfortunes of a disabled soldier—including his miserable childhood, his imprisonment, his forced engagement in the war, his terrible adventure on the privateer, etc. Here Goldsmith severely satirizes English society by exposing the cruelty, hypocrisy and other evils, and shows much sympathy for the misery of the poor and great admiration for their endurance in contrast with the rich.

No observation is more common, and at the same time more true, than that one half of the world are ignorant how the other half lives. The misfortunes of the great are held up to engage our attention; are enlarged upon in tones of declamation; and the world is called upon to gaze at the noble sufferers: the great, under the pressure of calamity, are conscious of several others sympathizing with their distress; and have, at once, the comfort of admiration and pity.

There is nothing magnanimous in bearing misfortunes with fortitude, when the whole world is looking on: men in such circumstances will act bravely even from motives of vanity: but he who, in the vale of obscurity, can brave adversity; who without friends to encourage, acquaintances to pity, or even without hope to alleviate his misfortunes, can behave with tranquility and indifference, is truly great: whether peasant or courtier, he deserves admiration, and should be held up for our imitation and respect.

While the slightest inconveniences of the great are magnified into calamities; while tragedy mouths out their sufferings in all the strains of eloquence, the miseries of the poor are entirely disregarded; and yet some of the lower ranks of people undergo more real hardships in one day, than those of a more exalted station suffer in their whole lives. It is inconceivable what difficulties the meanest of our common sailors and soldiers endure without murmuring or regret; without passionately declaiming against providence, or calling their fellows to be gazers on their intrepidity. Every day is to them a day of misery, and yet they entertain their hard fate without repining.

With what indignation do I hear an Ovid, a Cicero, or a Rabutin complain of their misfortunes and hardships, whose greatest calamity was that of being unable to visit a certain spot of earth, to which they had foolishly attached an idea of happiness. Their distresses were pleasures, compared to what many of the adventuring poor every day endure without murmuring. They ate, drank, and slept; they had slaves to attend them, and were sure of subsistence for life; while many of their fellow creatures are obliged to wander without a friend to comfort or assist them, and even without shelter from the severity of the season.

I have been led into these reflections from accidentally meeting, some days ago, a poor fellow, whom I knew when a boy, dressed in a sailor's jacket, and begging at one of the outlets of the town, with a wooden leg. I knew him to have been honest and industrious when in the country, and was curious to learn what had reduced him to his present situation. Wherefore, after giving him what I thought proper, I desired to know the history of his life and misfortunes, and the manner in which he was reduced to his present distress. The disabled soldier, for such he was, though dressed in a sailor's habit, scratching his head, and leaning on his crutch, put himself into an attitude to comply with my request, and gave me his history as follows:

"As for my misfortunes, master, I can't pretend to have gone through any more than other folks; for, except the loss of my limb, and my being obliged to beg, I don't know any reason, thank Heaven, that I have to complain. There is Bill Tibbs, of our regiment, he has lost both his legs, and an eye to boot; but, thank Heaven, it is not so bad with me yet.

"I was born in Shropshire; my father was a labourer, and died when I was five years old, so I was put upon the parish. As he had been a wandering sort of a man, the parishioners were not able to tell to what parish I belonged, or where I was born, so they sent me to another parish, and that parish sent me to a third. I thought in my heart, they kept sending me about so long, that they would not let me be born in any parish at all; but at last, however, they fixed me. I had some disposition to be a scholar, and was resolved at least to know my letters: but the master of the workhouse put me to business as soon as I was able to handle a mallet; and here I lived an easy kind of life for five years. I only wrought ten hours in the day, and had my meat and drink provided for my labour. It was true, I was not suffered to stir out of the house, for fear, as they said, I should run away; but what of that? I had the liberty of the whole house, and the yard before the door, and that was enough for me. I was then bound out to a farmer, where I was up both early and late; but I ate and drank well; and liked my business well enough, till he died, when I was obliged to provide for myself; so I was resolved to go seek my fortune.

"In this manner I went from town to town, worked when I could get employment, and starved when I could get none; when, happening one day to go through a field belonging to a justice of peace, I spied a hare crossing the path just before me; and I believe the devil put it into my head to fling my stick at it. Well, what will you have on't? I killed the hare, and was bringing it away, when the justice himself met me; he called me a poacher and a villain, and collaring me, desired I would give an account of myself. I fell upon my knees, begged his worship's pardon, and began to give a full account of all that I knew of my breed, seed, and generation; but though I gave a very true account, the justice said I could give no account; so I was indicted at the sessions, found guilty of being poor, and sent up to London to Newgate, in order to be transported as a vagabond.

"People may say this and that of being in jail, but for my part, I found Newgate as agreeable a place as ever I was in all my life. I had my belly full to eat and drink, and did no work at all. This kind of life was too good to last forever; so I was taken out of prison, after five months, put on board of ship, and sent off, with two hundred more, to the plantations. We had but an indifferent passage, for being all confined in the hold, more than a hundred of our people died for want of sweet air; and those that remained were sickly enough, God knows. When we came ashore we were sold to the planters, and I was bound for seven years more. As I was no scholar, for I did not know my letters, I was obliged to work among the Negroes; and I served out my time, as in duty bound to do.

"When my time was expired, I worked my passage home, and glad I was to see old England again, because I loved my country. I was afraid, however, that I should be indicted for a vagabond once more, so did not much care to go down into the country, but kept about the town, and did little jobs when I could get them.

"I was very happy in this manner for some time till one evening, coming home from work, two men knocked me down, and then desired me to stand. They belonged to a press-gang. I was carried before the justice, and as I could give no account of myself, I had my choice left, whether to go on board a man-of-war, or list for a soldier. I chose the latter, and in this post of a gentleman, I served two campaigns in Flanders, was at the battles of Val and Fontenoy, and received but one wound through the breast here; but the doctor of our regiment soon made me well again.

"When the peace came on I was discharged; and as I could not work, because my wound was sometimes troublesome, I listed for a landman in the East India Company's service. I have fought the French in six pitched battles; and I verily believe that if I could read or write, our captain would have made me a corporal. But it was not my good fortune to have any promotion, for I soon fell sick, and so got leave to return home again with forty pounds in my pocket. This was at the beginning of the present war, and I hoped to be set on shore, and to have the pleasure of spending my money; but the Government wanted men, and so I was pressed for a sailor, before ever I could set a foot on shore.

"The boatswain found me, as he said, an obstinate fellow: he swore he knew that I understood my business well, but that I shammed Abraham to be idle; but God knows, I knew nothing of sea-business, and he beat me without considering what he was about. I had still, however, my forty pounds, and that was some comfort to me under every beating; and the money I might have had to this day, but that our ship was taken by the French, and so I lost all.

"Our crew was carried into Brest, and many of them died, because they were not used to life in a jail; but, for my part, it was nothing to me, for I was seasoned. One night, as I was asleep on the bed of boards, with a warm blanket about me, for I always loved to lie well, I was awakened by the boatswain, who had a dark lantern in his hand. 'Jack,' says he to me, 'will you knock out the French sentry's brains?' 'I don't care,' says I, striving to keep myself awake, 'if I lend a hand.' 'Then follow me,' says he, 'and I hope we shall do business.' So up I got, and tied my blanket, which was all the clothes I had, about my middle, and went with him to fight the Frenchman. I hate the French, because they are all slaves, and wear wooden shoes.

"Though we had no arms, one Englishman is able to beat five French at any time; so we went down to the door where both the sentries were posted, and rushing upon them, seized their arms in a moment, and knocked them down. From thence nine of us ran together to the quay, and seizing the first boat we met, got out of the harbour and put to sea. We had not been here three days before we were taken up by the *Dorset* privateer, who were glad of so many good hands; and we consented to run our chance. However, we had not as much luck as we expected. In three days we fell in with the *Pompadour* privateer of forty guns, while we had but twenty-three, so to it we went, yard-arm and yard-arm. The fight lasted three hours, and I verily believe we should have taken the Frenchman, had we but had some more men left behind; but unfortunately we lost all our men just as we were going to get the victory.

"I was once more in the power of the French, and I believe it would have gone hard with me had I been brought back to Brest; but by good fortune we were retaken by the *Viper*. I had almost forgotten to tell you, that in that engagement, I was wounded in two places: I lost four fingers off the left hand, and my leg was shot off. If I had had the good fortune to have lost my leg and use of my hand on board a king's ship, and not aboard a privateer, I should have been entitled to clothing and maintenance during the rest of my life; but that was not my chance: one man is born with a silver spoon in his mouth, and another with a wooden ladle. However, Blessed be God, I enjoy good health, and will for ever love liberty and old England. Liberty, property, and Old England, for ever, huzza!"

Thus saying, he limped off, leaving me in admiration at his intrepidity and content; nor could I avoid acknowledging that an habitual acquaintance with misery serves better than philosophy to teach us to despise it.

Questions

1. In what ways does the narrator contrast the great and the poor in the first four paragraphs? What attitude does the narrator have toward them respectively?
2. How miserable is the disabled soldier's life? To what extent is the disabled soldier content with life?
3. According to the narrator, why does the disabled soldier deserve our admiration and respect?
4. Who should be blamed for the disabled soldier's misfortunes? What does the author intend to disclose?
5. What is the story's point of view? How effectively does it work?

奥利弗·哥尔德斯密斯
（约1730—1774）

奥利弗·哥尔德斯密斯，英国剧作家、小说家、诗人及散文家，出生于爱尔兰的帕拉斯，父亲是英国国教副牧师。哥尔德斯密斯曾在都柏林三一学院学习神学和法律，并在1749年获文学学士学位。随后他先后就读于爱丁堡大学和来登大学学习医学，之后开始欧洲之旅，靠演奏笛子和乞讨为生。他回国后定居于伦敦，成为一位药剂师的助手。由于一直债务缠身而又嗜赌如命，哥尔德斯密斯作为雇佣文人为伦敦出版商撰写了大量作品，但其中几部力作赢得了塞缪尔·约翰森的赏识，从而成为其文学社团的一员。到了晚年，虽然哥尔德斯密斯的收入比较可观，但由于他挥霍无度，对朋友有求必应，所以总是过着入不敷出的生活。哥尔德斯密斯逝世于伦敦。

哥尔德斯密斯的作品包括小说《威克菲尔德的牧师》（1766），它辛辣讽刺了社会、政治现状，将乡村生活中的诚实、仁慈和忍耐凌驾于都市价值观之上。哥尔德斯密斯的其他作品还包括两首重要的诗歌：一首为《旅行者》（1674），该诗充满了哲理，奠定了他重要的文学地位；另一首为《荒村》（1770），该诗标志着英国文学由新古典主义向浪漫主义的过渡。同时哥尔德斯密斯也有一些戏剧作品问世：《委曲求全》（1773）曾一炮走红，至今仍是英国戏剧界最受欢迎的喜剧之一。

伤残士兵苦难记

下面的故事讲述了一个伤残士兵的不幸遭遇，包括他悲惨的童年、他的监禁生涯、他被逼参战的历史、他在私掠船上的恐怖经历等等。借此短篇，哥尔德斯密斯辛辣讽刺了英国社会，揭露了其残酷性、虚伪性以及其他罪恶。同时通过与富人对比，哥尔德斯密斯对穷人所遭受的苦难给予极大的同情，并高度赞赏他们在困难面前的忍耐力。

世上有一半的人并不知晓世上另一半人的境况，这句话再平凡也再真实不过了。大人物们所遭受的不幸往往会被当作典范大肆宣扬，甚至不惜慷慨激昂地夸大其词，弄得全世界都得瞩目这些受苦受难的高等人士。灾难当头的大人物们能够享受到他人的同情，同时也会从他们的赞赏和怜悯中得到慰藉。

在世人瞩目下坚韧地去承受痛苦算不上什么崇高：在这种情况之下人人都会表现英勇，甚至出于虚荣也会如此。然而那些虽然一文不名却仍能在逆境中百折不挠的人；那些虽无朋友给予鼓励，虽无相识施与同情，甚至虽无希望减轻痛苦却仍能泰然处之、漠然置之的人，才是名副其实的伟大。无论他是农夫还是伺臣，都值得我们赞赏。这样的人才应该被立为典范，让人仿效、受人尊敬。

　　当大人物们一丁大点的不顺被夸大成灾难的时候，当这些灾难以悲剧的形式言不由衷地穷其雄辩之能事大谈这些大人物们有多么不幸的时候，穷苦人们所承受的痛苦却丝毫无人问津。然而，有些下等人一天所经历的痛苦要比那些上等人一生所经历的来得更为真实。无法想象出身微贱的普通水手和士兵们承受了何等的痛苦。他们毫无怨言或是懊悔；没有大张旗鼓地去对抗天命或是招来同胞目睹他们的英勇无畏。对他们来说，每一天都意味着苦难，但是他们却接受着这一切，无怨无悔。

　　当我听到奥维德、西塞罗或是拉布汀之流的人抱怨他们的不幸和苦难时，我真是气愤不已。他们最大的灾难不过是无法到地球的某一景点观光而已。这些人愚蠢地认为能去那里就等于实现了幸福。他们所谓的苦难跟那些每日险里求生的穷苦人默默承受的苦难相比简直就是享乐。他们吃得好、喝得好、睡得香；他们有奴隶服侍左右，毫无生计之忧。相比之下，他们许多同胞们却被迫四处流浪。他们得不到朋友的鼓励，也看不到援助之手，甚至连个遮风挡雨的栖身之所都没有。

　　我的这一番感想还得从几天前我与一位可怜同乡的邂逅说起。他是我儿时的旧相识，当时他穿着水手上衣，拖着一条木制的假肢，正在城里一家商店乞讨。记得在乡下的时候，他是一个诚实又勤奋的人。我很好奇他为何落得如此下场，因而在适当地给了他一点接济之后，我便开始询问起他的生活和不幸的来龙去脉。眼下这位伤残士兵，身穿水手服，斜靠在拐杖上，挠着头，答应了我的请求，向我述说了以下的苦难史。

　　"说起我的不幸，先生，我可不能假装比别人经历得更多。除了断了条腿，被迫成了乞丐之外，我真不知道我有任何理由，谢天谢地，可抱怨的。我们团的比尔·比波兹两条腿都没了，一只眼还瞎了。但是，谢天谢地，我还没那么惨。

　　"我出生在什罗普郡，父亲是个出苦力的，在我五岁时就过世了，之后我就被送到了教区那里。由于我父亲居无定所，所以教区的教徒们搞不清我到底属于哪一个区，也不知道我具体生于何地，所以他们就把我不断地从一个教区送到另一个教区。我心想，他们这样送来送去这么长时间，肯定不想接受我在任何一个教区出生。不管怎样，最终他们还是收养了我。我的愿望是想当个文化人，至少不应该目不识丁，但我刚刚能拿得动木槌，劳动救济院的院长就把我拉去干活了。在那里我待了五年，日子还算轻松自在。白天只要干上10个小时的活就能有肉吃，有喝的。说真的，他们不让我踏出救济院一步，理由是怕我逃跑。我干嘛要跑？在救济院里我不受约束，门前的院子也可以自由活动，这就足够了。从救济院出来后我就去给一个农场主干活了。在他那儿虽然没日没夜地干，但吃喝不愁。我还是很喜欢那里的生活，直到农场主过世了，我才被逼无奈开始自谋生路。于是我决定出去闯荡闯荡。

"就这样，我从一个城市走到另一个城市。如果能找到活的话，就干上一阵子，找不到的话就只能饿肚子了。有一天，我从治安官家的一块地上经过，碰巧看见一只兔子从眼前跑过去，当时我肯定是中了邪了，随手把手里的棍子朝它扔了过去，你猜怎么着？竟然一下把它砸死了。我刚要把兔子拎走，却跟治安官撞个正着。他骂我是个窃贼、恶棍，并揪住我的衣领让我交代一下身份。我跪了下来，求他饶了我，并一五一十地自述了我的身份、家系和祖辈的情况。虽然我所说的并无半点虚假，可治安官根本不相信，说我压根就澄清不了自己。于是我就被告上了治安法庭，因为贫穷而被判有罪，随后又被关进了伦敦纽盖特监狱，从那里被当作流浪汉流放海外。

"说到坐牢人们可能会众说纷纭，但我倒觉得纽盖特是我一生中待过的快乐之所。起码我能吃饱喝足，而且啥活不用干。然而好景不长，五个月之后我被带出监狱，押上了一艘船。同行的还有其他两百多人，我们将被流放到各大种植园。我们的旅途真是糟透了，由于被关押在货舱里，我们中的一百多人因缺氧而死，而那些存活下来的人也虚弱之极，上帝可以作证。上岸时，我们被卖给大种植园主们，我得服7年多的劳役。由于没什么文化，大字不识一个，我只得跟黑人们一起干活。最终我服满了刑期，责无旁贷嘛。

"刑满释放之后，我靠打工回归了故里。再次见到久违了的英格兰还真是高兴，因为我热爱自己的故土。然而，为了避免再次被当作流浪汉而告上法庭，我没再去乡下，而是选择在城镇里漂泊，可能的话打点零工。

"我就这样生活着，觉得很幸福，但是这种幸福只维持了一段时间就走到了尽头。有天晚上我正走在下班回家的路上，突然冒出了两个人将我打倒在地，然后又命令我站起来，他们是征兵队的。我被带到了法官面前，无法证明身份的我别无选择：要么上军舰，要么参加陆军。我选择了后者，在这个绅士般光荣的岗位上，我参加了佛兰德的两次战役，还参加了瓦尔战役和封特诺伊战役，只受过一次伤，在胸前这个地方。但我们团的军医很快就让我康复了。

"战争结束时，我退役了。由于胸部的伤痛时而发作，我无法再干体力活了。于是我报名到东印度公司当了一名陆地业务员。我曾在六次战斗中与法国人对决。我敢说要不是文化水平低，我们长官肯定会提升我为下士。然而，我的命没那么好，因为没多久我就病倒了。于是，兜里揣着40英镑，我再次踏上了归途。那时正值这场战争爆发的初期,我满怀希望地盘算着上岸后要好好享受一下花钱的乐趣。但是政府需要人手参战,我还没来得及上岸就被迫成了一名水手。

"水手长发现,如他所说,我是一个顽固分子:他发誓他看得出我对水手的职责是一清二楚的,而我却在装病偷懒。但上帝作证,我对海上作业根本一窍不通。他对我大打出手,全然不考虑自己的所作所为。不管怎样,那40英镑还在我身上,每次挨打,这多少还能给我一些慰藉。这些钱原本可以保留至今,但我们的船被法国人俘去了,钱也就分文没有了。

"我们全体船员一起被带到了布勒斯特,其中很多人由于无法适应监狱生活而丧命;但这一切对我来说却没什么,因为我早已对此习以为常了。一天晚上,我裹着毯子躺在木板上睡得正香,我总是喜欢规规矩矩地躺着,水手长过来把我叫醒,他手里拿着一盏昏暗的提灯对我说,'杰克,想不想把那些法国哨兵的脑袋打昏?''我愿意效劳帮一把,'我回答道,竭力保持清醒。'那么就跟我来,'他说,'希望我们能干成事儿。'于是我就起了床,将毯子围在腰间,这可是我唯一的衣服,跟着他去找法国人拼命去了。我憎恨法国人,因为他们都是些奴才,而且还穿着木头鞋子。

"尽管我们手无寸铁,但无论何时一个英国人都能干掉五个法国人。我们向门口走去,那儿有两个哨兵把守,我们向他们猛扑过去,一眨眼的工夫就缴了他们的械,并将其击倒在地。之后我们9个人一起逃向码头,看到一艘船就跳了上去,驶向大海。然而我们在海上不到三天就被抓上了一艘叫盗赛号的私掠船,他们很高兴又弄来了这么多的得力人手。我们达成一致再冒一次险,但事情却没像我们预想得那么走运。三天后,我们的船就遭遇了珀姆帕德号私掠船,他们有40条枪,而我们却只有23条。我们就这样冲了过去,桁端对着桁端。这一仗足足打了三个小时。要是我们的人手再多点,我敢肯定法国人不是我们的对手。但不幸的是,眼看胜利近在眼前,我们的人却全军覆没了。

"我们再次落到了法国人手里,要是被送回布勒斯特监狱,肯定会吃不少苦头。幸运的是我们又被送上了一艘名叫维坡号的船上。差点忘了告诉你,在那场交战中,我两处受伤:左手断了四根手指,还被打断了一条腿。当时要是我命好在皇家船队上效力而不是为私掠船卖命的话,那么我的下半辈子肯定会衣食无忧,可惜我没那个命。有些人生来富贵,用的是银勺子,而有些人则生来贫苦,用的是木勺子。不管怎样,上帝保佑,我的身体还很健康,还可以永远享受自由,永远热爱这古老的英格兰。自由、财富、古老的英格兰,万岁!"

说完这番话,他一瘸一拐地走了。我却沉浸于对他的仰慕之中,对他那种英勇无畏而又知足常乐的精神赞叹不已。我不得不承认这一事实:只有习于亲身体验不幸之苦方能懂得如何去蔑视苦难,这要比空谈哲学大道理奏效得多。

Walter Scott
(1771—1832)

Sir Walter Scott, Scottish novelist and poet, is most famous for his historical novels. Scott had strong interest in the old Border tales and ballads since his early childhood. He attended Edinburgh High School and studied arts and law at Edinburgh University. He practiced law and was appointed sheriff depute of the county of Selkirk and then he became clerk to the Court of Session in Edinburgh. He died three years later after he had a stroke in 1830.

Scott started his literary career by translating and writing poems. He completed a series of novels on the Scottish theme known as "The Waverley Novels" such as *Waverley* (1814), *Rob Roy* (1817), and *The Heart of Midlothian* (1818). Then he turned to English history and other themes including *Ivenhoe* (1819), the best known of Scott's novels today, and *The Monastery* (1820), *Kenilworth* (1821), and *Quentin Durward* (1823) etc. With his deep knowledge of the Scottish history and society, Scott presented his mastery of storytelling and dialogues in his novels. He focused on the lives of both great and ordinary people caught up in violent, dramatic changes in history. His rich and ornate literary style combined energy with decorum, lyric beauty with clarity of description. In addition, Scott was also one of the earliest short story writers in English.

The Tapestried Chamber or The Lady in the Sacque

The following story is about a most brave and experienced general who is yet ironically scared almost to death in a tapestried chamber haunted by his friend's ancestral infamous lady in the sacque. By Scott's rich and elaborate descriptions, we experience the pastoral landscape, the antique castle, the chivalrous gentlemen and the thrilling suspense of the story.

The following narrative is given from the pen, so far as memory permits, in the same character in which it was presented to the author's ear; nor has he claim to further praise, or to be more deeply censured, than in proportion to the good or bad judgment which he has employed in selecting his materials, as he has studiously avoided any attempt at ornament which might interfere with the simplicity of the tale.

At the same time, it must be admitted that the particular class of stories which turns on the marvellous, possesses a stronger influence when told than when committed to print. The volume taken up at noonday, though rehearsing the same incidents, conveys a much more feeble impression than is achieved by the voice of the speaker on a circle of fireside auditors, who hang upon the narrative as the narrator details the minute incidents which serve to give it authenticity, and lowers his voice with an affectation of mystery while he approaches the fearful and wonderful part. It was with such advantages that the present writer heard the following events related, more than twenty years since, by the celebrated Miss Seward, of Litchfield, who, to her numerous accomplishments, added, in a remarkable degree, the power of narrative in private conversation. In its present form the tale must necessarily lose all the interest which was attached to it, by the flexible voice and intelligent features of the gifted narrator. Yet still, read aloud, to an undoubting audience by the doubtful light of the closing evening, or, in silence, by a decaying taper, and amidst the solitude of a half-lighted apartment, it may redeem its character as a good ghost story. Miss Seward always affirmed that she had derived her information from an authentic source, although she suppressed the names of the two persons chiefly concerned. I will not avail myself of any particulars I may have since received concerning the localities of the detail, but suffer them to rest under the same general description in which they were first related to me; and, for the same reason, I will not add to or diminish the narrative, by any circumstance, whether more or less material, but simply rehearse, as I heard it, a story of supernatural terror.

About the end of the American war, when the officers of Lord Cornwallis's army, which surrendered at Yorktown, and others, who had been made prisoners during the impolitic and ill-fated controversy, were returning to their own country, to relate their adventures, and repose themselves after their fatigues, there was amongst them a general officer, to whom Miss S. gave the name of Browne, but merely, as I understood, to save the inconvenience of introducing a nameless agent in the narrative. He was an officer of merit, as well as a gentleman of high consideration for family and attainments.

Some business had carried General Browne upon a tour through the western counties, when, in the conclusion of a morning stage, he found himself in the vicinity of a small country town, which presented a scene of uncommon beauty, and of a character peculiarly English.

The little town, with its stately old church, whose tower bore testimony to the devotion of ages long past, lay amidst pastures and corn-fields of small extent, but bounded and divided with hedgerow timber of great age and size. There were few marks of modern improvement. The environs of the place intimated neither the solitude of decay nor the bustle of novelty; the houses were old, but in good repair; and the beautiful little river murmured freely on its way to the left of the town, neither restrained by a dam, nor bordered by a towing-path.

Upon a gentle eminence, nearly a mile to the southward of the town, were seen, amongst many venerable oaks and tangled thickets, the turrets of a castle, as old as the wars of York and Lancaster, but which seemed to have received important alterations during the age of Elizabeth and her successor. It had not been a place of great size; but whatever accommodation it formerly afforded was, it must be supposed, still to be obtained within its walls; at least such was the inference which General Browne drew from observing the smoke arise merrily from several of the ancient chimney-stacks. The wall of the park ran alongside of the highway for two or three hundred yards; and through the different points by which the eye found glimpses into the woodland scenery, it seemed to be well stocked. Other points of view opened in succession; now a full one, of the front of the old castle, and now a side glimpse at its particular towers; the former rich in all the bizarrerie of the Elizabethan school, while the simple and solid strength of other parts of the building seemed to show that they had been raised more for defence than ostentation.

Delighted with the partial glimpses which he obtained of the castle through the woods and glades by which this ancient feudal fortress was surrounded, our military traveller was determined to inquire whether it might not deserve a nearer view, and whether it contained family pictures or other objects of curiosity worthy of a stranger's visit; when, leaving the vicinity of the park, he rolled through a clean and well-paved street, and stopped at the door of a well-frequented inn.

Before ordering horses to proceed on his journey, General Browne made inquiries concerning the proprietor of the château which had so attracted his admiration; and was equally surprised and pleased at hearing in reply a nobleman named, whom we shall call Lord Woodville. How fortunate! Much of Browne's early recollections, both at school and at college, had been connected with young Woodville, whom, by a few questions, he now ascertained to be the same with the owner of this fair domain. He had been raised to the peerage by the decease of his father a few months before, and, as the

General learned from the landlord, the term of mourning being ended, was now taking possession of his paternal estate, in the jovial season of merry autumn, accompanied by a select party of friends to enjoy the sports of a country famous for game.

This was delightful news to our traveller. Frank Woodville had been Richard Browne's fag at Eton, and his chosen intimate at Christ Church; their pleasures and their tasks had been the same; and the honest soldier's heart warmed to find his early friend in possession of so delightful a residence, and of an estate, as the landlord assured him with a nod and a wink, fully adequate to maintain and add to his dignity. Nothing was more natural than that the traveller should suspend a journey, which there was nothing to render hurried, to pay a visit to an old friend under such agreeable circumstances.

The fresh horses, therefore, had only the brief task of conveying the General's travelling carriage to Woodville Castle. A porter admitted them at a modern Gothic lodge, built in that style to correspond with the castle itself, and at the same time rang a bell to give warning of the approach of visitors. Apparently the sound of the bell had suspended the separation of the company, bent on the various amusements of the morning; for, on entering the court of the château, several young men were lounging about in their sporting dresses, looking at and criticizing the dogs which the keepers held in readiness to attend their pastime. As General Browne alighted, the young lord came to the gate of the hall, and for an instant gazed, as at a stranger, upon the countenance of his friend, on which war, with its fatigues and its wounds, had made a great alteration. But the uncertainty lasted no longer than till the visitor had spoken, and the hearty greeting which followed was such as can only be exchanged betwixt those who have passed together the merry days of careless boyhood or early youth.

"If I could have formed a wish, my dear Browne," said Lord Woodville, "it would have been to have you here, of all men, upon this occasion, which my friends are good enough to hold as a sort of holiday. Do not think you have been unwatched during the years you have been absent from us. I have traced you through your dangers, your triumphs, your misfortunes, and was delighted to see that, whether in victory or defeat, the name of my old friend was always distinguished with applause."

The General made a suitable reply, and congratulated his friend on his new dignities, and the possession of a place and domain so beautiful.

"Nay, you have seen nothing of it as yet," said Lord Woodville, "and I trust you do not mean to leave us till you are better acquainted with it. It is true, I confess, that my present party is pretty large, and the old house, like other places of the kind, does not possess so much accommodation as the extent of the outward walls appears to promise. But we can give you a comfortable old-fashioned room, and I venture to suppose that your campaigns have taught you to be glad of worse quarters."

The General shrugged his shoulders, and laughed. "I presume," he said, "the worst apartment in your château is considerably superior to the old tobacco-cask, in which I was fain to take up my night's lodging when I was in the bush, as the Virginians call it, with the light corps. There I lay, like Diogenes himself, so delighted with my covering from the elements, that I made a vain attempt to have it rolled on to my next quarters; but my commander for the time would give way to no such luxurious provision, and I took farewell of my beloved cask with tears in my eyes."

"Well, then, since you do not fear your quarters," said Lord Woodville, "you will stay with me a week at least. Of guns, dogs, fishing-rods, flies, and means of sport by sea and land, we have enough and to spare: you cannot pitch on an amusement but we will find the means of pursuing it. But if you prefer the gun and pointers, I will go with you myself, and see whether you have mended your shooting since you have been amongst the Indians of the back settlements."

The General gladly accepted his friendly host's proposal in all its points. After a morning of manly exercise, the company met at dinner, where it was the delight of Lord Woodville to conduce to the display of the high properties of his recovered friend, so as to recommend him to his guests, most of whom were persons of distinction. He led General Browne to speak of the scenes he had witnessed; and as every word marked alike the brave officer and the sensible man, who retained possession of his cool judgment under the most imminent dangers, the company looked upon the soldier with general respect, as on one who had proved himself possessed of an uncommon portion of personal courage—that attribute, of all others, of which everybody desires to be thought possessed.

The day at Woodville Castle ended as usual in such mansions. The hospitality stopped within the limits of good order. Music, in which the young lord was a proficient, succeeded to the circulation of the bottle; cards and billiards, for those who preferred such amusements, were in readiness; but the exercise of the morning required early hours, and not long after eleven o'clock the guests began to retire to their several apartments.

The young lord himself conducted his friend, General Browne, to the chamber destined for him, which answered the description he had given of it, being comfortable, but old-fashioned. The bed was of the massive form used in the end of the seventeenth century, and the curtains of faded silk, heavily trimmed with tarnished gold. But then the sheets, pillows, and blankets looked delightful to the campaigner, when he thought of his "mansion, the cask." There was an air of gloom in the tapestry hangings, which, with their worn-out graces, curtained the walls of the little chamber, and gently undulated as the autumnal breeze found its way through the ancient lattice-window, which pattered and whistled as the air gained entrance. The toilet, too, with its mirror, turbaned, after the manner of the beginning of the century, with a coiffure of murrey-coloured silk, and its hundred strange-shaped boxes, providing for arrangements which had been obsolete for more than fifty years, had an antique, and in so far a melancholy, aspect. But nothing could blaze more brightly and cheerfully than the two large wax candles; or if aught could rival them, it was the flaming bickering fagots in the chimney that sent at once their gleam and their warmth through the snug apartment, which, notwithstanding the general antiquity of its appearance, was not wanting in the least convenience that modern habits rendered either necessary or desirable.

"This is an old-fashioned sleeping apartment, General," said the young lord; "but I hope you find nothing that makes you envy your old tobacco-cask."

"I am not particular respecting my lodgings," replied the General; "yet were I to make any choice, I would prefer this chamber by many degrees to the gayer and more modern rooms of your family mansion. Believe me, that when I unite its modern air of comfort with its venerable antiquity, and recollect that it is your lordship's property, I shall feel in better quarters here, than if I were in the best hotel London could afford."

"I trust—I have no doubt—that you will find yourself as comfortable as I wish you, my dear General," said the young nobleman; and once more bidding his guest good-night, he shook him by the hand, and withdrew.

The General once more looked around him, and internally congratulating himself on his return to peaceful life, the comforts of which were endeared by the recollection of the hardships and dangers he had lately sustained, undressed himself, and prepared for a luxurious night's rest.

Here, contrary to the custom of this species of tale, we leave the General in possession of his apartment until the next morning.

The company assembled for breakfast at an early hour, but without the appearance of General Browne, who seemed the guest that Lord Woodville was desirous of honouring above all whom his hospitality had assembled around him. He more than once expressed himself surprised at the General's absence, and at length sent a servant to make inquiry after him. The man brought back information that General Browne had been walking abroad since an early hour of the morning, in defiance of the weather, which was misty and ungenial.

"The custom of a soldier," said the young nobleman to his friends; "many of them acquire habitual vigilance, and cannot sleep after the early hour at which their duty usually commands them to be alert."

Yet the explanation which Lord Woodville thus offered to the company seemed hardly satisfactory to his own mind, and it was in a fit of silence and abstraction that he awaited the return of the General. It took place near an hour after the breakfast bell had rung. He looked fatigued and feverish. His hair—the powdering and arrangement of which was at this time one of the most important occupations of a man's whole day, and marked his fashion as much as, in the present time, the tying of a cravat, or the want of one—was dishevelled, uncurled, void of powder, and dank with dew. His clothes were huddled on with a careless negligence, remarkable in a military man, whose real or supposed duties are usually held to include some attention to the toilet; and his looks were haggard and ghastly in a peculiar degree.

"So you have stolen a march upon us this morning, my dear General," said Lord Woodville; "or you have not found your bed so much to your mind as I had hoped and you seemed to expect. How did you rest last night?"

"Oh, excellently well! remarkably well! never better in my life," said General Browne rapidly, and yet with an air of embarrassment which was obvious to his friend. He then hastily swallowed a cup of tea, and, neglecting or refusing whatever else was offered, seemed to fall into a fit of abstraction.

"You will take the gun to-day, General?" said his friend and host, but had to repeat the question twice ere he received the abrupt answer, "No, my lord; I am sorry I cannot have the opportunity of spending another day with your lordship: my post horses are ordered, and will be here directly."

All who were present showed surprise, and Lord Woodville immediately replied, "Post horses, my good friend! what can you possibly want with them, when you promised to stay with me quietly for at least a week?"

"I believe," said the General, obviously much embarrassed, "that I might, in the pleasure of my first meeting with your lordship, have said something about stopping here a few days; but I have since found it altogether impossible."

"This is very extraordinary," answered the young nobleman. "You seemed quite disengaged yesterday, and you cannot have had a summons to-day; for our post has not come up from the town, and therefore you cannot have received any letters."

General Browne, without giving any further explanation, muttered something about indispensable business, and insisted on the absolute necessity of his departure in a manner which silenced all opposition on the part of his host, who saw that his resolution was taken, and forbore all further importunity.

"At least, however," he said, "permit me, my dear Browne, since go you will or must, to show you the view from the terrace, which the mist, that is now rising, will soon display."

He threw open a sash window, and stepped down upon the terrace as he spoke. The General followed him mechanically, but seemed little to attend to what his host was saying, as, looking across an extended and rich prospect, he pointed out the different objects worthy of observation. Thus they moved on till Lord Woodville had attained his purpose of drawing his guest entirely apart from the rest of the company, when, turning round upon him with an air of great solemnity, he addressed him thus:

"Richard Browne, my old and very dear friend, we are now alone. Let me conjure you to answer me, upon the word of a friend, and the honour of a soldier. How did you in reality rest during last night?"

"Most wretchedly indeed, my lord," answered the General, in the same tone of solemnity; "so miserably, that I would not run the risk of such a second night, not only for all the lands belonging to this castle, but for all the country which I see from this elevated point of view."

"This is most extraordinary," said the young lord, as if speaking to himself; "then there must be something in the reports concerning that apartment." Again turning to the General, he said, "For God's sake, my dear friend, be candid with me, and let me know the disagreeable particulars which have befallen you under a roof where, with consent of the owner, you should have met nothing save comfort."

The General seemed distressed by this appeal, and paused a moment before he replied. "My dear lord," he at length said, "what happened to me last night is of a nature so peculiar and so unpleasant, that I could hardly bring myself to detail it even to your lordship, were it not that, independent of my wish to gratify any request of yours, I think that sincerity on my part may lead to some explanation about a circumstance equally painful and mysterious. To others, the communication I am about to make might place me in the light of a weak-minded, superstitious fool, who suffered his own imagination to delude and bewilder him; but you have known me in childhood and youth, and will not suspect me of having adopted in manhood the feelings and frailties from which my early years were free." Here he paused, and his friend replied:

"Do not doubt my perfect confidence in the truth of your communication, however strange it may be," replied Lord Woodville; "I know your firmness of disposition too well to suspect you could be made the object of imposition, and am aware that your honour and your friendship will equally deter you from exaggerating whatever you may have witnessed."

"Well, then," said the General, "I will proceed with my story as well as I can, relying upon your candour, and yet distinctly feeling that I would rather face a battery than recall to my mind the odious recollections of last night."

He paused a second time, and then perceiving that Lord Woodville remained silent and in an attitude of attention, he commenced, though not without obvious reluctance, the history of his night adventures in the Tapestried Chamber.

"I undressed and went to bed so soon as your lordship left me yesterday evening; but the wood in the chimney, which nearly fronted my bed, blazed brightly and cheerfully, and, aided by a hundred exciting recollections of my childhood and youth, which had been recalled by the unexpected pleasure of meeting your lordship, prevented me from falling immediately asleep. I ought, however, to say that these reflections were all of a pleasant and agreeable kind, grounded on a sense of having for a time exchanged the labour, fatigues, and dangers of my profession, for the enjoyments of a peaceful life, and the reunion of those friendly and affectionate ties, which I had torn asunder at the rude summons of war.

"While such pleasing reflections were stealing over my mind, and gradually lulling me to slumber, I was suddenly aroused by a sound like that of the rustling of a silken gown, and the tapping of a pair of high-heeled shoes, as if a woman were walking in the apartment. Ere I could draw the curtain to see what the matter was, the figure of a little woman passed between the bed and the fire. The back of this form was turned to me, and I could observe, from the shoulders and neck, it was that of an old woman, whose dress was an old-fashioned gown, which, I think, ladies call a sacque; that is, a sort of robe completely loose in the body, but gathered into broad plaits upon the neck and shoulders, which fall down to the ground, and terminate in a species of train.

"I thought the intrusion singular enough, but never harboured for a moment the idea that what I saw was anything more than the mortal form of some old woman about the establishment, who had a fancy to dress like her grandmother, and who, having perhaps (as your lordship mentioned that you were rather straitened for room) been dislodged from her chamber for my accommodation, had forgotten the circumstance, and returned by twelve to her old haunt. Under this persuasion, I moved myself in bed and coughed a little, to make the intruder sensible of my being in possession of the premises. She turned slowly round, but, gracious Heaven, my lord, what a countenance did she display to me! There was no longer any question what she was, or any thought of her being a living being. Upon a face which wore the fixed features of a corpse were imprinted the traces of the vilest and most hideous passions which had animated her while she lived. The body of some atrocious criminal seemed to have been given up from the grave, and the soul restored from the penal fire, in order to form, for a space, an union with the ancient accomplice of its guilt. I started up in bed, and sat upright, supporting myself on my palms, as I gazed on this horrible spectre. The hag made, as it seemed, a single and swift stride to the bed where I lay, and squatted herself down upon it in precisely the same attitude which I had assumed in the extremity of horror, advancing her diabolical countenance within half a yard of mine, with a grin that seemed to intimate the malice and the derision of an incarnate fiend."

Here General Browne stopped, and wiped from his brow the cold perspiration with which the recollection of his horrible vision had covered it.

"My Lord," he said, "I am no coward. I have been in all the mortal dangers incidental to my profession, and I may truly boast, that no man ever knew Richard Browne dishonour the sword he wears; but in these horrible circumstances, under the eyes, and, as it seemed, almost in the grasp of an incarnation of an evil spirit, all firmness forsook me, all manhood melted from me like wax in the furnace, and I felt my hair individually bristle. The current of my life-blood ceased to flow, and I sank back in a swoon, as very a victim to panic terror as ever was a village girl, or a child of ten years old. How long I lay in this condition I cannot pretend to guess.

"But I was roused by the castle clock striking one, so loud that it seemed as if it were in the very room. It was some time before I dared open my eyes, lest they should again encounter the horrible spectacle. When, however, I summoned courage to look up, she was no longer visible. My first idea was to pull my bell, wake the servants, and remove to a garret or a hay-loft, to be ensured against a second visitation. Nay, I will confess the truth, that my resolution was altered, not by the shame of exposing myself, but by the fear that, as the bell-cord hung by the chimney, I might, in making my way to it, be again crossed by the fiendish hag, who, I figured to myself, might be still lurking about some corner of the apartment.

"I will not pretend to describe what hot and cold fever-fits tormented me for the rest of the night, through broken sleep, weary vigils, and that dubious state which forms the neutral ground between them. An hundred terrible objects appeared to haunt me; but there was the great difference betwixt the vision which I have described, and those which followed, that I knew the last to be deceptions of my own fancy and over-excited nerves.

"Day at last appeared, and I rose from my bed ill in health and humiliated in mind. I was ashamed of myself as a man and a soldier, and still more so, at feeling my own extreme desire to escape from the haunted apartment, which, however, conquered all other considerations; so that, huddling on my clothes with the most careless haste, I made my escape from your lordship's mansion, to seek in the open air some relief to my nervous system, shaken as it was by this horrible encounter with a visitant, for such I must believe her, from the other world. Your lordship has now heard the cause of my discomposure, and of my sudden desire to leave your hospitable castle. In other places I trust we may often meet; but God protect me from ever spending a second night under that roof!"

Strange as the General's tale was, he spoke with such a deep air of conviction, that it cut short all the usual commentaries which are made on such stories. Lord Woodville never once asked him if he was sure he did not dream of the apparition, or suggested any of the possibilities by which it is fashionable to explain supernatural appearances, as wild vagaries of the fancy, or deceptions of the optic nerves. On the contrary, he seemed deeply impressed with the truth and reality of what he had heard; and after a considerable pause, regretted, with much appearance of sincerity, that his early friend should in his house have suffered so severely.

"I am the more sorry for your pain, my dear Browne," he continued, "that it is the unhappy, though most unexpected, result of an experiment of my own. You must know that, for my father and grandfather's time at least, the apartment which was assigned to you last night had been shut on account of reports that it was disturbed by supernatural sights and noises. When I came, a few weeks since, into possession of the estate, I thought the accommodation which the castle afforded for my friends was not extensive enough to permit the inhabitants of the invisible world to retain possession of a comfortable sleeping apartment. I therefore caused the Tapestried Chamber, as we call it, to be opened; and, without destroying its air of antiquity, I had such new articles of furniture placed in it as became the modern times. Yet as the opinion that the room was haunted very strongly prevailed among the domestics, and was also known in the neighbourhood and to many of my friends, I feared some prejudice might be entertained by the first occupant of the Tapestried Chamber, which might tend to revive the evil report which it had laboured under, and so disappoint my purpose of rendering it an useful part of the house. I must confess, my dear Browne, that your arrival yesterday, agreeable to me for a thousand reasons besides, seemed the most favourable opportunity of removing the unpleasant rumours which attached to the room, since your courage was indubitable, and your mind free of any preoccupation on the subject. I could not, therefore, have chosen a more fitting subject for my experiment."

"Upon my life," said General Browne, somewhat hastily, "I am infinitely obliged to your lordship—very particularly indebted indeed. I am likely to remember for some time the consequences of the experiment, as your lordship is pleased to call it."

"Nay, now you are unjust, my dear friend," said Lord Woodville. "You have only to reflect for a single moment, in order to be convinced that I could not augur the possibility of the pain to which you have been so unhappily exposed. I was yesterday morning a complete sceptic on the subject of supernatural appearances. Nay, I am sure that had I told you what was said about that room, those very reports would have induced you, by your own choice, to select it for your accommodation. It was my misfortune, perhaps my error, but really cannot be termed my fault, that you have been afflicted so strangely."

"Strangely indeed!" said the General, resuming his good temper; "and I acknowledge that I have no right to be offended with your lordship for treating me like what I used to think myself—a man of some firmness and courage. But I see my post horses are arrived, and I must not detain your lordship from your amusement."

"Nay, my old friend," said Lord Woodville, "since you cannot stay with us another day, which, indeed, I can no longer urge, give me at least half an hour more. You used to love pictures and I have a gallery of portraits, some of them by Vandyke, representing ancestry to whom this property and castle formerly belonged. I think that several of them will strike you as possessing merit."

General Browne accepted the invitation, though somewhat unwillingly. It was evident he was not to breathe freely or at ease till he left Woodville Castle far behind him. He could not refuse his friend's invitation, however; and the less so, that he was a little ashamed of the peevishness which he had displayed towards his well-meaning entertainer.

The General, therefore, followed Lord Woodville through several rooms, into a long gallery hung with pictures, which the latter pointed out to his guest, telling the names, and giving some account of the personages whose portraits presented themselves in progression. General Browne was but little interested in the details which these accounts conveyed to him. They were, indeed, of the kind which are usually found in an old family gallery. Here, was a cavalier who had ruined the estate in the royal cause; there, a fine lady who had reinstated it by contracting a match with a wealthy Roundhead. There, hung a gallant who had been in danger for corresponding with the exiled Court at Saint Germain's; here, one who had taken arms for William at the Revolution; and there, a third that had thrown his weight alternately into the scale of whig and tory.

While Lord Woodville was cramming these words into his guest's ear, "against the stomach of his sense," they gained the middle of the gallery, when he beheld General Browne suddenly start, and assume an attitude of the utmost surprise, not unmixed with fear, as his eyes were caught and suddenly riveted by a portrait of an old, old lady in a sacque, the fashionable dress of the end of the seventeenth century.

"There she is!" he exclaimed; "there she is, in form and features, though inferior in demoniac expression, to the accursed hag who visited me last night!"

"If that be the case," said the young nobleman, "there can remain no longer any doubt of the horrible reality of your apparition. That is the picture of a wretched ancestress of mine, of whose crimes a black and fearful catalogue is recorded in a family history in my charter-chest. The recital of them would be too horrible; it is enough to say, that in yon fatal apartment incest and unnatural murder were committed. I will restore it to the solitude to which the better judgment of those who preceded me had consigned it; and never shall any one, so long as I can prevent it, be exposed to a repetition of the supernatural horrors which could shake such courage as yours."

Thus the friends, who had met with such glee, parted in a very different mood; Lord Woodville to command the Tapestried Chamber to be unmantled, and the door built up; and General Browne to seek in some less beautiful country, and with some dignified friend, forgetfulness of the painful night which he had passed in Woodville Castle.

Questions

1. How did the narrator emphasize the truthfulness and vividness of the tale at the beginning? And what effect did he create by such an introduction?
2. What was introduced about General Browne? What were the little town and the castle like on the General's tour through the western countries? And who was the owner of Woodville Castle?
3. What did Lord Woodville offer to do for his old friend, General Browne?
4. What was the chamber like, in which the General was going to spend the night? And how did the General feel about it? Why did he suddenly decide to leave earlier? What happened to the General in the chamber?
5. How did the writer create the super suspense by the plot construction, characterization and dialogues?

瓦尔特·司各特
（1771—1832）

苏格兰小说家、诗人瓦尔特·司各特爵士最著名的作品是历史小说。司各特从小就对古老的边塞故事与民谣情有独钟。他上过爱丁堡中学，并在爱丁堡大学学过艺术与法律。他当过律师，曾被指派为委托塞尔科克郡副郡长，后又成为爱丁堡判决法庭法务助理。司各特于1830年患中风，三年后去世。

司各特以翻译和创作诗歌开始其文学生涯。他完成了一系列有关苏格兰主题的小说，统称为"威弗利小说"，例如《威弗利》（1814）、《罗布·罗伊》（1817）以及《中洛锡安郡之心脏》（1818）。之后他转向英国历史以及其他主题，包括至今仍为人津津乐道的小说《艾凡赫》（1819）、《修道院》（1820）、《肯尼威斯城堡》（1821）以及《昆丁·达沃德》等。凭借他对苏格兰历史与社会的深刻了解，司各特在小说中展现了他讲故事和编对话的精湛技艺。他着重描写大人物和小人物的人生如何卷入历史的暴力与巨变之中。他丰富与华丽的文体体现了活力与规范、抒情美与描述的明晰性的有机结合。与此同时，司各特还是最早的英语短篇小说家之一。

挂毯卧房（别名"长袍夫人"）

下面的故事讲述了一位英勇善战、阅历丰富的将军的遭遇。该将军一世英名，却遭遇其朋友的一位臭名昭著的长袍女祖先在挂毯卧房闹鬼，结果被吓得半死。通过司各特细腻、繁复的描写，读者领略了其中的田园风光、古老的城堡、侠义的绅士，以及故事令人毛骨悚然的悬念。

以下叙述付诸笔端，其特征依作者亲耳所听，凭记忆精略所限；作者既无受褒奖之奢望也不期指责之鞭挞，只靠自我判断，掌握分寸，精心选材，竭尽全力绝不雕琢，以保故事简洁之原味。

与此同时，众所周知，此类传奇故事以口相传的效果要强于阅读文字。正当午，手持一卷，纵使照例讲述同一奇闻逸事，给人之印象总归微弱，远不如听者围坐火炉亲耳聆听故事之真传。此时，听者全神贯注于说者所描述的细枝末节，那真是如临其境；每当讲到恐怖、神奇之处，说者便压低嗓音，造成一种神秘气氛。正是在此理想氛围中，本作者聆听到以下事情的讲述，那已经是二十多年前的事了，讲述者为利奇菲尔德大名鼎鼎的苏厄德小姐，她在自己众多的才艺之上，又锦上添花地增加了私下里聊天时讲故事的本领。本故事眼下这形式定然保全不了这位天才说手当时所赋予故事的变化多端的嗓音以及足智多谋的意蕴。尽管如此，在黄昏时分，光线明暗不定之时，面对虔诚的听众，或在万籁寂静之时，借着即将燃尽的蜡烛，在半昏半明的寓室孤寂的气氛中，这也不失为一个典型、生动的鬼故事。苏厄德小姐一直肯定该故事的内容取自真实的来源，只是她删去了两个主要当事人的真实姓名。对于故事发生地的细节，我可以了解到更多的内容，但并不想给予更多特别的交代，只烦大家听任我以我自己第一次所听到的同样方式给予笼统的描述；同理，我对这段叙述也不做任何增减，在任何情况下，无论材料是多是少，都不做任何更改，而是按照我所听到的那样，只复述一遍这个超级恐怖的故事。

大约在北美战争结束之际，康沃利斯勋爵军队的军官们在约克城缴械投降，还有其他人在那次失策、倒霉的争斗中成为俘虏，之后他们都回到自己国家，讲述各自的冒险经历，在极端疲惫之后进行休整。其中有一位将级军官，苏小姐取名为布朗，我认为取这个名字只是为了讲故事方便而已，不至于连主人公都无名无姓。这位主人公是一名功勋卓著的军官，也是一位重家庭的博学之士。

由于某桩事情，布朗行至西部各郡；在早上行将结束之际，他不觉来到乡下一座小城的边缘，此地的景致美不胜收，呈现出典型的英格兰风貌。

此城坐落在牧场与小片玉米地之中，周边由高大而年久的木篱笆墙隔开，其中有古老而庄严的教堂，教堂的钟楼见证了人们对久远年代的忠诚。城里没有多少现代化改造的痕迹。城郊既没显示出衰落之荒凉也没有新生之喧嚣；房屋虽然古旧但修缮良好；美丽的小河沿着城左侧的河道，自由自在地涓涓流淌，毫无堤坝阻拦，也无纤道为伍。

离城南将近一英里有一处平缓的高地，在那儿可以望见一座城堡的塔楼映衬在古老的橡树和繁茂的灌木丛中，其年代可以追溯到约克和兰开斯特战争期间，但城堡似乎在伊丽莎白以及其继承者时代进行过重大改造。城堡规模一直不算太大，无论它过去接待过何种住客，今天仍旧足以在其内笑纳八方来客。看见从几个古老的大烟囱袅袅生起的炊烟，至少布朗将军是如此推断的。古堡领地的围墙顺着大路延伸有二三百码；透过几个不同的位置，可以瞥见墙内林地的景色，那儿看起来牧草丰美；随着目光的移动，一系列的景致展现在眼前；一会儿，古老城堡的正面一览无余，另一会儿，其独特的塔楼若隐若现；前者呈现出浓重的伊丽莎白时代的奇异风格，城堡其他部分简朴、厚重的结构表现出其建筑目的在于防卫而不是炫耀。

这位将军旅行至此，透过环绕这座古代领地要塞的树林与空地，瞥见古堡部分真容，感到十分欣喜，他决意要进一步探明古堡是否值得近前一看，里面是否藏有家族肖像或者其他什么有趣物品，值得来客一观。将军离开领地的边缘，乘车直入，通过一条干净整洁的街道，在一家住客频频出入的客栈前停了下来。

　　布朗将军还没等预订马匹继续他的旅程，就先问起如此令他艳羡的城堡的主人是谁；待听说主人是一位叫伍德维尔勋爵的绅士时，将军感到又惊有喜。真是太巧了！布朗在校期间以及大学早期的种种回忆都与年轻的伍德维尔联系在一起。将军问了几个问题之后，很快就确信当时的小伍德维尔正是这座漂亮城堡的主人。几个月前，他由于父亲去世而继承了贵族头衔。将军从客栈老板处得知，现在丧期结束，伍德维尔接管其父产业，在欢快愉悦的秋季，与几个挚友为伍，共享此地声明远扬的狩猎活动。

　　这位旅者对此消息真是喜出望外。弗兰克·伍德维尔曾是理查德·布朗在伊顿公学的学弟，也是他在基督教堂学院的密友。他们当时的志趣与功课都相同。得知自己年轻时的朋友拥有这么迷人的住宅与地产，恰如其分地与其高贵的身份相匹配、相增益，同时客栈老板也点头、眨眼表示赞许，这位正直的军人不禁心胸充满温暖。此时，这位旅者决定延迟旅行就再自然不过了，他不必再匆匆而过，而是要在此欢娱的场合去会一会老友。

　　因而，新换马匹的任务也缩短到只把将军的马车拉到伍德维尔古堡。门房的建筑风格与古堡本身相呼应，守门人在那现代哥特式的门房接待了他们，同时响铃通报有客来访。铃声显然暂缓了一伙人出去各自从事早晨的种种娱乐活动。几位年轻人一身猎装来到古堡的庭院，他们信步于院中，观察并品评着主人们各自牵着的蓄以待发的猎狗。布朗将军下了车，年轻的勋爵来到大厅门口，他像待陌生人那样凝视了一会儿朋友的面容：由于战争造成的疲惫与创伤，朋友的面容改变了许多。不过还没等来者说话，疑惑就顿然散去，紧接着就是亲热的问候，其交流的方式只有在彼此共同度过了少年与青年时代快乐时光的朋友之间才见得到。

　　"亲爱的布朗，假如我许过什么愿的话，"伍德维尔勋爵说，"那就是在所有人中首先请您到场，与朋友们一起庆贺这一节日。别以为在我们缺您的岁月里，您就被忽视了。我一直在关注您，关注您的危险，您的胜利，以及您的不幸，我很欣慰地看到，无论处于胜利还是失败，我老朋友的名字总是那么响当当地备受欢迎。"

　　将军施礼以答，祝贺朋友加封头衔并继承了如此堂皇的领地与产业。

　　"过奖了，您还没看呢，"伍德维尔勋爵说，"我想您一定不会在熟悉此地之前就离开吧。我承认，我目前的队伍确实很大，这座老宅就像其他类似的地方一样，并不能像从其外墙看起来能容纳那么多人住宿。不过我可以给您提供一间老式、舒适的房间，同时恕我冒昧，您的战地经历一定教会了您欣然接受更差的居所。"

将军耸了耸肩，笑了起来。"我觉得，"他说，"您城堡中最差的房间也比那旧烟草桶强得多。我在弗吉尼亚人所谓的丛林地带与轻装备军团在一起的时候，就是夜晚宿营在烟草桶里。我当时在桶里躺着，就像戴奥真尼斯一样，心满意足地以周围最简单的东西来遮盖自己。我甚至都试图让人将桶滚到下一个宿营地，只是当时的司令官不允许那么奢侈的供给，我也就只好双眼含泪告别我那可爱的桶。"

"那好吧，既然您不在乎住处，"伍德维尔勋爵说，"您就至少和我呆一个礼拜。至于猎枪、猎狗、钓鱼竿、马车，以及海上、路地运动器具，我这里绰绰有余；您自己如果选不出什么娱乐活动，我们会想方设法帮您尽兴。要是您喜欢猎枪和猎狗，我就与您同去打猎，既然您曾去过内陆的印第安部落，我倒要看一看您的枪法长进如何。"

将军愉快地全盘接受了好客主人的建议。在一早上雄赳赳气昂昂的演练之后，这帮人在进餐时相会，此时伍德维尔勋爵欣喜地借机让他失而复得的朋友大显身手，同时把他介绍给每位客人，大多数客人都声名显赫。勋爵让布朗将军讲述他的亲眼所见，将军的字字句句都表现出一位指挥官的果敢与男子汉的明智。将军在危险来临之际，保持了冷静的判断力。在座的对将军都肃然起敬，就像对待一位证明了自己拥有超人胆量的勇士——那种品格是所有品格中人人都希望别人认为自己所拥有的。

伍德维尔古堡一天的活动在其寓所里照常结束了。一切井然有序，好客之情恰如其分。倒酒庆饮之后，音乐奏响，年轻的勋爵精通此道；纸牌与台球也为好此游戏者备齐；只是早晨的活动需要早起，因此十一点刚过，客人们就开始各自回房就寝。

年轻的勋爵亲自带朋友布朗将军来到指定的卧房，卧房的状况正如勋爵所描述的一样，舒适而古色古香。房中宽大而厚实的床是流行于17世纪的样式，褪色丝质床帏装饰着已失去光泽的金边。不过将军一想到他从前的"官邸，那木桶"，这些床单、枕头和毯子也就使这位出门在外之人心满意足了。挂毯帷帐装饰着小卧房的四壁，使室内气氛阴暗；这些装饰物早已失去了往日的优雅，秋风习习吹入古老的花格窗，啪啪、嘘嘘地作响，吹得饰物轻轻波动。梳妆台嵌有本世纪初包头巾样式的镜子，装饰着黑紫色的丝绸，还有上百个形状奇异的盒子；这些排列整齐的盒子已经有五十多年没人用了，这一切也都给人以古旧、阴郁的感觉。不过室内的两只大蜡烛明快地照耀着，压倒了一切；假如说有什么可与其抗衡，那就是壁炉中熊熊燃烧的柴木，不断放出光与热，温暖着卧房。虽然整个房间显得古旧，但却毫不缺乏现代生活所必须或渴望的方便与舒适。

"将军，这是所老式卧房，"年轻的勋爵说，"但我希望这儿的一切不会再让您羡慕您那旧烟草桶。"

"我对住处不太挑剔，"将军回答说，"不过假如让我选的话，比起您家城堡中其他那些更华美、现代的房间，我倒更喜欢这间卧房。相信我，每当我将这儿的现代舒适性与古代庄严性联系在一起，同时想起这就是阁下的宅第，我就会感到在这儿下榻比在伦敦最好的旅店都更惬意。"

"我确信——毫无疑问——您在这儿会感到像我所希望您那样舒服的，我亲爱的将军。"年轻的勋爵说。他再次向客人道晚安，握手，随后便退了出来。

将军再次环顾四周，暗自庆幸自己重新又回到平静的生活中；一想起自己近年来所经历的种种艰难险阻，他就感到这种舒适更加弥足珍贵。将军脱去衣服，准备奢华地休息一夜。

在此请恕我暂时违背此类故事的寻常讲法，且把将军在其寓所的情形留到后来叙述，先讲第二天早上。

一大早，勋爵就和朋友们共进早餐，可是没见布朗将军出现，而将军却是伍德维尔勋爵在其所有朋友中最尊敬的客人。面对将军的缺席，勋爵不止一次表现出惊讶，最后派仆人去问个清楚。仆人回来禀报说布朗将军一大早就一直在外面散步，尽管晨雾蒙蒙，天气不爽。

"军人的习惯，"年轻的勋爵对朋友们说，"很多军人都养成了警觉的习惯，他们凌晨很早就醒来，军人的责任感通常使他们这个时候就警惕起来。"

可是，伍德维尔勋爵如此对大家解释，就连他自己似乎都很难满意；在一阵缄默与恍惚之中，勋爵等待着将军的归来。直到早饭铃声敲响后一个钟头，将军才归来。他显得疲惫而焦躁。将军的头发——当时梳理和搽抹自己的头发在男人一天的活动中占有重要位置，同时显示出个人的风格，就如同当今扎领结或者不扎领结——蓬乱、僵直，毫无修饰，又被露水打湿。他身上的衣服由于疏忽而褶皱凌乱，而这对于军人却异乎寻常，军人无论在岗与否其职责一般都应包括军容部分；他的面容异常得憔悴和苍白。

"原来您今早背着我们行军来着，我亲爱的将军，"伍德维尔勋爵说，"也许您觉得床不尽如人意，不像我所希望、您所期待的那样。昨晚您歇息得如何？"

"哦，很好！好极了！今生今世再好不过了。"布朗将军匆匆地说，但他的朋友明显看出其脸上露出尴尬之情。将军随后急忙大口喝了一杯茶，他顾不上，或者说谢绝了其他送上来的早点，似乎陷入一阵茫然之中。

"您今天取枪吧，将军？"将军的朋友兼主人问道，但主人问了两遍才得到将军断然的答复:"不,勋爵。对不起,我不能有幸与勋爵大人再度一日,我定了驿马,即刻就到。"

在场的人皆感诧异,伍德维尔勋爵马上回问:"驿马?我的老友!您要驿马想干什么?您不是答应同我安安心心至少待上一个礼拜吗?"

将军面带难色地说:"初见勋爵大人之时颇感喜悦,我可能说了停留几天之意,可后来我发现那根本不可能。"

"这真是异乎寻常!"年轻的勋爵回答道。"昨天您还那么闲情逸致,今天也不可能接到什么命令,邮差还没从城里来,您不可能收到任何信件。"

布朗将军并没有进一步解释,他嘀咕说有急事要办,坚持必须离开,那坚定的架势使主人无言以留。将军决心已定,不容再留。

"那至少,"勋爵说,"我亲爱的布朗,既然您非走不可,请允许我从露台向您展示一下这里的景象,雾气正在升腾,美景尽收眼底。"

主人向上拉开窗门,边说边步入露台。将军机械地跟随其后,眼前富饶的景象伸向远方,主人指点着值得关注的各处景致,但将军却似乎很少注意主人在说什么。他们就这样走着,直到伍德维尔勋爵有意将客人完全引离其他人,这时勋爵转身面对将军,极严肃地问道:

"理查德·布朗,我亲爱的老友,现在就咱俩。我求您,以老朋友的信誉和军人的荣誉,回答我。您昨晚到底歇息得怎样?"

"说实话,糟糕透了,勋爵大人。"将军同样严肃地回答道。"太可怕了,我实在不敢再待上一晚,尽管这城堡周围,还有从这高处所看到的乡村,景致如此怡人。"

"这也太异乎寻常了吧!"年轻的勋爵好像在自言自语,"那一定是有关那间卧房传说的事情。"勋爵又转向将军说:"看在上帝的份上,我亲爱的朋友,您就直说吧,好让我确切地知晓,在这屋顶下,到底何种可恶之事降临在您头上。本来我向您许诺过,这间卧房只会使您感到舒适。"

将军似乎对这一请求黯然神伤,他停顿了一会儿才答话。"我亲爱的勋爵大人,"他终于回答说,"昨晚发生的一切实在是太离奇、太可怖了,甚至对勋爵大人您,我都很难述说细节。否则,假若我不希望顾及您的感受,而是实话实说,那么我对当时情形的解释会是既痛苦又神秘。其他人听了我的述说,可能会认为我是一个意志薄弱、疑神疑鬼的白痴。只有这样的白痴才会受自己胡思乱想的蛊惑与困扰。可是您从青少年时期就了解我,自然不会怀疑我到了成年反而养成了年轻时所没有的脆弱情感与意志。"将军说到这儿停顿下来,他的勋爵朋友回应道:

"丝毫不要怀疑我对您所传达内容的真实性,无论此事多怪我都信。"伍德维尔勋爵回答道，"我对您的坚毅性格再了解不过了，绝不会怀疑您会屈服于任何事情。同时我也清楚您的名誉和友谊也会阻止您对任何亲眼见到之事言过其实。"

"那么，好吧，"将军说，"我就尽可能如实说来。我相信您的公正，但同时也切身地感到，我宁愿挨一顿揍，也不愿意再回顾昨晚所发生的可怕之事。"

将军又停顿了一会儿，发觉伍德维尔勋爵一直沉默不语，专心听着，于是他显然不太情愿地开始讲述自己在挂毯卧房的夜间历险。

"昨晚勋爵您一离开，我就脱衣就寝了。当时靠近我床头壁炉里的木头正燃得欢，再加上由于见到勋爵您喜出望外而想起自己童年、青年时期多少令人激动的回忆，这些使我一时难以入眠。然而我必须先说明，这些回忆都是令人愉快、惬意的；这一切使我感到一时忘却了劳作、疲乏以及军旅生涯的危险，享受到了和平生活的幸福、老友重逢的喜悦与热情，只是当时战争残酷的号令突然将我与此分离。

"这些愉快的回忆悄悄溜进脑海，渐渐催我入眠，突然我被某种滑软睡袍的沙沙声惊醒，还听见高跟鞋轻轻作响，好像有妇人在屋里走动。没等我拉开床帷看个究竟，一个小妇人的身影从床头与壁炉间经过。身影的背部朝我，我从其肩膀与脖颈看出那是一位老妇人的身影，穿的是老式睡袍，我想就是女士们称作长袍的那种，也就是那种全身完全宽松而只是在脖颈和肩膀处扎紧成粗辫状，下身垂直落地，然后一直落到地上拖开的那种。

"我感到此人的闯入真怪，但也并没有其他猜测，只是以为我所看见的只是本住宅周围某个老妇人的凡人之躯，她只是喜欢穿老奶奶的衣着，也许是她为我腾出了卧房（勋爵您提到过房间很紧张），但却忘了这码事儿，半夜又回到老地儿来了。我如此劝慰自己，就在床上动了动，又轻轻咳嗽了几下，只是想让不速之客意识到卧房现在归我。那妇人慢慢转过身来，我的天哪！勋爵大人，瞧她那张脸！现在确确实实，毫无疑问地看见她是什么，她绝不是活人！瞧那脸上确凿的僵尸特征，脸上还印记着她活着时被激发的最可憎、可恶的怒气的痕迹。这就好像残暴罪犯的肉体被抛出坟墓，灵魂从惩罚之火中复原，为了争夺一片空间去与远古的同谋罪犯团聚。我腾地坐了起来，直直地坐着，双掌支撑着身体，直愣愣地看着那可怕的幽灵。那女魔似乎一下子就飞快地迈到我躺着的床前，蹲下身就坐在床上，那姿态同我在极度恐惧中的姿态简直一模一样，那恶魔般的面孔靠近我只有半码远，龇牙咧嘴地似乎要表现其魔鬼化身的轻蔑与恶毒。"

布朗将军讲到这儿停下来，擦去额头上的冷汗，回想起那可怕的幻觉仍心有余悸。

"勋爵大人，"将军说，"我非懦夫。我戎马生涯，出生入死，我敢毫不夸张地说,人人知晓我理查德·布朗从未有辱于自己的佩剑;可在那可怖的情形之下,就在那近乎恶魔幽灵化身的掌控中,在其眼皮底下,一切坚毅皆抛弃了我,一切阳刚之质就像熔炉中的蜡化为乌有,我感到毛骨悚然。我周身的血液凝固了,昏厥中我瘫倒下去,就像遭受剧烈恐惧的村姑或是十岁的孩子。我也想不清楚就这样躺了多久。

"后来我被古堡一点的钟声惊醒,那钟声格外响,就好像在我房里。过了一会儿我才敢睁眼,唯恐再看见那可怖的景象。不过当我鼓起勇气抬眼看去,那女子已不见了。我第一个念头就是拽铃铛叫醒仆人,搬到顶楼或顶棚,以防不速之客再来造访。不仅如此,说老实话,我对这一行动却迟疑不决,倒不是怕暴露自己的举动而丢人,而是由于铃绳就系在壁炉旁,生怕过去拽铃会再遭遇那可恶的妖婆;我默默地思忖,也许那妖婆仍隐藏在卧房的哪个角落。

"我实在不愿意描绘当时的感受,后半夜浑身忽冷忽热,备受折磨,没睡过整觉,疲惫不堪地熬着,一直处于半睡半醒、心神不定之中。周围似乎出现无数奇型怪物向我袭来,不过我前面所描绘的情景与后来的情形大不相同,我清楚那后来的只是自己的幻觉与过分受刺激的神经所造成的假象。

"天终于亮了,我从床上起来,感到又疲惫又羞耻。我感到不配做一个男子汉、一名军人,尤其是感到一心想要逃离闹鬼的卧房胜过一切之时,我倍感羞愧。于是我急匆匆地胡乱穿上衣服,逃离勋爵您的府邸,找一个空阔处缓解我紧张的神经。这位我深信来自另一个世界的可怕不速之客着实震动了我整个神经系统。勋爵您现在听见了我狼狈不堪的窘境和急于要离开您好客的古堡的原因了吧。在别处我希望咱们可以常见面,但上帝保佑我绝不要在那个屋顶下再过一晚。"

将军的故事虽然怪,但他说话的语气令人深信不疑,所以也就阻止了对此类故事的所有寻常的解释。伍德维尔勋爵从未问过将军他能否确信不是梦到了鬼怪,也从未提出任何其他解释的可能性,因为当时时兴以奇思怪想引起的狂乱行为或者以由视神经造成的错觉来解释奇异现象。相反,勋爵似乎对所听之事的真实性深有同感;停顿了好长时间,他才以十分真诚的姿态对自己早年的朋友在自己家里竟遭受如此之痛而表示歉意。

"我对您所遭之痛越发感到抱歉了,我的布朗将军,"勋爵接着说,"因为此事是我的实验所产生的不幸结果,实属意料之外。您一定知道,至少在我父亲和祖父时代,昨晚给您住的房间就早已关闭,其原因是传说里面有奇怪景象和异响惊扰。我几个星期前来接收这份房产,觉得这座为我朋友们在物质世界提供住宿的城堡不足以为他们的心灵世界提供宽裕、舒适的卧室空间。于是我就下令将所谓的'挂毯卧房'打开,在总体不破坏其古雅风格的前提下,搬入了一些现代的新家具。但由于此屋闹鬼的传说在佣人间人人知晓，街坊邻里以及许多朋友也有所耳闻，我怕第一位入住'挂毯卧房'者会心存疑虑，因而可能会重新使那可怕的传说死而复生，那样也就达不到我利用它的目的了。我必须承认，我的好布朗，您昨天的到来使我万分地高兴，也成了我消除对那房间的可恶谣言的绝好机会，因为您的勇气坚定无疑，同时头脑里对此事也未存任何偏见。因此，我为此实验选择了再合适不过的对象。"

"我以命担保，"布朗将军说，口气有点急，"我万分感谢您，我的勋爵大人，实在是太感谢您了。我将会铭记您所谓的这项实验的后果，这够我记一阵子了。"

"瞧，这您就不应该了，我的好朋友，"伍德维尔勋爵说，"您只需要静下来想一会儿，然后就会相信我不可能预想到会给您造成如此巨大的痛苦。我昨天早上对于鬼怪出没之事还是持完全怀疑的态度。而且，我相信假如我告诉您那房间的事，那些传言也会促使您自愿选择它为下榻之处。这件事是我的不幸，也许是失误，但真的不能称之为我的错误，它使您如此莫名其妙地遭受痛苦。"

"真是莫名其妙！"将军说，他又恢复了之前的好心情；"我得承认，我从前认为自己是坚毅、刚强之人，在此事上勋爵您自己也是如此待我的，因此我无权对此感到冒犯。"

"好了，我的老朋友，"伍德维尔勋爵说，"既然您不能同我们再待一天，对此我也确实不能再坚持，就再给我至少半个钟头吧。记得您从前喜欢画儿，我有一个肖像画廊，其中有一些是范戴克画的，代表了这片领地和古堡从前拥有者的家族谱系。我觉得其中有一些会使您印象深刻，觉得有价值。"

布朗将军接受了邀请，不过有点儿不情愿。显然，不远离伍德维尔古堡，他是不会自由自在地喘口气，放松下来的。然而，他也不能拒绝朋友的邀请；一想到之前对好意款待自己的朋友发火，就更不能拒绝了。

将军因此跟随伍德维尔勋爵穿过几个房间，来到一个长长的挂有肖像的画廊。勋爵向客人指点着画像，给出人名，并边走边介绍画像中的人物。不过布朗将军对介绍的细节并不太感兴趣。这些细枝末节也无非是在老家族画廊通常所听到的那种。这儿有个骑士为了皇家的事业毁了自己的庄园，那儿有个淑女通过与一个富裕的园颅党分子联姻又恢复了那庄园。那儿挂着一幅豪侠的画像，他冒险与流亡在圣·杰曼的皇室私通；这儿有个在革命期间为威廉拿起武器之人；那儿还有一个在辉格党与托利党之间来回权衡左右逢源之人。

伍德维尔勋爵滔滔不绝地向客人介绍着，也不管"客人是否真有兴趣"，此间他们到了画廊的中部，勋爵看见布朗将军突然呈现出极为惊讶的态度，其中无不夹杂着恐惧。将军的双眼被一幅身穿长袍的年迈妇人的肖像所吸引，并突然被定格在那里，她那身长袍是17世纪末流行的女装。

"就是她！"布朗将军叫起来，"就是她，外形与相貌都是如此，只是表情没那么可怕，就是这个可憎的女魔头昨晚拜访了我！"

"如果真是这样，"年轻的勋爵说，"您的幻觉毫无疑问就是可怕的现实了。那就是我一位不幸女祖先的画像，在我的文件柜里的家族史中记载着她一系列悲惨、可怖的罪恶行为。再叙述一番那些行为就太吓人了，我只说到此为止，在那间不幸的卧房里发生了乱伦与凶杀。我要听从前辈们真知灼见的叮嘱，将房间重新空置起来；只要我能阻止得了，任何人都将不会再遭受那莫名其妙的恐怖之苦啦；就连您的勇气都被动摇了，真是太可怕了！"

结果，本来幸会的朋友，却以完全不同的气氛分手。伍德维尔勋爵下令撤掉了挂毯卧房中所有家具，并砌封了房门；布朗将军另寻景致稍次的乡间，同另一位显赫的朋友在一起，渐渐也就忘却了在伍德维尔古堡度过的痛苦夜晚。

Elizabeth Gaskell
(1810—1865)

Elizabeth Gaskell was one of the most famous female novelists of Victorian England, short-story writer and first biographer of Charlotte Brontë. She was born in Chelsea, London, and educated at a boarding school in Warwickshire. In 1829 she went to Newcastle-upon-Tyne, where she met William Gaskell and married him in 1832. They had four children. When the only boy, Willie, died of scarlet fever in 1845, William encouraged his wife to write a long story as a way to get through her grief. The resulting novel is *Mary Barton* (1848), which revealed the desperate poverty of the millworkers of Manchester.

The much-loved novel, *Cranford* (1853), was Gaskell's favorite among her books. The most controversial of Gaskell's novels, *Ruth* (1853), tells of an unmarried woman who has a child. *North and South* (1855), which contrasts life in the rural south of England with conditions in the industrial city of Manchester, depicts the creation of a union and a violent strike. *The Life of Charlotte Brontë* (1857), the first biography of her contemporary novelist, is considered one of the better known of literary biographies in England. The unfinished *Wives and Daughters* (1866), known as her last, longest and perhaps the finest work, concerns the interlocking fortunes of several families in the country town of Hollingford. At the age of fifty-five, Elizabeth Gaskell died suddenly of a heart attack in Holybourne, Hampshire.

The Half-Brothers

This short story is about a boy called Gregory, his mother Helen, and his younger half brother—the narrator. The story contains great sorrow, bravery and neglect. It takes the reader on an emotional roller coaster. Elizabeth manages to use many different writing skills and techniques. She tells quite a complex story in only a dozen of pages.

My mother was twice married. She never spoke of her first husband, and it is only from other people that I have learnt what little I know about him. I believe she was scarcely seventeen when she was married to him: and he was barely one-and-twenty. He rented a small farm up in Cumberland, somewhere towards the sea-coast; but he was perhaps too young and inexperienced to have the charge of land and cattle: anyhow, his affairs did not prosper, and he fell into ill health, and died of consumption before they had been three years man and wife, leaving my mother a young widow of twenty, with a little child only just able to walk, and the farm on her hands for four years more by the lease, with half the stock on it dead, or sold off one by one to pay the more pressing debts, and with no money to purchase more, or even to buy the provisions needed for the small consumption of every day. There was another child coming, too; and sad and sorry, I believe, she was to think of it. A dreary winter she must have had in her lonesome dwelling with never another near it for miles around; her sister came to bear her company, and they two planned and plotted how to make every penny they could raise go as far as possible. I can't tell you how it happened that my little sister, whom I never saw, came to sicken and die; but, as if my poor mother's cup was not full enough, only a fortnight before Gregory was born the little girl took ill of scarlet fever, and in a week she lay dead. My mother was, I believe, just stunned with this last blow. My aunt has told me that she did not cry; Aunt Fanny would have been thankful if she had; but she sat holding the poor wee lassie's hand, and looking in her pretty, pale, dead face, without so much as shedding a tear. And it was all the same, when they had to take her away to be buried. She just kissed the child, and sat her down in the window-seat to watch the little black train of people (neighbours—my aunt, and one far-off cousin, who were all the friends they could muster) go winding away amongst the snow, which had fallen thinly over the country the night before. When my aunt came back from the funeral, she found my mother in the same place, and as dry-eyed as ever. So she continued until after Gregory was born; and, somehow, his coming seemed to loosen the tears, and she cried day and night, till my aunt and the other watcher looked at each other in dismay, and would fain have stopped her if they had but known how. But she bade them let her alone, and not be over-anxious, for every drop she shed eased her brain, which had been in a terrible state before for want of the power to cry. She seemed after that to think of nothing but her new little baby; she had hardly appeared to remember either her husband or her little daughter that lay dead in Brigham churchyard—at least so Aunt Fanny said; but she was a great talker, and my mother was very silent by nature, and I think Aunt Fanny may have been mistaken in believing that my mother never thought of her husband and child just because she never spoke about them. Aunt Fanny was older than my mother, and had a way of treating her like a child; but, for all that, she was a kind, warmhearted creature, who thought more of her sister's welfare than she did of her own and it was on her bit of money that they principally lived, and on what the two could earn by working for the great Glasgow sewing-merchants. But by-and-by my mother's eyesight began to fail. It was not that she was exactly blind, for she could see well enough to guide herself about the house, and to do a good deal of domestic work; but she could no longer do fine sewing and earn money. It must have been with the heavy crying she had had in her day, for she was but a young creature at this time, and as pretty a young woman, I have heard people say, as any on the country side. She took it sadly to heart that she could no longer gain anything towards the keep of herself and her child. My aunt Fanny would fain have persuaded her that she had enough to do in managing their cottage and minding Gregory; but my mother knew that they were pinched, and that Aunt Fanny herself had not as much to eat, even of the commonest kind of food, as she could have done with; and as for Gregory, he was not a strong lad, and needed, not more food— for he always had enough, whoever went short—but better nourishment, and more flesh meat. One day—it was Aunt Fanny who told me all this about my poor mother, long after her death—as the sisters were sitting together, Aunt Fanny working, and my mother hushing Gregory to sleep, William Preston, who was afterwards my father, came in. He was reckoned an old bachelor; I suppose he was long past forty, and he was one of the wealthiest farmers thereabouts, and had known my grandfather well, and my mother and my aunt in their more prosperous days. He sat down, and began to twirl his hat by way of being agreeable; my Aunt Fanny talked, and he listened and looked at my mother. But he said very little, either on that visit, or on many another that he paid before he spoke out what had been the real purpose of his calling so often all along, and from the very first time he came to their house. One Sunday, however, my Aunt Fanny stayed away from church, and took care of the child, and my mother went alone. When she came back, she ran straight upstairs, without going into the kitchen to look at Gregory or speak any word to her sister, and Aunt Fanny heard her cry as if her heart was breaking; so she went up and scolded her right well through the bolted door, till at last she got her to open it. And then she threw herself on my aunt's neck, and told her that William Preston had asked her to marry him, and had promised to take good charge of her boy, and to let him want for nothing, neither in the way of keep nor of education, and that she had consented. Aunt Fanny was a good deal shocked at this; for, as I have said, she had often thought that my mother had forgotten her first husband very quickly, and now here was proof positive of it, if she could so soon think of marrying again. Besides, as Aunt Fanny used to say, she herself would have been a far more suitable match for a man of William Preston's age than Helen, who, though she was a widow, had not seen her four-and-twentieth summer. However, as Aunt Fanny said, they had not asked her advice; and there was much to be said on the other side of the question. Helen's eyesight would never be good for much again, and as William Preston's wife she would never need to do anything, if she chose to sit with her hand before her; and a boy was a great charge to a widowed mother, and now there would be a decent steady man to see after him. So, by-and-by, Aunt Fanny seemed to take a brighter view of the marriage than did my mother herself, who hardly ever looked up, and never smiled after the day when she promised William Preston to be his wife. But much as she had loved Gregory before, she seemed to love him more now. She was continually talking to him when they were alone, though he was far too young to understand her moaning words, or give her any comfort, except by his caresses.

At last William Preston and she were wed; and she went to be mistress of a well-stocked house, not above half-an-hour's walk from where Aunt Fanny lived. I believe she did all that she could to please my father; and a more dutiful wife, I have heard him himself say, could never have been. But she did not love him, and he soon found it out. She loved Gregory, and she did not love him. Perhaps, love would have come in time, if he had been patient enough to wait; but it just turned him sour to see how her eye brightened and her colour came at the sight of that little child, while for him who had given her so much she had only gentle words as cold as ice. He got to taunt her with the difference in her manner, as if that would bring love: and he took a positive dislike to Gregory,—he was so jealous of the ready love that always gushed out like a spring of fresh water when he came near. He wanted her to love him more, and perhaps that was all well and good; but he wanted her to love her child less, and that was an evil wish. One day, he gave way to his temper, and cursed and swore at Gregory, who had got into some mischief, as children will; my mother made some excuse for him; my father said it was hard enough to have to keep another man's child, without having it perpetually held up in its naughtiness by his wife, who ought to be always in the same mind that he was; and so from little they got to more; and the end of it was, that my mother took to her bed before her time, and I was born that very day. My father was glad, and proud, and sorry, all in a breath; glad and proud that a son was born to him;

and sorry for his poor wife's state, and to think how his angry words had brought it on. But he was a man who liked better to be angry than sorry, so he soon found out that it was all Gregory's fault, and owed him an additional grudge for having hastened my birth. He had another grudge against him before long. My mother began to sink the day after I was born. My father sent to Carlisle for doctors, and would have coined his heart's blood into gold to save her, if that could have been; but it could not. My Aunt Fanny used to say sometimes, that she thought that Helen did not wish to live, and so just let herself die away without trying to take hold on life; but when I questioned her, she owned that my mother did all the doctors bade her do, with the same sort of uncomplaining patience with which she had acted through life. One of her last requests was to have Gregory laid in her bed by my side, and then she made him take hold of my little hand. Her husband came in while she was looking at us so, and when he bent tenderly over her to ask her how she felt now, and seemed to gaze on us two little half-brothers, with a grave sort of kindness, she looked up in his face and smiled, almost her first smile at him; and such a sweet smile! as more besides Aunt Fanny have said. In an hour she was dead. Aunt Fanny came to live with us. It was the best thing that could be done. My father would have been glad to return to his old mode of bachelor life, but what could he do with two little children? He needed a woman to take care of him, and who so fitting as his wife's elder sister? So she had the charge of me from my birth; and for a time I was weakly, as was but natural, and she was always beside me, night and day watching over me, and my father nearly as anxious as she. For his land had come down from father to son for more than three hundred years, and he would have cared for me merely as his flesh and blood that was to inherit the land after him. But he needed something to love, for all that, to most people, he was a stern, hard man, and he took to me as, I fancy, he had taken to no human being before, as he might have taken to my mother, if she had had no former life for him to be jealous of. I loved him back again right heartily. I loved all around me, I believe, for everybody was kind to me. After a time, I overcame my original weakliness of constitution, and was just a bonny, strong-looking lad whom every passer-by noticed, when my father took me with him to the nearest town.

At home I was the darling of my aunt, the tenderly-beloved of my father, the pet and plaything of the old domestics, the "young master" of the farm-labourers, before whom I played many a lordly antic, assuming a sort of authority which sat oddly enough, I doubt not, on such a baby as I was.

Gregory was three years older than I. Aunt Fanny was always kind to him in deed and in action, but she did not often think about him, she had fallen so completely into the habit of being engrossed by me, from the fact of my having come into her charge as a delicate baby. My father never got over his grudging dislike to his step-son, who had so innocently wrestled with him for the possession of my mother's heart. I mistrust me, too, that my father always considered him as the cause of my mother's death and my early delicacy; and utterly unreasonable as this may seem, I believe my father rather cherished his feeling of alienation to my brother as a duty, than strove to repress it. Yet not for the world would my father have grudged him anything that money could purchase. That was, as it were, in the bond when he had wedded my mother. Gregory was lumpish and loutish, awkward and ungainly, marring whatever he meddled in, and many a hard word and sharp scolding did he get from the people about the farm, who hardly waited till my father's back was turned before they rated the step-son. I am ashamed—my heart is sore to think how I fell into the fashion of the family, and slighted my poor orphan step-brother. I don't think I ever scouted him, or was wilfully ill-natured to him; but the habit of being considered in all things, and being treated as something uncommon and superior, made me insolent in my prosperity, and I exacted more than Gregory was always willing to grant, and then, irritated, I sometimes repeated the disparaging words I had heard others use with regard to him, without fully understanding their meaning. Whether he did or not I cannot tell. I am afraid he did. He used to turn silent and quiet—sullen and sulky, my father thought it: stupid, Aunt Fanny used to call it. But every one said he was stupid and dull, and this stupidity and dullness grew upon him. He would sit without speaking a word, sometimes, for hours; then my father would bid him rise and do some piece of work, maybe, about the farm. And he would take three or four tellings before he would go. When we were sent to school, it was all the same. He could never be made to remember his lessons; the schoolmaster grew weary of scolding and flogging, and at last advised my father just to take him away, and set him to some farm-work that might not be above his comprehension. I think he was more gloomy and stupid than ever after this, yet he was not a cross lad; he was patient and good-natured, and would try to do a kind turn for any one, even if they had been scolding or cuffing him not a minute before. But very often his attempts at kindness ended in some mischief to the very people he was trying to serve, owing to his awkward, ungainly ways. I suppose I was a clever lad; at any rate, I always got plenty of praise; and was, as we called it, the cock of the school. The schoolmaster said I could learn anything I chose, but my father, who had no great learning himself, saw little use in much for me, and took me away betimes, and kept me with him about the farm. Gregory was made into a kind of shepherd, receiving his training under old Adam, who was nearly past his work. I think old Adam was almost the first person who had a good opinion of Gregory. He stood to it that my brother had good parts, though he did not rightly know how to bring them out; and, for knowing the bearings of the Fells, he said he had never seen a lad like him. My father would try to bring Adam round to speak of Gregory's faults and shortcomings; but, instead of that, he would praise him twice as much, as soon as he found out what was my father's object.

One winter-time, when I was about sixteen, and Gregory nineteen, I was sent by my father on an errand to a place about seven miles distant by the road but only about four by the Fells. He bade me return by the road whichever way I took in going, for the evenings closed in early, and were often thick and misty; besides which, old Adam, now paralytic and bed-ridden, foretold a downfall of snow before long. I soon got to my journey's end, and soon had done my business; earlier by an hour, I thought, than my father had expected, so I took the decision of the way by which I would return into my own hands, and set off back again over the Fells, just as the first shades of evening began to fall. It looked dark and gloomy enough; but everything was so still that I thought I should have plenty of time to get home before the snow came down. Off I set at a pretty quick pace. But night came on quicker. The right path was clear enough in the daytime, although at several points two or three exactly similar diverged from the same place; but when there was a good light, the traveller was guided by the sight of distant objects,—a piece of rock,—a fall in the ground—which were quite invisible to me now. I plucked up a brave heart, however, and took what seemed to me the right road. It was wrong, nevertheless, and led me whither I knew not, but to some wild boggy moor where the solitude seemed painful, intense, as if never footfall of man had come thither to break the silence. I tried to shout—with the dimmest possible hope of being heard—rather to reassure myself by the sound of my own voice; but my voice came husky and short, and yet it dismayed me; it seemed so weird and strange, in that noiseless expanse of black darkness. Suddenly the air was filled thick with dusky flakes, my face and hands were wet with snow. It cut me off from the slightest knowledge of where I was, for I lost every idea of the direction from which I had come, so that I could not even retrace my steps; it hemmed me in, thicker, thicker, with a darkness that might be felt. The boggy soil on which I stood quaked under me if I remained long in one place, and yet I dared not move far. All my youthful hardiness seemed to leave me at once. I was on the point of crying, and only very shame seemed to keep it down. To save myself from shedding tears, I shouted— terrible, wild shouts for bare life they were. I turned sick as I paused to listen; no answering sound came but the unfeeling echoes. Only the noiseless, pitiless snow kept falling thicker, thicker—faster, faster! I was growing numb and sleepy. I tried to move about, but I dared not go far, for fear of the precipices which, I knew, abounded in certain places on the Fells. Now and then, I stood still and shouted again; but my voice was getting choked with tears, as I thought of the desolate helpless death I was to die, and how little they at home, sitting round the warm, red, bright fire, wotted what was become of me,—and how my poor father would grieve for me—it would surely kill him—it would break his heart, poor old man! Aunt Fanny too—was this to be the end of all her cares for me? I began to review my life in a strange kind of vivid dream, in which the various scenes of my few boyish years passed before me like visions. In a pang of agony, caused by such remembrance of my short life, I gathered up my strength and called out once more, a long, despairing, wailing cry, to which I had no hope of obtaining any answer, save from the echoes around, dulled as the sound might be by the thickened air. To my surprise I heard a cry—almost as long, as wild as mine—so wild, that it seemed unearthly, and I almost thought it must be the voice of some of the mocking spirits of the Fells, about whom I had heard so many tales. My heart suddenly began to beat fast and loud. I could not reply for a minute or two. I nearly fancied I had lost the power of utterance. Just at this moment a dog barked. Was it Lassie's bark—my brother's collie?—an ugly enough brute, with a white, ill-looking face, that my father always kicked whenever he saw it, partly for its own demerits, partly because it belonged to my brother. On such occasions, Gregory would whistle Lassie away, and go off and sit with her in some outhouse. My father had once or twice been ashamed of himself, when the poor collie had yowled out with the suddenness of the pain, and had relieved himself of his self-reproach by blaming my brother, who, he said, had no notion of training a dog, and was enough to ruin any collie in Christendom with his stupid way of allowing them to lie by the kitchen fire. To all which Gregory would answer nothing, nor even seem to hear, but go on looking absent and moody.

Yes! there again! It was Lassie's bark! Now or never! I lifted up my voice and shouted "Lassie! Lassie! for God's sake, Lassie!" Another moment, and the great white-faced Lassie was curving and gambolling with delight round my feet and legs, looking, however, up in my face with her intelligent, apprehensive eyes, as if fearing lest I might greet her with a blow, as I had done oftentimes before. But I cried with gladness, as I stooped down and patted her. My mind was sharing in my body's weakness, and I could not reason, but I knew that help was at hand. A grey figure came more and more distinctly out of the thick, close-pressing darkness. It was Gregory wrapped in his maud.

"Oh, Gregory!" said I, and I fell upon his neck, unable to speak another word. He never spoke much, and made me no answer for some little time. Then he told me we must move, we must walk for the dear life—we must find our road home, if possible; but we must move, or we should be frozen to death.

"Don't you know the way home?" asked I.

"I thought I did when I set out, but I am doubtful now. The snow blinds me, and I am feared that in moving about just now, I have lost the right gait homewards."

He had his shepherd's staff with him, and by dint of plunging it before us at every step we took—clinging close to each other, we went on safely enough, as far as not falling down any of the steep rocks, but it was slow, dreary work. My brother, I saw, was more guided by Lassie and the way she took than anything else, trusting to her instinct. It was too dark to see far before us; but he called her back continually, and noted from what quarter she returned, and shaped our slow steps accordingly. But the tedious motion scarcely kept my very blood from freezing. Every bone, every fibre in my body seemed first to ache, and then to swell, and then to turn numb with the intense cold. My brother bore it better than I, from having been more out upon the hills. He did not speak, except to call Lassie. I strove to be brave, and not complain; but now I felt the deadly fatal sleep stealing over me.

"I can go no farther," I said, in a drowsy tone. I remember I suddenly became dogged and resolved. Sleep I would, were it only for five minutes. If death were to be the consequence, sleep I would. Gregory stood still. I suppose, he recognized the peculiar phase of suffering to which I had been brought by the cold.

"It is of no use," said he, as if to himself. "We are no nearer home than we were when we started, as far as I can tell. Our only chance is in Lassie. Here! roll thee in my maud, lad, and lay thee down on this sheltered side of this bit of rock. Creep close under it, lad, and I'll lie by thee, and strive to keep the warmth in us. Stay! hast gotten aught about thee they'll know at home?"

I felt him unkind thus to keep me from slumber, but on his repeating the question,

I pulled out my pocket-handkerchief, of some showy pattern, which Aunt Fanny had hemmed for me—Gregory took it, and tied it round Lassie's neck.

"Hie thee, Lassie, hie thee home!" And the white-faced ill-favoured brute was off like a shot in the darkness. Now I might lie down—now I might sleep. In my drowsy stupor, I felt that I was being tenderly covered up by my brother; but what with I neither knew nor cared—I was too dull, too selfish, too numb to think and reason, or I might have known that in that bleak bare place there was naught to wrap me in, save what was taken off another. I was glad enough when he ceased his cares and lay down by me. I took his hand.

"Thou canst not remember, lad, how we lay together thus by our dying mother. She put thy small, wee hand in mine—I reckon she sees us now; and belike we shall soon be with her. Anyhow, God's will be done."

"Dear Gregory," I muttered, and crept nearer to him for warmth. He was talking still, and again about our mother, when I fell asleep. In an instant—or so it seemed—there were many voices about me—many faces hovering round me—the sweet luxury of warmth was stealing into every part of me. I was in my own little bed at home. I am thankful to say, my first word was "Gregory?"

A look passed from one to another—my father's stern old face strove in vain to keep its sternness; his mouth quivered, his eyes filled with unwonted tears.

"I would have given him half my land—I would have blessed him as my son,—Oh God! I would have knelt at his feet, and asked him to forgive my hardness of heart."

I heard no more. A whirl came through my brain, catching me back to death.

I came slowly to my consciousness, weeks afterwards. My father's hair was white when I recovered, and his hands shook as he looked into my face.

We spoke no more of Gregory. We could not speak of him; but he was strangely in our thoughts. Lassie came and went with never a word of blame; nay, my father would try to stroke her, but she shrank away; and he, as if reproved by the poor dumb beast, would sigh, and be silent and abstracted for a time.

Aunt Fanny—always a talker—told me all. How, on that fatal night, my father,—irritated by my prolonged absence, and probably more anxious than he cared to show, had been fierce and imperious, even beyond his wont, to Gregory; had upbraided him with his father's poverty, his own stupidity which made his services good for nothing—for so, in spite of the old shepherd, my father always chose to consider them. At last, Gregory had risen up, and whistled Lassie out with him—poor Lassie, crouching underneath his chair for fear of a kick or a blow. Some time before, there had been some talk between my father and my aunt respecting my return; and when Aunt Fanny told me all this, she said she fancied that Gregory might have noticed the coming storm, and gone out silently to meet me. Three hours afterwards, when all were running about in wild alarm, not knowing whither to go in search of me, not even missing Gregory, or heeding his absence, poor fellow—poor, poor fellow!—Lassie came home, with my handkerchief tied round her neck. They knew and understood, and the whole strength of the farm was turned out to follow her, with wraps, and blankets, and brandy, and everything that could be thought of. I lay in chilly sleep, but still alive, beneath the rock that Lassie guided them to. I was covered over with my brother's plaid, and his thick shepherd's coat was carefully wrapped round my feet. He was in his shirt-sleeves—his arm thrown over me—a quiet smile (he had hardly ever smiled in life) upon his still, cold face.

My father's last words were, "God forgive me my hardness of heart towards the fatherless child!"

And what marked the depth of his feeling of repentance, perhaps more than all, considering the passionate love he bore my mother, was this: we found a paper of directions after his death, in which he desired that he might lie at the foot of the grave, in which, by his desire, poor Gregory had been laid with OUR MOTHER.

Questions

1. How does Gaskell use Lassie to reveal the natures of the characters?
2. Why does the father (William Preston) unreasonably favour one brother over the other? In what ways is he like the typical step-parent of fairy-tales? How does he differ?
3. Why has Gaskell chosen the first-person, major character narrative point of view?
4. Explain whether you find the conclusion of this story tragic or merely sentimental.
5. After using considerable narration, in the last stage of the story Gaskell switches to dialogue. Why?

伊丽莎白·盖斯凯尔
（1810—1865）

伊丽莎白·盖斯凯尔是英国维多利亚时代著名女作家之一，短篇小说家，同时也是第一位夏洛蒂·勃朗特的传记作者。伊丽莎白·盖斯凯尔出生在伦敦切尔西，后在沃克里郡的寄宿学校学习。1829年她在泰恩河上的纽卡斯尔与威廉·盖斯凯尔相识，并于1832年和他结婚。婚后他们一共生了四个孩子。1845年，当家中唯一的男孩威利死于猩红热的时候，丈夫威廉鼓励妻子通过写一部长篇小说来减轻丧子的痛苦。于是便有了揭露曼彻斯特工人悲惨生活的《玛丽·巴顿》。

深受欢迎的《克兰福德》是作者本人最喜欢的作品。小说《鲁思》因为讲述的是一个未婚母亲生子的故事而引起巨大争议。在《北方与南方》中，作者把英国南方的乡村生活与曼彻斯特的工业城市的生活进行对比，描述了工会的产生和激烈的罢工现象。第一部同时代作家的传记《夏洛蒂·勃朗特的一生》被认为是英国著名的文学传记之一。最后一部未完成的小说《妻子和女儿》被认为是她最长，也许是最优秀的一部，讲述的是在霍岭福德乡村几个家庭命运的故事。伊丽莎白·盖斯凯尔在汉普郡的豪里伯恩因突发心脏病去世，享年55岁。

同母异父兄弟

下面的短篇小说讲述的是一个叫格雷戈里的男孩，他妈妈海伦还有叙述者——他的同母异父弟弟的故事。故事充满了无尽的悲伤情感、勇敢的品质和疏忽的后果。它带给读者的是跌宕起伏的情感思绪。作者运用多种不同的写作技巧和方法，在短短十几页纸里讲述了一个非常复杂的故事。

我妈妈结过两次婚。她从没说起过自己的第一任丈夫，我只是从其他人那里才对他略知一二。我想她嫁给他的时候还不到17岁，他也就刚刚21岁。他在靠海滩的嵌伯兰郡租了一个小农场，可能是太年轻而且对耕地、饲养牲口也没有经验，不管怎样他的事业不是很好，在结婚还不到三年就死于肺病，让我妈妈20岁就成了年轻寡妇，留下一个刚刚会走路的小孩，租赁的农场还有四年才到期。一半的牲口死了，要不就是一个个卖掉以偿还债务。家里根本没钱购买什么，哪怕是每天所需要的少量生活用品。还有一个即将降临的小生命，我想她一想到这些就会悲伤、沮丧。在一个方圆几里都没有人家的孤寂的住所里，她一定感到那个冬天格外凄凉。好在她姐姐过来陪她，俩人计划着，精打细算怎样才能让每一分钱尽可能地得到充分利用。不知是怎么回事，好像我那可怜的妈妈的痛苦还不够多似的，在格雷戈里出生前两周，我那从没见过面的小姐姐染上了猩红热，一周后夭折了。我想，妈妈一定是被这最后的打击彻底击垮了。我姨妈曾告诉我说，妈妈没有哭。范妮姨姨倒希望她能哭出来，但她坐在那儿，握着小女儿的手，看着她那已经死去的漂亮而苍白的脸，没有一滴眼泪。而且他们把她带走去埋葬的时候，她也一样欲哭无泪。她只是亲吻孩子，坐在窗前的椅子上看着一帮人（邻居、我姨妈，还有一个远房亲戚、一些他们可以召集的朋友）在雪中蜿蜒前行。雪是前一天晚上下的，稀疏地落满大地。我姨妈从葬礼回来的时候，发现妈妈仍坐在原处，眼里干枯无泪。妈妈就一直这样，直到格雷戈里出生。而格雷戈里的到来似乎打开了妈妈的泪囊，她整日哭泣不止，我姨妈以及其他人真是面面相觑，不知所措。他们是多么想知道如何让她停下来别哭了。但她吩咐不用管她，不用过度担心，因为每一滴眼泪都会缓解她在此之前因无力哭泣而处于麻木的大脑。在那之后，她看起来什么都不想了似的，一心想着她的新生儿。她似乎已经记不得安睡在伯明翰墓地的丈夫和小女儿，至少范妮姨妈是这么说的。姨妈格外健谈，可我妈天生寡言少语。而我觉得只是因为她从来都不提到他们，范妮姨妈就一直错误地认为，我妈妈从来不想她的丈夫和孩子。范妮姨妈比我妈妈大，并且对她像对孩子一样。但总的说来，她是一个善良、热心肠的人，总是考虑到她妹妹的利益多于考虑她自己。而且是靠她仅有的一些钱，还有两人靠为格拉斯哥缝纫商做工所得，他们才勉强度日。但渐渐地，妈妈的视力开始下降。倒不是她什么都看不见，她还可以在家里自由出入，做很多家务事，但她却不能再做针线活和挣钱了。一定是以前她哭得太厉害了。那时她很年轻，而且我听人家说在村里也算是一个漂亮姑娘。她很伤心，因为不能再为她自己和孩子养家糊口。范妮则劝她说，在家里做家务和照顾格雷戈里，她已经做得很多了，但我妈妈知道他们很难度日，范妮自己也不够吃，哪怕是最普通的食物都不够，而格雷戈里也不是很强壮，需要不是很多，谁不够吃他都够，只是缺乏更好的营养和能有肉吃。妈妈去世很久以后，是范妮姨妈告诉了我关于我那可怜妈妈的这一切。那一天，姐妹俩坐在一起，范妮姨妈忙着，妈妈哄格雷戈里睡觉，这时威廉·普雷斯顿进来了，他后来成了我父亲。他算是一个老光棍，我想他一定40多岁了，是周围比较富有的农场主之一。在我妈和姨妈生活得不错的日子里，他与我姥爷很熟悉。他坐下后就开始转动他的帽子，以示友好。我姨妈一直在讲，而他则听着并看着我妈妈。他此次来访，或是以前的许多次来访，每次话都不多，最终他说出了每一次来访的真正目的。有一个礼拜天，我姨妈没去教堂，在家照看孩子，我妈妈自己去的。她回来的时候，也没去厨房看看格雷戈里或对她姐姐说句话，就直接跑到楼上。随后范妮姨妈就听到她的哭声，好像心碎了似的。姨妈上楼隔着闩着的门开始责备妈妈，直到她自己把门打开。她搂住姨妈的脖子，告诉她威廉·普雷斯顿向她求婚，并保证好好照顾她的儿子，保证她的儿子生活上无忧无虑，读书也不是问题，她就答应了。范妮姨妈对此感到非常震惊，就像我说过的，因为她总是以为我妈妈很快就忘记了自己第一个丈夫，而如果她这么快就决定再结婚的话，这不就是最好的证明。另外，像范妮姨妈常说的，她自己而不是海伦更适合和威廉·普雷斯顿这样年龄的男人结婚，尽管海伦是个寡妇，她也还不到24岁。然而，正如范妮姨妈所说的，虽然她有很多要说的，他们并没征求她的意见。海伦的视力再也不会恢复了，而作为威廉·普雷斯顿的妻子，假如她选择无所事事地坐在那儿，不再做任何事情，那也是理所应当的。对于一个寡母来说，照顾一个男孩就已经是个很大的负担了，而现在可以有一个正派、沉稳的男人来照顾孩子了。所以，不久以后，范妮姨妈比我妈妈自己更看好这桩婚姻。但我妈妈自从答应嫁给威廉·普雷斯顿之后，就很少抬眼看人，再也没露过笑容。但像以前她爱格雷戈里一样，她现在更爱儿子了。她和孩子独处的时候，总是不停地和他说话，尽管他还太小，不知道她说的什么，除了爱抚她，也不能给她什么安慰。

　　终于威廉·普雷斯顿和她结婚了。她成了一个有着殷实家产的女主人，住的地方离范妮姨妈家走路只有半个小时的路程。我想她在尽其所能去取悦我爸爸，做一个再本分不过的妻子，这是爸爸亲口说的。但她不爱爸爸，而且爸爸不久就发现了。她爱的是格雷戈里，不爱爸爸。如果爸爸有耐心去等，或许爱情总会到来，但他生气地发现，她一看到孩子，目光就会变得明亮而神采飞扬，而对给予她那么多的丈夫，她的言辞彬彬有礼却冷若冰霜。他开始用与她不同的方式奚落她，好像那样可以带来爱；并且他表现出非常的不喜欢格雷戈里。他格外嫉妒那种母亲对孩子随时随地的爱；每当孩子在跟前，那种母爱总是像清澈的泉水一样涌出。他想让妻子多爱他一点，这倒是可以理解，也正当，但他想让母亲少爱一点自己的孩子，那可真是罪过。一天，爸爸大发脾气，朝着格雷戈里大骂，直接原因是格雷戈里淘气，所有孩子都这样，这本来没什么。我妈妈替儿子找借口，我爸爸则说抚养另一个男人的孩子已经够难的了，而这孩子又总是调皮却被他妻子护着，做妻子的就该同丈夫一条心。为此他们争吵起来，而且小事化大，结果妈妈当天就早产生下了我。爸爸一时间既高兴，又骄傲，同时又感到懊悔。高兴、骄傲的是他有了自己的儿子；懊悔的是他妻子现在可怜的状况，想着他愤怒的话语是如何造成妻子现在的状况。但他是一个更喜欢生气而不是懊悔的人。很快他就发现这都是格雷戈里的错，都是因为他才使得我成了早产儿。于是不久他就找到对格雷戈里不满的另一条理由。妈妈从我出生那天起身体就一天不如一天。爸爸到卡莱尔找医生；如果可能，他宁愿用自己的心血来换取金钱去救治她，但那不可能。我范妮姨妈有时就说，她觉得海伦是自己不想活下去了，那就让她去吧，她是丧失了生的勇气和希望。但我问她的时候，她承认我妈妈确实是按照医生吩咐去做的。她用一种一生都是毫无怨言的忍耐遵守医生的吩咐。她最后的请求是让格雷戈里在她床上，躺在我身边，然后她让他握着我的小手。她丈夫进来的时候，她正看着我们这么做。当他俯身问她感觉怎么样的时候，并似乎用一种庄严、慈爱的目光凝视我们两个同母异父兄弟的时候，她抬眼看着丈夫的脸，笑了，这几乎是对丈夫的第一次微笑。多么甜美的微笑！比范妮姨妈所描述的微笑还要甜美。一小时后，她就死了。范妮姨妈来和我们住在一起。这再好不过了。我爸爸或许应该高兴又回到了快乐的单身生活，但对我们两个小孩他能做什么呢？爸爸需要女人照顾，妻子的姐姐难道不是最佳人选吗？所以我一出生范妮姨妈就照顾我。有段时间我很虚弱，这很正常，她总是在我身边日夜守候。我爸爸几乎和她一样焦虑不安，因为他的土地是子承父业已经三百多年了，他非常担心我这个亲生骨肉能否承担起继承土地的重任。但他也需要去爱什么。虽然如此，对大多数人来说，他是一个严厉、难以相处的人，他从未喜欢过谁，但我感觉，他喜欢我，像喜欢我妈妈一样，假如她没有二婚前的生活使他感到嫉妒的话。我也真心地回报他的爱。我爱周围的每一个人，我觉得他们对我都很好。过了一段时间，我克服了天生的虚弱体质，长成一个漂亮、健壮的小伙子。爸爸带我到附近镇上的时候，过路人都对我刮目相看，在家里我是姨妈的宝贝儿，爸爸疼爱的孩子，家里备受宠爱的公子哥，农场工人的"小少爷"，在他们面前我俨然就是贵族气派，摆出一副有权威的架势，我承认，这些落在我这样一个孩子身上实在滑稽。

　　格雷戈里比我大三岁，范妮姨妈行动上一直对他很好，但她并非常想着他，而总是习惯性地对我全神贯注，因为她自从我是个弱小的婴儿起就照顾我。我爸爸还是不喜欢这个无辜地和他争夺我妈妈心的继子。我怀疑，爸爸总是认为是格雷戈里才导致我妈妈的死亡、我早期的体弱多病。我觉得，虽然这似乎完全没有道理，但我爸爸宁愿把他对我哥哥疏远的情感当作责任，也不愿压抑它。然而，我爸爸给他任何钱可以买到的东西，因为那是他和我妈妈结婚时的约定。格雷戈里迟钝而粗野，笨拙又难看，碰什么什么坏。他总是招来农场周围人们尖刻的言辞和严厉的责骂。那些人没等我爸爸转过身去就开始对他这个继子评头品足。我很难过，我痛苦地想，我是如何赢得家人欢心的，如何又冷落了我可怜的孤儿哥哥。我想虽然我从没嘲笑过他，或任性地恶意对他，但我已习惯于一切先考虑自己，习惯于被与众不同地、高人一等地对待，而这些使我变得傲慢无礼、春风得意。我的需求往往超出格雷戈里总是愿意接受的限度。每当我恼羞成怒，有时也会重复那些我所听到别人说他时候使用的蔑视之词，可我并不能完全明白那些话的意思。他是否明白，我不敢确定，恐怕他是明白的。他常常沉默不语。我爸爸觉得他闷闷不乐，范妮姨妈把那称作愚笨。人人都说他愚笨，反应迟钝，他也就越发愚笨、迟钝起来。他会坐在那里一言不发，有时几个小时。这时爸爸会叫他起来，干点活儿，也许是些农活儿。而他会在你叫了三四遍后才去。我们上学读书的时候，他还是这样。他从来也记不住功课。校长也懒得再责骂和鞭打他，最后建议我爸爸把他带走，让他干些力所能及的农活儿。我想从那以后他更郁闷和愚钝了。但他不是一个乖戾的孩子，他有耐心而且心地善良，他会对任何人给予帮助，即使是他们刚刚责骂过他或打过他。由于他的笨拙、不灵活的方式，他对那些人想要表示好意的尝试总是以失败告终。我觉得自己是个聪明的小伙子，不管这样，我总是得到很多表扬，就像大家所称呼的，我是"一校之雄"。校长说我能学好任何一科，但我爸爸他自己没有多少文化，觉得我学多了也没用，没多久就把我带走了，让我跟他在农场干活。他让格雷戈里牧羊，跟已经几乎不能干活的老亚当学本领。我觉得老亚当是第一个称赞格雷戈里的人。他坚信我哥哥有潜力，尽管他不知道怎样把这些潜力挖掘出来。他说他从来没见过像他这样了解这片丘陵沼泽地的人。我爸爸会试着让亚当说些格雷戈里的缺点和短处，但他一旦发现我爸爸的目的，反倒加倍称赞他。

一个冬天，我大概16岁的时候，格雷戈里19岁，爸爸派我去一个地方办事。去那个地方走大路要七英里，但走丘陵沼泽地只有四英里。不管去的时候怎么走，爸爸让我回来的时候一定要走大路，因为夜晚来得早，而且常常天色漆黑、雾气蒙蒙。另外，现在瘫痪在床的老亚当预测不久之后会有暴风雪。我很快就到了目的地，比我爸爸预计的提前了一个小时就办完了事，因此我决定自己选路回去。天刚刚暗下来，我就动身穿过丘陵沼泽地往家赶。很快天就黑下来，很暗，一切都很寂静，我觉得在降雪前我有足够时间到家。我上路时已经加快了步伐，但黑夜来临得更快。白天的时候回家的小路很清晰，尽管有几处两、三条完全相同的路都是从同一个地方分叉的，但光线好的时候，行人可以通过远处物体做向导，比如一块岩石，地上一段斜坡，可现在这一切对我来说都看不见了。我鼓起勇气选择了一条我觉得是正确的路。但实际上那是条错路，我也不知道它通向哪里，而只是通向一片荒凉、孤寂的沼泽地，那儿让人似乎感到无比的孤独和痛苦，好像从来没人来过此地，无人打破这沉寂。我试着大喊，被听见的希望很渺茫，我只是用声音给自己壮胆罢了。我的声音变得沙哑、短促，我感到惊慌。在寂静、黑暗的旷野中，这声音听起来那么怪异和陌生。突然，朦胧的天空飘起了厚厚的雪花，我的脸和手都被雪弄湿了。大雪完全妨碍了我仅有的一点方向感，因为我根本就不知道我从哪个方向过来的了，现在我连返回到原路都不可能了。越来越大的雪把我包围，我能感受的只是黑夜。如果我在一个地方站的时间久了，脚下的沼泽地就会震动，但我不敢挪动太远。年轻人那股子顽强劲儿在我身上似乎立刻荡然无存。我就要哭出来了，只是觉得有点儿丢人而克制住了。为防止我流泪，我疯狂地大喊大叫，那只是求救的喊叫。我停下来听着，心里一阵恶心，没人回答，只有冷酷无情的回音。雪花无声、无情不停地下着，越来越大，越来越急。我开始感觉麻木和困倦。我试着挪动挪动，但又不敢走太远，担心这片高沼泽地带，我知道，有些地方有悬崖。我时而站着不动，时而又大声呼喊，我想到了在荒无人烟的地方无助地死去，想到他们在家里，围坐在暖暖的、火苗又红又旺的火炉旁边，对我发生的事情一无所知，又想到我那可怜的父亲因我的死去而伤心不已，那就等于要他的命一样，让他心碎，可怜的老人！想到这些我的声音哽咽了，满眼泪水。还有范妮姨妈，难道这就是她对我长期操劳的最终结果吗？我开始以奇怪的非常清晰的梦境方式回忆我的生活，那些童年时光的各种情景在我眼前历历在目。想起我这短暂的一生，内心一阵剧痛。我用尽全身力气再一次大声呼救，一声绝望的悲嚎，我自己都不抱什么希望能有回答，除了周围的回声，这声音因厚重的空气而显得呆滞，了无生机。就在这时，我惊奇地听到一声呼喊，几乎和我那悠长、疯狂的喊叫声一样。那疯狂的喊声好像不是尘世的声音一样；我甚至觉得那一定是沼泽旷野中幽灵的声音。对此我已经听过很多传说故事。我的心突然咚咚地狂跳不止。有那么一、两分钟，我都无法答应。我差一点以为自己失去了说话的能力。就在这时，传来一声狗吠。那是莱西的吠声吗？是哥哥的牧羊犬，一条丑陋无比的白脸狗。我爸爸每次看见它都会踢它一脚，部分原因是它自身的缺点，另一个原因是因为它属于我哥哥的。每当这时，格雷戈里会用口哨声让莱西走开，然后和她到外屋坐下来。当可怜的牧羊犬因突然的疼痛而吼叫的时候，我爸爸也曾有一两次感到很内疚，但很快他就用责备我哥哥来缓解他的自我谴责。他说哥哥根本不懂怎么训练狗，像他那样愚蠢地让狗躺在厨房灶台旁，天底下再好的狗也会毁在他手里。对这一切，格雷戈里什么也不说，好像什么也没听见，只是一直表现为心不在焉、闷闷不乐。

是的，又一声！是莱西的叫声！不能错失良机！我提高了嗓门大喊："莱西！莱西！感谢上帝，莱西！"又过了一会儿，了不起的白脸莱西在我周围高兴得又转又跳，然后抬起头用她那聪明智慧的眼睛看着我，好像担心我会像以前一样用拳头迎接她似的。可这次我兴奋地哭了，弯下腰，抚摸着她。我的内心体验着我身体的软弱，我无以言表，但我知道帮手就在眼前。一个灰色的人影从厚重的黑暗中越来越清晰，是格雷戈里裹着灰呢子披风。

"哎，格雷戈里！"我说着，扑向他的脖子，再也说不出话了。他从来也不多说什么，这使得我一时也没话可说。然后他说我们必须马上起来离开。如果可能，我们必须为了活命马上走，我们必须找到回家的路；我们必须动起来，否则会被冻死。"

"你不知道回家的路吗？"我问。

"我出门的时候觉得知道，但现在我也说不准了。大雪让我没法判断，刚才我到处走动，我担心我也不知道回家的方向了。"

他带着牧羊人所需的那些工具，在我们面前击打出凹痕，我们紧搂在一起，一步一步前行。我们安全地往前走，至少没有掉下岩石峭壁，但走得很慢，很艰苦。我看到哥哥基本上是靠莱西引路，没其他办法，只能相信她的直觉。天太黑了，根本看不见太远，于是他不停地把莱西叫回来，根据她回来的方向来调整我们缓慢的步子。但单调乏味的动作简直无法阻止我冻僵。我浑身上下都开始疼，然后是肿，最后是因刺骨的寒冷变得麻木。我哥哥因经常在山上比我耐受力好一些。他除了叫莱西，什么话也不说；我尽力表现得勇敢，不抱怨，但现在我觉得致命的倦意向我袭来。

"我一步也不能走了，"我昏昏欲睡地说。我记得自己突然变得顽强、决然。我想睡觉，哪怕就睡五分钟。如果那结果是死亡的话，我也要睡一会儿。格雷戈里站着没动。我觉得哥哥意识到因为寒冷我所遭受的特殊状态了。

"没有用的，"他好像自言自语地说。"我敢断定，我们从开始到现在根本就没走多远。我们的机会全在莱西身上了。来，把我的披风给你裹上，小弟，躺在这块岩石的避风一面。尽可能地往下爬近些，我躺在你旁边，尽量保持暖和些。别动！你有没有什么东西，家里人一看就知道是你的？"

我觉得他这样不体谅我，不让我睡觉。但听到他不断重复的问题以后，我拿出口袋里带着漂亮图案，范妮姨妈为我缝制的手帕。格雷戈里拿了过去，系在莱西的脖子上。

"快，莱西，快回家！"这条长着白脸又不受宠爱的狗，像离弦的箭一样消失在夜幕中。现在我可以躺下了，现在我可以睡觉了。在我昏睡中，我感到我轻轻地被哥哥遮挡着，但我既不想知道也不关心是用什么遮挡的。我太迟钝、太自私、太麻木，已经不会思考，没有理智。或者我本该清楚在那样一个荒凉无遮蔽的地方，除了从另一个人身上脱下的衣服能有什么可以遮盖的呢。我很高兴他不再照顾我了，而只是躺在了我身边。我拉住他的手。

"你不记得吗，小弟，我们是怎样一起躺在奄奄一息的妈妈身边的。她把你的小手放在我手里，我想她现在一定看见我们了，或许我们很快就会和她在一起了。不管怎么说，上帝的意愿是会实现的。"

"亲爱的格雷戈里，"我咕哝着，又向他靠近一些好能感觉暖和点儿。他还在说着，又讲起妈妈，这时我睡着了。一会儿，好像是过了一会儿，我听到周围

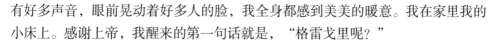

有好多声音,眼前晃动着好多人的脸,我全身都感到美美的暖意。我在家里我的小床上。感谢上帝,我醒来的第一句话就是,"格雷戈里呢?"

目光从一个人到另一个人的脸上,我爸爸严厉苍老的脸尽力保持着威严,他的嘴角颤动着,眼里充满了罕见的泪水。

"我宁愿把我一半的土地给他,我会像保佑自己的儿子一样保佑他。啊,上帝!我将跪倒在他的脚下,请求他宽恕我的铁石心肠。"

我再没听见什么。大脑一阵眩晕,把我带回死亡。

几周以后,我慢慢恢复意识。我康复的时候,爸爸的头发全白了,看着我的时候他的双手不停地颤抖。

我们不再提起格雷戈里。我们不能提起他,但他却总是怪怪的在我们的意识里。莱西在眼前来来回回,不再受责骂,而且爸爸会试着抚摸她,但她总躲闪。好像是受到这可怜、无言动物的责备,我爸爸常常会叹气、沉默,心不在焉一阵子。

范妮姨妈还是那么健谈,她告诉了我一切。在那个不幸的夜晚,爸爸是如何因为我的迟迟不归而心急如焚。可能是太担心而不愿表现出来,他对格雷戈里变得格外暴躁、专横;他因哥哥亲生父亲的贫困而责备他,虽然老牧羊人称赞他,但爸爸还是认为他的愚蠢使得他一无是处。最后,格雷戈里站起身,叫上莱西出了门。可怜的莱西一直蜷缩在椅子下,担心又会遭到一顿拳脚。在格雷戈里出门之前,爸爸和姨妈谈起过我回来的事。当范妮姨妈告诉我这一切的时候,她说,她猜想格雷戈里可能已经注意到即将到来的暴风雪,而悄悄地出去接你。三个小时以后,我们都惊慌地出去的时候,根本不知道到哪儿去找你,没人注意到格雷戈里的失踪,也不知道到哪儿去找他,可怜的人儿,好可怜的人儿!这时莱西回家了,脖子上系着我的手帕。他们知道了,也清楚了,农场上所有的人力都用上了,人们带着外套、毯子、白兰地酒,以及所有能想到的东西,跟随着莱西。莱西把他们带到了山岩下,我在寒冷中睡着了,但还活着。我盖着哥哥的羊毛呢披风,他厚厚的牧羊人大衣包裹着我的双脚。他只穿着衬衣,他的胳膊搂着我,一丝从容的微笑挂在他安静、冰冷的脸上(他一生中几乎很少有过笑容)。

我父亲临终时说:"请上帝饶恕我那么铁石心肠地对待一个没有父亲的孩子吧!"

鉴于他对我妈妈的深深眷恋,只有以下这件事或许更能表明他这种深深的悔恨之情:他死后,我们发现一张纸,上面有他的遗嘱,他希望躺在可怜的格雷戈里和妈妈合葬墓的脚下。

William Makepeace Thackeray
(1811—1863)

William Makepeace Thackeray, English novelist and satirist, is most often compared to one other great novelist of Victorian literature, Charles Dickens. Born in Calcutta, India, Thackeray was educated at Charterhouse and then at Trinity College, Cambridge. In 1836 in Paris he married Isabella Shawe, an Irish girl who later suffered a mental breakdown until her death, which profoundly affected his character and work. Back in England in 1837 and suffering massive financial losses, Thackeray started his career as a journalist. He was a notable early contributor to *Fraser's Magazine* and to *Punch*. In 1860 he became the editor of *Cornhill Magazine*, but died suddenly three years later.

Thackeray's early novel *The Luck of Barry Lyndon* (1844), a portrait of an adventurer, opportunist and gambler, made him arrive as a novelist. He achieved widespread popularity with *The Book of Snobs* (1848), a series of satirical character sketches. *Vanity Fair* (1847—1848), a satirical panorama of upper-middle-class London life and manners at the beginning of the 19th century, established Thackeray's fame permanently. With *The History of Pendennis* (1850), his semi-autobiographical novel, Thackeray's success as a satirist was confirmed. His other notable novels are *The History of Henry Esmond* (1852), *The Newcomers* (1853—1855) and *The Virginians* (1857—1859).

Snobs and Marriage

The following story from The Book of Snobs tells about how Mr. Gray, a briefless barrister-at-law, prepares dinner in his tiny mansion for Mr. Goldmore, a Croesus. With sharp satirical touches, the story vividly depicts Mr. Gray's living conditions and marriage in contrast to Mr. Goldmore's social status, talking and behavior. It makes a critical survey of the manners of a period in which old standards of behavior and social relationships were shaken by the redistribution of wealth and power affected by industrialism.

In that noble romance called *Ten Thousand a Year*, I remember a profoundly pathetic description of the hero, Mr. Aubrey's, Christian manner of bearing his misfortunes. After making a display of the most florid and grandiloquent resignation, and quitting his country mansion, the delightful writer supposes Aubrey to come to town in a post-chaise and pair sitting bodkin probably between his wife and sister. It is at about seven o'clock, carriages are rattling about, knockers are thundering, and tears bedim the fine eyes of Kate and Mrs. Aubrey as they think that in happier times at this hour—their Aubrey used formerly to go out to dinner to the houses of the aristocracy his friends. This is the gist of the passage—the elegant words I forget. But the noble, noble sentiment I shall always cherish and remember. What can be more sublime than the notion of a great man's relatives in tears about—his dinner? With a few unconscious touches, what author ever so happily described a SNOB?

We were reading the passage lately at the house of my friend Raymond Gray, Esquire, Barrister-at-Law, an ingenuous youth without the least practice, but who has luckily a great share of good spirits, which enables him to bide his time, and bear laughingly his humble position in the world. Meanwhile, until it is altered, the stern laws of necessity and the expenses of the Northern Circuit oblige Mr. Gray to live in a very tiny mansion in a very queer small square in the airy neighbourhood of Gray's Inn.

What is the more remarkable is, that Gray has a wife there. Mrs. Gray was a Miss Harley Baker: and I suppose I need not say *that* is a respectable family. Allied to the Cavendishes, the Oxfords, the Marrybones, they still, though rather *déchus* from their original splendour, hold their heads as high as any. Mrs. Harley Baker, I know, never goes to church without John behind to carry her prayer-book; nor will Miss Welbeck, her sister, walk twenty yards a shopping without the protection of Figby, her sugar-loaf page; though the old lady is as ugly as any woman in the parish, and as tall and whiskery as a Grenadier. The astonishment is, how Emily Harley Baker could have stooped to marry Raymond Gray. She, who was the prettiest and proudest of the family; she, who refused Sir Cockle Byles, of the Bengal Service; she, who turned up her little nose at Essex Temple, Q.C., and connected with the noble house of Albyn; she, who had but 4000 *pour tout potage*, to marry a man who had scarcely as much more. A scream of wrath and indignation was uttered by the whole family when they heard of this *mésalliance*. Mrs. Harley Baker never speaks of her daughter now but with tears in her eyes, and as a ruined creature. Miss Welbeck says, "I consider that man a villain;"—and has denounced poor good-natured Mrs. Perkins as a swindler, at whose ball the young people met for the first time.

Mr. and Mrs. Gray, meanwhile, live in Gray's Inn, aforesaid, with a maid-servant and a nurse, whose hands are very full, and in a most provoking and unnatural state of happiness. They have never once thought of crying about their dinner, like the wretchedly puling and Snobbish womankind of my favourite Snob Aubrey, of *Ten Thousand a Year*; but, on the contrary, accept such humble victuals as Fate awards them with a most perfect and thankful good grace—nay, actually have a portion for a hungry friend at times—as the present writer can gratefully testify.

I was mentioning these dinners, and some admirable lemon puddings which Mrs. Gray makes, to our mutual friend the great Mr. Goldmore, the East India Director, when that gentleman's face assumed an expression of almost apoplectic terror, and he gasped out, "What! Do they give dinners?" He seemed to think it a crime and a wonder that such people should dine at all; or that it was their custom to huddle round their kitchen fire over a bone and a crust. Whenever he meets them in society, it is a matter of wonder to him (and he always expresses his surprise very loud) how the lady can appear decently dressed, and the man have an unpatched coat to his back. I have heard him enlarge upon this poverty before the whole room at the Conflagrative Club, to which he and I and Gray have the honour to belong.

We meet at the Club on most days. At half-past four, Goldmore arrives in St. James's Street, from the City, and you may see him reading the evening papers in the bow window of the Club, which enfilades Pall Mall—a large plethoric man, with a bunch of seals in a large bow-windowed light waistcoat. He has large coat-tails, stuffed with agents' letters and papers about companies of which he is a Director. His seals jingle as he walks. I wish I had such a man for an uncle, and that he himself were childless. I would love and cherish him, and be kind to him.

At six o'clock in the full season, when all the world is in St. James's Street, and the carriages are cutting in and out among the cabs on the stand, and the tufted dandies are showing their listless faces out of White's; and you see respectable grey-headed gentlemen waggling their heads to each other through the plate-glass windows of Arthur's; and the red-coats wish to be Briarean, so as to hold all the gentlemen's horses; and that wonderful red-coated royal porter is sunning himself before Marlborough House at the noon of London time: you see a light-yellow carriage with black horses, and a coachman in a tight floss-silk wig, and two footmen in powder and white and yellow liveries, and a large woman inside in shot silk, a poodle, and a pink parasol, which drives up to the gate of the Conflagrative, and the page goes and says to Mr. Goldmore (who is perfectly aware of the fact, as he is looking out of the windows with about forty other Conflagrative bucks), "Your carriage, sir." Mr. Goldmore wags his head. "Remember, eight o'clock precisely," says he to Mulligatawney, the other East India Director, and ascending the carriage, plumps down by the side of Mrs. Goldmore for a drive in the Park, and then home to Portland Place. As the carriage whirls off, all the young bucks in the Club feel a secret elation. It is a part of their establishment as it were. That carriage belongs to their Club, and their Club belongs to them. They follow the equipage with interest; they eye it knowingly as they see it in the Park. But halt! we are not come to the Club Snobs yet. O my brave Snobs, what a flurry there will be among you when those papers appear!

Well, you may judge, from the above description, what sort of a man Goldmore is. A dull and pompous Leadenhall Street Croesus, good-natured withal, and affable—cruelly affable. "Mr. Goldmore can never forget," his lady used to say, "that it was Mrs. Gray's grandfather who sent him to India; and though that young woman has made the most imprudent marriage in the world, and has left her station in society, her husband seems an ingenious and laborious young man, and we shall do everything in our power to be of use to him." So they used to ask the Grays to dinner twice or thrice in a season, when, by way of increasing the kindness, Buff, the butler, is ordered to hire a fly to convey them to and from Portland Place.

Of course I am much too good-natured a friend of both parties not to tell Gray of Goldmore's opinion regarding him, and the Nabob's astonishment at the idea of the briefless barrister having any dinner at all. Indeed Goldmore's saying became a joke against Gray amongst us wags at the Club, and we used to ask him when he tasted meat last? whether we should bring him home something from dinner? and cut a thousand other mad pranks with him in our facetious way.

One day, then, coming home from the Club, Mr. Gray conveyed to his wife the astounding information that he had asked Goldmore to dinner.

"My love," says Mrs. Gray, in a tremor, "how could you be so cruel? Why, the dining-room won't hold Mrs. Goldmore."

"Make your mind easy, Mrs. Gray, her ladyship is in Paris. It is only Croesus that's coming, and we are going to the play afterwards—to Sadler's Wells. Goldmore said at the Club that he thought Shakspeare was a great dramatist poet, and ought to be patronized; whereupon, fired with enthusiasm, I invited him to our banquet."

"Goodness gracious! what can we give him for dinner? He has two French cooks; you know Mrs. Goldmore is always telling us about them; and he dines with Aldermen every day."

> "A plain leg of mutton, my Lucy,
> I prythee get ready at three;
> Have it tender, and smoking, and juicy,
> And what better meat can there be?"

says Gray, quoting my favourite poet.

"But the cook is ill; and you know that horrible Pattypan, the pastrycook's...."

"Silence, Frau!" says Gray, in a deep-tragedy voice. "I will have the ordering of this repast. Do all things as I bid thee. Invite our friend Snob here to partake of the feast. Be mine the task of procuring it."

"Don't be expensive, Raymond," says his wife.

"Peace, thou timid partner of the briefless one. Goldmore's dinner shall be suited to our narrow means. Only do thou do in all things my commands." And seeing, by the peculiar expression of the rogue's countenance, that some mad waggery was in preparation, I awaited the morrow with anxiety.

Questions

1. By mentioning the noble romance *Ten Thousand a Year*, what does Thackeray try to convey to the reader?
2. Classify the characters in the story. What is Thackeray's point of view on these stratums?
3. Illustrate how Thackeray gives the reader a full-scale description of Mr. Goldmore's image and "good" nature with his satirical touches.
4. Thackeray is good at details narrating and circumstance rendering. Find two examples and explain.
5. What do you think of the title of the story? What does "snob" mean in the story? What character(s) can be included in the group of snobs?

威廉·梅克比斯·萨克雷
（1811—1863）

　　威廉·梅克比斯·萨克雷，英国小说家和讽刺作家，与维多利亚时期另一位伟大小说家查尔斯·狄更斯齐名。萨克雷生于印度加尔各答，在英国查特豪斯公学和剑桥大学三一学院接受教育。1836年在巴黎与爱尔兰女孩伊莎贝拉·萧结婚，妻子不久后患病，从此精神失常直至去世。此事对萨克雷的性格和作品均产生了深远影响。1837年他蒙受巨大经济损失，返回英国，开始了为报纸杂志撰稿的生涯。萨克雷是《弗雷泽杂志》和《笨拙》杂志早期著名的撰稿人。1860年他出任《康希尔杂志》主编，三年后猝然辞世。

　　萨克雷的早期作品《巴利·林顿的遭遇》（1844）描绘了一个集冒险家、投机者、赌徒为一身的人物，奠定了他小说家的地位。由一系列讽刺人物随笔组成的短篇小说集《势利鬼文集》（1848）使他获得了广泛的知名度。长篇小说《名利场》（1847—1848）是萨克雷的传世成名之作。该小说以辛辣讥讽的手法，细致入微地展示了19世纪初伦敦中上层阶级的生活和习俗的全景图。半自传体小说《彭登尼斯的历史》（1850）确立了他作为成功讽刺作家的地位。萨克雷的其他重要作品还有长篇小说《亨利·埃斯蒙德的历史》（1852）、《纽克姆一家》（1853—1855）和《弗吉尼亚人》（1857—1859）。

势利鬼与婚姻

　　下面的故事选自《势利鬼文集》，讲述了时运不济的律师格雷先生如何准备在自己的小公寓里宴请大款戈德莫尔先生的故事。作者通过尖锐讽刺的笔触，生动地刻画出格雷先生的生活处境和婚姻状况，与戈德莫尔先生的社会地位、言谈举止形成了鲜明的对比，批判性地再现了工业主义影响下财富与权力重新分配所引起的旧的行为准则和社会关系的大震荡这一社会面貌。

　　在那本名为《一年一万镑》的贵族罗曼史里，我记得有一段关于主人公奥伯利先生以一种基督徒的方式承受不幸的深刻感人的描述。那位可爱的作者猜想，奥伯利先生在显示了最华丽最夸张的忍让并离开他的乡村别墅之后，他是乘坐驿站马车，有可能并排挤坐在他妻子和姐姐中间来到镇上的。大约七点钟光景，镇上马车络绎不绝，门环声嘈杂如雷，凯特和奥伯利夫人的美目不禁被泪水模糊了，因为她们想起以前更幸福的时光，也是在这个钟点，她们的奥伯利经常去他的贵族朋友家中赴宴。这就是那一段叙述的要点——那些雅致的话语我忘记了。但是我将永远珍惜铭记那种高尚的伤感情绪。有什么能比大人物的亲戚们想到他的宴会而流泪更为崇高的念头呢？有哪个作者曾用寥寥数笔就这么痛快地描述过一个势力鬼呢？

最近我们是在我的朋友雷蒙德·格雷家里读的这段叙述。他是一位绅士，一位出庭律师，一个率直而毫无经验的年轻人，但幸好他拥有一个极好的心态，这使他能够等待时机，欣然忍受他在这世间的卑微处境。格雷先生在等待时来运转，但眼下由于严峻的生活所迫以及北方法庭巡回区高额的费用，格雷先生只能蜗居在一间狭小的公寓里。这间公寓坐落在自傲的格雷律师学院街区一个非常古怪的小区中。

更值得注意的是，格雷先生在那里有妻室。格雷夫人过去是哈雷·贝克家的小姐：我想用不着说，那是一个体面的家庭。与卡文迪西、牛津、玛丽伯恩斯几家同属一类，虽然他们已不像原先那样显赫，但他们走路时仍高高地昂着头。据我所知，哈雷·贝克夫人每次去教堂时总有个男仆跟在后面拿着她的祈祷书；她的姐姐，维尔贝克小姐，哪怕是去附近二十码地远买东西，也总有她那形似塔塘的侍从费格比护卫；尽管这位老妇人长得像教区内任何一位女士一样丑陋，像近卫兵一般身高，还长有胡须。令人吃惊的是，艾米丽·哈雷·贝克怎么就屈尊嫁给了雷蒙德·格雷！她，曾是家里最漂亮最高傲的女孩；她，曾拒绝了孟加拉服役的科克尔·拜尔斯爵士；她，曾对埃塞克斯·坦普尔御用大律师嗤之以鼻，也曾与阿鲁比恩的贵族之家颇有关系；她如今却带着总共只有四千英镑的嫁妆，嫁给了一个收入一点不比这个多的男人。当得知这桩门不当户不对的婚姻时，整个家族发出一连串愤怒与愤慨。现在，每当哈雷·贝克夫人谈起女儿时，眼里总含着泪，说她女儿被毁了。维尔贝克小姐说："我认为那个男的是个恶棍。"她还指责可怜、和蔼的铂金斯夫人是个骗子，因为就是在铂金斯夫人的舞会上，这两个年轻人初次相识。

格雷夫妇当时住在上面所提到的格雷律师学院区。家中雇有一个女仆和一个保姆，这两人手头都很忙，而且总是处于一种可气的违背常理的快乐状态。他们从未想过抱怨自己的晚餐，绝不像《一年一万镑》里我最喜爱的势利鬼奥伯利家可怜巴巴、如泣如诉的势利女人那样；而恰恰相反，他们以一种最完美的最感恩的优雅姿态接受着命运所恩赐的粗茶淡饭——非但如此，他们有时还接济饥饿的朋友——关于这一点，现在我这个作家可以满怀感激地作证。

当我向我们共同的朋友，担任东印度公司董事的大人物戈德莫尔先生，讲起他们的晚餐和格雷夫人做的绝妙的柠檬布丁时，这位绅士的脸上呈现出几乎像中风般的恐怖表情。他倒抽一口气道："什么？他们还请吃晚餐？"他似乎认为像这样的人家用餐本身就是一种罪过，一个奇迹；他似乎认为他们家一贯挤坐在厨房里的炉火旁啃骨头、吃面包渣儿。每当他在社交场合里遇见他们时，他都感到奇怪（而且总是非常大声地表现出他的惊奇）：那位女士怎能穿得那么体面，那位男士怎么披着一件没有补丁的外套！在我和他还有格雷有幸一起参加的火焰俱乐部里，我曾听到他当着整屋子人的面儿大肆夸大这种贫困。

大部分日子我们都在俱乐部里见面。四点半钟，戈德莫尔从城里来到圣·詹姆士大街。你可以透过俱乐部正对着堡尔商业街的弓形窗看到他在那里阅读晚报——一个身材高大多血质的人，身穿大号弓形开口式浅色马甲，里面挂着一大串印章。他那巨大的上衣后摆里塞满了代理商的信件和他担任董事的公司的文件。那些印章在他走路时叮当作响。我真希望有这么一个人当我的叔父，希望他本人没有子女。我会爱戴、珍惜并善待这样的人。

在社交旺季六点钟，圣·詹姆士大街上挤满了人，停车场出租马车之中不断有私家马车出入，头戴帽缨的纨绔子弟带着倦怠的面容从怀特俱乐部走出；透过阿瑟俱乐部的厚玻璃窗，你能看见令人尊敬的老绅士们彼此摇晃着脑袋；那些身穿红制服的英国士兵希望成为百手巨人布里阿柔斯，以便抓住所有绅士马车的缰绳；伦敦响午时分，那个非同寻常的皇家红衣门卫正在马尔伯勒宫门前晒太阳：也就在此时，你看到一辆黑色马匹拉的浅黄色马车来到了火焰俱乐部门口。车上的车夫头上紧箍着丝线假发，两个油头粉面的仆从身穿一白一黄制服，车里有一位身穿闪光绸衣的高大女人，一只狮子狗和一把粉色阳伞。男侍从走上前向戈德莫尔先生报告："先生，您的马车来了。"（戈德莫尔十分清楚这件事，因为他正和四十来个火焰俱乐部的纨绔子弟一起隔窗眺望）。戈德莫尔摇晃着脑袋。"记住，八点整，"他一边对东印度公司另一位董事马里盖多尼说，一边登上马车，一屁股坐在戈德莫尔夫人身旁。他们要先去公园兜风，然后回波特兰区家里。当马车疾驰而去时，俱乐部里所有的年轻纨绔子弟都感到一股内心的振奋。它仿佛是他们机构的一部分。那辆马车属于他们的俱乐部，而他们的俱乐部属于他们。他们兴致勃勃地目送马车离去；当他们在公园看到那辆车时，都心照不宣地注视它。但是打住！我们还未讲到俱乐部的势力鬼们哪。啊，勇敢的势力鬼们，当那些文章发出来时，你们中间将会发生怎样的轰动啊！

好了，从上面的描述你可以判断出戈德莫尔是怎样的一种人了。一个无趣又傲慢的伦敦肉类市场的大款，然而生性善良又和蔼可亲——可亲得要命。"戈德莫尔先生永远不会忘记，"他的夫人过去常常说，"正是格雷夫人的祖父派他到印度去的；尽管那位年轻的女士结下了世间最草率的一桩亲事，也脱离了她在上层社会的地位，但她的丈夫看上去是个机灵又勤劳的年轻人，我们将尽最大努力去帮助他。"所以,他们过去总在社交季节宴请格雷夫妇两三次。为了进一步显示殷勤,还派男管家巴菲雇一辆轻便马车接格雷夫妇来波特兰区,再送他们回去。

我作为此二人本性太过善良的朋友,自然不能不告诉格雷有关戈德莫尔对他的看法,也不能不向格雷提及那位大款对于这个无人委托诉讼律师也用正式晚餐一事的吃惊程度。实际上,戈德莫尔的话成了我们俱乐部这些爱说笑的人谈论格雷的一段笑话。我们常问他:上次吃肉是什么时候?需不需要我们从宴会上带些吃的给他?并搞出种种鬼名堂以开玩笑的方式戏弄他。

后来有一天,当格雷先生从俱乐部回到家后,他给妻子带回了已邀请戈德莫尔来家用餐这一惊人的消息。

"亲爱的,"格雷夫人声音颤抖,"你怎能这么狠心?要知道,整个儿饭厅都容纳不下戈德莫尔夫人。"

"放轻松,我的夫人,戈德莫尔夫人现在在巴黎。只是大款自己来,吃完后我们去看戏——去赛德勒的韦尔斯剧院。戈德莫尔在俱乐部说,他认为莎士比亚是一位伟大的戏剧诗人,应该前往赞助赞助;于是,出于一时热情,我就邀请他来家里赴宴了。"

"哎呀,天啊!我们能请他吃什么呢?他有两个法国厨师,你知道戈德莫尔夫人总跟我们提起他们,而且他每天都和大官们一起用餐。"

"普通羊腿就一只,我的夫人好露西,
　请你准备在三点整;
　做得鲜嫩,热气腾腾,又多汁,
　还有什么肉比这更好吃?"

格雷回答道,引用了我最喜爱的诗人的词儿。

"可是厨师生病了,你知道那个糟透了的烤饼锅,还有那糕点师傅的……"

"别说了,夫人!"格雷用一种悲壮的声音说。"我将去订这顿宴席。一切照我吩咐的去做。邀请我们的朋友势利鬼先生来参加宴会。筹办宴会瞧我的吧。"

"别花钱太多,雷蒙德,"妻子说。

"敬请安静,您这个无人委托律师的胆小侣伴。戈德莫尔的晚宴不会超出我们有限的支出。只要您一切按我的吩咐行事。"从这个家伙脸上的特殊表情看,他似乎在准备某出荒唐的恶作剧。我急切盼望第二天的到来。

Charles Dickens
(1812—1870)

Charles Dickens is the foremost English novelist of the Victorian era, as well as a vigorous social campaigner. The defining moment of Dickens's life occurred when he was 12 years old. Because of the family's financial difficulties he was set to work in a shoe-blacking factory. For a period of months he was also forced to live apart from his family due to his father's imprisonment for debts. This experience of lonely hardship was the most significant formative event in his life. It affected his view of the world in profound and varied ways and was described in a number of his novels.

His comic novel *The Pickwick Papers* (1837) made him the most popular English author of his time. *Oliver Twist* (1838) and *The Old Curiosity Shop* (1841) were followed by *A Christmas Carol* (1843) which he wrote in a few weeks after a trip to America. With *Dombey and Son* (1848), his novels began to express a heightened uneasiness about the evils of Victorian industrial society, which intensified in the semi-autobiographical *David Copperfield* (1850), as well as in *Bleak House* (1853), *Little Dorrit* (1857), *Great Expectations* (1861), and others. *A Tale of Two Cities* (1859) appeared in the period when he achieved great popularity for his public readings. Dickens showed his profound sympathy for the poor and described how the rich were converted after undergoing severe tests. He had a tendency to depict the grosteque characters or events. He was noted for his description of pathetic scenes that aimed to arouse people's sympathy.

The Signalman

The following is a famous tale of suspense. It is a ghost story about a lone signalman who is haunted by the image of a man who appears at the mouth of the railway tunnel to warn of the impending disaster. The story is about the life of a man from the lower class of the society, which expresses the writer's idea of humanism.

"Halloa! Below there!"

When he heard a voice thus calling to him, he was standing at the door of his box, with a flag in his hand, furled round its short pole. One would have thought, considering the nature of the ground, that he could not have doubted from what quarter the voice came; but instead of looking up to where I stood on the top of the steep cutting nearly over his head, he turned himself about, and looked down the Line. There was something remarkable in his manner of doing so, though I could not have said for my life what. But I know it was remarkable enough to attract my notice, even though his figure was foreshortened and shadowed, down in the deep trench, and mine was high above him, so steeped in the glow of an angry sunset, that I had shaded my eyes with my hand before I saw him at all.

"Halloa! Below!"

From looking down the Line, he turned himself about again, and, raising his eyes, saw my figure high above him.

"Is there any path by which I can come down and speak to you?"

He looked up at me without replying, and I looked down at him without pressing him too soon with a repetition of my idle question. Just then there came a vague vibration in the earth and air, quickly changing into a violent pulsation, and an oncoming rush that caused me to start back, as though it had force to draw me down. When such vapour as rose to my height from this rapid train had passed me, and was skimming away over the landscape, I looked down again, and saw him refurling the flag he had shown while the train went by.

I repeated my inquiry. After a pause, during which he seemed to regard me with fixed attention, he motioned with his rolled-up flag towards a point on my level, some two or three hundred yards distant. I called down to him, "All right!" and made for that point. There, by dint of looking closely about me, I found a rough zigzag descending path notched out, which I followed.

The cutting was extremely deep, and unusually precipitate. It was made through a clammy stone, that became oozier and wetter as I went down. For these reasons, I found the way long enough to give me time to recall a singular air of reluctance or compulsion with which he had pointed out the path.

When I came down low enough upon the zigzag descent to see him again, I saw that he was standing between the rails on the way by which the train had lately passed, in an attitude as if he were waiting for me to appear. He had his left hand at his chin, and that left elbow rested on his right hand, crossed over his breast. His attitude was one of such expectation and watchfulness that I stopped a moment, wondering at it.

I resumed my downward way, and stepping out upon the level of the railroad, and drawing nearer to him, saw that he was a dark sallow man, with a dark beard and rather heavy eyebrows. His post was in as solitary and dismal a place as ever I saw. On either side, a dripping-wet wall of jagged stone, excluding all view but a strip of sky; the perspective one way only a crooked prolongation of this great dungeon; the shorter perspective in the other direction terminating in a gloomy red light, and the gloomier entrance to a black tunnel, in whose massive architecture there was a barbarous, depressing, and forbidding air. So little sunlight ever found its way to this spot, that it had an earthy, deadly smell; and so much cold wind rushed through it, that it struck chill to me, as if I had left the natural world.

Before he stirred, I was near enough to him to have touched him. Not even then removing his eyes from mine, he stepped back one step, and lifted his hand.

This was a lonesome post to occupy (I said), and it had riveted my attention when I looked down from up yonder. A visitor was a rarity, I should suppose; not an unwelcome rarity, I hoped? In me, he merely saw a man who had been shut up within narrow limits all his life, and who, being at last set free, had a newly-awakened interest in these great works. To such purpose I spoke to him; but I am far from sure of the terms I used; for, besides that I am not happy in opening any conversation, there was something in the man that daunted me.

He directed a most curious look towards the red light near the tunnel's mouth, and looked all about it, as if something were missing from it, and then looked at me.

That light was part of his charge? Was it not?

He answered in a low voice: "Don't you know it is?"

The monstrous thought came into my mind, as I perused the fixed eyes and the saturnine face, that this was a spirit, not a man. I have speculated since, whether there may have been infection in his mind.

In my turn, I stepped back. But in making the action, I detected in his eyes some latent fear of me. This put the monstrous thought to flight.

"You look at me," I said, forcing a smile, "as if you had a dread of me."

"I was doubtful," he returned, "whether I had seen you before."

"Where?"

He pointed to the red light he had looked at.

"There?" I said.

Intently watchful of me, he replied (but without sound), "Yes."

"My good fellow, what should I do there? However, be that as it may, I never was there, you may swear."

"I think I may," he rejoined. "Yes; I am sure I may."

His manner cleared, like my own. He replied to my remarks with readiness, and in well-chosen words. Had he much to do there? Yes; that was to say, he had enough responsibility to bear; but exactness and watchfulness were what was required of him, and of actual work—manual labour—he had next to none. To change that signal, to trim those lights, and to turn this iron handle now and then, was all he had to do under that head. Regarding those many long and lonely hours of which I seemed to make so much, he could only say that the routine of his life had shaped itself into that form, and he had grown used to it. He had taught himself a language down here,—if only to know it by sight, and to have formed his own crude ideas of its pronunciation, could be called learning it. He had also worked at fractions and decimals, and tried a little algebra; but he was, and had been as a boy, a poor hand at figures. Was it necessary for him when on duty always to remain in that channel of damp air, and could he never rise into the sunshine from between those high stone walls? Why, that depended upon times and circumstances. Under some conditions there would be less upon the Line than under others, and the same held good as to certain hours of the day and night. In bright weather, he did choose occasions for getting a little above these lower shadows; but, being at all times liable to be called by his electric bell, and at such times listening for it with redoubled anxiety, the relief was less than I would suppose.

He took me into his box, where there was a fire, a desk for an official book in which he had to make certain entries, a telegraphic instrument with its dial, face, and needles, and the little bell of which he had spoken. On my trusting that he would excuse the remark that he had been well educated, and (I hoped I might say without offence) perhaps educated above that station, he observed that instances of slight incongruity in such wise would rarely be found wanting among large bodies of men; that he had heard it was so in workhouses, in the police force, even in that last desperate resource, the army; and that he knew it was so, more or less, in any great railway staff. He had been, when young (if I could believe it, sitting in that hut,—he scarcely could), a student of natural philosophy, and had attended lectures; but he had run wild, misused his opportunities, gone down, and never risen again. He had no complaint to offer about that. He had made his bed, and he lay upon it. It was far too late to make another.

All that I have here condensed he said in a quiet manner, with his grave dark regards divided between me and the fire. He threw in the word, "Sir," from time to time, and especially when he referred to his youth,—as though to request me to understand that he claimed to be nothing but what I found him. He was several times interrupted by the little bell, and had to read off messages, and send replies. Once he had to stand without the door, and display a flag as a train passed, and make some verbal communication to the driver. In the discharge of his duties, I observed him to be remarkably exact and vigilant, breaking off his discourse at a syllable, and remaining silent until what he had to do was done.

In a word, I should have set this man down as one of the safest of men to be employed in that capacity, but for the circumstance that while he was speaking to me he twice broke off with a fallen colour, turned his face towards the little bell when it did NOT ring, opened the door of the hut (which was kept shut to exclude the unhealthy damp), and looked out towards the red light near the mouth of the tunnel. On both of those occasions, he came back to the fire with the inexplicable air upon him which I had remarked, without being able to define, when we were so far asunder.

Said I, when I rose to leave him, "You almost make me think that I have met with a contented man."

(I am afraid I must acknowledge that I said it to lead him on.)

"I believe I used to be so," he rejoined, in the low voice in which he had first spoken; "but I am troubled, sir, I am troubled."

He would have recalled the words if he could. He had said them, however, and I took them up quickly.

"With what? What is your trouble?"

"It is very difficult to impart, sir. It is very, very difficult to speak of. If ever you make me another visit, I will try to tell you."

"But I expressly intend to make you another visit. Say, when shall it be?"

"I go off early in the morning, and I shall be on again at ten tomorrow night, sir."

"I will come at eleven."

He thanked me, and went out at the door with me. "I'll show my white light, sir," he said, in his peculiar low voice, "till you have found the way up. When you have found it, don't call out! And when you are at the top, don't call out!"

His manner seemed to make the place strike colder to me, but I said no more than, "Very well."

"And when you come down tomorrow night, don't call out! Let me ask you a parting question. What made you cry, 'Halloa! Below there!' tonight?"

"Heaven knows," said I. "I cried something to that effect—"

"Not to that effect, sir. Those were the very words. I know them well."

"Admit those were the very words. I said them, no doubt, because I saw you below."

"For no other reason?"

"What other reason could I possibly have?"

"You had no feeling that they were conveyed to you in any supernatural way?"

"No."

He wished me good night, and held up his light. I walked by the side of the down Line of rails (with a very disagreeable sensation of a train coming behind me) until I found the path. It was easier to mount than to descend, and I got back to my inn without any adventure.

Punctual to my appointment, I placed my foot on the first notch of the zigzag next night, as the distant clocks were striking eleven. He was waiting for me at the bottom, with his white light on. "I have not called out," I said, when we came close together; "may I speak now?" "By all means, sir." "Good night, then, and here's my hand." "Good night, sir, and here's mine." With that we walked side by side to his box, entered it, closed the door, and sat down by the fire.

"I have made up my mind, sir," he began, bending forward as soon as we were seated, and speaking in a tone but a little above a whisper, "that you shall not have to ask me twice what troubles me. I took you for some one else yesterday evening. That troubles me."

"That mistake?"

"No. That some one else."

"Who is it?"

"I don't know."

"Like me?"

"I don't know. I never saw the face. The left arm is across the face, and the right arm is waved,—violently waved. This way."

I followed his action with my eyes, and it was the action of an arm gesticulating, with the utmost passion and vehemence, "For God's sake, clear the way!"

"One moonlight night," said the man, "I was sitting here, when I heard a voice cry, 'Halloa! Below there!' I started up, looked from that door, and saw this someone else standing by the red light near the tunnel, waving as I just now showed you. The voice seemed hoarse with shouting, and it cried, 'Look out! Look out!' And then again, 'Halloa! Below there! Look out!' I caught up my lamp, turned it on red, and ran towards the figure, calling, 'What's wrong? What has happened? Where?' It stood just outside the blackness of the tunnel. I advanced so close upon it that I wondered at its keeping the sleeve across its eyes. I ran right up at it, and had my hand stretched out to pull the sleeve away, when it was gone."

"Into the tunnel?" said I.

"No. I ran on into the tunnel, five hundred yards. I stopped, and held my lamp above my head, and saw the figures of the measured distance, and saw the wet stains stealing down the walls and trickling through the arch. I ran out again faster than I had run in (for I had a mortal abhorrence of the place upon me), and I looked all round the red light with my own red light, and I went up the iron ladder to the gallery atop of it, and I came down again, and ran back here. I telegraphed both ways, 'An alarm has been given. Is anything wrong?' The answer came back, both ways, 'All well.'"

Resisting the slow touch of a frozen finger tracing out my spine, I showed him how that this figure must be a deception of his sense of sight; and how that figures, originating in disease of the delicate nerves that minister to the functions of the eye, were known to have often troubled patients, some of whom had become conscious of the nature of their affliction, and had even proved it by experiments upon themselves. "As to an imaginary cry," said I, "do but listen for a moment to the wind in this unnatural valley while we speak so low, and to the wild harp it makes of the telegraph wires."

That was all very well, he returned, after we had sat listening for a while, and he ought to know something of the wind and the wires,—he who so often passed long winter nights there, alone and watching. But he would beg to remark that he had not finished.

I asked his pardon, and he slowly added these words, touching my arm, —

"Within six hours after the Appearance, the memorable accident on this Line happened, and within ten hours the dead and wounded were brought along through the tunnel over the spot where the figure had stood."

A disagreeable shudder crept over me, but I did my best against it. It was not to be denied, I rejoined, that this was a remarkable coincidence, calculated deeply to impress his mind. But it was unquestionable that remarkable coincidences did continually occur, and they must be taken into account in dealing with such a subject. Though to be sure I must admit, I added (for I thought I saw that he was going to bring the objection to bear upon me), men of common sense did not allow much for coincidences in making the ordinary calculations of life.

He again begged to remark that he had not finished.

I again begged his pardon for being betrayed into interruptions.

"This," he said, again laying his hand upon my arm, and glancing over his shoulder with hollow eyes, "was just a year ago. Six or seven months passed, and I had recovered from the surprise and shock, when one morning, as the day was breaking, I, standing at the door, looked towards the red light, and saw the spectre again." He stopped, with a fixed look at me.

"Did it cry out?"

"No. It was silent."

"Did it wave its arm?"

"No. It leaned against the shaft of the light, with both hands before the face. Like this."

Once more I followed his action with my eyes. It was an action of mourning. I have seen such an attitude in stone figures on tombs.

"Did you go up to it?"

"I came in and sat down, partly to collect my thoughts, partly because it had turned me faint. When I went to the door again, daylight was above me, and the ghost was gone."

"But nothing followed? Nothing came of this?"

He touched me on the arm with his forefinger twice or thrice giving a ghastly nod each time:

"That very day, as a train came out of the tunnel, I noticed, at a carriage window on my side, what looked like a confusion of hands and heads, and something waved. I saw it just in time to signal the driver, Stop! He shut off, and put his brake on, but the train drifted past here a hundred and fifty yards or more. I ran after it, and, as I went along, heard terrible screams and cries. A beautiful young lady had died instantaneously in one of the compartments, and was brought in here, and laid down on this floor between us."

Involuntarily I pushed my chair back, as I looked from the boards at which he pointed to himself.

"True, sir. True. Precisely as it happened, so I tell it you."

I could think of nothing to say, to any purpose, and my mouth was very dry. The wind and the wires took up the story with a long lamenting wail.

He resumed. "Now, sir, mark this, and judge how my mind is troubled. The spectre came back a week ago. Ever since, it has been there, now and again, by fits and starts."

"At the light?"

"At the Danger-light."

"What does it seem to do?"

He repeated, if possible with increased passion and vehemence, that former gesticulation of "For God's sake, clear the way!"

Then he went on. "I have no peace or rest for it. It calls to me, for many minutes together, in an agonised manner, 'Below there! Look out! Look out!' It stands waving to me. It rings my little bell—"

I caught at that. "Did it ring your bell yesterday evening when I was here, and you went to the door?"

"Twice."

"Why, see," said I, "how your imagination misleads you. My eyes were on the bell, and my ears were open to the bell, and if I am a living man, it did NOT ring at those times. No, nor at any other time, except when it was rung in the natural course of physical things by the station communicating with you."

He shook his head. "I have never made a mistake as to that yet, sir. I have never confused the spectre's ring with the man's. The ghost's ring is a strange vibration in the bell that it derives from nothing else, and I have not asserted that the bell stirs to the eye. I don't wonder that you failed to hear it. But I heard it."

"And did the spectre seem to be there, when you looked out?"

"It was there."

"Both times?"

He repeated firmly: "Both times."

"Will you come to the door with me, and look for it now?"

He bit his under lip as though he were somewhat unwilling, but arose. I opened the door, and stood on the step, while he stood in the doorway. There was the Danger-light. There was the dismal mouth of the tunnel. There were the high, wet stone walls of the cutting. There were the stars above them.

"Do you see it?" I asked him, taking particular note of his face. His eyes were prominent and strained, but not very much more so, perhaps, than my own had been when I had directed them earnestly towards the same spot.

"No," he answered. "It is not there."

"Agreed," said I.

We went in again, shut the door, and resumed our seats. I was thinking how best to improve this advantage, if it might be called one, when he took up the conversation in such a matter-of-course way, so assuming that there could be no serious question of fact between us, that I felt myself placed in the weakest of positions.

"By this time you will fully understand, sir," he said, "that what troubles me so dreadfully is the question, What does the spectre mean?"

I was not sure, I told him, that I did fully understand.

"What is its warning against?" he said, ruminating, with his eyes on the fire, and only by times turning them on me. "What is the danger? Where is the danger? There is danger overhanging somewhere on the Line. Some dreadful calamity will happen. It is not to be doubted this third time, after what has gone before. But surely this is a cruel haunting of me. What can I do?"

He pulled out his handkerchief, and wiped the drops from his heated forehead.

"If I telegraph Danger, on either side of me, or on both, I can give no reason for it," he went on, wiping the palms of his hands. "I should get into trouble, and do no good. They would think I was mad. This is the way it would work,—Message: 'Danger! Take care!' Answer: 'What Danger? Where?' Message: 'Don't know. But, for God's sake, take care!' They would displace me. What else could they do?"

His pain of mind was most pitiable to see. It was the mental torture of a conscientious man, oppressed beyond endurance by an unintelligible responsibility involving life.

"When it first stood under the Danger-light," he went on, putting his dark hair back from his head, and drawing his hands outward across and across his temples in an extremity of feverish distress, "why not tell me where that accident was to happen,—if it must happen? Why not tell me how it could be averted,—if it could have been averted? When on its second coming it hid its face, why not tell me, instead, 'She is going to die. Let them keep her at home'? If it came, on those two occasions, only to show me that its warnings were true, and so to prepare me for the third, why not warn me plainly now? And I, Lord help me! A mere poor signalman on this solitary station!

Why not go to somebody with credit to be believed, and power to act?"

When I saw him in this state, I saw that for the poor man's sake, as well as for the public safety, what I had to do for the time was to compose his mind. Therefore, setting aside all question of reality or unreality between us, I represented to him that whoever thoroughly discharged his duty must do well, and that at least it was his comfort that he understood his duty, though he did not understand these confounding Appearances. In this effort I succeeded far better than in the attempt to reason him out of his conviction. He became calm; the occupations incidental to his post as the night advanced began to make larger demands on his attention: and I left him at two in the morning. I had offered to stay through the night, but he would not hear of it.

That I more than once looked back at the red light as I ascended the pathway, that I did not like the red light, and that I should have slept but poorly if my bed had been under it, I see no reason to conceal. Nor did I like the two sequences of the accident and the dead girl. I see no reason to conceal that either.

But what ran most in my thoughts was the consideration how ought I to act, having become the recipient of this disclosure? I had proved the man to be intelligent, vigilant, painstaking, and exact; but how long might he remain so, in his state of mind? Though in a subordinate position, still he held a most important trust, and would I (for instance) like to stake my own life on the chances of his continuing to execute it with precision?

Unable to overcome a feeling that there would be something treacherous in my communicating what he had told me to his superiors in the Company, without first being plain with himself and proposing a middle course to him, I ultimately resolved to offer to accompany him (otherwise keeping his secret for the present) to the wisest medical practitioner we could hear of in those parts, and to take his opinion. A change in his time of duty would come round next night, he had apprised me, and he would be off an hour or two after sunrise, and on again soon after sunset. I had appointed to return accordingly.

Next evening was a lovely evening, and I walked out early to enjoy it. The sun was not yet quite down when I traversed the field-path near the top of the deep cutting. I would extend my walk for an hour, I said to myself, half an hour on and half an hour back, and it would then be time to go to my signalman's box.

Before pursuing my stroll, I stepped to the brink, and mechanically looked down, from the point from which I had first seen him. I cannot describe the thrill that seized upon me, when, close at the mouth of the tunnel, I saw the appearance of a man, with his left sleeve across his eyes, passionately waving his right arm.

The nameless horror that oppressed me passed in a moment, for in a moment I saw that this appearance of a man was a man indeed, and that there was a little group of other men, standing at a short distance, to whom he seemed to be rehearsing the gesture he made. The Danger-light was not yet lighted. Against its shaft, a little low hut, entirely new to me, had been made of some wooden supports and tarpaulin. It looked no bigger than a bed.

With an irresistible sense that something was wrong,—with a flashing self-reproachful fear that fatal mischief had come of my leaving the man there, and causing no one to be sent to overlook or correct what he did,—I descended the notched path with all the speed I could make.

"What is the matter?" I asked the men.

"Signalman killed this morning, sir."

"Not the man belonging to that box?"

"Yes, sir."

"Not the man I know?"

"You will recognise him, sir, if you knew him," said the man who spoke for the others, solemnly uncovering his own head, and raising an end of the tarpaulin, "for his face is quite composed."

"O, how did this happen, how did this happen?" I asked, turning from one to another as the hut closed in again.

"He was cut down by an engine, sir. No man in England knew his work better. But somehow he was not clear of the outer rail. It was just at broad day. He had struck the light, and had the lamp in his hand. As the engine came out of the tunnel, his back was towards her, and she cut him down. That man drove her, and was showing how it happened. Show the gentleman, Tom."

The man, who wore a rough dark dress, stepped back to his former place at the mouth of the tunnel.

"Coming round the curve in the tunnel, sir," he said, "I saw him at the end, like as if I saw him down a perspective glass. There was no time to check speed, and I knew him to be very careful. As he didn't seem to take heed of the whistle, I shut it off when we were running down upon him, and called to him as loud as I could call."

"What did you say?"

"I said, 'Below there! Look out! Look out! For God's sake, clear the way!'"

I started.

"Ah! it was a dreadful time, sir. I never left off calling to him. I put this arm before my eyes not to see, and I waved this arm to the last; but it was no use."

Without prolonging the narrative to dwell on any one of its curious circumstances more than on any other, I may, in closing it, point out the coincidence that the warning of the engine-driver included, not only the words which the unfortunate Signalman had repeated to me as haunting him, but also the words which I myself—not he—had attached, and that only in my own mind, to the gesticulation he had imitated.

Questions

1. Try to visualize and describe the location of the Signalman's hut.
2. What was the Signalman's personal background?
3. What had been troubling his mind?
4. What was the spectre about?
5. What happened to the Signalman in the end? How and why?

查尔斯·狄更斯
（1812—1870）

查尔斯·狄更斯是英国维多利亚时期首屈一指的小说家，同时也是一位积极的社会活动家。十二岁那年，家里的变故对他产生了深远的影响。由于家境窘困，他不得不在一家皮鞋油厂工作。由于父亲欠债入狱，有几个月狄更斯只得被迫单独生活。这段孤独的艰苦生活成了他生命中最具影响力的阶段，从多方面深深地影响了他的世界观。这种人生体验表现在他的多部小说中。

他的喜剧小说《匹克威克外传》使他成为他那个时代最畅销的小说家。在《雾都孤儿》（1838）和《老古玩店》（1841）之后他又发表了《圣诞颂歌》（1843），那是他去美国后的几个星期内写成的。从《董贝父子》（1848）开始，他的小说开始描写维多利亚时期工业社会的罪恶所给人们带来的深深不安。这种不安在后来的作品中越来越多地体现出来，如《大卫·科波菲尔》（1850）、《荒凉山庄》（1853）、《小杜丽》（1857）、《远大前程》（1861），等等。《双城记》（1859）发表的时候，他当众朗读自己的作品，并且广受读者欢迎。狄更斯对穷人表现出深厚的同情，同时还描述了富人如何经过严峻考验而变好。他还倾向于描写光怪陆离的人物和事件。他以善于记述感伤的场面而唤起人们的同情心著称。

信号工

下面这篇鬼怪故事富于悬念。故事讲述了一名孤独的信号工在火车隧道口遭遇一个人影警告他即将发生灾难的怪事。故事还反映出社会底层人的生活，表达了作者的人文主义思想。

"嗨，下面当心！"

听见有声音这样叫他，他正站在信号岗门口，手里拿着面小旗，卷在短旗杆上。鉴于此处地形的特点，人们以为他对声音传来的方向不会有疑问。但他并没有抬头看我所站立之处，我的位置几乎就在他头顶上方那陡峭的铁道路堑顶端，而是转身向下朝铁路线望去。他这种举动十分奇怪，尽管我也说不出究竟奇怪在哪儿。但我知道他的奇怪举动足以引起我的注意。他身在深沟，显得矮小暗淡，而我则高高在上，袒露在晚霞暴怒的光芒之中，不得不用手遮住眼睛才能完全看清他。

"嗨，下面当心！"

他把目光从铁路线上收回，转过身来，抬起双眼，这才看见高处的我。

"我能从哪条路下去和你聊聊吗？"

他向上看看我，没回答，我也向下看看他，没有急于重复自己那个无关紧要的问题。正在这时，地面和空气隐隐震动，很快剧烈起来，一股猛烈的气流冲击而至，使我忽然后退，仿佛要把我拉倒在地。列车疾驰而过，喷出的蒸汽升到我所在的高处，再飘过去，从这块地方一掠而过。我又往下看，发现他已把刚才指挥列车通过时挥舞的旗子卷好了。

我又问了他一遍。他似乎注视了我一会儿，然后用卷好的旗子指着我水平高度的某个地点，大约有两三百码远。我向下朝着他大声叫道："谢谢啦！"就朝那里走去。我仔细环顾周围，发现有一条崎岖的凿出的锯齿形小路通往下面，于是我顺路而下。

路壑极深，也异常陡峭，是穿过一块冷湿的巨石开凿出来的。我越往下走，路越泥泞不堪，真觉得路漫长啊，长到使我有时间回味他为我指路时脸上所显露的勉强或不情愿的独特表情。

当我沿着崎岖的小路走到低得又能看见他时，发现他站在列车刚驶过的两条铁轨之间，那姿态仿佛是在等我出现。他左手捏着下巴边，右手横在胸前托着左肘。这是一种期待与戒备的姿态，我于是稍停片刻，对此感到疑惑。

我继续向下走，然后迈到与铁路高度持平的路上。靠近时，我发现他皮肤深黄、黑胡须、浓眉毛。他所在的信号亭位于我所见过的最寂寞、凄凉的地方。两边是湿漉漉参差不齐的石墙，除了一线天空外什么也见不到。一边只能见到如此巨大的"地牢"，弯曲地向前延伸；另一边视线较短，尽头是暗淡的红光，一个黑洞洞的隧道口更显阴沉——这个庞然大物造成一种原始粗野、阴森压抑、令人恐惧的气氛。这里几乎见不到阳光，散发着难闻的泥土气味，凛冽的寒风呼啸而过，使我不禁打了一个寒战，仿佛置身于世外。

还没等他动身，我很快就来到他跟前，只有一臂之远。此时他的视线还没有从我身上离开，他向后退了一步，举起手。

我刚才说过，坚守在这个岗亭相当寂寞，我高高在上往下看时，它就吸引了我的注意力。我想，来访此地是件稀奇的事，我也希望自己并非不速之客。在他看来，我只不过是在自己工作的狭小范围内一直受困的人，而最终获得自由，便重新激发出对这些伟大工程的兴趣。抱着这种想法，我与他交谈；但是我却不太熟知与他交谈的方式，除此之外，我也不愿意对他敞开心扉，因为这个人内在的某些东西使我害怕。

他的眼光好奇地落在了隧道口附近的红灯上,然后他看了看灯的周围,仿佛什么东西丢了,然后转向我。

那个灯也归他管？不是吗？

"难道你不知道吗？"他回答的声音很低。

我审视着他专注的眼神和忧郁的表情,一种可怕的想法出现在脑海,他是魂灵而非常人。随后我开始怀疑,他的脑袋是否感染了什么病症。

这时我也向后退了退。但向后退的时候,我发现他的眼中好像对我有一丝的恐惧。这反倒打消了我刚才那种可怕的想法。

"你看我时,"我强挤出一丝微笑,"好像有些害怕。"

"我怀疑,"他回答道,"是否在什么地方见过你。"

"什么地方？"我问道。

他指了指刚才看的红灯。

"在那儿？"我问道。

他特意地打量一下我,然后默念道,"是的。"

"伙计,我在那儿做什么？无论怎么说,我真的是从来没去过那儿,你应该相信。"

"我会相信的,"随后他又补充了一句,"是啊,我的确会相信。"

像我刚才一样,他重新整理了一下思路。他从容不迫地回答了我的问题,措辞精当。他在那里有很多活儿要干吗？是啊,事实上他责任重大；准确和细心是这份工作的要求,实际的活儿,也就是体力活儿,他几乎没有。改变信号,维修信号灯,还要不时转动这个铁杆,这些都是他工作的组成部分。这些工作在我看来时间又长又寂寞,但他只是说这种惯例性的工作模式使他的生活变得如此,并且他已经习惯了这一切。他在这下边教会自己一种语言——如果要用眼睛来懂得这种语言,并且用他简单的思维来形成它的发音,那就可以称之为在学习这种语言。他也学了些分数和小数,一点儿代数,只是幼年时,他数数就不灵。他是否有必要在上班时必须坚持在空气潮湿的通道中,难道他就永远都不能升到阳光普照之地,而只能留守在高耸的石壁之间吗？为什么？这要取决于时间和环境。在某些区域,铁道线上的阳光比别处就要少,同样道理,白天黑夜的某些时刻情况也不同。在晴朗的天气下,他有时也会选择待在高于大片阴冷之上的地方,但随时都会被电铃召唤,每当这时注意听电铃总会给他带来更多的不安,这样,阳光下的解脱我想对他也就大打折扣了。

他带我去了工作间,在那儿有一个火盆,一张桌子,桌子上边放着一本工作日志,他需要在日志里做记录,还有带表盘、指针的电报仪,还有他曾提及的小电铃。见我相信他受过良好教育,而且（希望我这样说不至于冒犯他）所受的教育还可能高于他现在的地位，于是他便评述道，此类不和谐的例子在芸芸众生之中并不少见；他听说在工厂、警察局里也是如此，甚至在最优越的部门军队里也是如此；他知道在大量的铁路员工中或多或少也存在此类不和谐因素。他年轻时（很难相信坐在那间棚子里，人还会年轻）曾经学过自然哲学，听过讲座；但他年少轻狂，没有把握住机会，最后一蹶不振。他对此并没有抱怨过。他酿的苦酒自己喝，再没有重新振作的机会。

我在这儿所概述的内容，只是通过他轻描淡写地聊出来的，他那阴郁的目光将火炉与我分隔开来。他时时叫声"先生"，尤其在他谈到自己年轻的时候——好像让我明白，他并无奢望，只要像现在的样子。他好几次都被铃声打断，读取信息并发送回复。一次他站在门外，向一辆行驶的火车挥舞着旗帜，并与司机进行言语交流。在工作时，我发现他出奇的精确和机警，一字一句，不折不扣，随后寂静无声，直到做完该做的事。

总之，我认为这个人是本岗位最牢靠的人选之一，但有两次在和我说话的时候，他突然停止交谈，面色沉重，把头转向电铃，而当时电铃并没有响。接着，他打开房门，望向那个离隧道口很近的红灯。有两次他回到屋内火盆边，脸上挂满了我所提到的谜团，但我们之间的差距如此之大，我无法猜到他在想什么。

我起身要离开，于是对他说，"你差不多使我相信你是我所遇见的最随遇而安的人了。"

（我得承认我是在套他的话。）

"我想我以前是，"接着他又用那种低沉的声音说道，"但现在我很不安，先生，很不安。"

他本该记起刚才说过的话，因为他已经说过了，于是我便很快接过了他的话。

"不安什么？你有什么不安的？"

"很难表述，先生。真的很难、很难说清楚。如果你下次再来，我会试着告诉你。"

"我的确想再来看你，说个时间吧。"

"我早晨一大早下班，明晚十点我会来这里值班，先生。"

"那我明晚十一点到。"

他表示谢意，送我到门口。"我来点亮白灯，先生，"接着他又以一种特殊的低音说道，"直到你找到这个路的出口，找到路口时，不要喊！到了顶上，也别喊！"

他的举止令我对此地不寒而栗，但我却只说了声，"好吧！"

"如果明晚你再来，别喊！现在你要走了，请告诉我，今晚你为什么喊那句话，'嗨，下面当心！'"

"天知道，"我说。"我只是叫了一声，大概是那个意思吧——"

"先生，不是大概，千真万确就是那几个词儿。我清楚得很。"

"好吧，就是那几个词儿，我的确说了，那是因为我看见你在下面。"

"没有别的原因？"

"我还能有什么别的原因？"

"难道你就没有感觉它在以超自然的方式告诉你一些事情？"

"没有。"

他祝我晚安，举起灯。我沿着铁路向下走，直到找到回去的路（悚然地感觉有一列火车正从后面向我驶来）。上山容易下山难，费了很大力气，我回到了客栈，没再出去。

第二天晚上，当远处的钟声敲响第十一下时，我准时来到约好的地方，双脚站在开凿成锯齿形的路口。他在下面等着我，手里的灯亮着白光。当我们靠近时，我说，"这次我可没出声，我现在可以说话了吗？""当然了，先生。""那么晚上好，握个手吧。""晚上好，先生，握握手。"之后我们并肩来到值班室，进了屋，关上门，坐在火炉旁。

"先生，我已经决定告诉你一切，"我们一坐下，他就向前探身开始对我说，嗓音只是稍高于耳语，"你没有必要再问我有什么不安了。我昨晚错把你当作另一个人了。这就是我的不安。"

"是认错了人？"

"不，是那另一个人叫我不安。"

"他是谁？"

"不知道。"

"长的像我？"

"不清楚，我从没见过那张脸。他左臂横挡着脸，右臂用力地挥舞，就像这样。"

我目不转睛地盯着他，他那强有力的动作似乎在说，"看在上帝的份上，让开！"

"在一个月色皎洁的夜晚，"他说，"我就坐在这儿，突然听见有人喊'嗨，下面当心！'我立即起身向门外看，只见那另一个人站在隧道附近的红灯边挥着手，就像我刚才向你演示的那样。那声音听起来有些沙哑，并且一直喊：'当心！当心！'然后又接着说：'嗨，下面当心！当心！'我抓起灯，把它调到红色就朝那个人影奔去：'怎么了？''出什么事了？在哪儿？'那影子就站在铁路黑暗的坑道外面，我走到离影子很近的地方，为了看清挡在袖子后面的脸。我直奔过去，刚伸出手要拉开袖子，影子就消失了。"

"消失在隧道里了？"我说。

"没有，我飞快地跑进去，大概有五百码。我停下来，把灯举过头顶，只看到标明距离的数字，以及拱顶和墙上慢慢流淌着的湿漉漉的污渍。于是我又以更快的速度跑了出来(因为这阴暗的隧道令我毛骨悚然)，我举着自己的红灯，环顾隧道红灯的四周，爬上铁梯走上廊台，然后又下来跑回原地。我给前后方都发出了信号：'收到警报，出什么事了吗？'两边都回复'一切正常。'"

我抵御着一只冰冷的手指正慢慢划过我的脊柱这般恐惧感，尽力让他相信这个人影一定是他视觉上的幻觉；这些人影幻觉是由支配眼功能敏感神经的疾病所造成的，经常困扰病人。他们中有些人已经意识到自己受折磨的原因，并通过实验证明了这一点。"至于那幻觉中的叫喊，"我接着说，"当我们轻轻说话时，只要听听这奇异山谷里的风声，还有电报线被风刮出的像竖琴般的声音就明白了。"

我们坐着听了一会儿后，然后他回答说，这些解释都很有道理。他经常独自凝望这漫长的冬夜，所以一定懂得我说的风声和电话线声。但他还是求我听他把话讲完。

我表示抱歉，请他继续说，于是他抓着我的手臂，慢慢地补充道：

"在那个人影出现后6小时，这条铁路上发生了可怕的事故，10小时之内死伤的人又从这个隧道里被抬出来，而且恰恰经过那个人影当时站立的地方。"

我不禁打了个冷战，但还是尽力让自己平静些。我接着他的话说，无可否认，这纯属一个异常的巧合，才这么深刻地印在他的脑海里。但毫无疑问，此类异常的巧合之事的确会接二连三地发生，在处理这个问题的时候也必须考虑在内。但我当然还是认为，我补充道（我想他会反对我的观点），有常识的人不会让这些巧合左右自己的人生计划。

他又一次求我听他把话讲完。

我再次抱歉打断了他的话。

他再一次抓住我的手臂，转过头，双眼茫然地望着我说："那只是一年前的事情。六七个月过去了，我已从惊恐中恢复过来，但一天清晨，我站在门口向红灯那里张望，突然又看见了那个幽灵。"他停止说话，死死地盯着我。

"它喊出声了吗？"

"没有，没出声。"

"那它挥动手臂了吗？"

"也没有，它只是靠向一束光，双手挡在脸前。像这样。"

我又一次目不转睛地盯着他的一举一动。那是某种哀悼的举动，我曾经在墓碑上的石雕上见过这种姿势。

"你没走过去吗？"

"没有，我回到屋里坐下，一是想冷静下来，同时也是因为我当时吓晕了。等我再走到门口，天已亮了，幽灵也消失了。"

"接下来怎么了？没有什么事情发生吗？"

他用食指捅了捅我的手臂，大概有两三次，每一次都是面色苍白地点头：

"就在那天，一辆火车正驶出隧道，我注意到，在我这边一个车厢的窗子边，有一个似乎像手和脸的东西，还有什么东西在挥动。我示意司机停车，司机师傅也立即踩住刹车，但列车还是前行了大概一百五十尺，我立即追过去，突然听到撕心裂肺的哭喊声，瞬间一位年轻貌美的姑娘死在一节车厢里。很快那女子被抬到这里，就放在你我之间的地板上。"

我不由自主地把椅子往后挪一点，看他所指的地面。

"真的，先生。是真事儿。千真万确，我说的都是实话。"

我感到口干舌燥，无论如何一个字也说不出来。呼呼的风声和电话线的摇曳声也在为这伤感的故事而痛哭。

他又接着说下去。"先生，请帮我分析一下，我心里为何忐忑不安。那个幽灵一周前回来过，打那以后，它就断断续续抽风似地来过几次。"

"在红灯那儿？"

"在'危险信号灯'那儿。"

"它来想做什么？"

他这次的情绪更强烈，用以前的手势重复着"看在上帝的份上，让开！"。

然后他接着说下去。"我被它搅得心神不定。它有时会极度痛苦地叫我，一叫就好几分钟：'下面当心！当心！当心！'它站在那里向我招手，响我的铃儿。"

我接着他的话问，"昨晚我在这儿时，你走到门那里，它是不是也响铃了？"

"嗯，两次。"

"瞧，这就对啦，"我说，"是你的想象力误导了你呀。我可是瞪着眼盯着铃儿，又竖起耳朵听着呢；我可是个大活人，那几次根本就没响过铃。不，它什么时候都没响过，除了火车站通知你时，铃儿发出自然的响声之外。"

他摇了摇头。"在这一点上，先生，我从没失误过。我从来没把鬼魂的铃音和人的铃声混淆过。鬼魂的铃音是铃本身的一种奇怪的震动，不是任何物体能发出的，何况我也没说可以用眼看到铃声震动呀。所以你听不到也不足为怪，但是我听到了。"

"那么你向外望时，鬼魂似乎在那儿吗？"

"在那儿。"

"两次都在？"

他肯定地重复说，"两次都在。"

"那你愿意跟我到门口，现在找找它？"

他咬着下嘴唇，似乎有些不乐意，但还是站了起来。我打开门，站在台阶上，他则站在门口。远处有"危险信号灯"，有昏暗的隧道入口，有路堑高高、潮湿的石壁，还有天上闪烁的群星。

"你看到了吗？"我问，特别注意他的面部。他双眼使劲睁大，不过我比他更用力地盯着那同一个地方。

"没有，"他回答，"不在那儿。"

"我看也是。"我说。

我们又进了屋，关上门，回到了座位上。我正在思考怎样才能发挥这一优势来说服他，如果这可以称得上是优势的话，突然他又自然而然地继续说起来，他自信我们对于这一事实彼此好像并没有什么重大分歧，这反而使我感到被置于最不利的位置。

"到这时你该彻底明白，先生，"他说，"是什么问题使我如此不安了吧，那就是：那鬼魂在指什么呢？"

我告诉他，我并不能确定是否彻底明白了。

"它在警告什么呢？"他说，反复想着，双眼似火，只是偶尔瞅瞅我。"危险是什么？危险在哪里？在线路之上某个地方将发生危险。会发生可怕的灾难。先前的经历让我们无法怀疑第三次预言。这当然使我心神不宁、心怀恐惧。我可怎么办呢？"

他拿出手绢，擦去滚烫额头上的汗滴。

"假如我发'危险'电报，报任何一方，或两方都报，但我却给不出理由。"他擦擦掌心，继续说，"我会碰到麻烦，而且不会有什么好结果。他们会认为我疯了。情形会是这样：信息：'危险！当心！'回应：'什么危险？在哪里？'信息：'不知道。不过，看在上帝的份上，一定要注意啊！'他们肯定得撤了我。要不然他们还能怎么做？"

他的心痛令我倍感怜惜。这种涉及生命，同时又令人费解的责任感对于一个尽职尽责的人的心理折磨，令他备受煎熬。

"当它第一次站在'危险信号灯'下时，"他说着，把黑发捋到脑后，极度苦恼地把手一次次掠过太阳穴，而后又继续说，"为什么不告诉我事故在那儿发生——如果注定要发生？为什么不告诉我怎样去避免——如果可以避免？当它第二次出现时，他没有露脸，为什么不告诉我'她会死的，让他们把她留在家里吧？'如果他前两次的出现只是为了证明它的警告的真实性，让我为第三次做好心理准备的话，那为什么不现在直接警告我呀？上帝帮帮我吧！我只是在这个孤独站上的一个可怜的信号工呀！为什么不去找有信誉度又有权力做出反应的人？"

看到他这种状态，我觉得为了这个可怜的人，也是为了公共安全，当下我应该做的就是稳定他的情绪。因此，把我们之间现实和不现实的问题都放到一边，我告诉他任何真正尽职的人都应该好好表现，至少他能懂得自己的职责，这就是一种安慰，虽然他并不理解这些奇怪的"影像"。我尽力向他讲明他的义务和责任，这点我做得很好，但很难说服他摆脱困惑。他平静下来。夜色深沉下来，他需要在工作中倾注更大的注意力。我是在凌晨两点钟走的。本来我说要陪他一整夜，可是他不同意。

我走上通道时，不时地回望那个红灯；我不喜欢那红灯，假如我的床就在它下面，我是睡不好觉的。这些我都没有理由隐瞒。同样，我也不喜欢这两起事故和那个死去的小姑娘。我也没有理由隐瞒这一点。

然而，此时我想得最多的是，既然已经听到了信号工的一番话，我应该怎么做？我虽然已经知道他聪明、警觉、辛苦而且严格，但是这样的心理状态，他又能维持多久呢？尽管职位不高，他的责任却十分重大，那么如果是我（比如说），我会以身家性命像他那样去继续严格地履行职责吗？

我总是觉得如果不先跟他坦白，也没能提出折中意见，就把他说的告诉他公司的上级们，这样做有点背信弃义，这挥之不去的感觉让我最终决定主动陪他去看当地最好的医师，听听医师的建议，除此之外就只能暂时为他保密了。他告诉我他第二天晚上换班，日出一两个小时后会下班，日落一会儿就又上班了。于是我跟他约好回去找他。

第二天的夜晚非常迷人，于是我提前出来欣赏美景。当我穿过陡峭路堑顶端附近的田野小路时，太阳还没下山。我心想，还可以再散步一小时，半小时走过去，半小时走回来，那时再去信号工的岗亭。

在还没散步之前，我走到路堑边缘，机械地从我第一次见到信号工的地点往下望去。就在靠近隧道入口处，我看到一个人影，他左袖捂着眼睛，一个劲儿地挥动右臂，此时我被一股难以名状的恐惧震慑住了。

那股莫名的恐惧瞬间就消散了，因为我马上发现那是一个真人，不远处还有一小群人。那个人像是在对那群人练习他的姿势。"危险信号灯"还没有打开。靠在杆子旁，有一个低矮棚子，由木头支架和雨布组成，我以前没有见过这东西。棚子看上去还没有一张床大。

我不禁感觉到出事了，心中升起一股自责感；我离开他是个致命的错误，没人监督他，也没人帮他纠正错误。于是我飞快跑下凹凸的路径。

"出什么事了？"我问那些人。

"信号工早晨死了，先生。"

"不是岗亭里的那个人吧？"

"是，先生。"

"不是我认识的那个人吧？"

"如果你认识他，自己来认吧，先生，"那个人代表其他人回答我说，他沉重地露出自己的头，并掀起雨布的一端，"他的脸很安详。"

"啊，这是怎么发生的呀，怎么发生的？"我朝在场的人不停地问，棚子又关上了。

"他被火车撞倒了，先生。英国再没有人比他更了解自己的工作了。可是不知怎的，他没躲开外轨。还是在大白天。他点亮了灯，就提在手上。火车出隧道时，他正背对着火车，结果就被撞倒了。那个人开的火车，他正在比划是怎么发生的。汤姆，给这位先生比划比划。"

一个身穿深色粗布衣服的人走回到隧道口，站到原来的位置。

"转过隧道里的弯道，先生，"他说，"我看见他在那一端，就像是从透视镜中看见他一样。没有时间减速了，我知道他十分小心。见他似乎没理睬汽笛的警示，当我们朝他驶去时，我关掉了笛声，竭尽全力朝他大喊。"

"你都喊什么了？"

"我喊，'下面当心！当心！当心！看在上帝的份上，让开！'"

我惊呆了。

"啊！好可怕呀，先生。我一直不停地向他喊。我用这只胳膊捂着眼不去看，自始至终都挥着手，可都没用。"

对于这些蹊跷的事再无须赘言。在结束这个故事之际，也许我可以指出，火车司机的警告之语，不仅与那不幸的信号工几次三番跟我提及的一直困扰他的那些话一模一样，而且还与我自己，而不是他，看到他模仿鬼影动作时脑子里联想到的话不谋而合。

The Boots at the Holly-Tree Inn

In the following story, the narrator tells about one of Cobbs's "curious" things in his life, that two children of higher social class run away from their families respectively and try to elope and get married, only to be brought back to their "normal" life. Fancy as it is, it is undeniably thought-provoking.

Where had he been in his time? he repeated, when I asked him the question, Lord, he had been everywhere! And what had he been? Bless you, he had been everything you could mention, a'most!

Seen a good deal? Why, of course he had. I should say so, he could assure me, if I only knew about a twentieth part of what had come in *his* way. Why, it would be easier for him, he expected, to tell what he hadn't seen than what he had. Ah! a deal, it would.

What was the curiousest thing he had seen? Well! He didn't know. He couldn't momently name what was the curiousest thing he had seen—unless it was a Unicorn—and he saw *him* once at a fair. But supposing a young gentleman not eight year old was to run away with a fine young woman of seven, might I think *that* a queer start? Certainly. Then that was a start as he himself had had his blessed eyes on, and he had cleaned the shoes they run away in—and they was so little he couldn't get his hand into 'em.

Master Harry Walmers' father, you see, he lived at the Elmses, down away by Shooter's Hill there, six or seven miles from Lunnon. He was a gentleman of spirit, and good-looking, and held his head up when he walked, and had what you call Fire about him. He wrote poetry, and he rode, and he ran, and he cricketed, and he danced, and he acted, and he done it all equally beautiful. He was uncommon proud of Master Harry as was his only child; but he didn't spoil him neither. He was a gentleman that had a will of his own and a eye of his own, and that would be minded. Consequently, though he made quite a companion of the fine bright boy, and was delighted to see him so fond of reading his fairy-books, and was never tired of hearing him say my name is Norval, or hearing him sing his songs about Young May Moons is beaming love, and when he as adores thee has left but the name, and that; still he kept the command over the child, and the child *was* a child, and it's to be wished more of 'em was.

How did Boots happen to know all this? Why, through being under-gardener. Of course he couldn't be under-gardener, and he always about, in the summer-time, near the windows on the lawn, a-mowing, and sweeping, and weeding, and pruning, and this and that, without getting acquainted with the ways of the family. Even supposing Master Harry hadn't come to him one morning early, and said, "Cobbs, how should you spell Norah, if you was asked?" and then began cutting it in print all over the fence.

He couldn't say that he had taken particular notice of children before that; but really it was pretty to see them two mites a-going about the place together, deep in love. And the courage of the boy! Bless your soul, he'd have thrown off his little hat, and tucked up his little sleeves, and gone in at a lion, he would, if they had happened to meet one, and she had been frightened of him. One day he stops, along with her, where Boots was hoeing weeds in the gravel, and says, speaking up, "Cobbs," he says, "I like *you*." "Do you, sir? I'm proud to hear it." "Yes, I do, Cobbs. Why do I like you, do you think, Cobbs?" "Don't know, Master Harry, I am sure." "Because Norah likes you, Cobbs." "Indeed, sir? That's very gratifying." "Gratifying, Cobbs? It's better than millions of the brightest diamonds to be liked by Norah." "Certainly, sir." "Would you like another situation, Cobbs?" "Well, sir, I shouldn't object if it was a good 'un." "Then, Cobbs," says he, "you shall be our Head Gardener when we are married." And he tucks her, in her little sky-blue mantle, under his arm, and walks away.

Boots could assure me that it was better than a picter, and equal to a play, to see them babies, with their long, bright, curling hair, their sparkling eyes, and their beautiful light tread, a-rambling about the garden, deep in love. Boots was of opinion that the birds believed they was birds, and kept up with 'em, singing to please 'em. Sometimes they would creep under the tulip-tree, and would sit there with their arms round one another's necks, and their soft cheeks touching, a-reading about the Prince and the Dragon, and the good and bad enchanters, and the king's fair daughter. Sometimes he would hear them planning about a house in a forest, keeping bees and a cow, and living entirely on milk and honey. Once he came upon them by the pond, and heard Master Harry say, "Adorable Norah, kiss me, and say you love me to distraction, or I'll jump in head foremost." And Boots made no question he would have done it if she hadn't complied. On the whole, Boots said it had a tendency to make him feel he was in love himself—only he didn't exactly know who with.

"Cobbs," said Master Harry, one evening, when Cobbs was watering the flowers, "I am going on a visit, this present midsummer, to my grandmamma's at York."

"Are you, indeed, sir? I hope you'll have a pleasant time. I am going into Yorkshire, myself, when I leave here."

"Are you going to your grandmamma's, Cobbs?"

"No, sir. I haven't got such a thing."

"Not as a grandmamma, Cobbs?"

"No, sir."

The boy looked on at the watering of the flowers for a little while, and then said, "I shall be very glad indeed to go, Cobbs—Norah's going."

"You'll be all right, then, sir," says Cobbs, "with your beautiful sweetheart by your side."

"Cobbs," returned the boy, flushing, "I never let anybody joke about it when I can prevent them."

"It wasn't a joke, sir," says Cobbs, with humility—"wasn't so meant."

"I am glad of that, Cobbs, because I like you, you know, and you're going to live with us. Cobbs!"

"Sir."

"What do you think my grandmamma gives me when I go down there?"

"I couldn't so much as make a guess, sir."

"A Bank-of-England five-pound note, Cobbs."

"Whew!" says Cobbs, "that's a spanking sum of money, Master Harry."

"A person could do a great deal with such a sum of money as that—couldn't a person, Cobbs?"

"I believe you, sir!"

"Cobbs," said the boy, "I'll tell you a secret. At Norah's house they have been joking her about me, and pretending to laugh at our being engaged—pretending to make game of it, Cobbs!"

"Such, sir," says Cobbs, "is the depravity of human natur."

The boy, looking exactly like his father, stood for a few minutes with his glowing face toward the sunset, and then departed with, "Good-night, Cobbs. I'm going in."

If I was to ask Boots how it happened that he was a-going to leave that place just at that present time, well, he couldn't rightly answer me. He did suppose he might have stayed there till now if he had been anyways inclined. But you see, he was younger then, and he wanted change. That's what he wanted—change. Mr. Walmers, he said to him when he gave him notice of his intentions to leave, "Cobbs," he says, "have you anything to complain of? I make the inquiry, because if I find that any of my people really has anything to complain of, I wish to make it right if I can." "No, sir," says

Cobbs; "thanking you, sir, I find myself as well sitiwated here as I could hope to be anywheres. The truth is, sir, that I'm a-going to seek my fortun'." "Oh, indeed, Cobbs!" he says; "I hope you may find it." And Boots could assure me—which he did, touching his hair with his bootjack, as a salute in the way of his present calling—that he hadn't found it yet.

Well, sir! Boots left the Elmses when his time was up, and Master Harry, he went down to the old lady's at York, which old lady would have given that child the teeth out of her head (if she had had any), she was so wrapped up in him. What does that Infant do—for Infant you may call him, and be within the mark—but cut away from that old lady's with his Norah, on a expedition to go to Gretna Green and be married!

Sir, Boots was at this identical Holly-Tree Inn (having left it several times to better himself, but always come back through one thing or another), when, one summer afternoon, the coach drives up, and out of the coach gets them two children. The Guard says to our Governor, "I don't quite make out these little passengers, but the young gentleman's words was, that they was to be brought here." The young gentleman gets out; hands his lady out; gives the Guard something for himself; says to our Governor, "We're to stop here to-night, please. Sitting-room and two bedrooms will be required. Chops and cherry-pudding for two!" and tucks her in her little sky-blue mantle, under his arm, and walks into the house much bolder than Brass.

Boots leaves me to judge what the amazement of that establishment was, when these two tiny creatures all alone by themselves was marched into the Angel—much more so when he, who had seen them without their seeing him, give the Governor his views upon the expedition they was upon. "Cobbs," says the Governor, "if this is so, I must set off myself to York, and quiet their friends' minds. In which case you must keep your eye upon 'em, and humor 'em till I come back. But before I take these measures, Cobbs, I should wish you to find from themselves whether your opinions is correct." "Sir, to you," says Cobbs, "that shall be done directly."

So Boots goes up-stairs to the Angel, and there he finds Master Harry, on a enormous sofa—immense at any time, but looking like the Great Bed of Ware, compared with him—a-drying the eyes of Miss Norah with his pocket-hankecher. Their little legs was entirely off the ground, of course, and it really is not possible for Boots to express to me how small them children looked.

"It's Cobbs! It's Cobbs!" cries Master Harry, and comes running to him on t'other side, and catching hold of his t'other hand, and they both jump for joy.

"I see you a-getting out, sir," says Cobbs. "I thought it was you. I thought I couldn't be mistaken in your height and figure. What's the object of your journey, sir? Matrimonial?"

"We're going to be married, Cobbs, at Gretna Green," returned the boy. "We have run away on purpose. Norah has been in rather low spirits, Cobbs; but she'll be happy, now we have found you to be our friend."

"Thank you, sir, and thank you, miss," says Cobbs, "for your good opinion. Did you bring any luggage with you, sir?"

If I will believe Boots when he gives me his word and honor upon it, the lady had got a parasol, a smelling-bottle, a round and a half of cold buttered toast, eight peppermint drops, and a hair-brush—seemingly a doll's. The gentleman had got about half a dozen yards of string, a knife, three or four sheets of writing-paper, folded up surprising small, a orange, and a Chaney mug with his name upon it.

"What may be the exact nature of your plans, sir?" says Cobbs.

"To go on," replied the boy—which the courage of that boy was something wonderful!— "in the morning, and be married to-morrow."

"Just so, sir," says Cobbs. "Would it meet your views, sir, if I was to accompany you?"

When Cobbs said this, they both jumped for joy again, and cried out, "Oh yes, yes, Cobbs! Yes!"

"Well, sir!" says Cobbs. "If you will excuse me having the freedom to give an opinion, what I should recommend would be this. I am acquainted with a pony, sir, which, put in a pheayton that I could borrow, would take you and Mrs. Harry Walmers, Junior (myself driving, if you approved), to the end of your journey in a very short space of time. I am not altogether sure, sir, that this pony will be at liberty to-morrow, but even if you had to wait over to-morrow for him, it might be worth your while. As to the small account here, sir, in case you was to find yourself running at all short, that don't signify; because I am a part proprietor of this inn, and it could stand over."

Boots assures me that when they clapped their hands, and jumped for joy again, and called him "Good Cobbs!" and "Dear Cobbs!" and bent across him to kiss one another in the delight of their confiding hearts, he felt himself the meanest rascal for deceiving 'em that ever was born.

"Is there anything you want just at present, sir?" says Cobbs, mortally ashamed of himself.

"We should like some cakes after dinner," answered Master Harry, folding his arms, putting out one leg, and looking straight at him, "and two apples and jam. With dinner we should like to have toast and water. But Norah has always been accustomed to half a glass of currant wine at dessert. And so have I."

"It shall be ordered at the bar, sir," says Cobbs; and away he went.

Boots has the feeling as fresh upon him this moment of speaking as he had then, that he would far rather have had it out in half a dozen rounds with the Governor than have combined with him; and that he wished with all his heart there was any impossible place where two babies could make an impossible marriage, and live impossibly happy ever afterward. However, as it couldn't be, he went into the Governor's plans, and the Governor set off for York in half an hour.

The way in which the women of that house—without exception—every one of 'em—married *and* single—took to that boy when they heard the story, Boots considers surprising. It was as much as he could do to keep 'em from dashing into the room and kissing him. They climbed up all sorts of places, at the risk of their lives, to look at him through a pane of glass. They was seven deep at the keyhole. They was out of their minds about him and his bold spirit.

In the evening, Boots went into the room to see how the runaway couple was getting on. The gentleman was on the window-seat, supporting the lady in his arms. She had tears upon her face, and was lying, very tired and half asleep, with her head upon his shoulder.

"Mrs. Harry Walmers, Junior, fatigued, sir?" says Cobbs.

"Yes, she is tired, Cobbs; but she is not used to be away from home, and she has been in low spirits again. Cobbs, do you think you could bring a biffin, please?"

"I ask your pardon, sir," says Cobbs. "What was it you—"

"I think a Norfolk biffin would rouse her, Cobbs. She is very fond of them."

Boots withdrew in search of the required restorative, and, when he brought it in, the gentleman handed it to the lady, and fed her with a spoon, and took a little himself; the lady being heavy with sleep, and rather cross. "What should you think, sir," says Cobbs, "of a chamber candlestick?" The gentleman approved; the chambermaid went first, up the great staircase; the lady, in her sky-blue mantle, followed, gallantly escorted by the gentleman; the gentleman embraced her at her door, and retired to his own apartment, where Boots softly locked him in.

Boots couldn't but feel with increased acuteness what a base deceiver he was, when they consulted him at breakfast (they had ordered sweet milk-and-water, and toast and currant jelly, over-night) about the pony. It really was as much as he could do, he don't mind confessing to me, to look them two young things in the face, and think what a wicked old father of lies he had grown up to be. Howsomever, he went on a-lying like a Trojan about the pony. He told 'em that it did so unfortunately happen that the pony was half clipped, you see, and that he couldn't be taken out in that state, for fear it should strike to his inside. But that he'd be finished clipping in the course of the day, and that to-morrow morning at eight o'clock the pheayton would be ready. Boots' view of the whole case, looking back on it in my room, is, that Mrs. Harry Walmers, Junior, was beginning to give in. She hadn't had her hair curled when she went to bed, and she didn't seem quite up to brushing it herself, and its getting in her eyes put her out. But nothing put out Master Harry. He sat behind his breakfast-cup, a-tearing away at the jelly, as if he had been his own father.

After breakfast Boots is inclined to consider they drawed soldiers—at least he knows that many such was found in the fireplace, all on horseback. In the course of the morning Master Harry rang the bell—it was surprising how that there boy did carry on—and said, in a sprightly way, "Cobbs, is there any good walks in this neighborhood?"

"Yes, sir," says Cobbs. "There's Love Lane."

"Get out with you, Cobbs!"—that was that there boy's expression—"you're joking."

"Begging your pardon, sir," says Cobbs, "there *really is* Love Lane. And a pleasant walk it is, and proud shall I be to show it to yourself and Mrs. Harry Walmers, Junior."

"Norah, dear," says Master Harry, "this is curious. We really ought to see Love Lane. Put on your bonnet, my sweetest darling, and we will go there with Cobbs."

Boots leaves me to judge what a Beast he felt himself to be, when that young pair told him, as they all three jogged along together, that they had made up their minds to give him two thousand guineas a year as Head Gardener, on account of his being so true a friend to 'em. Boots could have wished at the moment that the earth would have opened and swallowed him up, he felt so mean, with their beaming eyes a-looking at him, and believing him. Well, sir, he turned the conversation as well as he could, and he took 'em down Love Lane to the water-meadows, and there Master Harry would have drowned himself in half a moment more, a-getting out a water-lily for her—but nothing daunted that boy. Well, sir, they was tired out. All being so new and strange to 'em, they was tired as tired could be. And they laid down on a bank of daisies, like the children in the wood, leastways meadows, and fell asleep.

Boots don't know—perhaps I do—but never mind, it don't signify either way—why it made a man fit to make a fool of himself to see them two pretty babies a-lying there in the clear, still day, not dreaming half so hard when they was asleep as they done when they was awake. But, Lord! when you come to think of yourself, you know, and what a game you have been up to ever since you was in your own cradle, and what a poor sort of chap you are, and how it's always either Yesterday with you, or To-morrow, and never To-day, that's where it is!

Well, sir, they woke up at last, and then one thing was getting pretty clear to Boots—namely, that Mrs. Harry Walmerses, Junior's, temper was on the move. When Master Harry took her round the waist, she said he "teased her so"; and when he says, "Norah, my young May Moon, your Harry tease you?" she tells him, "Yes; and I want to go home."

A boiled fowl and baked bread-and-butter pudding brought Mrs. Walmers up a little; but Boots could have wished, he must privately own to me, to have seen her more sensible of the voice of love, and less abandoning of herself to currants. However, Master Harry, he kept up, and his noble heart was as fond as ever. Mrs. Walmers turned very sleepy about dusk, and began to cry. Therefore, Mrs. Walmers went off to bed as per yesterday; and Master Harry ditto repeated.

About eleven or twelve at night comes back the Governor in a chaise, along with Mr. Walmers and a elderly lady. Mr. Walmers looks amused and very serious, both at once, and says to our Missis: "We are much indebted to you, ma'am; for your kind care of our little children, which we can never sufficiently acknowledge. Pray, ma'am, where is my boy?" Our Missis says: "Cobbs has the dear child in charge, sir. Cobbs, show Forty!" Then he says to Cobbs: "Ah, Cobbs, I am glad to see *you*! I understood you was here!" And Cobbs says: "Yes, sir. Your most obedient, sir."

I may be surprised to hear Boots say it, perhaps; but Boots assures me that his heart beat like a hammer, going up-stairs. "I beg your pardon, sir," says he, while unlocking the door; "I do hope you are not angry with Master Harry. For Master Harry is a fine boy, sir, and will do you credit and honor." And Boots signifies to me that, if the fine boy's father had contradicted him in the daring state of mind in which he then was, he thinks he should have "fetched him a crack," and taken the consequences.

But Mr. Walmers only says: "No, Cobbs. No, my good fellow. Thank you!" And, the door being opened, goes in.

Boots goes in, too, holding the light, and he sees Mr. Walmers go up to the bedside, bend gently down, and kiss the little sleeping face. Then he stands looking at it for a minute, looking wonderfully like it (they do say he ran away with Mrs. Walmers); and then he gently shakes the little shoulder.

"Harry, my dear boy! Harry!"

Master Harry starts up and looks at him. Looks at Cobbs, too. Such is the honor of that mite, that he looks at Cobbs, to see whether he has brought him into trouble.

"I'm not angry, my child. I only want you to dress yourself and come home."

"Yes, pa."

Master Harry dresses himself quickly. His breast begins to swell when he has nearly finished, and it swells more and more as he stands, at last, a-looking at his father; his father standing a-looking at him, the quiet image of him.

"Please may I"—the spirit of that little creature, and the way he kept his rising tears down!—"please, dear pa—may I—kiss Norah before I go?"

"You may, my child."

So he takes Master Harry in his hand, and Boots leads the way with the candle, and they come to that other bedroom, where the elderly lady is seated by the bed, and poor little Mrs. Harry Walmers, Junior, is fast asleep. There the father lifts the child up to the pillow, and he lays his little face down for an instant by the little warm face of poor unconscious little Mrs. Harry Walmers, Junior, and gently draws it to him—a sight so touching to the chambermaids, who are peeping through the door, that one of them called out, "It's a shame to part 'em!" But this chambermaid was always, as Boots informs us, a soft-hearted one. Not that there was any harm in that girl. Far from it.

Finally, Boots says, that's all about it. Mr. Walmers drove away in the chaise, having hold of Master Harry's hand. The elderly lady and Mrs. Walmers, Junior, that was never to be (she married a Captain long afterward, and died in India), went off next day. In conclusion, Boots puts it to me whether I hold with him in two opinions: firstly, that there are not many couples on their way to be married who are half as innocent of guile as those two children; secondly, that it would be a jolly good thing for a great many couples on their way to be married, if they could only be stopped in time, and brought back separately.

Questions

1. Who is telling the story? Who is Mr. Boots?
2. Who are Harry and Norah? How old are they? What is their relationship?
3. What is Mr. Boots's attitude toward the puppy love?
4. What does the father do to the boy when he finds him?
5. What are Mr. Boot's lessons drawn from the elopement?

冬青树旅馆的布茨先生

在下面的故事中,叙述者向我们讲述了考布斯一生中经历过的"最离奇"的事——两个上层社会的孩子各自从家中逃出,一起去私奔结婚,结果却被家长带回到"正常"生活。尽管故事离奇,但却发人深省。

他当年都去过哪儿?当我问他的时候,他重复道,天哪,他哪儿都去过!他都做过什么?哎呀,你能想出的他都做过,差不多吧!

见多识广?那是当然。应该说他让我深信我连他这些年来经历的二十分之一都不及。呃,他估摸着,对他来说,讲讲他没有见过的反倒要比讲他见过的容易得多。啊,这么说还差不多。

他见过的最离奇的事是什么?嗨,他也不知道。他从来都说不清他见过的最离奇的事是什么——也许是那只他在集市上看到的独角兽。不过说起来,如果一个八岁的小绅士和一位七岁的小淑女私奔,这算不算是离奇事件的开端呢?当然是了。那就从这儿说起吧,既然他有幸目睹此事,并且擦过他们私奔时穿的鞋——他们的鞋太小了,他连手都伸不进去。

小主人哈利·沃马士的父亲,你知道的,住在艾尔梅斯,那儿离卢南六七英里,在舒特山脚下。他是一位精神抖擞的绅士,长相英俊,走路气宇轩昂,有些你们说的"激情"。他会作诗,擅骑马,能赛跑,会打板球,能舞蹈,擅长表演,而且样样精通。小主人哈利是他唯一的孩子,因此他为哈利感到非常骄傲;但他并没有惯坏孩子。他是位有主见又有眼光的绅士,这点可要记住。因此,尽管他经常陪伴在他可爱伶俐的孩子身边,看到孩子愿意读童话书而感到欣喜,听不够孩子说"我的名字叫诺维",或者听他唱有关"小五月坠爱河,爱您的他离开时,留下的只有他的名儿"之类的歌儿等等;但他还是保持着对孩子的掌控。孩子就是孩子,他希望孩子们都有孩子样儿。

布茨是怎么知道这些的?哎,因为他是沃马士家的副园丁。他总是在夏季的时候在草坪上挨着窗户的地方割草,打扫,除杂草,修剪,做这做那。作为他家里的副园丁,他怎么会跟沃马士一家不熟呢?不过要是小主人哈利那天一大清早没有走到他面前对他说"考布斯,怎么拼写诺拉的名字,你会吗?"并且开始在篱笆上一笔一画地刻写的话,事情也许就会是另外一番景象。

照他说,在那之前他并没有特别留意过那两个孩子,不过见这两个小人儿出双入对、深坠情网倒也是挺有意思。男孩子勇气可嘉!哎呀!如果他们俩真地遇到狮子，而她又感到害怕的话，他会扔掉小礼帽，卷起小袖子，奔着狮子就去，他会的。有一天，布茨正在锄沙砾路上的杂草，他和她停到布茨身边，他大声说："考布斯，我喜欢你。""是吗，先生，听您这么说我很荣幸。""考布斯，我真的喜欢你。你知道我为什么喜欢你吗，考布斯？""不知道，小主人哈利，我确实不知道。""因为诺拉喜欢你，考布斯。""真的吗，先生？这太让人高兴了。""高兴，考布斯？受到诺拉的喜爱要比得到上百万的最耀眼的钻石还好。""当然，先生。""你想另谋高就吗？""先生，如果有好地方我不会拒绝。""那好，考布斯，"他说，"等我们结婚的时候，你当我们的园丁长。"然后他为她披上天蓝色的小斗篷，搂着她，走开了。

布茨跟我说，看着这两个宝贝长着长长的、亮丽的卷发，眼睛炯炯有神，穿着漂亮的轻便鞋漫步在花园里，深坠情网的样子，真是比画儿还好看，跟看戏似的。布茨甚至觉得鸟儿们都把他们当作同类，跟着他们，唱歌取悦他们。有时候他们会悄悄走到百合树下，坐那里，互相搂着脖子，嫩脸蛋贴在一起，读着有关王子与恶龙，好坏巫师，以及国王的美丽女儿的故事。有时他会听到他们计划在森林里建一处房子，养蜜蜂和奶牛，只吃蜂蜜喝牛奶度日。有一次他在池塘边遇到他们，听到小主人哈利说："可爱的诺拉,亲亲我吧,对我说,你爱我爱得发狂,否则我就大头朝下跳下去。"布茨可以肯定要是她没答应他，他一定会跳下去的。总而言之，布茨说，他自己都觉得甜蜜，仿佛也坠入情网——只是不知道和谁。

一天傍晚，考布斯正在浇花，小主人哈利说："考布斯，这个仲夏，我要去约克郡我奶奶家。"

"是吗，先生？希望你过得愉快。我也要离开这里去约克郡。"

"你去看你奶奶吗，考布斯？"

"不，先生，没那事儿。"

"你没有奶奶吗，考布斯？"

"对，没有。"

男孩看了一会儿考布斯浇花，然后说："去奶奶家我的确应该很高兴，考布斯——诺拉也去。"

考布斯说："先生，有您美丽的情人在身边，您一定会快乐的。"

"考布斯，"男孩脸红了，回应道，"如果我能阻止，我从来不让任何人开这事儿的玩笑。"

"我并没有开玩笑，"考布斯谦逊地说，——"没有开玩笑的意思。"

"那就太好了，考布斯，因为我喜欢你，你是知道的，你将来得跟我们生活在一起，考布斯！"

"先生。"

"你猜猜我每次去奶奶那儿她给我什么?"

"我猜不出来,先生。"

"一张英格兰银行五英镑的钞票,考布斯。"

"呃!"考布斯说,"那可是不小的一笔钱呀,小主人哈利。"

"用这样一笔钱可以做很多事,是吧,考布斯?"

"您说的对,先生。"

"考布斯,"男孩说,"我告诉你一个秘密。诺拉他们家人一直在跟她开我的玩笑,试图笑话我们订婚——胆敢拿我们的事开心,考布斯!"

考布斯说,"这可真是人性的堕落,先生。"

男孩在那里站了几分钟,表情像极了他的父亲,红润的脸朝着夕阳,然后走开了,"晚安,考布斯。我进去了。"

如果问布茨他怎么会在那个时候打算离开沃马士家,呃,他不会很确切地告诉我。他的确以为,如果他自己愿意的话,他也许会在沃马士家一直干到现在。但是,你知道,他那时年轻,想要换种生活。他的确想要换换生活。布茨对沃马士先生表达去意的时候,沃马士先生问道,"考布斯,你有什么不满吗?我这样问是因为如果我发现我的人对我有什么不满,我可以改进。""没有不满,先生,"考布斯说,"谢谢您,先生,我希望到其他地方也能像在这里一样适应。其实,先生,我要去寻找发财的机会。""哦,是这样,考布斯!"他说,"希望你能找到发财的机会。"可是布茨向我确定他并没有找到什么机会——他还以自己职业特有的方式,用脱靴器碰了碰头发,来向我确定没有找到过什么机会。

好了,先生!布茨在艾尔梅斯干完后,离开了那里。小主人哈利去了约克郡他奶奶那儿。老奶奶对这孩子十分倾心,甚至会把嘴里的牙给他(如果她还有牙的话)。那个宝宝干什么了——可以叫他宝宝,他合乎标准——他跟诺拉从老奶奶那里跑了出来,大老远去格雷特纳格林结婚了!

先生,布茨当时正在那家一模一样的冬青树旅馆工作(他有几次离开了那里,试图改善自己的境况,但都因为这样那样的原因回来了)。夏天的一个下午,马车驶进,两个孩子从车里出来。马车夫对我们主管说,"我没太弄懂这两个孩子,但是那位小绅士说他们要到这里来。"小绅士走出来,扶他的淑女下车,给了车夫些钱。他对我们的主管说,"我们今晚在这里停留。请给我们准备带客厅和两个卧室的套间。还要两人份的排骨和樱桃布丁!"说完就为她披上天蓝色的小斗篷,搂着她,走进了旅馆,言行举止极其胆大妄为。

布茨让我想象一下,当那两个小东西独自走入安琪儿客房的时候,整个旅店的人都觉得这是多么令人惊讶啊；而鉴于布茨看到了两个孩子，而他们却没有看到他，所以当布茨告诉主管他猜想他们此行的目的时候，大家就更觉得惊讶。主管说，"考布斯，如果是这样的话，我得亲自动身去趟约克，让他们的朋友们冷静冷静。这样，你就得在我回来之前看住他们，哄着他们。但在我动身之前，我希望你能从他们那里证实你的猜测。"考布斯说，"我立即就办，先生。"

于是，布茨上楼去了安琪儿客房，在那里，他看到了小主人哈利。哈利正坐在一个很大的沙发上——沙发本身很大，跟他一比，简直像是一个巨大的床。他正在用他的手帕给诺拉小姐擦眼泪。他们的小腿完全离地，当然，布茨跟我说那两个孩子显得太小了，简直无法用语言形容。

"是考布斯！是考布斯！"小主人哈利喊道，他跑到他的身边，抓住了他另一边的手，他们都高兴地跳了起来。

"我看见您走出来，先生，"考布斯说。"我觉得是您。您的身高和体型，我想我是不会认错的。您此行的目的是什么？结婚？"

"我们要去格雷特纳格林结婚，考布斯，"男孩回答道。"我们是故意跑出来的。诺拉情绪有些低落，考布斯；不过我们现在有你这个朋友，她会高兴起来的。"

"谢谢，先生，谢谢，小姐，这样夸我，"考布斯说，"您带行李来了吗，先生？"

布茨向我发誓，用荣誉向我保证，小姐带了一把阳伞，一个香水瓶，一块半冷黄油圆吐司，八块薄荷硬糖和一把发刷——像是玩具发刷。小绅士带了六码长的绳子，一把刀，三四张叠得很小的书写纸，一个橘子和一个带有他名字的钱尼牌杯子。

"您到底怎么计划的呢，先生？"考布斯说。

"明早继续走，"男孩回答道——这孩子的勇气可嘉——"明天结婚。"

"这样的话，先生，"考布斯说，"如果我陪您去，是否中您的意？"

听到考布斯这样说，他们两个又都高兴地跳了起来，大喊道，"哦，太好啦，太好啦，考布斯！太好啦！"

考布斯说，"呃，先生，请允许我斗胆发表一下意见。我有一个提议。先生，我知道有一匹小马，我还可以借到一辆马车，用这匹小马套马车，您和小哈利·沃马士夫人乘坐这辆马车到达目的地可以节省很多时间（如果您同意，我亲自驾车）。先生，我不敢确定明天那匹马有没有安排，但是即便是明天要等一天，也是值得的。至于这小笔费用嘛，先生，如果您手头稍紧，就无所谓了，我在这个旅馆有股份，所以可以以后再说。"

布茨跟我说，他看到孩子们拍手、高兴地跳起来，叫他"好人考布斯！"

"亲爱的考布斯!"他们全身心地信任他,还弯身隔着他互相亲吻。他觉得自己欺骗了孩子,是有史以来最卑鄙的坏蛋。

"您现在还有什么需要的吗,先生?"考布斯十分羞愧地说。

小主人哈利交叉双臂,一条腿伸向前,直视着他回答道,"我们晚饭后想要些蛋糕,两个苹果和果酱。晚饭要吐司和水。不过诺拉已经习惯在吃甜点的时候喝半杯醋栗酒,我也要一份。"

"我会告诉吧台点上的,先生。"考布斯说,然后退下了。

布茨在告诉我这事儿时候的感觉就像当时一样,他宁可跟主管出去跑六圈,也不愿意这样和主管合谋;他全心全意地希望能有个世外桃源让这两个宝贝神仙眷侣般地共结连理,从此过上不食人间烟火的幸福生活。但是,不行。他得按照总管的计划行动。总管半小时后就出发了。

旅馆的所有女人——结婚的、单身的——所有女人,在听说这事的来龙去脉后无一例外地对男孩产生了好感。布茨对此感到十分不解。他想尽办法阻止她们冲进房间亲吻那男孩。她们甚至冒险爬上各处,为了就是能透过玻璃窗看到他。七个人使劲从钥匙孔往里看。她们为那男孩和他的勇敢精神而发狂。

傍晚,布茨去房间里看看这对逃亡者如何。小绅士坐在窗前的座上,怀里抱着小淑女。小淑女脸上带泪,头枕着小绅士的肩膀躺着,很累的样子,快睡着了。

"小哈利·沃马士太太很疲劳吧,先生?"考布斯说。

"是呀,她累了,考布斯。不过那是因为她不习惯离开家,而且她又闹情绪了。考布斯,请你拿个英国苹果来好吗?"

"什么,"先生,考布斯说,"您要什么——"

"也许诺福克苹果会使她好起来。考布斯。她很喜欢吃苹果。"

布茨出门去拿男孩要的"补药"。回来后,小绅士把苹果递给了女孩,用勺喂了她一口,自己吃了一点;女孩睡得很香,有些恼。考布斯说,"拿个夜用蜡台来,怎么样?"男孩同意了。客房女服务员先上了大楼梯,女孩跟在后面,她披着天蓝色的斗篷,男孩豪侠般地陪着她;男孩在她的房门口拥抱了她,然后走进了自己的房间。布茨轻轻地为他锁上门。

第二天早餐(头天晚上他们点了甜味稀释奶、吐司和醋栗果冻)他们问布茨有关小马的时候,布茨情不自禁地越发感到自己是一个无耻的骗子。他毫不保留地跟我坦白说,看着那两个小东西的脸,他觉得自己简直变成了邪恶的谎言之父。然而,他却像特洛伊人一样对有关小马的事继续撒谎。他告诉俩人说,很不幸,小马被剪了一半鬃毛,在这种状态下,他不适合出去,否则小马会伤自尊。不过,它今天白天就可以剪完鬃毛,明天一早八点马车就会准备好。布茨在我屋里回顾整个事件的时候认为，那时小哈利·沃马士太太已经开始妥协了。她睡觉前没有卷头发，她好像也不太会自己梳头，头发总是进眼睛让她烦躁。但是小主人哈利并不觉得烦躁。他坐在那里，前面摆着早餐杯，把果冻弄得细碎，活脱脱就是他自己的父亲。

早餐后，布茨觉得他们画起士兵来——反正在壁炉旁他发现了很多士兵的画像，都是骑着马的。上午小主人哈利按铃叫人——他能坚持下来很不容易——他精神抖擞地问，"考布斯，这附近有什么散步的好去处吗？"

"有啊，先生，"考布斯说，"有爱之巷。"

"去你的吧，考布斯！"那是男孩的表达法，意思是"你开玩笑吧。"

"您别见怪，先生，"考布斯说，"这里确实有个爱之巷。是一条很宜人的路。我将很荣幸亲自带您和小哈利·沃马士夫人去。"

小主人哈利说，"诺拉，亲爱的，真是神奇。我们真得去看看爱之巷。带上帽子，我最甜蜜的爱人，我们跟考布斯一起去那儿。"

他们三个人一起漫步的时候，这对年轻恋人告诉布茨，既然布茨是他们的真朋友，他们已经决定要雇布茨当园丁长，每年给他两千几尼。这时的布茨觉得自己真是个禽兽，他还让我去评判他当时的感受。那时布茨甚至希望地壳会裂开，把他吞进去。他们闪闪发亮的眼睛看着他，相信他，他觉得自己那么邪恶。然后呢，先生，布茨继续着话题，他带他们沿着爱之巷，去了草甸。在那儿小主人哈利为了给诺拉够睡莲，差点落水淹着。但是男孩毫无惧色。呃，先生，他们筋疲力尽。一切对他们都是全新的，从未体验过。他们累极了。他们在一片雏菊旁躺下，睡着了，这与一般小孩子在树林里，或在草地上玩累了睡着了别无二样。

布茨搞不懂，也许我能搞懂，不用介意，反正无所谓。布茨看着这两个孩子躺在晴朗宁静的天空下做着美梦，就如同他们清醒时也做美梦一样，不禁感慨。可是天呀！想想自己，要知道，从襁褓到现在我们都做了什么，我们是多么可怜的家伙，我们要么是生活在昨天，要么是生活在明天，从来都不是生活在今天。就是这样！

好了，先生，他们终于醒了，布茨认识到一件事——那就是，小哈利·沃马士夫人的脾气上来了。小主人哈利搂她的腰时，她说哈利"耍弄她"，而当哈利说，"诺拉，我的小五月，你的哈利怎么能耍弄你呢？"她回答说，"你就是耍弄我。我要回家。"

小哈利·沃马士夫人吃了炖鸡和烤面包奶油布丁后高兴了一些。布茨私下里向我坦白，他真希望诺拉能更敏感地回应一下爱的声音，而少贪吃一些黑醋栗果冻。然而，小主人哈利却一如既往，他那颗高尚的心还是充满了爱。小沃马士夫人在黄昏的时候开始困倦，哭泣起来。于是，跟前一天一样，小沃马士夫人回去睡觉，小主人哈利又重复了前一天的做法。

晚上十一二点的时候总管乘着马车回来了，跟他一起来的是沃马士先生和一位上了年纪的夫人。沃马士先生看起来既愉快又严肃，他对服务员说，"女士，您一定花了很多我们想不到的心思照顾我们的小孩，真是太感谢您了。请问，我的儿子在哪里？"服务员说，"先生，考布斯照看着可爱的孩子。考布斯，领先生去四十号房间！"于是沃马士先生对考布斯说，"哦，考布斯，真高兴见到你！我听说你在这儿！"考布斯说，"是的先生。愿为您效劳，先生。"

布茨跟我保证他们上楼的时候，他的心蹦得像个锤子，听他这样说我还觉得很奇怪，也许吧。"请原谅，先生，"他开门的时候说，"我希望您不要生小主人哈利的气。他是个好孩子，先生，他会为您带来荣誉的。"布茨还跟我表示，他当时正心气鲁莽，如果这好孩子的父亲反对他的话，他一定会"给他猛烈一击"，然后承担全部后果。

可是沃马士先生只是说："我不生气，考布斯。好伙计，我不会的。谢谢你！"门开了，他走了进去。

布茨也进去了，手里拿着灯。他看到沃马士先生走到床边，轻轻弯下腰，吻了吻孩子熟睡的小脸。然后他站直身子看了一会儿，看上去很欣赏的样子（有人说他当年与沃马士夫人也是私奔的）；然后他轻轻地摇晃孩子的肩膀。

"哈利，我的儿子！哈利！"

小主人哈利惊起，看了看父亲，也看了看考布斯。这就是这孩子的优秀品质，他看着考布斯，想弄清是不是他自己给人家带来了麻烦。

"我并没有生气，孩子。我只是想让你穿上衣服回家。"

"好的，爸。"

小主人哈利很快穿好衣服。快穿好的时候，他的胸部开始起伏，他站起来的时候他的胸部起伏得更明显，最后他激动地看着父亲。父亲站在那里看着他，俨然就是沉静的小哈利。

"请允许我，"——这小家伙真有勇气，看看他那努力抑制自己眼泪的样子——"请，好爸爸，允许我，在我走之前吻一下诺拉好吗？"

"好的，孩子。"

他领着小主人哈利的手，布茨举着蜡烛前面带路，他们来到了另一个卧室。那位年长一些的太太坐在床边，可怜的小哈利·沃马士太太睡得正香。父亲把孩子抱起来让他够得着枕头，孩子迅速地把自己的小脸贴到熟睡的小哈利·沃马士太太脸上，温柔地把她的脸拉向自己。那些从门缝儿里偷看的女仆们见到这一情景都很感动。她们其中一个喊道："把他们分开太残忍了！"不过据布茨讲，那位女仆总是面慈心软。女孩子没有受到一点伤害。绝对没有。

最后，布茨说，事情就这样结束了。沃马士先生驾车离开了，一直握着小主人哈利的手。那位年长的夫人和从未成为小沃马士夫人的女孩（多年后她嫁给了一位船长，死在了印度）第二天也离开了。布茨最后问我是否同意他的两条结论：第一，很多踏上结婚之路的情侣都不及这两个孩子一半真诚；第二，很多踏上结婚之路的情侣，如果他们也能中途被制止并被分别带回家，那将是皆大欢喜。

Thomas Hardy
(1840—1928)

Thomas Hardy, English novelist and poet, is well-known for his stories located in an imaginary area called Wessex. Living in a period of great changes that took place in England, Hardy revealed his pessimism and fatalism through his works. Born in Dorset, a rural region of Southwestern England, he was the son of a building contractor and a woman of some literary interest. His formal education ended at the age of 16 when he was apprenticed to a local architect, but he read a great deal and made his own study of music, painting and poetry. Even though he did very well in architecture, what really interested him was literature. In 1862, he went to London to work, where he began to write poems and novels. At first, he could not find publishers. When he could finally support himself by writing, he married Emma Lavinia Gifford in 1874. After Emma's death, he married Florence Emily Dugdale, his secretary in 1914. When Hardy died, his ashes were placed in Poet's Corner of Westminster Abbey for his great contribution to English literature.

Hardy's early writings were unsuccessful. His real fame came with the publication of *Far from the Madding Crowd* (1874). He continued to produce his best novels. *The Return of the Native* (1878) is a story about a beautiful girl who desires to find the mad love and escape the dull rural life. Its tragic ending reflects Hardy's pessimistic philosophy. *Tess of the D'Urberville* (1891) depicts the misfortune and tragedy of a poor country girl who struggles to find her place in society. Hardy's last and most famous novel *Jude the Obscure* (1895) questions the Victorian conventions through the hero's attempts to fulfill his aims, which reveals the helplessness of human beings under the mysterious power of nature. For the rest of his life, Hardy devoted himself to writing poems, dramas and short stories. He published several books of poems, an epic drama, *The Dynasts* (1903—1908), and some collections of short stories.

Absent-Mindedness in a Parish Choir

The following story is from Life's Little Ironies (1894). With simple and colloquial language, it tells about the members of a parish choir, who play irreverent *music in the church due to excessive drinking to keep warm. The humorous and ironical story depicts the bitter life of the lower class people and criticizes the class differences in the 19th century England.*

"It happened on Sunday after Christmas—the last Sunday they ever played in Longpuddle church gallery, as it turned out, though they didn't know it then. As you may know, sir, the players formed a very good band—almost as good as the Mellstock parish players that were led by the Dewys; and that's saying a great deal. There was Nicholas Puddingcome, the leader, with the first fiddle; there was Timothy Thomas, the bass-viol man; John Biles, the tenor fiddler; Dan'l Hornhead, with the serpent; Robert Dowdle, with the clarionet; and Mr. Nicks, with the oboe—all sound and powerful musicians, and strongwinded men—they that blowed. For that reason they were very much in demand Christmas week for little reels and dancing-parties; for they could turn a jig or a hornpipe out of hand as well as ever they could turn out a psalm, and perhaps better, not to speak irreverent. In short, one half-hour they could be playing a Christmas carol in the squire's hall to the ladies and gentlemen, and drinking tay and coffee with 'em as modest as saints; and the next, at the Tinker's Arms, blazing away like wild horses with the 'Dashing White Sergeant' to nine couple of dancers and more, and swallowing rum-and-cider hot as flame.

"Well, this Christmas they'd been out to one rattling randy after another every night, and had got next to no sleep at all. Then came the Sunday after Christmas, their fatal day. 'Twas so mortal cold that year that they could hardly sit in the gallery; for though the congregation down in the body of the church had a stove to keep off the frost, the players in the gallery had nothing at all. So Nicholas said at morning service, when 'twas freezing an inch an hour, 'Please the Lord I won't stand this numbing weather no longer; this afternoon we'll have something in our insides to make us warm if it cost a king's ramsom.'

"So he brought a gallon of hot brandy and beer, ready mixed, to church with him in the afternoon, and by keeping the jar well wrapped up in Timothy Thomas's bass-viol bag it kept drinkably warm till they wanted it, which was just a thimbleful in the Absolution, and another after the Creed, and the remainder at the beginning o' the sermon. When they'd had the last pull they felt quite comfortable and warm, and as the sermon went on—most unfortunately for 'em it was a long one that afternoon—they fell asleep, every man jack of 'em; and there they slept on as sound as rocks.

"'Twas a very dark afternoon, and by the end of the sermon all you could see of the inside of the church were the pa'son's two candles alongside of him in the pulpit, and his soaking face behind 'em. The sermon being ended at last, the pa'son gied out the Evening Hymn. But no choir set about sounding up the tune, and the people began to turn their heads to learn the reason why, and then Levi Limpet, a boy who sat in the gallery nudged Timothy and Nicholas, and said, 'Begin! Begin!'

"'Hey, what?' says Nicholas, starting up; and the church being so dark and his head so muddled he thought he was at the party they had played at all the night before, and away he went, bow and fiddle, at 'The Devil among the Tailors', the favorite jig of our neighborhood at that time. The rest of the band, being in the same state of mind and nothing doubting, followed their leader with all their strength, according to custom. They poured out that there tune till the lower bass notes of 'The Devil among the Tailors' made the cobwebs in the roof shiver like ghosts; then Nicholas, seeing nobody moved, shouted out as he scraped (in his usual commanding way at dances when folks didn't know the figures), 'Top couples cross hands! And when I make the fiddle squeak at the end, every man kiss his pardner under the mistletoe!'

"The boy Levi was so frightened that he bolted down the gallery stairs and out homeward like lightning. The pa'son's hair fairly stood on end when he heard the evil tune raging through the church; and thinking the choir had gone crazy, he held up his hand and said: 'Stop, stop, stop! Stop, stop! What's this?' But they didn't hear'n for the noise of their own playing, and the more he called the louder they played.

"Then the folks came out of their pews, wondering down to the ground, and saying: 'What do they mean by such a wickedness? We shall be consumed like Sodom and Gomorrah!'

"Then the squire came out of his pew lined wi' green baize, where lots of lords and ladies visiting at the house were worshipping along with him, and went and stood in front of the gallery, and shook his fist in the musicians' faces, saying, 'What! In this reverent edifice! What!'

"And at last they heard 'n through their playing, and stopped.

"'Never such an insulting, disgraceful thing—never!' says the squire, who couldn't rule his passion.

"'Never!' says the pa'son, who had come down and stood beside him.

"'Not if the angels of Heaven,' says the squire, (he was a wickedish man, the squire was, though now for once he happened to be on the Lord's side)— 'not if the angels of Heaven come down,' he says, 'shall one of you villainous players ever sound a note in this church again; for the insult to me, and my family, and my visitors, and God Almighty, that you've a-perpetrated this afternoon!'

"Then the unfortunate church band came to their senses, and remembered where they were; and 'twas a sight to see Nicholas Puddingcome and Timothy Thomas and John Biles creep down the gallery stairs with their fiddles under their arms, and poor Dan'l Hornhead with his serpent, and Robert Dowdle with his clarionet all looking as little as ninepins; and out they went. The pa'son might have forgi'ed 'em when he learned the truth o't, but the squire would not. That very week he sent for a barrel-organ that would play two-and-twenty new psalm tunes, so exact and particular that, however sinful inclined you was, you could play nothing but psalm tunes whatsomever. He had a really respectable man to turn the winch, as I said, and the old players played no more."

Questions

1. Who do you think is the narrator of the story?
2. Is the colloquial language well used? What does it contribute to the style?
3. Find the sentences which help express the theme of the story.
4. What is the squire's personality?
5. What tone does the narrator adopt to tell the story?

托马斯·哈代
（1840—1928）

英国小说家、诗人托马斯·哈代以"威塞克斯故事"闻名于世。哈代生活在英国的历史变革时期，作品主要反映了他悲观主义及宿命论的思想。他出生于英国西南部多塞特郡的一个小村庄，父亲是一个建筑包工头，母亲喜欢文学。哈代的正统教育在他16岁跟建筑师学徒时就结束了，但他读了很多书，自学了音乐、绘画和诗歌。尽管他在建筑业做得不错，但最感兴趣的还是文学。1862年，哈代去了伦敦工作，在那里他开始写诗歌和小说。起初，没有出版社愿意出他的作品。哈代直到1874年能以写作为生时，才与埃玛·拉维尼娅·吉福德结婚。埃玛去世后，他于1914年娶了自己的秘书，弗洛伦斯·埃米莉·达格代尔。哈代逝世时，鉴于他对英国文学的巨大贡献，他的骨灰被安葬在威斯敏斯特大教堂的"诗人角"。

哈代的早期作品不太成功，但《远离尘嚣》（1874）的发表使他名声大振。之后，他又创作了其他优秀的小说。《还乡》（1878）讲述的是一个漂亮姑娘追求疯狂的爱情，以逃离乏味乡村生活的故事。这篇小说悲剧性的结尾充分体现了哈代的悲观主义人生观。《德伯家的苔丝》（1891）叙述了一个命运多舛的乡下女孩为在社会寻求一席之地而付出巨大代价的故事。哈代最著名的小说当属《无名的裘德》（1895），也是哈代的最后一部小说。作品通过描述男主人公实现自己梦想的几番尝试，对维多利亚的传统观念提出了质疑，描写了在神秘自然力量面前人类的无助状态。此后，哈代就致力于诗歌、戏剧和短篇小说的创作。他先后出版了几本诗集，一部长篇历史诗剧《列王》（1902—1908），以及几部短篇小说集。

心不在焉的教区乐队

下面的故事选自哈代的短篇小说集《人生的小讽刺》（1894）。作者以简单、口语化的语言讲述了为取暖而喝多了的教区乐队成员在教堂演奏不敬音乐的故事。作品以幽默、讽刺的笔触描写了英国下层人民的困苦生活，批判了19世纪英国的阶级差别。

"故事发生在圣诞节后的礼拜天——但他们那时候并不知道这竟是最后一次在长池村教堂的廊台上演奏。先生，你可能有所耳闻，这些乐手组成了一个非常棒的乐队——几乎和杜伊一家带领的梅尔斯托克教区乐队一样出色，很不一般。乐队成员有队长，第一提琴手，尼古拉斯·普丁勘姆；低音提琴手，蒂莫西·托马斯；次中音提琴手，约翰·贝尔斯；蛇状管手，丹尼尔·霍恩海德；单簧管手，罗伯特·多德尔以及双簧管手，尼克斯先生——都是可靠、强劲的演奏家，吹管乐器的肺活量都很大。为此，圣诞节那周他们在小型里尔舞等各种舞会上备受欢迎，因为他们能把快步舞曲和号笛舞曲演奏得跟赞美诗一样优美，甚至更动听，更别说那些下里巴人的乐曲了。总之，他们前半个小时能在乡绅家的大厅里为先生和女士们演奏圣诞颂歌，彬彬有礼地和他们一起品茶，喝咖啡；而后半个小时，他们又在铁匠铺里如同野马一般为十几对舞者狂热地演奏《勇敢的士官》，喝烈性的朗姆苹果酒。

"唔，这个圣诞节他们每晚都赶好几个场，几乎没睡过觉。之后就是圣诞节后的礼拜天，给他们带来灾难的那一天。那年，天很冷。他们在教堂的廊台上冻得都坐不住。教堂的中央有一个火炉给参加礼拜的村民驱寒，但是廊台上的乐手们什么取暖设施也没有。做早礼拜时，天变得越来越冷。所以，尼古拉斯说：'老天啊，我再也受不了这冻死人的鬼天气了。今天下午就算花大价钱，我们也得弄点东西喝，来暖和暖和。'

"下午他带来了一加仑已经混合好的热白兰地和啤酒，封好了坛子放在蒂莫西·托马斯的低音提琴袋里。这样，直到他们想喝的时候，酒还是温的。在忏悔式上，每人喝了一小口；读经时又喝了一小口；剩下的留到了讲道开始时喝。当他们喝完最后一大口时感到非常舒服、暖和。牧师讲道还在继续——但不幸的是那天下午讲道的时间对于他们来说太长——他们全都睡着了，而且睡得像石头一样沉。

"那是一个昏暗的下午，讲道接近尾声时，教堂里只能看见讲坛上牧师旁边的两根蜡烛，还有蜡烛后面牧师那汗淋淋的脸。讲道终于结束了，牧师开始唱晚赞美诗。但是乐队没奏音乐。于是人们开始四处张望，想知道为什么乐队不演奏赞美诗音乐。这时候，一个站在廊台上叫利瓦伊·林佩特的小男孩轻轻推了一下蒂莫西和尼古拉斯，说：'开始了！开始了！'

"尼古拉斯被惊醒了，问道：'嘿，怎么了？'教堂里十分昏暗，再加上脑子里乱糟糟的，他以为还在前一晚演奏的舞会上，于是他走上前，提起弓和琴，开始拉我们村里人最喜欢的快步舞曲《恶魔在裁缝中》。乐队的其他人也都和尼古拉斯一样迷糊，按照惯例全力跟着队长演奏，丝毫没有怀疑过。他们流畅地演奏着曲子，《恶魔在裁缝中》的低重音把教堂棚顶的蜘蛛网震得像鬼魂一样抖个不停。尼古拉斯发现台下没人动，于是边拉边喊（每当舞会上的村民们还没弄清舞步时，他都以此惯用的命令方式指挥大家）：'舞王、舞后们挽起手！我拉最

后的高音时，男人们都在槲寄生枝下亲吻自己的舞伴！'

"那个男孩利瓦伊吓得从廊台的台阶上窜下来，闪电般地跑回家了。听到这邪恶的曲子响彻教堂，牧师的头发都竖起来了。他想乐队一定是疯了，于是举起手说：'停，停，停！停，停！这是什么？'但乐手们自己演奏的声音太大，根本没听见。牧师越是喊，他们演奏的声就越大。

"村民们纷纷从长凳上站出来，走到空地上惊奇地议论道：'他们演奏这么邪恶的音乐是什么意思？我们会像罪恶之都所多玛和俄摩拉里的人一样被神毁灭！'

"这时，村里的乡绅从用绿色台面呢隔开的长凳上站出来。这里有很多前来拜访他的地主及贵妇人们正和他一起做礼拜。他走到廊台前，挥着拳头对乐队说：'你们干什么？在这圣洁的殿堂！你们干什么？'

"最后他们终于在演奏中听到了乡绅的话，停了下来。

"'如此无礼、可耻之事永远不要再发生了。永远不要！'无法控制自己情绪的乡绅说道。

"'永远不要！'牧师也附和道，他早已走下讲坛站在乡绅的身旁。

"'就算天使下凡也不能，'乡绅说（此时此刻他第一次恰巧站在上帝一边，其实他是个大恶人）——'就算天使下凡，'他接着说，'你们这群罪人谁也不能再在这间教堂演奏一个音符。你们侮辱了我，我的家人，我的客人和万能的主，今天下午你们犯下了滔天大罪！'

"不幸的教堂乐队这时才清醒过来，想起他们在哪儿。只见尼古拉斯·普丁勘姆、蒂莫西·托马斯和约翰·贝尔斯夹着提琴悄悄地走下廊台的楼梯；可怜的丹尼尔·霍恩海德拿着他的蛇状管，罗伯特·多德尔提着他的单簧管走出了教堂。他们看起来是那么渺小、无助。如果牧师知道了真相还可能原谅他们，但是乡绅不会。就在那个星期，乡绅差人送来了一架能准确无误地演奏22首新赞美诗的手摇筒风琴。无论你有何罪过的企图，你都只能用它演奏出赞美诗来。他让一个正派人摇琴柄，就像我前面提到的那样，那些老乐手们再也没有在此演奏过！"

A Tradition of Eighteen Hundred and Four

As one of Hardy's Wessex tales, this story is set in Sussex of England, referring to an anticipation of Napoleon's invasion of Great Britain through a shepherd's story. It is also accepted as a historical tale since Napoleon and his preparation for the invasion of Great Britain were set as the centered event all through it. Like other famous Wessex tales of Thomas Hardy, this one has plenty of depiction of the author's tranquil countryside. The shift of the setting from Sussex to Dorset can be noticed and Hardy's intention can be associated with the landing place in Napoleon's coming invasion.

The widely discussed possibility of an invasion of England through a Channel tunnel has more than once recalled old Solomon Selby's story to my mind.

The occasion on which I numbered myself among his audience was one evening when he was sitting in the yawning chimney-corner of the inn-kitchen, with some others who had gathered there, and I entered for shelter from the rain. Withdrawing the stem of his pipe from the dental notch in which it habitually rested, he leaned back in the recess behind him and smiled into the fire. The smile was neither mirthful nor sad, not precisely humorous nor altogether thoughtful. We who knew him recognized it in a moment: it was his narrative smile. Breaking off our few desultory remarks we drew up closer, and he thus began :—

"My father, as you mid know, was a shepherd all his life, and lived out by the Cove four miles yonder, where I was born and lived likewise, till I moved here shortly afore I was married. The cottage that first knew me stood on the top of the down, near the sea; there was no house within a mile and a half of it; it was built o' purpose for the farm-shepherd, and had no other use. They tell me that it is now pulled down, but that you can see where it stood by the mounds of earth and a few broken bricks that are still lying about. It was a bleak and dreary place in winter-time, but in summer it was well enough, though the garden never came to much, because we could not get up a good shelter for the vegetables and currant bushes; and where there is much wind they don't thrive.

"Of all the years of my growing up the ones that bide clearest in my mind were eighteen hundred and three, four, and five. This was for two reasons: I had just then grown to an age when a child's eyes and ears take in and note down everything about him, and there was more at that date to bear in mind than there ever has been since with me. It was, as I need hardly tell ye, the time after the first peace, when Bonaparte was scheming his descent upon England. He had crossed the great Alp mountains, fought in Egypt, drubbed the Turks, the Austrians, and the Proossians, and now thought he'd have a slap at us. On the other side of the Channel, scarce out of sight and hail of a man standing on our English shore, the French army of a hundred and sixty thousand men and fifteen thousand horses had been brought together from all parts, and were drilling every day. Bonaparte had been three years a-making his preparations; and to ferry these soldiers and cannon and horses across he had contrived a couple of thousand flat-bottomed boats. These boats were small things, but wonderfully built. A good few of 'em were so made as to have a little stable on board each for the two horses that were to haul the cannon carried at the stern. To get in order all these, and other things required, he had assembled there five or six thousand fellows that worked at trades—carpenters, blacksmiths, wheelwrights, saddlers, and what not. O 'twas a curious time!

"Every morning Neighbour Boney would muster his multitude of soldiers on the beach, draw 'em up in line, practise 'em in the maneuver of embarking, horses and all, till they could do it without a single hitch. My father drove a flock of ewes up into Sussex that year, and as he went along the drover's track over the high downs thereabout he could see this drilling actually going on—the accoutrements of the rank and file glittering in the sun like silver. It was thought and always said by my uncle Job, sergeant of foot (who used to know all about these matters), that Bonaparte meant to cross with oars on a calm night. The grand query with us was, Where would my gentleman land? Many of the common people thought it would be at Dover; others, who knew how unlikely it was that any skilful general would make a business of landing just where he was expected, said he'd go either east into the River Thames, or west'ard to some convenient place, most likely one of the little bays inside the Isle of Portland, between the Beal and St. Alban's Head—and for choice the three-quarter-round Cove, screened from every mortal eye, that seemed made o' purpose, out by where we lived, and which I've climmed up with two tubs of brandy across my shoulders on scores o' dark nights in my younger days. Some had heard that a part o' the French fleet would sail right round Scotland, and come up the Channel to a suitable haven. However, there was much doubt upon the matter; and no wonder, for after-years proved that Bonaparte himself could hardly make up his mind upon that great and very particular point, where to land. His uncertainty came about in this wise, that he could get no news as to where and how our troops lay in waiting, and that his knowledge of possible places where flat-bottomed boats might be quietly run ashore, and the men they brought marshalled in order, was dim to the last degree. Being flat-bottomed, they didn't require a harbour for unshipping their cargo of men, but a good shelving beach away from sight, and with a fair open road toward London. How the question posed that great Corsican tyrant (as we used to call him), what pains he took to settle it, and, above all, what a risk he ran on one particular night in trying to do so, were known only to one man here and there; and certainly to no maker of newspapers or printer of books, or my account o't would not have had so many heads shaken over it as it has by gentry who only believe what they see in printed lines.

"The flocks my father had charge of fed all about the downs near our house, overlooking the sea and shore each way for miles. In winter and early spring father was up a deal at nights, watching and tending the lambing. Often he'd go to bed early, and turn out at twelve or one; and on the other hand, he'd sometimes stay up till twelve or one, and then turn into bed. As soon as I was old enough I used to help him, mostly in the way of keeping an eye upon the ewes while he was gone home to rest. This is what I was doing in a particular month in either the year four or five—I can't certainly fix which, but it was long before I was took away from the sheepkeeping to be bound prentice to a trade. Every night at that time I was at the fold, about half a mile, or it may be a little more, from our cottage, and no living thing at all with me but the ewes and young lambs. Afeard? No; I was never afeard of being alone at these times; for I had been reared in such an out-step place that the lack o' human beings at night made me less fearful than the sight of 'em. Directly I saw a man's shape after dark in a lonely place I was frightened out of my senses.

"One day in that month we were surprised by a visit from my uncle Job, the sergeant in the Sixty-first foot, then in camp on the downs above King George's watering-place, several miles to the west yonder. Uncle Job dropped in about dusk, and went up with my father to the fold for an hour or two. Then he came home, had a drop to drink from the tub of sperrits that the smugglers kept us in for housing their liquor when they'd made a run, and for burning 'em off when there was danger. After that he stretched himself out on the settle to sleep. I went to bed: at one o'clock father came home, and waking me to go and take his place, according to custom, went to bed himself. On my way out of the house I passed Uncle Job on the settle. He opened his eyes, and upon my telling him where I was going he said it was a shame that such a youngster as I should go up there all alone; and when he had fastened up his stock and waist-belt he set off along with me, taking a drop from the sperrit-tub in a little flat bottle that stood in the corner-cupboard.

"By and by we drew up to the fold, saw that all was right, and then, to keep ourselves warm, curled up in a heap of straw that lay inside the thatched hurdles we had set up to break the stroke of the wind when there was any. To-night, however, there was none. It was one of those very still nights when, if you stand on the high hills anywhere within two or three miles of the sea, you can hear the rise and fall of the tide along the shore, coming and going, every few moments like a sort of great snore of the sleeping world. Over the lower ground there was a bit of a mist, but on the hill where we lay the air was clear, and the moon, then in her last quarter, flung a fairly good light on the grass and scattered straw.

"While we lay there Uncle Job amused me by telling me strange stories of the wars he had served in and the wounds he had got. He had already fought the French in the Low Countries, and hoped to fight 'em again. His stories lasted so long that at last I was hardly sure that I was not a soldier myself, and had seen such service as he told of. The wonders of his tales quite bewildered my mind, till I fell asleep and dreamed of battle, smoke, and flying soldiers, all of a kind with the doings he had been bringing up to me.

"How long my nap lasted I am not prepared to say. But some faint sounds over and above the rustle of the ewes in the straw, the bleat of the lambs, and the tinkle of the sheep-bell brought me to my waking senses. Uncle Job was still beside me; but he too had fallen asleep. I looked out from the straw, and saw what it was that had aroused me. Two men, in boat-cloaks, cocked hats, and swords, stood by the hurdles about twenty yards off.

"I turned my ear thitherward to catch what they were saying, but though I heard every word o't, not one did I understand. They spoke in a tongue that was not ours—in French, as I afterward found. But if I could not gain the meaning of a word, I was shrewd boy enough to find out a deal of the talkers' business. By the light o' the moon I could see that one of 'em carried a roll of paper in his hand, while every moment he spoke quick to his comrade, and pointed right and left with the other hand to spots along the shore. There was no doubt that he was explaining to the second gentleman the shapes and features of the coast. What happened soon after made this still clearer to me.

"All this time I had not waked Uncle Job, but now I began to be afeared that they might light upon us, because uncle breathed so heavily through's nose. I put my mouth to his ear and whispered, 'Uncle Job.'

"'What is it, my boy?' he said, just as if he hadn't been asleep at all.

"'Hush!' says I. 'Two French generals—'

"'French ?' says he.

"'Yes,' says I. 'Come to see where to land their army!'

"I pointed 'em out ; but I could say no more, for the pair were coming at that moment much nearer to where we lay. As soon as they got as near as eight or ten yards, the officer with a roll in his hand stooped down to a slanting hurdle, unfastened his roll upon it, and spread it out. Then suddenly he sprung a dark lantern open on the paper, and showed it to be a map.

"'What be they looking at?' I whispered to Uncle Job.

"'A chart of the Channel, says the sergeant (knowing about such things).

"The other French officer now stooped likewise, and over the map they had a long consultation, as they pointed here and there on the paper, and then hither and thither at places along the shore beneath us. I noticed that the manner of one officer was very respectful toward the other, who seemed much his superior, the second in rank calling him by a sort of title that I did not know the sense of. The head one, on the other hand, was quite familiar with his friend, and more than once clapped him on the shoulder.

"Uncle Job had watched as well as I, but though the map had been in the lantern-light, their faces had always been in shade. But when they rose from stooping over the chart the light flashed upward, and fell smart upon one of 'em's features. No sooner had this happened than Uncle Job gasped, and sank down as if he'd been in a fit.

"'What is it—what is it, Uncle Job ?' said I.

"'O good God!' says he, under the straw.

"'What?' says I,

"'Boney!' he groaned out.

"'Who?' says I.

"'Bonaparty,' he said. 'The Corsican ogre. O that I had got but my new-flinted firelock, that there man should die! But I haven't got my new-flinted firelock, and that there man must live. So lie low, as you value your life!'

"I did lie low, as you mid suppose. But I couldn't help peeping. And then I too, lad as I was, knew that it was the face of Bonaparte. Not know Boney ? I should think I did know Boney. I should have known him by half the light o' that lantern. If I had seen a picture of his features once, I had seen it a hundred times. There was his bullet head, his short neck, his round yaller cheeks and chin, his gloomy face, and his great glowing eyes. He took off his hat to blow himself a bit, and there was the forelock in the middle of his forehead, as in all the draughts of him. In moving, his cloak fell a little open, and I could see for a moment his white-fronted jacket and one of his epaulets.

"But none of this lasted long. In a minute he and his general had rolled up the map, shut the lantern, and turned to go down toward the shore.

"Then Uncle Job came to himself a bit. 'Slipped across in the night-time to see how to put his men ashore,' he said. 'The like o' that man's coolness eyes will never again see! Nephew, I must act in this, and immediate, or England's lost!'

"When they were over the brow, we crope out, and went some little way to look after them. Half-way down they were joined by two others, and six or seven minutes brought them to the shore. Then, from behind a rock, a boat came out into the weak moonlight of the Cove, and they jumped in; it put off instantly, and vanished in a few minutes between the two rocks that stand at the mouth of the Cove as we all know. We climmed back to where we had been before, and I could see, a short way out, a larger vessel, though still not very large. The little boat drew up alongside, was made fast at the stern as I suppose, for the largest sailed away, and we saw no more.

"My uncle Job told his officers as soon as he got back to camp; but what they thought of it I never heard—neither did he. Boney's army never came, and a good Job for me; for the Cove below my father's house was where he meant to land, as this secret visit showed. We coast-folk should have been cut down one and all, and I should not have sat here to tell this tale."

We who listened to old Selby that night have been familiar with his simple gravestone for these ten years past. Thanks to the incredulity of the age his tale has been seldom repeated. But if anything short of the direct testimony of his own eyes could persuade an auditor that Bonaparte had examined these shores for himself with a view to a practicable landing-place, it would have been Solomon Selby's manner of narrating the adventure which befell him on the down.

Questions

1. What kind of smile rested on Selby's face before his narration? Who was Neighbour Boney?
2. What could be proved afterwards as to Bonaparte's doubt upon the landing place?
3. Why did Uncle Job think it was a shame that the narrator had to go to the fold all alone?
4. What caught Selby's eyes when he woke from his nap?

1804年的传说

这是托马斯·哈代的威塞克斯故事之一。故事的背景在英格兰的苏塞克斯郡，它通过一个牧羊人的讲述，展现了人们想象中的拿破仑入侵英国事件。由于拿破仑和他为发动侵略英国而做的准备构成了该短篇小说的主要情节，评论家认为这也是一部历史题材的作品。哈代的威塞克斯系列小说大都展现了作者家乡英国农村的恬静景象，这篇小说也是如此。此外，小说中从苏塞克斯到多西特不同地点的转换，体现了作者时刻将这些地点与拿破仑入侵登陆地点紧密联系的用意。

很多人都在讨论通过英吉利海峡海底隧道入侵英国是否可行，这些讨论也不止一次地让我回想起所罗门·塞尔比曾经讲过的故事。

一个夜晚，我和其他一群人听他讲故事。当时他就坐在客栈厨房令人发困的炉角旁，一些人围在他的周围，而我为了避雨也加入其中。所罗门把烟斗杆从牙槽中取出来，要在平时，他会把烟斗就搁在那儿。只见他靠向身后的壁凹，微笑着朝炉火望去。那微笑既不开心，也没有忧伤，既不十分幽默，也没若有所思。熟悉他的人都明白：这微笑藏满了故事。我们中断了闲聊，一起围上前来听他开始讲故事：

"大伙儿也许知道，我父亲住在四英里外的小海湾旁，一辈子都靠放牧为生。我从一出生就住在那儿，结婚前不久才搬来这里。我出生的小茅屋就在海边开阔高地的顶端，周围一英里半以内再也没有其他人家。茅屋只是为放牧所用。听说那茅屋现在已经拆了，但是从旁边堆着的小土墩和散乱四处的碎砖块仍可以看出它当年的位置。冬天，这里一片萧条，但夏天还不错。尽管如此，这里还是成不了什么园子，因为我们建不了什么遮挡设施来保护蔬菜和黑醋栗灌木的生长，风一大这些植物就长不好。

"在我长大的日子里，1803、1804、1805这三年让我记忆最深。这有两个原因：一是那时我正长到一个孩子的眼耳如饥似渴地摄取和记录周围一切的年龄，二是那几年里值得关注的事情比任何其他时候都多。那几年正是第一次休战期，这谁都知道；拿破仑密谋着入侵英格兰。他们的军队早已跨越了阿尔卑斯山，与埃及交了战，后来击败了土耳其、奥地利和普鲁士的军队，如今又野心勃勃地要向我们进攻。在海峡的另一端，四面八方汇集而来的法国军队有十六万士兵和一万五千匹马，大军日夜操练。而在这边的英国海岸，隐约可见一个人摇旗呐喊。三年以来，拿破仑一直在准备着，为了运送士兵和大炮、马匹渡海，他还设计了几千艘宽底船只。这些船只吨位不大却是设计精良。很多船只上都配有马厩，可供两匹拖拽船尾大炮的马使用。为安顿好马匹等的必需品，拿破仑召集了五六千人，各负其责，包括木匠、铁匠、车轮修理工、马鞍匠等不同行当的人。那真是个奇妙的时代！

"每天清晨，邻居波尼总会在海滩上集结士兵，整齐列队，练习登船出征等项目，其中就包括运送马匹。训练要等到士兵们达到十分娴熟、不出任何差错才能结束。当年，我父亲经常赶着羊向北去往苏塞克斯郡。当他沿途穿过附近开阔的高地时，总能看见训练中的军队，队伍在行进，军人不同级别的制服和徽章在阳光下闪耀着白银般的光芒。乔布叔叔以前是步兵中士，对行军打仗很是在行。他总是说，拿破仑预谋在一个风平浪静的夜晚挥军渡海。我们最关心的问题是：这位绅士将在何处登陆？许多百姓认为他会选择多佛尔；另外一些人则认为，经验丰富的将军是不会在路人皆知的地方登陆的，因此他们认为拿破仑要么会向东，进入泰晤士河，要么会向西，选择一处合适的地方，很有可能在位于比尔和圣·奥尔本之间的波特兰岛。如果还可以选择的话，那就是占四分之三圆面积的小海湾。谁都看得清，这小海湾好像是为此而生的，它离我家不远，小时候我经常在晚上肩背着两桶白兰地酒穿梭于此。有些人早就听说，部分法国舰船会绕行苏格兰，沿英吉利海峡北上，寻找适宜的登陆地点。然而，很多人都置疑这些说法，而且后来发生的事情的确证实了拿破仑本人也无法决定到底该在哪里登陆。他对此毫无把握的原因是这样：首先，他无法获知我军设防的地点及布阵情况；其次，他也不清楚哪里适合宽底船只登陆并进行人员调遣。宽底船只进行人员输送并不需要码头，但是需要较为隐蔽的带有缓坡的海岸，以此打通进军伦敦的通道。这个难题是如何困扰这个科西嘉大暴君的（我们当时都这么习惯地称呼他），为解决这一问题他承受了多少痛苦，那一晚他又是冒何种危险下令行动的，这些情况都不为人知晓，尤其是不为任何媒体所知，否则的话，我今天的故事就不会令在座的大为震惊了，因为很多人都相信媒体的言论。

"父亲在离家不远的山丘一带放牧，从那里可以俯瞰数英里远的海岸。在冬夜和早春的夜晚，父亲会起身照看羊羔们。通常父亲会很早入睡，然后在午夜或凌晨醒来，有时，父亲会忙到午夜或凌晨然后才入睡。我长大一些以后，就会在父亲去休息的时候帮忙看护牧群。记不清是1804年还是1805年，只记得是在我不再放牧而转做学徒之前的很长一段日子里，我一直这样帮着父亲。那时，每天夜里，我就待在离家不止半英里的山谷里，周围除了羊群，再也没有任何生灵。问我害怕吗？一点也不。那时，我从没因为独自一人而感到恐惧，大概是因为我是在这样一个远离市景生活的地方长大，所以在夜里看不见人比看见什么人反倒不那么害怕。在偏僻的地方，如果天黑后遇上什么人，我反倒会被吓傻的。

"那个月的一天，乔布叔叔的突然来访令我们大家吃惊不小，他是第61步兵团的中士，当时驻扎在向西几英里外的山丘开阔地带，那附近便是乔治国王的疗养地。乔布叔叔来的时候已经是黄昏时分，之后他和父亲去羊栏处转了两个小时。晚上回来，叔叔从酒桶里取了些酒喝了起来。那烈酒是酒贩子们逃亡时在我们家寄存的，如果出现危险，就将酒全部烧掉。喝完酒后，乔治叔叔舒展了筋骨，躺在那把长椅里呼呼大睡起来。我也睡觉了，大约一点的时候，父亲回来了，像往常一样，他叫醒我去接替他，然后自己也去睡了。我出门时经过乔治叔叔躺着的长椅。他睁开眼睛，听说我要去接替父亲放牧，就说，我这么小的孩子就被安排孤身一人去羊栏那边，真是不像话。于是他系好领带和腰带，在角落橱柜里的浅口瓶里取了些烈性酒喝了，然后和我一道出了门。

"过了一阵子，我们来到了羊栏处，看到一切安好，为了不挨冻，我们找到了平日里为遮风而搭建的茅草围栏，蜷缩在里面的草堆上。而那一晚却风平浪静。在如此寂静的夜晚，站在距离大海两、三英里处的山上就能听到岸边潮起潮落的声音，那时强时弱的潮汐声仿佛就是整个沉睡着的世界在发出的阵阵鼾声。山谷的凹地处有些雾气，而我们躺着的山上空气清新，一轮下弦月照耀着草地和四周的麦秆。

"为了逗我开心，我们一边躺着，乔治叔叔一边给我讲着离奇的故事，都是关于他参加过的战争和他负伤的经历。他曾经在低地国家参加过抗法战争，现在仍希望重返战场。他一讲起故事来就滔滔不绝，直到后来我真觉得自己也参了军，也目睹了他故事中的那些场景。我着迷于他的神奇故事，到后来渐渐睡去，竟然梦到他讲给我听的各种景象、战斗、硝烟，还有飞快行进的士兵。

"先不说我到底睡了多久。这时草堆里母羊们发出的'沙沙'声，羊羔们的'咩咩'声，还有羊铃铛发出的'叮铃'声让我从梦中醒来。乔布叔叔还在我身边，只不过也进入了梦乡。我向草堆外张望，看到了到底是什么惊醒了我。在离围栏二十码开外的地方，站着两个人，身披斗篷，戴着竖起的帽子，斜佩着剑。

"我转向他们，竖着耳朵想搞清楚他们说什么，可是尽管我听清了每个字，还是搞不懂他们在说什么。因为他们不是用英语在交谈，后来才知道他们说的是法语。虽然我无法弄明白他们说的话，但是凭我的智慧，还能够猜到他们在干什么。借着月光，我看到其中的一个人手持一卷纸，一边向其同伴飞快地说着什么，一边用手朝岸边比划着。可以肯定的是，他一定在向对方介绍海边的地形及特点。紧接着发生的事情更清楚地表明了这一切。

"整个过程，我都没有叫醒乔布叔叔，但是现在我担心他睡着时鼻子发出的

巨大声响会让他们照着我们。我把嘴巴放在他的耳旁，轻声说：'乔布叔叔。'

"'怎么了，孩子？'他说这话时就像一直很清醒一样。

"'嘘，'我说，'有两个法国将军……'

"'法国人？'他说。

"'是的，'我说，'他们是来侦察登陆地点的。'

"我指了指他们，就不再说话了，因为那两个法国人正向我们一点点走来。当他们走到离我们仅剩八九码时，手拿卷纸的那个军官在一处倾斜的围栏处，将纸卷解开，铺展开来。忽然间，他拿出灯点上，照在纸面上，摆在面前的原来是一幅地图。

"'他们在看什么？'我悄声问乔布叔叔。

"'是英吉利海峡地形图。'身为中士的乔布叔叔对此很了解。

"另一个法国军官也跟着俯下身，对着地图他们讨论了很长时间，不停地在地图上比划着，同时也指着我们下方海岸上的一些地方。我注意到一个军官对另一个军官始终毕恭毕敬，看起来后者是个长官，因为那个下属一直在用某个职位称呼他，可惜我搞不明白是什么职务。而那个长官和他的下级也十分熟悉，时不时地会在他的肩上拍上一下。

"乔布叔叔和我一直在旁边看着，虽然地图始终在灯光下，但是他们的面部一直都处于黑暗中。而当他们起身时，灯光向上反射在其中一个人的脸上。就在这时，乔布叔叔倒吸一口气，好像要昏倒似地沉沉地坐在地。

"'怎么了，乔布叔叔？'我问道。

"'我的天啊！'他在草堆下说道。

"'怎么了，是什么呀！'

"'波尼！'他叹着气。

"'是谁？'我问。

"'是拿破仑，'他说，'是那个科西嘉魔鬼。噢，要是我带着那把火石扳枪，他今天就必死无疑了。可是我没带枪来，他还死不了。所以我们得藏好，不然会遭杀身之祸。'

"大家想想，我当时一定是藏得好好的，可是我还是忍不住偷偷往外看。尽管当时年幼，我也认出那人是拿破仑。不认识波尼？我想我是认识的。借着微弱的灯光我是可以认出他的。看过一次他的照片，我会永生难忘。他圆头，脖子较短，脸颊和下巴也是圆圆的，肤色偏黄，脸色阴郁，但双眼却是炯炯有神。他摘下帽子透透气，露出了额头中央的头发，嘴里不停地喘着气。他走动的时候，斗篷滑落了一些，露出了正面为白色的上衣和其中的一个肩章。

"不一会儿工夫，他和他的将军便卷起地图，熄灭了灯，转身向山下的海岸走去。

"乔布叔叔恢复了点儿精神。'借夜幕掩护溜过来看看他如何调兵上岸,'叔叔说。'不能再让那冷漠的双眼发现任何东西。好侄子,我必须这么做,而且要迅速,否则英国就会战败无疑。'

"当他们翻过山脊后,我们探出头来,远远地跟着他们。下山的半路上,另外两人迎了上来,又过了六七分钟,他们来到了岸边。随后,在一个礁石后面,一艘船借着月光缓缓驶出。他们上了船,船立刻启航,几分钟后就消失在海湾口处大家都熟悉的两块礁石间。我们又回到了刚才的位置,我能够看到不远处有一艘大一点的船,其实也并不太大。小船在一旁前行,在大船的船尾部较快地行驶,大船走得很快,不久就不见了。

"乔布叔叔一回到营地就将此事汇报给了他的长官,可是我和乔布叔叔都没有得到回应。波尼的军队并没再来,这对我可是件幸事,因为从那次秘密之行来看,父亲家下面的海湾便是计划登陆的地方。真是那样的话,我们这些牧羊人全部都会被杀死的,我现在也不会坐在这儿给你们讲这段故事了。"

那天夜里的听众这十年来经常去老塞尔比的墓碑前。由于故事发生的年代令人怀疑,因此这段故事并没有流传开去。但是,假如非亲眼所见也能使人信服拿破仑当年果真视察过这里的海岸来寻找合适的登陆地点的话,那么也只有塞尔比才能够做得到,他以如此生动的风格讲述了自己当时在开阔高地上的冒险经历。

Robert Louis Stevenson
(1850—1894)

Robert Louis Stevenson, Scottish short story writer, travel writer, novelist, playwright, and poet, had fallen victim to tuberculosis since his childhood and he spent much of his time in bed composing stories even before he could read. In 1867, he was enrolled by Edinburgh University to study engineering, intending to follow his father's footsteps, where later he also studied law. Due to his strong interest in the letters and poor health, he turned to writing. Stevenson died in Samoa.

Stevenson was especially known for his novels of adventures. Many of Stevenson's stories were set in colorful locations, containing some horror and supernatural elements. Arguing against realism, Stevenson underlined the "nameless longings of the reader", the desire for experience. Stevenson made his name known with the romantic adventure story *Treasure Island* (1883). His other popular works include *Kidnapped* (1886), *The Strange Case of Dr. Jekyll And Mr. Hyde* (1886), and *The Master of Ballantrae* (1889). Fascinated by the Polynesian culture, Stevenson also published novels like *The Beach of Falesa* (1893) and *The Ebb-Tide* (1894) in an attempt to condemn European colonial exploitation. His last yet unfinished work, *Weir of Hermiston* (1896) was published posthumously.

Markheim

The following tale ranks among Stevenson's most celebrated short stories. It reveals a murder for profit, a crime which ends up in confession and surrender. The theme of the story is the struggle within human soul between good and evil and between predestination and freewill. "Markheim" is typical of Stevenson's horror and supernatural stories and bears the strong influence of Edgar Allan Poe. To some extent, this short story can stand comparison with Fedor Dostoevsky's novel Crime and Punishment (1866) because of its probe into benevolence and iniquity within a man's conscience.

"Yes," said the dealer, "our windfalls are of various kinds. Some customers are ignorant, and then I touch a dividend on my superior knowledge. Some are dishonest," and here he held up the candle, so that the light fell strongly on his visitor, "and in that case," he continued, "I profit by my virtue."

Markheim had but just entered from the daylight streets, and his eyes had not yet grown familiar with the mingled shine and darkness in the shop. At these pointed words, and before the near presence of the flame, he blinked painfully and looked aside.

The dealer chuckled. "You come to me on Christmas Day," he resumed, "when you know that I am alone in my house, put up my shutters, and make a point of refusing business. Well, you will have to pay for that; you will have to pay for my loss of time, when I should be balancing my books; you will have to pay, besides, for a kind of manner that I remark in you to-day very strongly. I am the essence of discretion, and ask no awkward questions; but when a customer cannot look me in the eye, he has to pay for it." The dealer once more chuckled; and then, changing to his usual business voice, though still with a note of irony, "You can give, as usual, a clear account of how you came into the possession of the object?" he continued. "Still your uncle's cabinet? A remarkable collector, sir!"

And the little pale, round-shouldered dealer stood almost on tip-toe, looking over the top of his gold spectacles, and nodding his head with every mark of disbelief. Markheim returned his gaze with one of infinite pity, and a touch of horror.

"This time," said he, "you are in error. I have not come to sell, but to buy. I have no curios to dispose of; my uncle's cabinet is bare to the wainscot; even were it still intact, I have done well on the Stock Exchange, and should more likely add to it than otherwise, and my errand to-day is simplicity itself. I seek a Christmas present for a lady," he continued, waxing more fluent as he struck into the speech he had prepared; "and certainly I owe you every excuse for thus disturbing you upon so small a matter. But the thing was neglected yesterday; I must produce my little compliment at dinner; and, as you very well know, a rich marriage is not a thing to be neglected."

There followed a pause, during which the dealer seemed to weigh this statement incredulously. The ticking of many clocks among the curious lumber of the shop, and the faint rushing of the cabs in a near thoroughfare, filled up the interval of silence.

"Well, sir," said the dealer, "be it so. You are an old customer after all; and if, as you say, you have the chance of a good marriage, far be it from me to be an obstacle. Here is a nice thing for a lady now," he went on, "this hand-glass—fifteenth century, warranted; comes from a good collection, too; but I reserve the name, in the interests of my customer, who was just like yourself, my dear sir, the nephew and sole heir of a remarkable collector."

The dealer, while he thus ran on in his dry and biting voice, had stooped to take the object from its place; and, as he had done so, a shock had passed through Markheim, a start both of hand and foot, a sudden leap of many tumultuous passions to the face. It passed as swiftly as it came, and left no trace beyond a certain trembling of the hand that now received the glass.

"A glass," he said hoarsely, and then paused, and repeated it more clearly. "A glass? For Christmas? Surely not?"

"And why not?" cried the dealer. "Why not a glass?"

Markheim was looking upon him with an indefinable expression. "You ask me why not?" he said. "Why, look here—look in it—look at yourself! Do you like to see it? No! nor I—nor any man."

The little man had jumped back when Markheim had so suddenly confronted him with the mirror; but now, perceiving there was nothing worse on hand, he chuckled. "Your future lady, sir, must be pretty hard-favoured," said he.

"I ask you," said Markheim, "for a Christmas present, and you give me this—this damned reminder of years, and sins and follies—this hand-conscience! Did you mean it? Had you a thought in your mind? Tell me. It will be better for you if you do. Come, tell me about yourself. I hazard a guess now, that you are in secret a very charitable man."

The dealer looked closely at his companion. It was very odd, Markheim did not appear to be laughing; there was something in his face like an eager sparkle of hope, but nothing of mirth.

"What are you driving at?" the dealer asked.

"Not charitable?" returned the other, gloomily. "Not charitable; not pious; not scrupulous; unloving, unbeloved; a hand to get money, a safe to keep it. Is that all? Dear God, man, is that all?"

"I will tell you what it is," began the dealer, with some sharpness, and then broke off again into a chuckle. "But I see this is a love match of yours, and you have been drinking the lady's health."

"Ah!" cried Markheim, with a strange curiosity. "Ah, have you been in love? Tell me about that."

"I," cried the dealer. "I in love! I never had the time, nor have I the time to-day for all this nonsense. Will you take the glass?"

"Where is the hurry?" returned Markheim. "It is very pleasant to stand here talking; and life is so short and insecure that I would not hurry away from any pleasure—no, not even from so mild a one as this. We should rather cling, cling to what little we can get, like a man at a cliff's edge. Every second is a cliff, if you think upon it—a cliff a mile high—high enough, if we fall, to dash us out of every feature of humanity. Hence it is best to talk pleasantly. Let us talk of each other; why should we wear this mask? Let us be confidential. Who knows? we might become friends."

"I have just one word to say to you," said the dealer. "Either make your purchase, or walk out of my shop."

"True, true," said Markheim. "Enough fooling. To business. Show me something else."

The dealer stooped once more, this time to replace the glass upon the shelf, his thin blond hair falling over his eyes as he did so. Markheim moved a little nearer, with one hand in the pocket of his greatcoat; he drew himself up and filled his lungs; at the same time many different emotions were depicted together on his face—terror, horror, and resolve, fascination and a physical repulsion; and through a haggard lift of his upper lip, his teeth looked out.

"This, perhaps, may suit," observed the dealer; and then, as he began to rearise, Markheim bounded from behind upon his victim. The long, skewer-like dagger flashed and fell. The dealer struggled like a hen, striking his temple on the shelf, and then tumbled on the floor in a heap.

Time had some score of small voices in that shop—some stately and slow as was becoming to their great age; others garrulous and hurried. All these told out the seconds in an intricate chorus of tickings. Then the passage of a lad's feet, heavily running on the pavement, broke in upon these smaller voices and startled Markheim into the consciousness of his surroundings. He looked about him awfully. The candle stood on the counter, its flame solemnly wagging in a draught; and by that inconsiderable movement the whole room was filled with noiseless bustle and kept heaving like a sea: the tall shadows nodding, the gross blots of darkness swelling and dwindling as with respiration, the faces of the portraits and the china gods changing and wavering like images in water. The inner door stood ajar, and peered into that leaguer of shadows with a long slit of daylight like a pointing finger.

From these fear-stricken rovings, Markheim's eyes returned to the body of his victim, where it lay, both humped and sprawling, incredibly small and strangely meaner than in life. In these poor, miserly clothes, in that ungainly attitude, the dealer lay like so much sawdust. Markheim had feared to see it, and, lo! it was nothing. And yet, as he gazed, this bundle of old clothes and pool of blood began to find eloquent voices. There it must lie; there was none to work the cunning hinges or direct the miracle of locomotion; there it must lie till it was found. Found! ay, and then? Then would this dead flesh lift up a cry that would ring over England, and fill the world with the echoes of pursuit. Ay, dead or not, this was still the enemy. "Time was that when the brains were out," he thought; and the first word struck into his mind. Time, now that the deed was accomplished— time, which had closed for the victim, had become instant and momentous for the slayer.

The thought was yet in his mind, when, first one and then another, with every variety of pace and voice—one deep as the bell from a cathedral turret, another ringing on its treble notes the prelude of a waltz, —the clocks began to strike the hour of three in the afternoon.

The sudden outbreak of so many tongues in that dumb chamber staggered him. He began to bestir himself, going to and fro with the candle, beleaguered by moving shadows, and startled to the soul by chance reflections. In many rich mirrors, some of home design, some from Venice or Amsterdam, he saw his face repeated and repeated, as it were an army of spies; his own eyes met and detected him; and the sound of his own steps, lightly as they fell, vexed the surrounding quiet. And still, as he continued to fill his pockets, his mind accused him with a sickening iteration, of the thousand faults of his design. He should have chosen a more quiet hour; he should have prepared an alibi; he should not have used a knife; he should have been more cautious, and only bound and gagged the dealer, and not killed him; he should have been more bold, and killed the servant also; he should have done all things otherwise; poignant regrets, weary, incessant toiling of the mind to change what was unchangeable, to plan what was now useless, to be the architect of the irrevocable past. Meanwhile, and behind all this activity, brute terrors, like the scurrying of rats in a deserted attic, filled the more remote chambers of his brain with riot; the hand of the constable would fall heavy on his shoulder, and his nerves would jerk like a hooked fish; or he beheld, in galloping defile, the dock, the prison, the gallows, and the black coffin.

Terror of the people in the street sat down before his mind like a besieging army. It was impossible, he thought, but that some rumour of the struggle must have reached their ears and set on edge their curiosity; and now, in all the neighbouring houses, he divined them sitting motionless and with uplifted ear—solitary people, condemned to spend Christmas dwelling alone on memories of the past, and now startlingly recalled from that tender exercise; happy family parties struck into silence round the table, the mother still with raised finger: every degree and age and humour, but all, by their own hearths, prying and hearkening and weaving the rope that was to hang him. Sometimes it seemed to him he could not move too softly; the clink of the tall Bohemian goblets rang out loudly like a bell; and alarmed by the bigness of the ticking, he was tempted to stop the clocks. And then, again, with a swift transition of his terrors, the very silence of the place appeared a source of peril, and a thing to strike and freeze the passer-by; and he would step more boldly, and bustle aloud among the contents of the shop, and imitate, with elaborate bravado, the movements of a busy man at ease in his own house.

But he was now so pulled about by different alarms that, while one portion of his mind was still alert and cunning, another trembled on the brink of lunacy. One hallucination in particular took a strong hold on his credulity. The neighbour hearkening with white face beside his window, the passer-by arrested by a horrible surmise on the pavement—these could at worst suspect, they could not know; through the brick walls and shuttered windows only sounds could penetrate. But here, within the house, was he alone? He knew he was; he had watched the servant set forth sweet-hearting, in her poor best, "out for the day" written in every ribbon and smile. Yes, he was alone, of course; and yet, in the bulk of empty house above him, he could surely hear a stir of delicate footing; he was surely conscious, inexplicably conscious of some presence. Ay, surely; to every room and corner of the house his imagination followed it; and now it was a faceless thing, and yet had eyes to see with; and again it was a shadow of himself; and yet again behold the image of the dead dealer, reinspired with cunning and hatred.

At times, with a strong effort, he would glance at the open door which still seemed to repel his eyes. The house was tall, the skylight small and dirty, the day blind with fog; and the light that filtered down to the ground story was exceedingly faint, and showed dimly on the threshold of the shop. And yet, in that strip of doubtful brightness, did there not hang wavering a shadow?

Suddenly, from the street outside, a very jovial gentleman began to beat with a staff on the shop door, accompanying his blows with shouts and railleries in which the dealer was continually called upon by name. Markheim, smitten into ice, glanced at the dead man. But no! he lay quite still; he was fled away far beyond earshot of these blows and shoutings; he was sunk beneath seas of silence; and his name, which would once have caught his notice above the howling of a storm, had become an empty sound. And presently the jovial gentleman desisted from his knocking and departed.

Here was a broad hint to hurry what remained to be done, to get forth from this accusing neighbourhood, to plunge into a bath of London multitudes, and to reach, on the other side of day, that haven of safety and apparent innocence—his bed. One visitor had come; at any moment another might follow and be more obstinate. To have done the deed, and yet not to reap the profit, would be too abhorrent a failure. The money—that was now Markheim's concern; and as a means to that, the keys.

He glanced over his shoulder at the open door, where the shadow was still lingering and shivering; and with no conscious repugnance of the mind, yet with a tremor of the belly, he drew near the body of his victim. The human character had quite departed. Like a suit half-stuffed with bran, the limbs lay scattered, the trunk doubled, on the floor; and yet the thing repelled him. Although so dingy and inconsiderable to the eye, he feared it might have more significance to the touch. He took the body by the shoulders, and turned it on its back. It was strangely light and supple, and the limbs, as if they had been broken, fell into the oddest postures. The face was robbed of all expression; but it was as pale as wax, and shockingly smeared with blood about one temple. That was, for Markheim, the one displeasing circumstance. It carried him back, upon the instant, to a certain fair day in a fishers' village: a gray day, a piping wind, a crowd upon the street, the blare of brasses, the booming of drums, the nasal voice of a ballad singer; and a boy going to and fro, buried overhead in the crowd and divided between interest and fear, until, coming out upon the chief place of concourse, he beheld a booth and a great screen with pictures, dismally designed, garishly coloured: Brownrigg with her apprentice, the Mannings with their murdered guest, Weare in the death-grip of Thurtell, and a score besides of famous crimes. The thing was as clear as an illusion He was once again that little boy; he was looking once again, and with the same sense of physical revolt, at these vile pictures; he was still stunned by the thumping of the drums. A bar of that day's music returned upon his memory; and at that, for the first time, a qualm came over him, a breath of nausea, a sudden weakness of the joints, which he must instantly resist and conquer.

He judged it more prudent to confront than to flee from these considerations, looking the more hardily in the dead face, bending his mind to realise the nature and greatness of his crime. So little a while ago that face had moved with every change of sentiment, that pale mouth had spoken, that body had been all on fire with governable energies; and now, and by his act, that piece of life had been arrested, as the horologist, with interjected finger, arrests the beating of the clock. So he reasoned in vain; he could rise to no more remorseful consciousness; the same heart which had shuddered before the painted effigies of crime, looked on its reality unmoved. At best, he felt a gleam of pity for one who had been endowed in vain with all those faculties that can make the world a garden of enchantment, one who had never lived and who was now dead. But of penitence, no, not a tremor.

With that, shaking himself clear of these considerations, he found the keys and advanced toward the open door of the shop. Outside, it had begun to rain smartly, and the sound of the shower upon the roof had banished silence. Like some dripping cavern, the chambers of the house were haunted by an incessant echoing, which filled the ear and mingled with the ticking of the clocks. And, as Markheim approached the door, he seemed to hear, in answer to his own cautious tread, the steps of another foot withdrawing up the stair. The shadow still palpitated loosely on the threshold. He threw a ton's weight of resolve upon his muscles, and drew back the door.

The faint, foggy daylight glimmered dimly on the bare floor and stairs; on the bright suit of armour posted, halbert in hand, upon the landing; and on the dark wood-carvings, and framed pictures that hung against the yellow panels of the wainscot. So loud was the beating of the rain through all the house that, in Markheim's ears, it began to be distinguished into many different sounds. Footsteps and sighs, the tread of regiments marching in the distance, the chink of money in the counting, and the creaking of doors held stealthily ajar, appeared to mingle with the patter of the drops upon the cupola and the gushing of the water in the pipes. The sense that he was not alone grew upon him to the verge of madness. On every side he was haunted and begirt by presences. He heard them moving in the upper chambers; from the shop, he heard the dead man getting to his legs; and as he began with a great effort to mount the stairs, feet fled quietly before him and followed stealthily behind. If he were but deaf, he thought, how tranquilly he would possess his soul! And then again, and hearkening with ever fresh attention, he blessed himself for that unresting sense which held the outposts and stood a trusty sentinel upon his life. His head turned continually on his neck; his eyes, which seemed starting from their orbits, scouted on every side, and on every side were half rewarded as with the tail of something nameless vanishing. The four and twenty steps to the first floor were four and twenty agonies.

On that first story, the doors stood ajar—three of them, like three ambushes, shaking his nerves like the throats of cannon. He could never again, he felt, be sufficiently immured and fortified from men's observing eyes; he longed to be home, girt in by walls, buried among bedclothes, and invisible to all but God. And at that thought he wondered a little, recollecting tales of other murderers and the fear they were said to entertain of heavenly avengers. It was not so, at least, with him. He feared the laws of nature, lest, in their callous and immutable procedure, they should preserve some damning evidence of his crime. He feared tenfold more, with a slavish, superstitious terror, some scission in the continuity of man's experience, some wilful illegality of nature. He played a game of skill, depending on the rules, calculating consequence from cause; and what if nature, as the defeated tyrant overthrew the chess-board, should break the mould of their succession? The like had befallen Napoleon (so writers said) when the winter changed the time of its appearance. The like might befall Markheim: the solid walls might become transparent and reveal his doings like those of bees in a glass hive; the stout planks might yield under his foot like quicksands and detain him in their clutch. Ay, and there were soberer accidents that might destroy him; if, for instance, the house should fall and imprison him beside the body of his victim, or the house next door should fly on fire, and the firemen invade him from all sides. These things he feared; and, in a sense, these things might be called the hands of God reached forth against sin. But about God himself he was at ease; his act was doubtless exceptional, but so were his excuses, which God knew; it was there, and not among men, that he felt sure of justice.

When he had got safe into the drawing-room, and shut the door behind him, he was aware of a respite from alarms. The room was quite dismantled, uncarpeted besides, and strewn with packing-cases and incongruous furniture; several great pier-glasses, in which he beheld himself at various angles, like an actor on a stage; many pictures, framed and unframed, standing, with their faces to the wall; a fine Sheraton sideboard, a cabinet of marquetry, and a great old bed, with tapestry hangings. The windows opened to the floor; but by great good fortune the lower part of the shutters had been closed, and this concealed him from the neighbours. Here, then, Markheim drew in a packing-case before the cabinet, and began to search among the keys. It was a long business, for there were many; and it was irksome, besides; for, after all, there might be nothing in the cabinet, and time was on the wing. But the closeness of the occupation sobered him. With the tail of his eye he saw the door—even glanced at it from time to time directly, like a besieged commander pleased to verify the good estate of his defences. But in truth he was at peace. The rain falling in the street sounded natural and pleasant. Presently, on the other side, the notes of a piano were wakened to the music of a hymn, and the voices of many children took up the air and words. How stately, how comfortable was the melody! How fresh the youthful voices! Markheim gave ear to it smilingly, as he sorted out the keys; and his mind was thronged with answerable ideas and images: church-going children, and the pealing of the high organ; children afield, bathers by the brookside, ramblers on the brambly common, kite-flyers in the windy and cloud-navigated sky; and then, at another cadence of the hymn, back again to church, and the somnolence of summer Sundays, and the high genteel voice of the parson (which he smiled a little to recall) and the painted Jacobean tombs, and the dim lettering of the Ten Commandments in the chancel.

And as he sat thus, at once busy and absent, he was startled to his feet. A flash of ice, a flash of fire, a bursting gush of blood, went over him, and then he stood transfixed and thrilling. A step mounted the stair slowly and steadily, and presently a hand was laid upon the knob, and the lock clicked, and the door opened.

Fear held Markheim in a vice. What to expect he knew not—whether the dead man walking, or the official ministers of human justice, or some chance witness blindly stumbling in to consign him to the gallows. But when a face was thrust into the aperture, glanced round the room, looked at him, nodded and smiled as if in friendly recognition, and then withdrew again, and the door closed behind it, his fear broke loose from his control in a hoarse cry. At the sound of this the visitant returned.

"Did you call me?" he asked, pleasantly, and with that he entered the room and closed the door behind him.

Markheim stood and gazed at him with all his eyes. Perhaps there was a film upon his sight, but the outlines of the new comer seemed to change and waver like those of the idols in the wavering candle-light of the shop; and at times he thought he knew him; and at times he thought he bore a likeness to himself; and always, like a lump of living terror, there lay in his bosom the conviction that this thing was not of the earth and not of God.

And yet the creature had a strange air of the commonplace, as he stood looking on Markheim with a smile; and when he added, "You are looking for the money, I believe?" it was in the tones of everyday politeness.

Markheim made no answer.

"I should warn you," resumed the other, "that the maid has left her sweetheart earlier than usual and will soon be here. If Mr. Markheim be found in this house, I need not describe to him the consequences."

"You know me?" cried the murderer.

The visitor smiled. "You have long been a favourite of mine," he said; "and I have long observed and often sought to help you."

"What are you?" cried Markheim; "the devil?"

"What I may be," returned the other, "cannot affect the service I propose to render you."

"It can," cried Markheim; "it does! Be helped by you? No, never; not by you! You do not know me yet; thank God, you do not know me!"

"I know you," replied the visitant, with a sort of kind severity or rather firmness. "I know you to the soul."

"Know me!" cried Markheim. "Who can do so? My life is but a travesty and slander on myself. I have lived to belie my nature. All men do; all men are better than this disguise that grows about and stifles them. You see each dragged away by life, like one whom bravos have seized and muffled in a cloak. If they had their own control—if you could see their faces, they would be altogether different, they would shine out for heroes and saints! I am worse than most; myself is more overlaid; my excuse is known to me and God. But, had I the time, I could disclose myself."

"To me?" inquired the visitant.

"To you before all," returned the murderer. "I supposed you were intelligent. I thought—since you exist—you would prove a reader of the heart. And yet you would propose to judge me by my acts! Think of it—my acts! I was born and I have lived in a land of giants; giants have dragged me by the wrists since I was born out of my mother—the giants of circumstance. And you would judge me by my acts! But can you not look within? Can you not understand that evil is hateful to me? Can you not see within me the clear writing of conscience, never blurred by any wilful sophistry, although too often disregarded? Can you not read me for a thing that surely must be common as humanity—the unwilling sinner?"

"All this is very feelingly expressed," was the reply, "but it regards me not. These points of consistency are beyond my province, and I care not in the least by what compulsion you may have been dragged away, so as you are but carried in the right direction. But time flies; the servant delays, looking in the faces of the crowd and at the pictures on the hoardings, but still she keeps moving nearer; and remember, it is as if the gallows itself was striding towards you through the Christmas streets! Shall I help you—I, who know all? Shall I tell you where to find the money?"

"For what price?" asked Markheim.

"I offer you the service for a Christmas gift," returned the other.

Markheim could not refrain from smiling with a kind of bitter triumph. "No," said he, "I will take nothing at your hands; if I were dying of thirst, and it was your hand that put the pitcher to my lips, I should find the courage to refuse. It may be credulous, but I will do nothing to commit myself to evil."

"I have no objection to a death-bed repentance," observed the visitant.

"Because you disbelieve their efficacy!" Markheim cried.

"I do not say so," returned the other; "but I look on these things from a different side, and when the life is done my interest falls. The man has lived to serve me, to spread black looks under colour of religion, or to sow tares in the wheat-field, as you do, in a course of weak compliance with desire. Now that he draws so near to his deliverance, he can add but one act of service: to repent, to die smiling, and thus to build up in confidence and hope the more timorous of my surviving followers. I am not so hard a master. Try me; accept my help. Please yourself in life as you have done hitherto; please yourself more amply, spread your elbows at the board; and when the night begins to fall and the curtains to be drawn, I tell you, for your greater comfort, that you will find it even easy to compound your quarrel with your conscience, and to make a truckling peace with God. I came but now from such a death-bed, and the room was full of sincere mourners, listening to the man's last words; and when I looked into that face, which had been set as a flint against mercy, I found it smiling with hope."

"And do you, then, suppose me such a creature?" asked Markheim. "Do you think I have no more generous aspirations than to sin and sin and sin and at last sneak into heaven? My heart rises at the thought. Is this, then, your experience of mankind? or is it because you find me with red hands that you presume such baseness? And is this crime of murder indeed so impious as to dry up the very springs of good?"

"Murder is to me no special category," replied the other. "All sins are murder, even as all life is war. I behold your race, like starving mariners on a raft, plucking crusts out of the hands of famine and feeding on each other's lives. I follow sins beyond the moment of their acting; I find in all that the last consequence is death, and to my eyes, the pretty maid who thwarts her mother with such taking graces on a question of a ball, drips no less visibly with human gore than such a murderer as yourself. Do I say that I follow sins? I follow virtues also. They differ not by the thickness of a nail; they are both scythes for the reaping angel of Death. Evil, for which I live, consists not in action but in character. The bad man is dear to me, not the bad act, whose fruits, if we could follow them far enough down the hurtling cataract of the ages, might yet be found more blessed than those of the rarest virtues. And it is not because you have killed a dealer, but because you are Markheim, that I offer to forward your escape."

"I will lay my heart open to you," answered Markheim. "This crime on which you find me is my last. On my way to it I have learned many lessons; itself is a lesson—a momentous lesson. Hitherto I have been driven with revolt to what I would not; I was a bond-slave to poverty, driven and scourged. There are robust virtues that can stand in these temptations; mine was not so; I had a thirst of pleasure. But to-day, and out of this deed, I pluck both warning and riches—both the power and a fresh resolve to be myself. I become in all things a free actor in the world; I begin to see myself all changed, these hands the agents of good, this heart at peace. Something comes over me out of the past—something of what I have dreamed on Sabbath evenings to the sound of the church organ, of what I forecast when I shed tears over noble books, or talked, an innocent child, with my mother. There lies my life; I have wandered a few years, but now I see once more my city of destination."

"You are to use this money on the Stock Exchange, I think?" remarked the visitor; "and there, if I mistake not, you have already lost some thousands?"

"Ah," said Markheim, "but this time I have a sure thing."

"This time, again, you will lose," replied the visitor quietly.

"Ah, but I keep back the half!" cried Markheim.

"That also you will lose," said the other.

The sweat started upon Markheim's brow. "Well then, what matter?" he exclaimed. "Say it be lost, say I am plunged again in poverty, shall one part of me, and that the worse, continue until the end to override the better? Evil and good run strong in me, hailing me both ways. I do not love the one thing; I love all. I can conceive great deeds, renunciations, martyrdoms; and though I be fallen to such a crime as murder, pity is no stranger to my thoughts. I pity the poor; who knows their trials better than myself? I pity and help them. I prize love; I love honest laughter; there is no good thing nor true thing on earth but I love it from my heart. And are my vices only to direct my life, and my virtues to lie without effect, like some passive lumber of the mind? Not so; good, also, is a spring of acts."

But the visitant raised his finger. "For six and thirty years that you have been in this world," said he, "through many changes of fortune and varieties of humour, I have watched you steadily fall. Fifteen years ago you would have started at a theft. Three years back you would have blenched at the name of murder. Is there any crime, is there any cruelty or meanness, from which you still recoil? Five years from now I shall detect you in the fact! Downward, downward, lies your way; nor can anything but death avail to stop you."

"It is true," Markheim said huskily, "I have in some degree complied with evil. But it is so with all; the very saints, in the mere exercise of living, grow less dainty, and take on the tone of their surroundings."

"I will propound to you one simple question," said the other; "and as you answer I shall read to you your moral horoscope. You have grown in many things more lax; possibly you do right to be so; and at any account, it is the same with all men. But granting that, are you in any one particular, however trifling, more difficult to please with your own conduct, or do you go in all things with a looser rein?"

"In any one?" repeated Markheim, with an anguish of consideration. "No," he added, with despair; "in none! I have gone down in all."

"Then," said the visitor, "content yourself with what you are, for you will never change; and the words of your part on this stage are irrevocably written down."

Markheim stood for a long while silent, and, indeed, it was the visitor who first broke the silence. "That being so," he said, "shall I show you the money?"

"And grace?" cried Markheim.

"Have you not tried it?" returned the other. "Two or three years ago did I not see you on the platform of revival meetings, and was not your voice the loudest in the hymn?

"It is true," said Markheim; "and I see clearly what remains for me by way of duty. I thank you for these lessons from my soul; my eyes are opened, and I behold myself at last for what I am."

At this moment, the sharp note of the door-bell rang through the house; and the visitant, as though this were some concerted signal for which he had been waiting, changed at once in his demeanour. "The maid!" he cried. "She has returned, as I forewarned you, and there is now before you one more difficult passage. Her master, you must say, is ill; you must let her in, with an assured but rather serious countenance; no smiles, no overacting, and I promise you success! Once the girl within, and the door closed, the same dexterity that has already rid you of the dealer will relieve you of this last danger in your path. Thenceforward you have the whole evening—the whole night, if needful—to ransack the treasures of the house and to make good your safety. This is help that comes to you with the mask of danger. Up!" he cried; "up, friend. Your life hangs trembling in the scales; up, and act!"

Markheim steadily regarded his counsellor. "If I be condemned to evil acts," he said, "there is still one door of freedom open: I can cease from action. If my life be an ill thing, I can lay it down. Though I be, as you say truly, at the beck of every small temptation, I can yet, by one decisive gesture, place myself beyond the reach of all. My love of good is damned to barrenness; it may, and let it be! But I have still my hatred of evil; and from that, to your galling disappointment, you shall see that I can draw both energy and courage."

The features of the visitor began to undergo a wonderful and lovely change: they brightened and softened with a tender triumph, and, even as they brightened, faded and dislimned. But Markheim did not pause to watch or understand the transformation. He opened the door and went downstairs very slowly, thinking to himself. His past went soberly before him; he beheld it as it was, ugly and strenuous like a dream, random as chance medley—a scene of defeat. Life, as he thus reviewed it, tempted him no longer; but on the further side he perceived a quiet haven for his bark. He paused in the passage, and looked into the shop, where the candle still burned by the dead body. It was strangely silent. Thoughts of the dealer swarmed into his mind, as he stood gazing. And then the bell once more broke out into impatient clamour.

He confronted the maid upon the threshold with something like a smile.

"You had better go for the police," said he; "I have killed your master."

Questions

1. How do Markheim's reflections in the mirror foreshadow his supernatural encounter with the mysterious visitant?
2. Why does this horrible story take place on a rainy Christmas day? How does this fact help to reveal the theme of the story, that is, the struggle between good and evil within human soul?
3. What symbolic meaning does the visitant convey? Does he symbolize Markheim's

self-awareness and self-accusation?
4. Many a time the author describes various shadows in the story. What purposes do these descriptions serve?
5. Who do you think the visitant is? If you were Markheim, would you accept his offer? And why or why not?

罗伯特·路易斯·史蒂文森
(1850—1894)

罗伯特·路易斯·史蒂文森是苏格兰著名小说家、剧作家、诗人,他自童年时代就患有肺结核,识字前便在病床上编故事。他1867年入爱丁堡大学主修工程学,旨在继承父业,后来又在那里学习法律。由于对文学情有独钟,也出于健康原因,他转向写作。史蒂文森病逝于萨摩亚。

史蒂文森以擅长创作冒险题材的小说而著称,故事背景绚丽多彩,故事中经常穿插一些恐怖情节和超自然元素。不同于现实主义文学创作,史蒂文森于创作中强调"读者对故事情节难以名状的憧憬",即读者渴望身临其境的阅读情结。1883年出版的浪漫主义冒险小说《金银岛》使得史蒂文森一举成名,随后他又发表了《绑架》《化身博士》《巴兰特里的主人》等脍炙人口的小说。史蒂文森曾一度痴迷于波利尼西亚文化,所发表的小说《弗丽莎海滩》与《落潮》旨在抨击欧洲的殖民主义剥削。他的未完成也是最后一部著作《赫米斯顿的魏尔》于他逝世后得以发表。

马克海姆

以下的作品是史蒂文森所创作的著名短篇小说之一。主要故事情节围绕着一起谋财害命案展开,故事结尾杀人者良心悔悟并主动投案自首。小说主题鲜明,故事情节围绕着人性的善与恶层层铺开。"个人的命运已前世注定还是掌握在自己手中?"这个主题贯穿于故事的始终。根据小说中的恐怖情节及超自然主义因素可以看出,史蒂文森的文学创作受埃德加·爱伦·坡影响颇深。在一定程度上,这部小说可以媲美俄国大作家陀思妥耶夫斯基的名著《罪与罚》,因为两部著作都深入而细致地挖掘了人性中善与恶的激烈冲突。

"是啊,"当铺老板说道,"能让我们发点儿财的这些主儿呀,什么样的都有。有的根本不懂行情,那我肯定得看准宰他一把。有的呢,跟我玩奸耍滑。"他边说边擎起蜡烛,烛光明晃晃地照在马克海姆的脸上,"要是那样,"老板继续说道,"我更要捞上一笔,让他们知道我的厉害。"

大白天刚从街上进来,店里若明若暗,马克海姆的眼睛很不适应。烛焰就在眼前燃着,听到老板若有所指的话,他眨了眨难受的眼睛,侧脸看着别处。

老板轻轻笑了笑，接着说道："你知道今天是圣诞节，店里就我一个人，关上百叶窗本无意做生意，可你却偏偏今天来，就冲这一点，你得额外支付我费用，因为你占用了我的时间，我本打算核对账目的时间。还有，你得为你今天的态度付我钱，我可是行事谨慎，也没出言不逊，可你却不正眼看我，所以你必须得给我钱。"老板又笑笑，接着就恢复了生意人惯有的语气，尽管声音里还是有那么点儿讽刺味儿，"又从你那了不起的叔叔那倒腾到什么收藏品了？既然要当，必要的程序还是要走的，请你原原本本地说说你是怎么弄到这东西的？"

这老板个头不高，躬肩曲背的，脸色苍白，站在那儿，踮着脚，抬着眼皮儿掠过金边眼镜上方盯着马克海姆，晃悠个脑袋好像谁都不信。马克海姆也回视盯着他，觉得眼前这家伙太可怜巴巴了，可不知为什么又有点儿害怕他。

"这回你可说错了。今天我不是来当东西的，相反，我是来买东西的。最近我可弄不到什么古董了，我叔叔的收藏室虽然还在那儿，但也差不多空得只剩下四壁了。倒是我玩股票挣着些钱，看情形赔不了，还能接着挣下去。今天来你这没别的事儿，就是想给一位女士买个圣诞礼物，"马克海姆事先已想好了说词儿，所以越说越流利，"当然，为这么一件小事大过节的打扰您，我确实欠您个好借口。但是昨天我忙着忙着就把这件事给疏忽了，可今天晚餐时，我必须得跟人家有所表示。要知道，能娶个有钱老婆，这样的机会可疏忽不得。"

听了这番话，老板不再言语，心里掂量着他这话有几分可信。一时间两人都默不作声，除了摆在形态怪异的货架上的钟表发出的滴答声外，屋里静悄悄的，静得甚至都能听清店外不远处的街道上有马车在来回行驶。

"哦，先生，"待了一会儿，老板说，"好吧。怎么说您也是小店的老主顾了。这会儿你有了成家立业的好机会，我说什么也不能当绊脚石。这儿有一件送女人的好东西，"他接着说，"这个小镜子可以随身携带，是15世纪的呢，保证是真的，也是来自某人的珍藏。出于尊重客户利益的考虑，我不能公开顾客的名字。他和您一样，也是某个大收藏家的侄子，也是唯一的财产继承人。"

老板自顾自地说着恭维话，可语气干干巴巴的让人听了极不舒服。他边说边弯腰从货架上取货，没留意顾客脸上的惊惧之色。马克海姆手脚猛地抖动了一下，脸上的神情剧烈地变化着，可这一切来得快去得也快，当他伸出微微颤抖的手接过老板递过的镜子时，面部神色已恢复如初。

"你说是个镜子，"马克海姆声音变得有些沙哑，停顿了一下，接着说道："拿镜子当圣诞礼物？这怎么行？"

"为什么不行啊？送镜子有什么不对头的吗？"

马克海姆神情复杂，难以言表，他盯着店老板说："你还问我为什么不能送镜子？你说为什么呀，看这儿，你自己照照！你愿意照吗？没人愿意照这破玩意儿,没人!"

他猛地把镜子推到店老板面前,老板不禁后退了一步,可随即意识到顾客此举并无恶意,嘴角又浮现出惯有的笑容,"先生,您未来的夫人一定是相貌很难看吧。"

"我来你这儿可是要买圣诞礼物的,你却给我这么一面破镜子,镜子有什么好?它只能折射出人内心深处的蒙昧与罪恶,只能使照镜子的人觉得自己青春不再、垂垂老矣。只要端起它照照自己,内心世界便永无宁日。你是不是有意的?你是不是存心的?告诉我。你最好如实说来!快点儿,说说你的心里话。让我斗胆猜猜,您私底下该不是个大善人吧?"

老板目不转睛地看着马克海姆。说来也怪,马克海姆倒不像是在嘲笑他;相反,他的眼中闪耀着火花,给人以希望,但却叫人快乐不起来。

"你到底是什么意思?"老板问道。

"这么说你不是大善人了,"马克海姆神情阴郁地反问道,"不是什么大善人,并不虔诚,也不谨小慎微,没爱心,也没人爱。你所在意的只是拼命捞钱,然后把钱锁到保险柜里。这就是你生活的全部吗?我亲爱的上帝,先生,这就是你生活的全部吧?"

"你真想知道,那我就告诉你,"老板的说话声变得有些刺耳,可随即又咯咯笑起来,"不过我看你们的结合还真是为了爱,你不是一直在祝福这位女士身体健康吗?"

"啊!"马克海姆好奇地叫道,"啊,你也爱过?快和我说说。"

"我,"老板叫道,"我爱过!我从没有那闲工夫,今天也没工夫听你胡扯。你到底想不想买镜子?"

"急什么?"马克海姆回敬道,"其实站在这儿聊天挺愉快的。要知道人生如此之短暂,而且随时都有不测风云,所以只要有高兴事,我们就一定要把握住,即便像今天咱俩聊天这么件小事也得把握住。我们的生活中就这么点儿快乐,我们一定要把握好。想象一下,站在悬崖边上的人有什么感受,其实生活中我们每分每秒都像是站在悬崖边,悬崖只有一英里那么高,但掉下去足以把我们摔得支离破碎,不复人形了。所以说,难得今天聊得开心。你说说你的事儿,我说说我的,咱们为何要戴着面具说话啊!咱俩都保密。天知道,也许咱俩还能成为好朋友呢。"

"我只有一句话对你说,"老板说,"要么买点儿什么,要么立即离开我的铺子。"

"说真的,说真的,"马克海姆说,"玩笑归玩笑,生意是生意,还有没有别的东西拿来看看。"

老板弯下腰去把镜子放回到货架上。就在他弯腰找东西的时候，他头上稀稀拉拉的金发耷拉下来挡住了他的视线。马克海姆稍稍靠近了他一些，一只手插在大衣口袋中，挺了挺胸膛，深吸了一口气。与此同时，他脸上的神情快速地变化着，时而恐惧，时而决然，时而厌憎，时而又痴醉。最后，他上唇略略抬起，露出一行白牙。

"这件东西也许你会中意，"老板边说边准备直起腰来，刹那间，马克海姆一步蹿到他身后，拔出一柄长长的匕首，寒光一闪，手起刀落。店老板扑棱棱地挣扎着，像只母鸡，太阳穴一下子撞到了货架上，然后就瘫倒在地上，堆作一团。

此刻店内钟表走针声滴答作响，交错起伏，就好像有人在轻声低语。有的声音严肃舒缓，好像上了年纪，有的喋喋不休匆匆忙忙，一分一秒都在以复杂的合唱形式滴答作响。尔后店外人行道上一个小伙子跑过时的沉重脚步声驱散了马克海姆耳际的低语声，惊得他回过神儿来，意识到了自己的处境。他环顾四周，面带惧色。烛台静静地立在柜台上，室内气流暗动，烛火摇曳不定，光芒肃然。烛光闪烁，室内忽明忽暗，如波涛般翻转起伏。屋内光影好像正魁然而立，摇头晃脑，庞然的黑暗也晃动着，好似一呼一吸地喘着气，店里画像和瓷像上的一张张面庞也变幻波动起来，宛如水中倒影。里屋的门虚掩着，从门缝间隐约透进一束白光，好像一根细长的手指，直戳内心。

透过恐惧的阴霾，马克海姆的目光又一次落到了店老板的身上，他手脚摊开躺在地上，身形出奇地枯干瘦小，显得比活着的时候更猥琐。他破衣烂衫的，死相难看，躺在那儿简直就像一堆烂木屑。眼前的情景令马克海姆有点儿害怕，瞧！其实也没什么可怕的。可是盯着看了一会儿后，马克海姆突然觉得死者又开始和他侃侃而谈了。不对呀！他肯定是死了，死了的人就应该不能说，不能动，更不能耍奸弄滑了呀。他肯定是死了，当然，尸体有朝一日总是会被发现的。发现之后呢？这堆死肉会不会突然一声尖叫，震彻英伦，让全世界人都听到他"捉拿凶手"的惨厉哀号声呢？不管他现在是死是活，他是敌人这一点不容置疑。"时间就是灵魂出窍之时，"马克海姆想着，那第一个词突然闪过脑海。既然事情已经做出来了，被杀者再也不知时间为何物了，而对于杀人者来说，时间变得刻不容缓、至关重要。

沉思中的马克海姆被钟表报时的声音惊醒了，已经是下午三点钟了。店里的钟表一个接一个地响了起来，节奏音色五花八门，有的低沉，如教堂钟声从远方钟楼缓缓飘来；有的高昂，如管弦高音拉开华尔兹轻快的舞步。

静悄悄的店里一下子声音大作，令他头晕目眩，脚步飘忽。马克海姆强打精神，手持烛台行走于光影明暗之间，灵魂深处的梦魇不时惊出他一身冷汗。环视周遭，装饰华丽的镜子比比皆是，其中一些是本国设计的，还有一些是来自威尼斯或阿姆斯特丹的舶来品。一面又一面镜子反反复复地映出马克海姆的脸庞，他觉得自己似乎被无数间谍包围着，无论走到哪儿，相互交对竟然都是自己的目光，自己的目光又都在监视着自己。他轻挪脚步，声音虽轻，可却依然能够激怒死一般的静寂。马克海姆尽量把值钱的东西往兜里塞，心里却一遍又一遍地责骂自己怎么设计了这么一个漏洞百出的计划。本该在更静一点的时间下手；事先就应该编好案发时自己不在现场的理由；甚至不该用刀；本该更小心点儿的，拿绳子捆住他，堵上他的嘴不就行了，不一定非得杀了他呀。如果非得杀人，那就该一不做、二不休，连仆人一起干掉；这一切都该换个方式做才对。要是这些都做到了，也不至于现在懊悔不迭，筋疲力尽，苦苦思索着该如何去改变已发生了的既成事实，扭转已不可扭转的被动局面，而这一切看来都是徒劳的。他思来想去，极度恐惧，脑袋里就像有一群老鼠在废弃的阁楼里窜来窜去，搅得他脑腔子里一团糟。他脑海中迅速闪过可怕的一幕：警察的手重重落下，按住他的肩膀；自己每根神经都挣扎抽搐，像是要挣脱铁钩的鱼儿，接着就当庭受审，锒铛入狱，之后被推上绞架，最后躺进那黑乎乎的棺材……

　　恐惧感无情地折磨着马克海姆，另一幕情景又悄然浮现于脑际：街坊邻居如潮水般从四面八方向他涌来，黑压压的如大军压境。不可能啊！怎么这么快风言风语就传遍了大街小巷？怎么所有人都在好奇地四处打听？直觉告诉他，人们这回再也不会像以前那样独处家中，关起门来自扫门前雪，于圣诞之夕追忆逝去的似水流年，再也不会了。相反，凶杀案带来的震惊取代了温馨的回忆；欢乐的家庭晚宴一下子陷入死一般的沉寂，母亲竖起手指示意大家不要作声。所有的人无论身份地位、年龄次序、脾气禀性，都在打探、倾听着事情的经过，激愤之余，恨不得立即把杀人者送上绞架。回到现实中，马克海姆觉得再怎么放轻脚步也不可能不被听见，货架上波希米亚风格的高脚杯叮叮当当碰个不停，撞击声比摇铃还要响；钟表走针的滴答声不时惊出他一身冷汗，真恨不得干脆关掉它们。一阵惊恐忽地闪过，他马上意识到，此时此地周围真静下来才危险呢，会引得路人注意停下脚步；他得煞有介事，假模假样地在店里忙活开，把架上的物品碰得大声响，就像主人在自己家里那样踏踏实实地进出忙碌。

　　可是现在马克海姆惶恐不安，他的神经被撕扯着，好像裂成两半，一半仍要诡秘警觉着，可另一半则战栗不已几近崩溃。此时脑海中的一个幻觉让他坚信不疑。幻觉中一个脸色惨白的邻居正趴在窗边倾听着室内发生的一切，一个路人站在那里，好像已猜到发生了什么，脸现惊恐之色。他们不可能知道的，往坏处想，他们至多也只是怀疑。厚厚的砖墙，紧闭的百叶窗，顶多能传出点儿声音，室外的人是什么也看不见的。可室内呢？就马克海姆一个人吗？是的，肯定就他一人,他亲眼看见店里的女仆赶着和情人约会去了,穿着寒酸但却是她最好的,那甜甜的笑颜,飘飘的衣带好像都在说"过圣诞去了!"是的,当然只有他一个人;可是,偌大的店里,空无他人,置身于此,他觉得自己确实听到脚步搅扰,窸窸窣窣。他就是觉得屋里还有别人,可说不清为什么会有这种感觉。哎呀,这屋里确实有人啊!马克海姆思绪游走,轻轻地滑过每间屋子,飘过每个角落。看见了!确实有人!看不清这家伙的脸,可他一双眼睛却在死死盯着自己。突然间他发现那竟是自己的影子;马科海姆的神智随即被机警和仇恨激醒,目光再次投向店老板的那副死相。

好几次,马克海姆鼓起勇气把目光投向里屋那扇半开的门,不知为什么,一直好像有股力量迫使他不敢正视那扇门。屋顶离地面很高,天窗又小又脏,透窗而望,灰蒙蒙的,好像大雾弥天;勉强照进来的阳光落到地面时已不剩什么光亮了,只能影影绰绰地在门槛附近晃出那么点儿亮。光亮若有若无,该不会是什么人冤魂不散吧?

突然,外面街上兴冲冲地来了个男人,一边不知用什么敲门,一边又吼又骂,不停喊着老板的名字。马克海姆扫了一眼地上的死尸,吓得一动也不敢动,如同冻僵了一样。可别再敲了!他可还躺在那儿呀!其实店老板已经到很远的地方去了,远得再也听不见这里的打门声和呼喊声了,或者已经沉入静寂的海底。曾几何时,就算室外狂风怒嚎,只要有人喊他的名字,他也一定会听见。可现在,那只不过是空洞的声响,对他而言已毫无意义。不一会儿,敲门声停了,男人走了。

这个小插曲对马克海姆来说可是个明确的提示,必须速战速决,赶紧离开这个是非之地,冲入伦敦熙攘的人群,晚上就可以躺在自己的床上了,在那儿他才能感到安全和无罪。已经来了一个人,随时可能再有人来,而且不会敲一会儿门就走。然而人都杀了,不拿钱就这么走了岂非大大的失败。马克海姆当下最关心的事儿就是拿到钱,可要拿到钱就不能不先找到保险柜的钥匙。

他转头又瞧了瞧里屋那扇半开的门,里面的影子还在那儿哆哆嗦嗦、晃晃悠悠。马克海姆走近尸体,心里还没感到怎么厌恶,胃里却一阵绞痛,恶心得要命。身已死,人不再。店老板散着胳膊腿儿佝偻在地上,活像空皮囊里塞了半下子谷糠。可马克海姆还是不太敢看,店老板那样子很是瘆人,不堪入目,可要不挪一挪也没办法呀。最终,马克海姆鼓起勇气,双手抓住死尸的肩膀把他翻转过来面朝上。真难以置信,尸体轻飘飘软绵绵的,四肢的骨头好像早被敲碎了,扭曲成活人不可能做出的古怪形态。死者面无表情,脸色苍白如蜡,太阳穴上一片血迹触目惊心。马克海姆感到极不舒服,此情此景突然把他带回到一个渔村,那天正好开鱼市,天是灰蒙蒙的,风呜呜地刮,街上人头攒动,锣鼓喧天;一个卖艺的正在唱民谣，歌声中掺杂着浓浓的鼻音；一个小男孩跑来跑去，一钻到人群里就没了人影，消失在人群里的男孩既兴奋又害怕，被人流操到了一个广场处，在那儿他看到了一个棚子和一个巨大的牌子，样式沉闷，颜色刺目，上面的画让人看了心情沉重：布洛瑞格暴虐女学徒，曼宁一家谋害宾客，韦尔命丧瑟特尔之手，还记着其他一些触目惊心的案件。这一切如同梦魇般清晰地浮现在马克海姆的脑海中，他又成了那个小男孩，看着罪恶的画面，身体和心理上的感受惊人地相似，喧天锣鼓响彻耳畔，震得他头晕目眩，记忆里又回响起那天的一段乐声。那一刻，马克海姆第一次感到心悸，恶心，四肢无力，他知道这种感觉可要不得，必须立刻压制住。

马克海姆思来想去，当前情况下与其逃避，不如勇敢地面对，顾虑重重于事无补。他鼓起勇气正视死者的脸，把恐惧扔到一边，努力去发现自己罪行中"了不起"的一面。想想吧！不久前那张脸还能折射出喜怒哀乐，那毫无血色的双唇还能吐出声音，那身体还生机无限、活动自如，可现在，这一切都被掳走了。就如同钟表匠毫不费力就能让表停下来一样，他就这么轻而易举让一颗心脏停止了跳动。马克海姆竭力想理出个头绪来，但做不到，反正不能再无谓地懊悔了；在罪恶面前胆战心惊的日子已经一去不复返了，该学会在血淋淋的现实面前无动于衷了。马克海姆做到了，现在他心里至多只剩下一丝怜惜。可惜呀！上帝赋予人建人间为乐土、化腐朽为神奇的伟力，就这么轻易地被剥夺了，刚才还活蹦乱跳的一个人现在就这么死者已矣了。怜惜也就罢了，懊悔千万要不得，一丝一毫也要不得。

想到这儿，马克海姆打定了主意，抛开一切顾虑，找到钥匙后径直向里屋敞开的门走去。这时外面哗哗下起了大雨，雨点打在屋顶上发出的噼啪声驱散了四周死一般的沉寂。房间如同一个滴水的岩洞，始终有声音在回荡，那声音与钟表的滴答声交织在一起，在他耳边响个不停。马克海姆向门口走着，他好像听到了另一个人上楼的脚步声，他每向门跨前一步，那个人就向楼上走一步，一步步和着自己谨慎的步履，节奏一丝不差。门槛上的影像依旧若明若暗，马克海姆暗自咬紧牙关，把全身的力量都集中到了手臂上，猛地一下把门拽开。

日光透过浓雾照进屋里时已不甚明亮，勉强照到空荡荡的地板和楼梯上，让他看到了立在一边顶盔贯甲、手持长戟的骑士像，也让他看到了黑色的木雕，凭墙而立的黄色木架，还有摆在木架上镶有边框的画像。雨滴敲打屋顶的声音清晰可闻，听在马克海姆耳里，它已不再是简单的噼啪声，而是脚步声、叹息声、远处军队行进的步伐声、数钱时钱币碰撞发出的叮当声、轻轻开门门轴转动时发出的吱嘎声，同时还混杂着雨滴敲打圆屋顶的噼啪声和水管里流水的哗哗声。马克海姆总觉得屋里不止他一个人，这种可怕的感觉越来越强烈，使他已濒临崩溃的边缘。感觉最强烈时,好像自己四面八方都被人包围了,痛苦不堪。他听到楼上屋子里有人走动,大堂里死尸从地板上站了起来,而当他终于鼓足气力拾级而上时,却听到自己身前身后都有脚步声,前面的人悄悄地躲着他,后面的人鬼鬼祟祟地跟着他。有时他想,自己要是个聋子该多好啊!那样他的灵魂深处就会得到永久的安宁。可当他再一次凝神倾听时,又不禁感激上帝赐予自己的敏锐听觉,它从不休息,就如同一个不知疲倦的哨兵,永远坚守着自己的岗位。马克海姆瞪大眼睛不停地四下张望,眼球瞪得好像要从眼眶里鼓出来一样,视线所及之处不无所获,总好像看到了什么难以名状的东西一闪而过。一楼到二楼共二十四级台阶,他每跨上一级,就要经历一次痛苦的挣扎。

二楼所有房间的门都虚掩着,其中三个房间里漆黑一片,让他毛骨悚然,觉得进去就可能遭到伏击,半开的房门在他眼中赫然就是三个黑洞洞的炮口。他总觉得周围有一双双眼睛在盯着自己,逃也逃不了,躲也躲不掉。他极想回家,躲在屋里,裹在被里,除了上帝谁也看不见自己。想了一会儿,脑子里又开始搜罗起以往犯案者的故事,据说杀人后都是惶惶终日,怕遭天谴。可至少他不是这样。他惧怕的是自然之法,怕它们绝不网开一面,从不改弦更张,让自己所犯罪恶无可遁形。让他更惧怕十倍的是行事生枝节,晴天遭霹雳,就像迷信的人敬畏神明一样。他以为自己沿因究果,干得很有路数,玩儿了个很有技术含量的游戏,可是怎能保证老天不会像输了棋的暴君突然掀翻棋盘,万一发生变数怎么办?有书记载,拿破仑兵败,就是因为发生了寒冬改了时令这样的变数。不测风云也会降临到马克海姆身上,坚固的墙壁万一变透明了怎么办?那他不就变成了玻璃蜂箱里的蜜蜂,所作所为无人不知、无人不晓了吗?结实的地板万一塌陷了怎么办?那自己不就如同脚陷流沙难以自拔?唉!还有更可怕的意外呢,那足以毁了马克海姆:比如说,突然房倒屋塌,自己有可能成了店老板的陪葬;隔壁失火,消防员从四面八方冲进来正好逮他个现形。这些都是他所惧怕的,从某种意义上说,他所惧怕的这些可能就是人们所说的罪有天惩。如果真能站在上帝面前,他反而会觉得自在心安,毫无疑问,自己所为异常,但也是情非得已呀,这恐怕只有上帝才晓得。也只有跟上帝在一起,脱离俗世,他才能真正感觉到公正。

马克海姆步入客厅,随手关上了客厅门,屋里一切正常,他紧绷的神经终于可以松一会儿了。客厅里杂乱不堪,没铺地毯,到处都是装东西的箱子。家具无论是颜色还是样式都与周围的环境格格不入。靠墙立着几面高大的穿衣镜,由于摆放角度的不同,他能看到自己各个不同的侧面轮廓,这种感觉就好像站在舞台上表演一样。画像有的镶了框,有的没有,都正面朝里靠墙而立。屋里还有一个谢拉顿风格的餐具柜,一个镶木细工的壁橱和一张很大的旧床,床上支着带有锦缎的帐幔。大大的窗户是落地式的，但万幸的是下半截儿的百叶窗是拉上的，这样邻居就看不见屋里发生什么事了。马克海姆拖开壁橱前的一个箱子，然后开始试哪把钥匙是开壁橱的。这么试可是又费时又费力，因为钥匙太多，一个一个地试着实麻烦，最后即便是找到了，柜里也完全有可能空无一物，可时间是不等人的。看到门窗紧闭，马克海姆心里踏实多了，事实上，即便他忙着试钥匙的时候，眼角的余光也始终瞄着门，有时不放心，干脆转过头去看看，这感觉就像一个将军所率的部队已被敌人包围，但看到自己坚固的阵地牢不可破，又不免内心暗自高兴。确实，这一刻他内心很平静，雨滴落在街面上，声音听起来自然又惬意。不一会儿，街对面传来了钢琴的乐声，孩子们正和着琴声唱着赞美诗，琴声、歌声弥漫在空气里，掩盖了街上嘈杂的人声。乐声那么庄重，歌声那么清新稚嫩，简直让人心旷神怡！马克海姆面带微笑，一边找着钥匙，一边侧耳倾听。由此萌发的感觉和想象在他脑海里纷纷涌现：教堂里，孩子们在做礼拜，高大的风琴，呜呜作响旋律悠长；田野上，孩子们在溪畔戏水，在莓儿草间漫步，风吹云动，高飞的风筝在蓝天中游弋。没多久，赞美诗的旋律又在耳际响起，思绪一下又被带回教堂。夏日炎炎，礼拜者昏昏欲睡，牧师布道声浑厚优雅，想到这里，他情不自禁地笑了，眼前浮现出詹姆士一世的陵墓，墓穴的墙壁上布满彩绘，而刻在圣坛上的"十诫"字迹模糊。

马克海姆出神地坐在那里，脑海中的画面一个接一个，不停地切换着。突然，有个声音吓得他一激灵跳了起来。他浑身一阵冰冷，紧接着是一团火热，全身的血液刹那间沸腾了起来，他定在那里如同凝固了一般，全身汗毛都竖了起来。楼梯上响起了缓慢而沉稳的脚步声，不一会儿就到了门口，一只手放在了门把手上，门锁咯噔一响，门开了。

恐惧如同一把钢钳紧紧地攫住了马克海姆。紧接着该发生什么了，他无从得知，是死人复活来向他索命，还是警察赶到来将他绳之以法，抑或是什么人误打误撞地闯了进来，随即宣布了他的"死刑"？门开了，一张面孔从门后探了出来，四下打量了一圈，看到他后点点头，微微一笑，以示友好，就像和熟人打招呼一样，随即退出门外，还随手关上了门。此刻，马克海姆的恐惧感如同决堤的江水般再也无法控制，他大叫了一声，声音撕心裂肺。听见了叫声，那个人又转身回来了。

"你是在叫我吗？"那人愉悦地问，进屋后随手又把门关上了。

马克海姆呆呆地站着，双眼死死盯着眼前这个人。不知为什么，他眼前朦朦胧胧的，只能看见一个晃动的模糊轮廓，这一幕让他想到了不久前大堂里烛光下那似有若无的幻象。他时而觉得自己应该认识这个人，时而又觉得眼前这个人或多或少和自己有几分相似。可有一点马克海姆是确信不疑的，这个人既非尘世凡胎，亦非天神降临，一定是魔鬼的化身，彰显着邪恶与恐怖。

可这家伙看起来实在没什么与众不同的地方，就跟普通人没什么两样，他看着你时嘴角始终挂着笑模样，和你说话时就如同日常打招呼一样彬彬有礼，"我想，你是要找钱吧？"

马克海姆没有作声

"我必须提醒你，"那人继续说，"女仆人已经会完情人就快回来了，当然，和以往相比，她今天回来得早了些。要是她进屋发现了马克海姆先生的话，会有什么样的后果，我想就无须赘言了吧。"

"你认识我？"马克海姆情不自禁地大叫。

那人又笑了笑，"岂止是认识？这么久以来，我一直是那么欣赏你，我一直在观察着你，总在想方设法在你有些需要时帮助你。"

"那你到底是什么人？你是魔鬼吗？"

"不管我是什么人，我对你始终是善意的，我只想帮助你。"

"我能相信吗？你帮助我？不，这不可能。你是谁啊？上帝啊！你根本就不了解我。"

"我了解你，"说这话时那人流露出诚挚、严肃且确信不疑的神情，"我了解你的一切，包括你的内心。"

"你了解我？怎么可能？"马克海姆大声叫道。"我所过的日子不过就是对我自己的歪曲诽谤。活着就得把自个儿掩饰起来。人人不都是如此吗，把自己伪装得严严实实，透不过气来，虽然脱掉伪装会好得多。想想被生活所累的人吧，想想斗篷扣在头上被歹徒欺负是什么感觉？要是他们都能够左右自己的生活，要是你能看到他们的真实的一面，情景将会完全不同，他们一定会像英雄圣人般光芒四射。而我的情况更糟，掩饰得更深，我的理由只有自己和神知道。要是有机会，我会表白我自己的。"

"是向我表白吗？"那人问。

"你应该是第一个，"马克海姆说，"因为我觉得你有头脑。如果你不是幻象的话，我想你能读懂我的心。也许你和大多数人一样，看了我的所作所为就断定我是个恶人吧。唉！看我都做了些什么？我降生的这个世界是由'巨人'所主宰的，从我出娘胎的那一刻起，'现实'这个可怕的'巨人'就紧紧地抓住我不放手。难道你就只凭我做了什么就断定我是怎样的人吗？你就不会看看我的内心吗？你难道看不出我是多么痛恨罪恶吗？你难道就看不见我内心深处明明白白写着'良知'二字吗？它没有被任何强言诡辩玷污过，尽管我的行为总是背弃这两个字。你难道就没发现我也有着常人的慈悲，杀人获罪也是迫不得已吗？"

"你表白的很清楚了，而且声情并茂，"那人答道，"但这一切与我无关。

我不在意你的行为是否符合心理或社会发展的必然规律,我也丝毫不关心是什么力量驱使你误入歧途的。我只想告诉你,时间不等人,女仆人也许路上会耽搁一会儿,旁人的穿着打扮和广告牌上的图片文字都有可能让她驻足片刻,但她毕竟离这里越来越近了。别忘了,她的到来就意味着绞刑架和她一起穿过圣诞时节的街道向你走来。还是让我这个无所不知的人来帮帮你吧,想知道钱放哪儿了吗?"

"我接受你帮助的代价是什么?"马克海姆问道。

"就当是我送你的圣诞礼物吧。"那人回答道。

马克海姆禁不住笑了,笑容里有一丝胜利的满足,也有一丝苦涩的难堪。"不,我不会接受你的任何东西。"马克海姆接着说道,"即便有一天我快渴死了,你把水壶都端到了我嘴边,我也一定会有勇气拒绝你的帮助。也许有人会很轻易地相信你刚才的那番话,我决计不会委身邪恶!"

"我并不是不相信一个人临终前会幡然悔悟。"那人说道。

"那是因为你不相信临终悔悟有什么意义!"马克海姆大叫着。

"我可没这个意思,"那人反唇相讥,"我只不过是从另一个角度来看待这件事情的。生命一旦结束,我对它的兴致也就走到了尽头。你杀的这个人活着的时候就是我的奴仆,他要么披着圣徒的外衣在人前板起脸来假道学,要么把野草仔撒到别人的麦田里,尽不干好事。他的所作所为和你没什么两样,都是因为意志力薄弱,屈从了欲望的左右,干出格的事。现在他死了,差不多可以完全解脱了,但我的身后还有许多和他差不多的追随者依然活着,他们需要信心和希望,所以他还要为我做最后一件事,那就是悔悟,那就是微笑着死去。我并不是一个难伺候的主人,事实会证明这一点的。请接受我的帮助吧!接受了我的帮助,你就能继续像以前那样,高兴怎么活就怎么活,而且活得更潇洒、更无拘无束、更随心所欲。而当夜幕降临,家家户户关窗拉帘之后,我向你保证你会感觉更棒,因为你的良知再也不会向你发难,因为你知道自己是在按'上帝'的旨意行事,内心将获得永恒的宁静。我刚才还在一位死者身边,那屋里满是诚挚的哀悼者,聆听着死者的临终之音,而当我望向他的脸孔时,却看不到以往的冷酷无情,相反,我看到的是充满希望的笑容。"

"你当真认为我和他,还有你的那些追随者们是一路人吗?"马克海姆问,"你当真认为我这个人不可能有什么更高境界的追求,而只会一再地犯罪,并寄希望于在生命的最后一刻偷偷混入天堂吗?这就是你所阅历的人生百态吗?是不是因为我双手沾满鲜血地站在你面前,你就断定我是个卑鄙邪恶的人吗?是不是这桩谋杀当真罪大恶极之至,以至于令你认为世人再无半点'仁爱'之心了?"

"谋杀在我看来没什么特别邪恶之处,"那人回答道。

"谋杀确实邪恶,但很平常,就像人一生都在你争我夺一样,再平常不过了。我发现人类或可比为饥肠辘辘的水手,驾着筏子飘荡在海上,饿极了就从比他还饿的人手中抢夺面包屑,甚至不惜自相残杀。当罪恶还处于萌芽状态时我就开始密切注意它了,我发现所有罪恶最终必然导致死亡,在我看来,一个举止优雅的漂亮姑娘看见母亲受邀参加舞会便百般阻挠,其心地之卑污丝毫不亚于谋财害命。我刚说过我密切关注罪恶了吧?同样,我也关注仁善。'善'与'恶'有时只是一线之隔,它们都是死神手中用来'收获'生命的镰刀。我就是为邪恶而生的,我深知邪恶并不体现在行动中,而是深藏于人性之中。我喜欢恶人,不是恶行,要知道恶行往往结出恶果,如果你能沿着时间的长河顺流而下,长时间地关注它的话,你就会发现相比起那些少得可怜的善行的结局,恶果往往更受上帝的'青睐'。我主动提出帮你逃脱,不是因为你杀了人,而是因为你是马克海姆,这一点希望你能明白。"

"听听我的心声吧,"马克海姆说,"今天是我最后一次犯罪了,以后你再也看不到了。这次犯罪让我学到了很多,其实这罪行本身对我而言就是一堂课,别有深意的一堂课。迄今为止,我总是被一种违心的力量驱使着,做的都是我不想做的事情,因为我和'贫穷'签了卖身契,成了它的奴隶,受它的奴役,历尽了磨难。如果我有一颗坚定的仁善之心,今天也不会沦落至此,但我没做到,我太渴望享乐了。今天这件事警醒了我,让我收获了真正的财富,那就是重新找回作自己的勇气和力量。在这个世上,我终于可以自由地演绎我的人生了。我脱胎换骨了,这双手从此远离邪恶,这颗心从此永享安宁。心间会再次萦绕起美好的往昔岁月:是伴着安息夜教堂风琴声飘出的梦想;是佳卷在手潸然泪下时的遐想;是孩提时与母亲交谈时的天真无邪。那儿才是我生命所在;多年来,我迷失彷徨,如今,我终于再次找到了生命的归宿。"

"我猜你急需这笔钱炒股对吧?"那人接着说,"如果我没猜错,你在股市已经损失好几千块钱了吧?"

"啊!可这次我一定稳操胜券。"马克海姆回答道。

"这次你还是会输的。"那人语气平淡地说。

"那我就投一半,留一半。"马克海姆大声喊道。

"留下的那一半你照样会输光。"那人说道。

马克海姆的额头沁出了汗水。"输光了又如何?"他大叫道,"就算我又变得一文不名,就算我又变得穷困潦倒,我就永远要受灵魂中邪恶一面的支配,直到将我最后的一丝仁善之念挤得干干净净吗?善与恶在我灵魂中对峙鏖战,二者不停撕扯着我。我不厚此薄彼,我两个都爱。我向往成就丰功伟业,为了这一伟大目标我可以克制自己的私欲,我也甘愿为之献出我的生命,尽管我现在堕落成了一个杀人犯，但我不乏悲天悯人的情怀。我同情穷苦人，还有谁比我更了解他们的苦痛呢？我愿意帮助穷苦人，因为我珍视爱，我喜欢那挚诚的笑脸。虽然现实中我从没见过所谓的真善美，但我还是由衷地向往。是不是我这一生注定只能像魔鬼般作'恶'，而我心中的'善'念就永远无法开花结果呢？不，不会是这样的。善念一旦迸发，必然会表现出一连串儿可歌可泣的行动。"

那人用手指着马克海姆说道："你在这个世上已经度过三十六个春秋了。在这三十六年里，你时运、性情几经起伏变化，我可是眼看着你一步一步地堕落下去了。十五年前，看到别人偷东西你会感到震惊；三年前，一听到'杀人凶手'这个词就会把你吓得转身就跑；而如今，为非作歹还会让你震惊吗？干起残忍卑鄙的勾当还会畏缩吗？打今天起，五年后的你是什么样子我已经看到了，除了堕落还是堕落，一直堕落下去，直到死的那一天。"

"你说的对，"马克海姆嘶声地说，"一定程度上我是向邪恶屈膝低头了，可现实中谁不是这样呢？圣人也得活着啊，只要活着他就不可能不食人间烟火，只要活着他就不可能不被环境所同化，圣人也就不那么'神圣'了。"

"我有一个简单的问题请你回答，"那人接着说，"通过你的回答，我就能解读你的道德密码，判断你的道德观。的确，你在很多方面变得越来越无所谓了，做事情也越来越随意了。你变成这样也无可厚非，毕竟绝大多数人和你也没什么两样。但请你告诉我，你是否觉得有些事情根本无足轻重，很难劳您大驾，还是无论什么事你都放任自流？"

"你是说任何事吗？"马克海姆痛苦地思索着，表情很绝望，"是的，我做什么都是一团糟。"

"那么，你还是面对现实，别再牢骚满腹了吧。因为你永远也无法改变现实，而在人生的舞台上，你所扮演角色的台词早已写好，想改也改不了。"

马克海姆站在原地，久久没有作声，最后，还是那人的声音打破了沉寂，"既然这样，让我告诉你钱在哪里好吗？"

"难道你就不能发发慈悲吗？"马克海姆大喊着。

"难道你自己没努力过吗？结果又如何呀？"那人反唇相讥，"两三年前，在福音布道会的唱诗台上，扯开喉咙高唱赞美诗的那位就是你吧？"

"你说的没错，"马克海姆说，"现在我终于明白了有些事情对我来说是责无旁贷的。我得衷心地感谢你呀，和你这番交谈让我受益匪浅啊，是你擦亮了我的眼睛，让我在最后一刻认识了我自己。"

就在这一刻，门外传来刺耳的门铃声，响彻了整个房子。铃声就好像是一个事先安排好了的同步信号，那人一直在等待它的出现。铃声响起的一瞬间，那人立刻神色为之一变。

"女仆回来了,我已经警告过你了。唉!你接下来的路将更难走了。你必须对她说主人病了,说这话时要严肃、自信,千万不要笑,太做作了反而过犹不及。只要你照做,我保证你会成功的。她一进来,你就关上门,再用除掉店老板那招对付她,那招你再熟悉不过了。之后,你便再无后患,接下来的时间任你支配,如果需要,你有整晚的时间将这店里的财物洗劫一空,然后安全离开。尽管这么做看起来很危险,但我确实是在帮你。快行动吧,朋友,你已经命悬一线了,没时间磨蹭了!"

马克海姆眼睛一眨不眨地看着他说:"就算老天要责罚我的恶行,还会有一扇门向我敞开的,穿过这扇门,我将重获自由。我可以给我以前的所作所为画一个句号。如果我活着就是个祸害,那我可以就此了结它。诚如你所言,一直以来,面对大大小小的诱惑,我总是唯利是图,但我仍决定一搏,让自己摆脱种种诱惑的束缚。虽然我的善念没让我做出什么善行义举,也许永远都是如此,那就顺其自然吧!然而,我还是那么憎恨邪恶,这也许会令你大失所望,但却让我获得勇气和力量。"

那人的神情开始发生奇妙而有趣的变化,开始时容光焕发,逐渐变得柔和,然后慢慢模糊淡去,但却一直带着些许胜利的神采。马克海姆没有去观察他神情的变化,也没思考这其中的意义。他推开门,慢慢向楼下走去,边走边思索着,心潮澎湃。往事一幕幕闪现心头,如噩梦般丑陋沉重,如大杂烩般零乱狼藉,真是太失败了!往事不堪回首,生活于他已魅力不再,可这时,他好像看见远处有一个静静的港湾,也许那里就是他停泊之处吧。马克海姆在过道里停下来,向店堂里望了一眼,尸体旁烛光闪烁,周围出奇地安静。他盯着那里,站着不动,脑袋里挤满了店老板被害前的一幕又一幕。刺耳的铃声再度响起,按铃的人已经不耐烦了。

马克海姆打开门,站在门口,面对女仆似笑非笑。

"你最好马上去报警,"马克海姆说,"我把你主人杀了。"

Oscar Wilde
(1854—1900)

Oscar Wilde, Irish wit, poet, and dramatist, spokesman for the late 19th-century Aesthetic Movement in England, was born in Dublin, Ireland. His father, Sir William Wilde, was an eye surgeon, and his mother, a poet and writer. Oscar Wilde went to Trinity College, Dublin (1871—1874), and Magdalen College, Oxford (1874—1878), which awarded him a degree with honours. In 1884 Wilde married Constance Lloyd and soon had two sons. His years of triumph ended dramatically, when his intimate association with Alfred Douglas led to his trial on charges of homosexuality. He was sentenced to two years of hard labor. He died of acute meningitis, penniless, in a cheap Paris hotel.

Wilde's reputation rests on his best-known novel, *The Picture of Dorian Gray* (1891), his comic masterpieces *Lady Windermere's Fan* (1892), *A Woman of No Importance* (1893), *The Importance of Being Earnest* (1895) and *An Ideal Husband*(1895), and his fairy tales *The Happy Prince and Other Tales* (1888). *The Picture of Dorian Gray* is a story about a handsome young man, Dorian Gray, and the painter Howard Basil. When Dorian meets a hedonist, Lord Henry, he becomes a hedonist himself until he kills Howard. *Lady Windermere's Fan* deals with a blackmailing divorcée driven to self-sacrifice by maternal love. In *A Woman of No Importance*, an illegitimate son is torn between his father and mother. *An Ideal Husband* deals with blackmail, political corruption and public and private honor. *The Importance of Being Earnest* is about two fashionable young gentlemen and their eventually successful courtship.

The Sphinx without a Secret

The following story is about the love affair between Lord Murchison and Lady Alroy who is thought to be charming and mysterious to Murchison. In the end, the author reveals that Lady Alroy "just had a passion for secrecy, but she herself was merely a Sphinx without a secret." The story is beautifully written with irony.

One afternoon I was sitting outside the Café de la Paix, watching the splendour and shabbiness of Parisian life, and wondering over my vermouth at the strange panorama of pride and poverty that was passing before me, when I heard some one call my name. I turned round, and saw Lord Murchison. We had not met since we had been at college together, nearly ten years before, so I was delighted to come across him again, and we shook hands warmly. At Oxford we had been great friends. I had liked him immensely, he was so handsome, so high-spirited, and so honourable. We used to say of him that he would be the best of fellows, if he did not always speak the truth, but I think we really admired him all the more for his frankness. I found him a good deal changed. He looked anxious and puzzled, and seemed to be in doubt about something. I felt it could not be modern scepticism, for Murchison was the stoutest of Tories, and believed in the Pentateuch as firmly as he believed in the House of Peers; so I concluded that it was a woman, and asked him if he was married yet.

"I don't understand women well enough," he answered.

"My dear Gerald," I said, "women are meant to be loved, not to be understood."

"I cannot love where I cannot trust," he replied.

"I believe you have a mystery in your life, Gerald," I exclaimed; "tell me about it."

"Let us go for a drive," he answered, "it is too crowded here. No, not a yellow carriage, any other colour—there, that dark-green one will do;" and in a few moments we were trotting down the boulevard in the direction of the Madeleine.

"Where shall we go to?" I said.

"Oh, anywhere you like!" he answered—"to the restaurant in the Bois; we will dine there, and you shall tell me all about yourself."

"I want to hear about you first," I said. "Tell me your mystery."

He took from his pocket a little silver-clasped morocco case, and handed it to me. I opened it. Inside there was the photograph of a woman. She was tall and slight, and strangely picturesque with her large vague eyes and loosened hair. She looked like a clairvoyante, and was wrapped in rich furs.

"What do you think of that face?" he said; "is it truthful?"

I examined it carefully. It seemed to me the face of some one who had a secret, but whether that secret was good or evil I could not say. Its beauty was a beauty moulded out of many mysteries—the beauty, in face, which is psychological, not plastic—and the faint smile that just played across the lips was far too subtle to be really sweet.

"Well," he cried impatiently, "what do you say?"

"She is the Gioconda in sables," I answered. "Let me know all about her."

"Not now," he said; "after dinner;" and began to talk of other things.

When the waiter brought us our coffee and cigarettes I reminded Gerald of his promise. He rose from his seat, walked two or three times up and down the room, and, sinking into an armchair, told me the following story: —

"One evening," he said, "I was walking down Bond Street about five o'clock. There was a terrific crush of carriages, and the traffic was almost stopped. Close to the pavement was standing a little yellow brougham, which, for some reason or other, attracted my attention. As I passed by there looked out from it the face I showed you this afternoon. It fascinated me immediately. All that night I kept thinking of it, and all the next day. I wandered up and down that wretched Row, peering into every carriage, and waiting for the yellow brougham; but I could not find ma belle inconnue, and at last I began to think she was merely a dream. About a week afterwards I was dining with Madame de Rastail. Dinner was for eight o'clock; but at half-past eight we were still waiting in the drawing-room. Finally the servant threw open the door, and announced Lady Alroy. It was the woman I had been looking for. She came in very slowly, looking like a moon-beam in grey lace, and, to my intense delight, I was asked to take her in to dinner. After we had sat down I remarked quite innocently, 'I think I caught sight of you in Bond Street some time ago, Lady Alroy.' She grew very pale, and said to me in a low voice, 'Pray do not talk so loud; you may be overheard.' I felt miserable at having made such a bad beginning, and plunged recklessly into the subject of French plays. She spoke very little, always in the same low musical voice, and seemed as if she was afraid of some one listening. I fell passionately, stupidly in love, and the indefinable atmosphere of mystery that surrounded her excited my most ardent curiosity. When she was going away, which she did very soon after dinner, I asked her if I might call and see her. She hesitated for a moment, glanced round to see if any one was near us, and then said, 'Yes; to-morrow at a quarter to five.' I begged Madame de Rastail to tell me about her; but all that I could learn was that she was a widow with a beautiful house in Park Lane, and as some scientific bore began a dissertation of widows, as exemplifying the survival of the matrimonially fittest, I left and went home.

"The next day I arrived at Park Lane punctual to the moment, but was told by the butler that Lady Alroy had just gone out. I went down to the club quite unhappy and very much puzzled, and after long consideration wrote her a letter, asking if I might be allowed to try my chance some other afternoon. I had no answer for several days, but at last I got a little note saying she would be at home on Sunday at four, and with this extraordinary postscript: 'Please do not write to me here again; I will explain when I see you.' On Sunday she received me, and was perfectly charming; but when I was going away she begged of me, if I ever had occasion to write to her again, to address my letter to 'Mrs. Knox, care of Whittaker's Library, Green Street.' 'There are reasons,' she said, 'why I cannot receive letters in my own house.'

"All through the season I saw a great deal of her, and the atmosphere of mystery never left her. Sometimes I thought that she was in the power of some man, but she looked so unapproachable that I could not believe it. It was really very difficult for me to come to any conclusion, for she was like one of those strange crystals that one sees in museums, which are at one moment clear, and at another clouded. At last I determined to ask her to be my wife: I was sick and tired of the incessant secrecy that she imposed on all my visits, and on the few letters I sent her. I wrote to her at the library to ask her if she could see me the following Monday at six. She answered yes, and I was in the seventh heaven of delight. I was infatuated with her: in spite of the mystery, I thought then—in consequence of it, I see now. No; it was the woman herself I loved. The mystery troubled me, maddened me. Why did chance put me in its track?"

"You discovered it, then?" I cried.

"I fear so," he answered. "You can judge for yourself."

"When Monday came round I went to lunch with my uncle, and about four o'clock found myself in the Marylebone Road. My uncle, you know, lives in Regent's Park. I wanted to get to Piccadilly, and took a short cut through a lot of shabby little streets. Suddenly I saw in front of me Lady Alroy, deeply veiled and walking very fast. On coming to the last house in the street, she went up the steps, took out a latch-key, and let herself in. 'Here is the mystery,' I said to myself; and I hurried on and examined the house. It seemed a sort of place for letting lodgings. On the doorstep lay her handkerchief, which she had dropped. I picked it up and put it in my pocket. Then I began to consider what I should do. I came to the conclusion that I had no right to spy on her, and I drove down to the club. At six I called to see her. She was lying on a sofa, in a tea-gown of silver tissue looped up by some strange moonstones that she always wore. She was looking quite lovely. 'I am so glad to see you,' she said; 'I have not been out all day.' I stared at her in amazement, and pulling the handkerchief out of my pocket, handed it to her. 'You dropped this in Cumnor Street this afternoon, Lady

Alroy,' I said very calmly. She looked at me in terror, but made no attempt to take the handkerchief. 'What were you doing there?' I asked. 'What right have you to question me?' she answered. 'The right of a man who loves you,' I replied; 'I came here to ask you to be my wife.' She hid her face in her hands, and burst into floods of tears. 'You must tell me,' I continued. She stood up, and , looking me straight in the face, said, 'Lord Murchison, there is nothing to tell you.'—'You went to meet some one,' I cried; 'this is your mystery.' She grew dreadfully white, and said, 'I went to meet no one,'—'Can't you tell the truth?' I exclaimed. 'I have told it,' she replied. I was mad, frantic; I don't know what I said, but I said terrible things to her. Finally I rushed out of the house. She wrote me a letter the next day; I sent it back unopened, and started for Norway with Alan Colville. After a month I came back, and the first thing I saw in the Morning Post was the death of Lady Alroy. She had caught a chill at the Opera, and had died in five days of congestion of the lungs. I shut myself up and saw no one. I had loved her so much, I had loved her so madly. Good god! How I had loved that woman!"

"You went to the street, to the house in it?" I said.

"Yes," he answered.

"One day I went to Cumnor Street. I could not help it; I was tortured with doubt. I knocked at the door, and a respectable-looking woman opened it to me. I asked her if she had any rooms to let. "Well, sir," she replied, "the drawing-rooms are supposed to be let; but I have not seen the lady for three months, and as rent is owing on them, you can have them."—"Is this the lady?" I said, showing the photograph. "That's her, sure enough," she exclaimed; "and when is she coming back, sir?"—"The lady is dead," I replied. "Oh, sir, I hope not!" said the woman; "she was my best lodger. She paid me three guineas a week merely to sit in my drawing-rooms now and then."—"She met some one here?" I said; but the woman assured me that it was not so, that she always came alone, and saw no one. "What on earth did she do here?" I cried. "She simply sat in the drawing-room, sir, reading books, and sometimes had tea," the woman answered. I did not know what to say, so I gave her a sovereign and went away. Now, what do you think it all meant? You don't believe the woman was telling the truth?"

"I do."

"Then why did Lady Alroy go there?"

"My dear Gerald," I answered, "Lady Alroy was simply a woman with a mania for mystery. She took these rooms for the pleasure of going there with her veil down, and imagining she was a heroine. She had a passion for secrecy, but she herself was merely a Sphinx without a secret."

"Do you really think so?"

"I am sure of it," I replied.

He took out the morocco case, opened it, and looked at the photograph. "I wonder?" he said at last.

Questions

1. What is the author's purpose of using the word "the Sphinx" rather than "a Lady" in the title?
2. Do you think Lady Alroy deliberately dropped her handkerchief on the door step?
3. Do you find the ending tragic or sentimental?
4. How does the writer use suspense in developing the plot of this story?
5. What is the climax of the story?

奥斯卡·王尔德
(1854—1900)

爱尔兰著名诗人、戏剧家、19世纪英国唯美主义运动的倡导者奥斯卡·王尔德出生于爱尔兰的都柏林。父亲威廉·王尔德爵士是眼科医生,母亲是诗人、作家。王尔德自都柏林圣三一学院毕业后,于1874年进入牛津大学莫德林学院学习并获得荣誉学位。1884年王尔德与康斯坦斯·劳埃德结婚并有两个儿子。他因被控与阿尔弗莱德·道格拉斯同性恋而在监狱服了两年苦役。他因急性脑膜炎死在巴黎的一家旅馆,当时身无分文。

王尔德享誉盛名的作品有:小说《道林·格雷的画像》(1891),喜剧《少奶奶的扇子》(1892)、《无足轻重的女人》(1893)、《认真的重要性》(1895)、《理想丈夫》(1895)、童话《快乐王子》(1888)。《道林·格雷的画像》讲述的是一个漂亮的年轻人道林·格雷、画家霍华德·巴兹尔以及享乐主义者亨利男爵之间的故事。《少奶奶的扇子》讲的是一个离了婚的女人敲诈勒索,最后因母爱而自我牺牲的故事。《无足轻重的女人》是一个私生子在父母之间备受折磨的故事。《理想丈夫》讲述的是公、私名义上的敲诈和政治腐败。《认真的重要性》讲述的是两个时尚的年轻男子最终求婚成功的故事。

没有秘密的斯芬克斯

下面的故事是关于穆奇森男爵和阿罗瑞夫人之间的爱情故事。对穆奇森来说阿罗瑞夫人充满了迷人和神秘色彩。作者最后才揭示出一个结果,阿罗瑞夫人其实没有秘密,所有一切不过是她努力营造的神秘气氛而已。故事技法优美,笔调颇具反讽之韵。

一天下午,我悠闲地坐在和平咖啡馆外面,注视巴黎人生活中的光彩华丽与贫穷困苦。一边品尝着我杯中的味美斯酒,一边感叹眼前骄傲和贫穷并存的奇异景象。忽然,我听见有人叫我的名字,回头一看,原来是穆奇森男爵。我们自从十年前大学毕业之后,就未曾谋面。因此我很高兴能与他不期而遇,我们热情地相互握手。在牛津读书的时候,我们就是挚友。我非常欣赏他。他是那么英俊潇洒、生气勃勃而且诚实正直。我们常说,要不是他总是实话实说,还真是一流的好人。其实我想我们真正欣赏他的,正是他的坦诚。此次相见我发现他有很大变化。他看上去忧心忡忡，似乎对什么事情感到困惑不解。凭我的感觉，我觉得应该与当今的怀疑主义无关。因为，穆奇森是坚定的保守党，他对贵族院的信任就像对摩西五经一样坚定不移。所以我推断那一定是与女人有关。于是我问他结婚了没有。

"我对女人还不够了解。"他回答道。

"我亲爱的杰尔拉德，"我说，"女人是要去爱的，不是要了解的。"

"可是不能让我信任的人，我是没法爱的。"他回答说。

"我想你一定是有什么秘密吧，杰尔拉德，"我断言道，"跟我说说。"

"我们去兜兜风吧，"他说，"这里人多嘈杂。不，不要坐黄马车，其他什么颜色都行，就那辆深绿色的吧。"不一会儿，我们就奔驰在通往马德林方向的林荫大道上了。

"我们去哪儿？"我问。

"随便你。"他回答道，"就去波瓦斯那里的餐厅吧。我们在那里吃饭，然后聊聊你的情况。"

"我倒是想先听听你的情况，"我说，"告诉我你心中的秘密。"

他从衣袋里掏出一个有银链扣的羊皮夹子递给我。我打开皮夹子，里面是一个女人的照片。她身材高挑纤细，一双有着朦胧眼神的大眼睛和蓬松的头发，这使她有种奇特的魅力。她全身裹在昂贵的裘皮大衣里，看起来像是具有超越常人的洞察力。

"你觉得她长得怎么样？"他问，"看着诚实吗？"

我仔细地端详那张照片。在我看来，这人似乎有什么秘密，至于那秘密是好还是坏，我就不得而知了。因为那个女人的美是由种种神秘的东西构成的，实际上，那种美是一种内在的，而不是外在的。就连她挂在唇边的那一抹微笑，因为太过微妙，而根本称不上甜美。

"什么，"他不耐烦地喊道，"你说什么？"

"她是身穿黑貂皮的蒙娜丽莎，"我回答说，"和我说说她吧。"

"不是现在，"他说，"晚饭以后吧。"然后我们开始谈论其他事情。

侍者给我们送来咖啡和香烟的时候，我提醒杰尔拉德别忘了他刚才的承诺。他从椅子上站起来，在房间里来回走了两三次，又坐回椅子，给我讲了下面的故事：

"一天晚上，"他说，"大约五点钟左右，我走在邦德大街上。有一起撞车事故，交通几乎瘫痪了。不知是什么原因，靠近人行道边停着的一辆黄色小车引起我的注意。我走过的时候，正巧下午我给你看的照片上的那个女人从车里往外看。我立刻被她迷住了。整个晚上我都想着那张美丽忧郁的面孔。第二天我又惦念了一整天,在那条街上来来回回地闲逛,向每一辆过往的马车里张望,期待着那辆黄色小车的出现,但没能看到美女。最后我开始觉得她只不过是一场梦吧。大约一周后,我应邀和瑞斯塔夫人共进晚餐。晚餐是八点钟,但八点半的时候我们还在客厅里等着呢。终于佣人推开大门,宣布阿罗瑞夫人的光临。她正是我一直在寻找的女人。她缓缓地走进来,宛如银灰蕾丝中的一缕月光,更令我兴奋不已的是,我被邀请带她入座。我们刚一落座,我便天真地说,'那天在邦德大街上我看到过你,阿罗瑞夫人。'她脸色变得苍白,然后低声说,'拜托不要这么大声说话,别人会听到的。'如此的开场使我感到很窘,于是我便很快转向法国戏剧的话题。她很少说话,而且总是用那悦耳的声音低声说,好像是担心有人听到似的。我疯狂而盲目地爱上了她,笼罩在她周围的无法言表的神秘气氛更激发了我强烈的好奇心。晚餐不久她就离开了。在临行前,我问她能否和她联系,去看她。她犹豫了一会儿,看了看我们周围是否有人,然后说,'好吧,明天差一刻钟五点。'我请求瑞斯塔夫人告诉我关于她的事情,但结果我只知道,她住在帕克大街一所漂亮房子里,是寡妇。接着她们开始喋喋不休地谈论起有关寡妇以及婚姻中未亡人的处境,于是我便起身回家了。

"第二天,我准时到达帕克大街,但管家告诉我说,阿罗瑞夫人刚出去。我感到困惑不解,于是去了俱乐部。考虑了很久后我给她写了封信,询问能否在哪天的下午再给我一次拜访的机会。我好几天也没得到回音,但最后我收到一张便条。她说星期天下午四点在家,而且特别附上:'请不要再往这儿给我写信,见面的时候我再解释。'星期天我见到了她,她真是非常迷人。可我要离开的时候她请求我能否再给她写信,地址写'格林大街,威特太克图书馆诺克斯夫人转交。''我为什么不能在自己的住处收信,'她说,'这是有原因的。'

"整个季节我们经常见面,但神秘的气氛从没有消失。有时我觉得她有着某些男人的威慑力。但我真不敢相信她看起来是那么无法接近,我确实也很难得出结论,因为她就像是那些博物馆里的水晶体似的,一会儿清澈,一会儿迷蒙。最终我还是决定向她求婚。我讨厌也厌倦了每次和她见面还有写信带给我的不断的神秘感。我在图书馆给她写信,问她能否在下周一的晚上六点见面。她回答说,可以。我兴奋不已。虽然神秘,但她还是把我迷住了。我想,不管怎么说,这下子我可以知道结果了。我爱的是这个女人,她本人。但这种种神秘困扰着我,令我发狂。为什么命运把我带到这条路上呢?"

"你发现秘密了吗?"我问。

"恐怕没有,"他回答,"这你自己可以看得出来。"

"星期一的时候我和叔叔去吃午饭,四点钟左右的时候,我走到马里林堡路。我叔叔就住在摄政公园附近。我想抄近道通过几条小路去皮卡迪利大街。

突然，我看见阿罗瑞夫人头戴面纱，行色匆匆在前面走。在大街尽头的一所房子前，她走上台阶，拿出钥匙，走了进去。'这就是秘密'，我自言自语地说。我疾走几步仔细察看，这房子看起来好像是用来出租的。在门阶上有她刚刚掉落的手帕。我拾起来放进口袋。然后我就开始想该怎么办。结论是，我无权跟梢她，于是我便去了俱乐部。六点钟的时候我去见她，她正躺在沙发上，身穿一件银色薄纱的茶会礼服，上面镶嵌着她喜欢佩带的几圈有些怪异的月长石配饰。她看起来很可爱。'很高兴能见到你，'她说，'我一整天都没出去。'我惊愕地盯着她，从口袋里拿出手帕，递给她，很平静地说，'今天下午你把它掉在卡姆诺大街了，阿罗瑞夫人。'她惊恐地看着我，但并没有想拿回手帕的意思。'你在那儿干什么？'我问。'你有什么权力问我？'她反问道。'我有爱着你的一个男人的权利，'我回答道，'我来这里是让你做我的妻子。'她双手捂着脸，突然大哭起来。'你必须告诉我，'我接着说。她站起来，直视着我，说，'穆奇森男爵，我没什么可以告诉你的。''你是去见别人了，'我大叫着说，'这是你的秘密。'她的脸色变得苍白可怕，说道，'我谁也没见。''你说的是真话吗？'我大声问。'我已经告诉你了，'她回答。我暴跳如雷，我也不知道我都说了些什么，但我对她说了很多难听的话，最后冲出房门。第二天，她写给我一封信，我没拆开看就给寄回去了。然后就和爱伦·科乐威尔出发去挪威了。一个月后我回来的时候，在晨报上看到的第一条内容就是阿罗瑞夫人的讣告。她去看歌剧的时候染上风寒，五天后死于肺病。我把自己关在房里，谁也不见。我是那么爱她，爱她爱得那么痴情。上帝啊，我是多么爱那个女人啊！"

"你到那条大街，进到房子里看了吗？"我问。

"是的，"他回答。

"有一天，我来到卡姆诺大街。我实在忍不住，这种疑惑折磨着我。敲门后，一位文雅漂亮的女士打开门。我问是否有房子出租。'嗯，先生，'她说。'客厅本来是租出去了，但我已经有三个多月没看见那位夫人了，房租又是欠着的，您可以租用。''是这位夫人吗？'我说着，拿出照片给她看。'就是她，'她大声说，'她什么时候回来，先生？''她去世了，'我说。'哦，先生。不会吧？'那个女人说，'她是我最好的房客。她每星期付给我三基尼，只是偶尔到我这客厅坐一会儿。''她来这儿是见什么人吗？'我问，那女人很确信地说，不是。她总是一个人来，没见别人。'那她到底来这儿做什么？'我大声问。'她只是坐在客厅看看书，有时候喝喝茶，先生，'那女人回答说。我不知道该说什么，我给了她一个金币（值一英镑），就离开了。现在，你觉得这意味着什么？你不相信那个女人说的是真的？"

"我相信。"

"可为什么阿罗瑞夫人去那里呢?"

"我亲爱的杰尔拉德,"我说,"阿罗瑞夫人只不过是一个有神秘感癖好的女人。她戴上面纱到那些房间去只是为了感受愉悦的心情,想象自己是女主人公。她对秘密有瘾,其实她自己只是一个没有秘密的斯芬克斯。"

"你真是这么认为的吗?"

"我肯定,"我回答说。

他拿出那个羊皮夹子,打开,看着里面的照片,最后说:"我还是不明白?"

Joseph Rudyard Kipling
(1865—1936)

Joseph Rudyard Kipling, English short story writer, poet, and novelist, was born in Bombay, India. He was sent to school in England at six like most children of English citizens living in India. But he was not happy in his foster home. His experience there played an important part in his literary imagination. He had better experiences at a military training school where he was a student beginning in 1878. When he returned to India in 1882, he worked as a newspaper reporter and a part-time writer. This helped him to gain rich experience of colonial life which he later described in his stories and poems. Death of both his children left a profound impression on his life which was displayed in his works published in the following years. Between 1919 and 1932 he traveled intermittently, and continued to publish stories, poems, sketches and historical works. As he grew older, his works displayed his preoccupation with physical and psychological strain, breakdown, and recovery. He passed away due to illness, leaving behind a legacy that would live for the following centuries.

Kipling was chiefly remembered for his celebration of British imperialism, his tales and poems of British soldiers in India, and his tales for children. He was famous for volumes of stories, beginning with *Plain Tales from the Hills* (1888), and later for the poetry collection *Barrack-Room Ballads* (1892). His poems, often strongly rhythmic, were frequently narrative ballads. During a residence in the U.S., he published a novel, *The Light That Failed* (1890), two *Jungle Books* (1894, 1895), stories of the wild boy Mowgli in the Indian jungle that had become children's classics, the adventure story *Captains Courageous* (1897), and *Kim* (1901), one of the great novels of India. He wrote six other volumes of short stories and several other verse collections. His children's books include the famous *Just So Stories* (1902) and the fairy-tale collection *Puck of Pook's Hill* (1906). He was awarded the Nobel Prize for Literature in 1907.

The Limitations of Pambé Serang

The following is a story of a determined revenge. Stoker Nurkeed eats Pambé Serang's food and stabs him in the leg when Nurkeed is drunk. Pambé waits an unusually long time for the opportunity to revenge. He waits at Nyanza Docks, a busy port for Nurkeed despite his poverty from giving up his lascar career. At the end, the revenge is taken and Pambé is hanged. Different characteristics such as Pambé's extremity, Nurkeed's simple-mindedness and the kind gentleman's naivety are depicted and contrasted in the story.

If you consider the circumstances of the case, it was the only thing that he could do. But Pambé Serang has been hanged by the neck till he is dead, and Nurkeed is dead also.

Three years ago, when the Elsass-Lothringen steamer *Saarbruck* was coaling at Aden and the weather was very hot indeed, Nurkeed, the big fat Zanzibar stoker who fed the second right furnace thirty feet down in the hold, got leave to go ashore. He departed a "Seedee boy", as they call the stokers; he returned the full-blooded sultan of Zanzibar—His Highness Sayyid Burgash, with a bottle in each hand. Then he sat on the fore-hatch grating, eating salt fish and onions, and singing the songs of a far country. The food belonged to Pambé, the Serang or head man of the lascar sailors. He had just cooked it for himself, turned to borrow some salt, and when he came back Nurkeed's dirty black fingers were spading into the rice.

A Serang is a person of importance, far above a stoker, though the stoker draws better pay. He sets the chorus of "Hya! Hulla! Hee-ah! Heh!" when the captain's gig is pulled up to the davits; he heaves the lead too; and sometimes, when all the ship is lazy, he puts on his whitest muslin and a big red sash, and plays with the passengers' children on the quarter-deck. Then the passengers give him money, and he saves it all up for an orgy at Bombay or Calcutta, or Pulu Penang.

"Ho! You fat black barrel, you're eating my food!" said Pambé, in the other lingua franca that begins where the Levant tongue stops, and runs from Port Said eastward till east is west, and the sealing-brigs of the Kurile Islands gossip with the strayed Hakodate junks.

"Son of Eblis, monkey-face, dried shark's liver, pig-man, I am the sultan Sayyid Burgash and the commander of all this ship. Take away your garbage," and Nurkeed thrust the empty pewter rice-plate into Pambé's hand.

Pambé beat it into a basin over Nurkeed's woolly head. Nurkeed drew his sheath-knife and stabbed Pambé in the leg. Pambé drew his sheath-knife; but Nurkeed dropped down into the darkness of the hold and spat through the grating at Pambé, who was staining the clean fore-deck with his blood.

Only the white moon saw these things; for the officers were looking after the coaling, and the passengers were tossing in their close cabins. "All right," said Pambé—and went forward to tie up his leg— "we will settle the account later on."

He was a Malay born in India: married once in Burma, where his wife had a cigar-shop on the Shwe-Dagon road; once in Singapore, to a Chinese girl; and once in Madras, to a Mohammedan woman who sold fowls. The English sailor cannot, owing to postal and telegraph facilities, marry as profusely as he used to do; but native sailors can, being uninfluenced by the barbarous inventions of the Western savage. Pambé was a good husband when he happened to remember the existence of a wife; but he was also a very good Malay; and it is not wise to offend a Malay, because he does not forget anything. Moreover, in Pambé's case blood had been drawn and food spoiled.

Next morning Nurkeed rose with a blank mind. He was no longer Sultan of Zanzibar, but a very hot stoker. So he went on deck and opened his jacket to the morning breeze, till a sheath-knife came like a flying-fish and stuck into the woodwork of the cook's galley half an inch from his right armpit. He ran down below before his time, trying to remember what he could have said to the owner of the weapon. At noon, when all the ship's lascars were feeding, Nurkeed advanced into their midst, and being a placid man with a large regard for his own skin, he opened negotiations, saying, "Men of the ship, last night I was drunk, and this morning I know that I behaved unseemly to someone or another of you. Who was that man, that I may meet him face to face and say that I was drunk?"

Pambé measured the distance to Nurkeed's naked breast. If he sprang at him he might be tripped up, and a blind blow at the chest sometimes only means a gash on the breast-bone. Ribs are difficult to thrust between unless the subject be asleep. So he said nothing; nor did the other lascars. Their faces immediately dropped all expression, as is the custom of the Oriental when there is killing on the carpet or any chance of trouble. Nurkeed looked long at the white eyeballs. He was only an African, and could not read characters. A big sigh—almost a groan—broke from him, and he went back to the furnaces. The lascars took up the conversation where he had interrupted it. They talked of the best methods of cooking rice.

Nurkeed suffered considerably from lack of fresh air during the run to Bombay. He only came on deck to breathe when all the world was about; and even then a heavy block one dropped from a derrick within a foot of his head, and an apparently firm-lashed grating on which he set his foot began to turn over with the intention of dropping him on the cased cargo fifteen feet below; and one insupportable night the sheath-knife dropped from the fo'c's'le, and this time it drew blood. So Nurkeed made complaint; and, when the *Saarbruck* reached Bombay, fled and buried himself among eight hundred thousand people, and did not sign articles till the ship had been a month gone from the port. Pambé waited too; but his Bombay wife grew clamorous, and he was forced to sign in the *Spicheren* to Hongkong, because he realized that all play and no work gives Jack a ragged shirt. In the foggy China seas he thought a great deal of Nurkeed, and, when Elsass-Lothringen steamers lay in port with the *Spicheren*, enquired after him and found he had gone to England via the Cape, on the *Graveloyte*. Pambé came to England on the *Worth*. The *Spicheren* met her by the Nore Light. Nurkeed was going out with the *Spicheren* to the Calicut coast.

"Want to find a friend, my trap-mouthed coal-scuttle?" said a gentleman in the mercantile service. "Nothing easier. Wait at the Nyanza Docks till he comes. Everyone comes to the Nyaza Docks. Wait, you poor heathen." The gentleman spoke truth. There are three great doors in the world where, if you stand long enough, you shall meet anyone you wish. The head of Suez Canal is one; but there Death comes also; Charing Cross Station is the second—for inland wok; and the Nyana Docks is the third. At each of these places are men and women looking eternally for those who will surely come. So Pambé waited at the docks. Time was no object to him; and the wives could wait, as he did from day to day, week to week, and month to month, by the Blue Diamond funnels, the Red Dot smoke-stacks, the Yellow Streaks, and the nameless dingy gypsies of the sea that loaded and unloaded, jostled, whistled, and roared in the everlasting fog. When money failed, a kind gentleman told Pambé to become a Christian; and Pambé became one with great speed, getting his religious teachings between ship and ship's arrival and six or seven shillings a week for distributing tracts to mariners. What the faith was Pambé did not in the least care; but he knew if he said "Native Ki-lis-tian, Sar" to men with long black coasts he might get a few coppers; and the tracts were vendible at a little public-house that sold shag by the "dottle", which is even smaller weight than the "half-screw", which is less than the half-ounce, and a most profitable retail trade.

But after eight month Pambé fell sick with pneumonia, contacted from long standing still in slush; and much against his will he was forced to lie down in his two-and-sixpenny room raging against Fate.

The kind gentleman sat by his bedside, and grieved to find that Pambé talked in strange tongues, instead of listening to good books, and almost seemed to become a benighted heathen again—till one day he was roused from semi-stupor by a voice in the street by the dock-head. "My friend—he," whispered Pambé, "Call now—call Nurkeed. Quick! God has sent him!"

"He wanted one of his own race," said the kind gentleman; and, going out, he called "Nurkeed!" at the top of his voice. An excessively coloured man in a rasping white shirt and brand-new slops, a shining hat and a breast-pin, turned around. Many voyages had taught Nurkeed how to spend his money and made him a citizen of the world.

"Hi! Yes!" said he, when the situation was explained. "Command him—black nigger—when I was in the *Saarbuck*. Ole, Pambé, good ole Pambé. Damn lascar. Show him up, Sar," and he followed into the room. One glance told the stoker what the kind gentleman had overlooked. Pambé was desperately poor. Nurkeed drove his hands deep into his pockets, then advanced with clenched fists on the sick, shouting, "Hya, Pambé. Hya! Hee-ah! Hulla! Heh! Taliko! Taliko! Make fast aft, Pambé. You know, Pambé. You know me. Dekho, jee! Look! Damn big fat lazy lascar!"

Pambé beckoned with his left hand. His right was under his pillow. Nurkeed removed his gorgeous hat and stooped over Pambé till he could catch a faint whisper "How beautiful!" said the kind gentleman. "How these Orientals love like children!"

"Spit him out," said Nurkeed, leaning over Pambé yet more closely.

"Touching the matter of that fish and onions—" said Pa Pambé—and sent the knife home under the edge of the rib-bone upwards and forwards.

There was a thick sick cough, and the body of the African slid slowly from the bed, his clutching hand letting fall a shower of silver pieces that ran across the room.

"Now I can die!" said Pambé.

But he did not die. He was nursed back to life with all the skill that money could buy, for the Law wanted him; and in the end he grew sufficiently healthy to be hanged in due and proper form.

Pambé did not care particularly; but it was a sad blow to the kind gentleman.

Questions

1. What does the author imply by saying "it was the only thing he could do" in paragraph 1?

2. Describe the author's view on the Orientals.
3. Why is it that "it was a sad blow to the kind gentleman" in the last paragraph?
4. Describe Pambé's personality.
5. How are the Orientals contrasted with the "kind gentleman?" Are they representative of the races or are they biased portrayals?

约瑟夫·鲁德亚德·吉卜林
（1865—1936）

英国短篇小说家、诗人兼长篇小说家约瑟夫·鲁德亚德·吉卜林生于印度孟买。像大多数居住在印度的英国公民一样，他在六岁时被送去英国的学校读书。但他在寄养家庭里并不快乐。他的这些经历在他后来的文学想象中起了很大的作用。他从1878年起在一所军事训练学校读书，那里的生活更快乐一些。1882年回到印度之后，他成为一名记者和兼职作家。这期间他对殖民地的生活有了更丰富的感受，这在他后来的小说和诗歌中都有所体现。他的两个孩子的早逝极大地影响了他的生活，这体现在其随后几年的作品中。1919年到1932年间，他断断续续地旅行并继续发表小说、诗歌、随笔和历史著作。随着年龄渐长，他的作品展现了对身体和心理压力、崩溃和康复的关注。他因病去世，留下的丰富文学遗产在此后的几个世纪里经久不衰。

吉卜林的作品颂扬了大英帝国，并以描写驻印度的英国士兵的故事和诗歌以及儿童故事而闻名。他先是以几部短篇小说集闻名，其中最早的一部是《山间的简单故事》（1888），此后又有诗集《巴拉可房间民谣》（1892）出版。他的诗通常很有节奏感，多是叙事民谣。在旅居美国期间他发表了小说《未能点亮的灯》（1890），两部《丛林故事》（1894，1895），故事描述了野男孩牟哥利在印度丛林的经历，已成为儿童文学的经典。同时他还发表了《勇气船长》（1897）和《吉姆》（1901），其中《吉姆》是有关印度的最著名的小说之一。他的作品还包括六部短篇小说集和其他几部诗集。他的儿童文学作品包括著名的《如此故事》（1902）和童话集《普克山的顽童》（1906）。吉卜林于1907年获得诺贝尔文学奖。

潘贝·赛朗的局限

下面是一篇誓死复仇的故事。司炉工努尔凯埃德喝醉了酒，吃了潘贝的食物并刺伤了潘贝的腿。潘贝为了报复等待了很长时间。尽管由于放弃了水手的工作一贫如洗，潘贝还是在繁忙的尼安萨码头等待报复努尔凯埃德。最后，潘贝终于报了仇，而他也被绞死。故事刻画了不同人物的性格特点，如潘贝的极端，努尔凯埃德的头脑简单，以及和蔼绅士的天真等。

如果你考虑到这件事的具体经过，就知道这是他唯一的选择。潘贝·赛朗被处以绞刑，一命呜呼，努尔凯埃德也死了。

三年前，从阿尔萨斯·洛林来的轮船撒布拉克号在亚丁装煤的时候，天儿热得很。桑给巴尔岛人大胖子努尔凯埃德，这个掌管三十英尺底舱下右边第二个锅炉的司炉工，请假上了岸。他离开时还是一个"西地男孩"——人们都这么叫司炉工，回来时就变成了血统纯正的桑给巴尔之王——至高无上的赛义德·博戈什，一手拿一瓶酒。然后坐在舱口的隔栅上一边吃咸鱼和洋葱一边哼着异国的小曲儿。他吃的这些是潘贝的，潘贝是这些东印度水手的赛朗，也就是他们的头儿。潘贝刚给自己弄好了吃的，出去借点儿盐，回来时却发现努尔凯埃德又脏又黑的手指正伸到米饭里。

赛朗是很重要的人物，比司炉工重要得多，尽管司炉工挣得更多。当船长的快艇被拉上吊艇柱的时候，赛朗领头喊号子"嘿呀！呼啦！嘿啊！嘿！"他也投水砣测水的深度。有时候，当船上不忙的时候，他就穿上最白的平纹细布衣服，披上红色大肩带，到后甲板上跟旅客的孩子们玩儿。旅客会给他一点儿钱，他就攒起来留着到孟买、加尔各答或槟城痛快地喝一顿。

"嘿！你这个胖黑桶，你在吃我的东西！"潘贝嚷道，他的话是很多方言的混合语，刚说完赖凡特方言，又从赛德港往东一直说到东边变成了西边，同时混杂着千岛群岛帆船和漂泊着的日本函馆的舢板上的流言蜚语。

"恶魔的龟儿子，猴子脸，风干的鲨鱼肝，蠢猪，我就是国王赛义德·博戈什，是这艘船的头儿。拿走你的垃圾。"努尔凯埃德把空的白镴盘子塞到潘贝手里。

潘贝把盘子扔了过去，盘子越过努尔凯埃德毛茸茸的脑袋上方，掉进了盆里。于是努尔凯埃德抽出刀刺进潘贝的腿里。潘贝也拔出了刀，而努尔凯埃德这时却钻进了黑洞洞的底舱里，隔着隔栅冲潘贝吐口水，潘贝的血弄脏了干净的前甲板。

只有白色的月亮看到了这一切，当官的都去看着装煤去了，旅客们也在狭小的船舱里翻来覆去。"好吧，"潘贝边说边去包扎他的腿去了，"以后再找你算账。"

潘贝是马来人，出生在印度；曾在缅甸结过一次婚，老婆在施伟-道根路上开着一家雪茄店；曾在新加坡结过一次婚，老婆是个中国姑娘；曾在马德拉斯结过一次婚，老婆是个卖家禽的穆斯林。由于有邮政和电报设施，英国水手就不能像以前那样到处结婚，但是本地的水手却能，因为他们不受那些西方野蛮人的野蛮发明所影响。当潘贝偶尔记起老婆时他是个好丈夫，但他也是一个好马来人；惹怒马来人可不是个聪明的举动，因为马来人记得一切事儿，更何况，就潘贝而言，已经见血了，吃的也被糟蹋了。

第二天早晨，努尔凯埃德起床后头脑一片空白，他再也不是桑给巴尔的国王，而是一个燥热的司炉工。他来到甲板上，迎着晨风敞开了外套，直到一把刀像飞鱼一样飞过来，从离他右腋窝半英寸的地方擦过，插进了厨房的木头墙里。他还没到上班时间就下到底舱了，努力地想记起自己曾对这武器的主人说过什么话。中午水手们吃饭的时候，努尔凯埃德走过去，因为意识到自己的肤色而十分平和地用商量的口吻说道："水手们，昨儿晚上我喝醉了，今天早上我才知道我对某个人或者你们当中的一位做了不该做的事，那个人是谁？我愿意跟他面对面，说我喝醉了。"

潘贝约莫了一下到努尔凯埃德裸露的胸膛的距离，如果他跳起来扑向他可能会被绊倒，向他的胸前随便一击也只能把胸骨打出一个裂缝，从两根肋骨之间刺进去也很不容易，除非在对方睡着的时候。所以他什么也没说，别的水手也没说什么。他们的脸立刻毫无表情，就像发生了地毯上的谋杀案或其他麻烦时东方人惯常的做法一样。努尔凯埃德盯着那些白眼球看了半天，他只是个非洲人，不识字。他发出了一声叹息——几乎是呻吟——回到了锅炉那里。水手们继续刚才被打断的谈话，议论着什么方法做米饭最好吃。

在去孟买的途中努尔凯埃德严重缺乏新鲜空气，只有甲板上没人的时候他才出来透透气，就在那时候起重机上掉下来一件重物从离他的头不到一英尺的地方落下来，并且一个看上去很结实的隔栅在他一踩上去就翻转过来，目的是要把他扔到15英尺下的密封货舱里去；在一个莫名其妙的晚上，一把匕首从前甲板掉下来，这次见血了。所以努尔凯埃德一直抱怨。撒布拉克号一到孟买努尔凯埃德就逃上了岸把自己淹没在八万人中，直到这艘船离开一个月后才又签了另一艘船。潘贝也在等待，但是他的孟买老婆越闹越凶，他只好与到香港的斯皮彻伦号签了合同，因为他意识到光玩乐不工作只能穿破衬衫。在雾气笼罩的中国海域他念念不忘努尔凯埃德。当从阿尔萨斯·洛林来的轮船跟斯皮彻伦号一起停在港口的时候，他向船上的人问起努尔凯埃德，得知他已经跟格拉拜洛特号经好望角到英国去了，潘贝就跟沃斯号到了英国。斯皮彻伦号在诺尔赖特遇见了沃斯号，努尔凯埃德正跟着斯皮彻伦号到卡利卡特海岸。

"想找朋友吗，深嘴煤斗？"一位商务部门的绅士问他。"没有比这再简单的了。在尼安萨码头等他。人人都到尼安萨码头来，等着吧，可怜的异教徒。"这位绅士说的是实话。世界上有三个大门，如果你在门边站得足够长，就能见到任何你想见到的人。苏伊士运河的头是一个，但是那也是死神光顾的地方；查林十字车站是第二个——是内陆门户；尼安萨码头就是第三个。在上述的任何一个地方都有男人女人在长久地等待那些一定会来的人。所以潘贝就在码头等着。时间对他不是问题，老婆们也可以等待，于是他日复一日，周复一周，月复一月地等着，等来了蓝宝石的船烟囱，等来了红斑点的大烟囱，等来了黄条船，等来了不知名的衣衫褴褛的海上吉普赛人，装货又卸货，在永不散去的雾气里推搡着，吹着口哨，咆哮着。后来钱花光了，一位和蔼的绅士劝潘贝成为基督徒，他就以惊人的速度成了一名基督徒，在船与船到来的间隙里接受传教，靠给海员们发传单一星期领上六七个先令。潘贝丝毫不关心他的信仰是什么，但是他知道只要他对那些穿着黑色长大衣的男人说："本地的'交'督徒，先生"，他就能拿到几个铜板。在一家卖劣质残烟丝的酒馆这些传单很畅销，因为它比小纸卷还轻，半盎司还不到，所以是挺赚钱的小买卖。

但是八个月后潘贝得了肺炎病倒了，这病是长时间站在烂泥地里得的，他极不情愿地躺在他那间2先令6便士的出租屋里跟命运怄气。

那位好心的绅士坐在他的床边，很伤心地发现潘贝胡言乱语，不再听《圣经》的教诲，好像又变成了愚昧的异教徒——直到有一天码头方向传来的一个声音把他从半昏迷中叫醒。"我的朋友——他，"潘贝耳语道，"快叫他——叫努尔凯埃德。快！上帝已经把他送来了！"

"他想见自己人，"那位和蔼的绅士说着就出去了，扯开嗓子喊到，"努尔凯埃德！"一个很黑的男人出现了，穿着嚓嚓作响的白衬衫，崭新的外套，闪亮的帽子，还戴着个胸针。多次的航海已经教会努尔凯埃德怎样花钱把自己打扮成一个世界公民。

"嗨，是的！"听完绅士的解释，努尔凯埃德说。"他是头儿——黑鬼——那是我在撒布拉克号上的时候。好样的潘贝，好人潘贝。该死的水手。带我去见他，先生。"他就跟那位绅士进了屋。只一眼，司炉工就看出了那位和蔼的绅士所忽略的事实，潘贝穷困潦倒。努尔凯埃德把手深深地伸进口袋里，然后握着拳头走向病人潘贝，嚷道："嘿呀！呼啦！嘿啊！嘿！特基洛！特基洛！船尾快点，潘贝。你认识，潘贝。你认识我。德克霍，嘿！看！该死的大胖子懒水手！"

潘贝招了招左手，右手在枕头底下。努尔凯埃德摘下他的大帽子弯腰伏向潘贝以便能听清楚他微弱的耳语。"多美啊！"和蔼的绅士叹道，"这些东方人像孩子一样相爱！"

"大声说，"努尔凯埃德说着更凑近一些。

"关于鱼和洋葱那件事——"潘贝说着——同时把刀沿着肋骨的边缘向上向前猛插进去。

随着病人大声地咳嗽，这个非洲人的身体沿着床边慢慢滑下来，紧握着的手松开了，一大把银币纷纷落下，滚得满屋都是。

"现在我可以死了！"潘贝说。

但是他并没有死，而是被各种用钱能买到的办法救活了，因为法律需要他；最后，他健康到足以在适当的时候以适当的形式被绞死。

这个结果潘贝并不在乎，但是对那位和蔼的绅士却是一个伤心的打击。

John Galsworthy
(1867—1933)

John Galsworthy is an English novelist and playwright, winner of the Nobel Prize for Literature in 1932. He is well known for his portrayal of the British upper middle class and for his social satire. His most famous work is *The Forsyte Saga* trilogy (1906—1928). Galsworthy is a representative of the literary tradition which regards the novel as a lawful instrument of social propaganda. He believes that it is the duty of an artist to state a problem, to throw light upon it, but not to provide a solution.

John Galsworthy was born in Kingston Hill, Surrey, into an upper-middle-class family. He studied law at Harrow and New College, Oxford. However, his favorite authors were Thackeray, Dickens, and Melville, and his favorite composer was Beethoven. In 1893 he met the writer Joseph Conrad on a South Sea voyage. This meeting convinced him to give up law and become a writer. He married Ada Person Cooper in 1905. She became the inspiration for many of Galsworthy's female characters. *The Man of Property* (1906) established Galsworthy's reputation as an important writer. He also gained recognition as a dramatist with his plays that dealt directly with the unequal division of wealth and the unfair treatment of poor people, such as *The Silver Box* (1906), *Strife* (1909) and *Justice* (1910).

Compensation

The following story tells about a youth called Tchuk–Tchuk who makes money very carefully and seriously in order to go back to his hometown to find his girlfriend. Unfortunately, on the eve before his departure, all his money is robbed while he is drunk and asleep. The story exposes the evils of unfairness, greed and unscrupulousness of the society.

If, as you say (said Ferrand), there is compensation in this life for everything, do tell me where it comes in here.

Two years ago I was interpreter to an hotel in Ostend, and spent many hours on the Plage waiting for the steamers to bring sheep to my slaughter. There was a young man about that year who had a stall of cheap jewellery; I don't know his name, for among us he was called Tchuk-Tchuk; but I knew him—for we interpreters know everybody. He came from Southern Italy and called himself an Italian, but by birth he was probably an Algerian Jew; an intelligent boy, who knew that, except in England, it is far from profitable to be a Jew in these days. After seeing his nose and his beautiful head of frizzly hair, however, there was little more to be said on the subjects. His clothes had been given him by an English tourist—a pair of flannel trousers, an old frock coat, a bowler hat. Incongruous? Yes, but think, how cheap! The only thing that looked natural to him was his tie; he had unsewn the ends and wore it without a collar. He was little and thin which was not surprising, for all he ate a day was half a pound of bread, or its equivalent in macaronis, with a little piece of cheese, and on a feast day a bit of sausage. In those clothes, which were made for a fat man, he had the appearance of a scarecrow with a fine, large head. The conditions of life down there being impossible, they are driven out like locusts or the old inhabitants of Central Asia—a regular invasion. In every country they have a kind of Society which helps them to make a start. When once provided with organs, jewellery, or whatever their profession, they live on nothing, drink nothing, spend no money. Smoke? Yes, they smoke; but you have to give them the tobacco. Sometimes they bring their women; more often they come alone—they make money more quickly without. The end they have in view is to scrape together a treasure of two or three hundred pounds and go back to Italy rich men. If you're accustomed to the Italian at home, it will astonish you to see how he works when he's out of his own country, and how provident he is— Tchuk-Tchuk was alone, and he worked like a slave. He was at his stand, day in, day out; if the sun burned, if there was a gale; he was often wet through, but no one could pass without receiving a smile from his teeth and a hand stretched out with some gimcrack or other. He always tried to impress the women, with whom he did most of his business—especially the cocotterie. Ah! how he looked at them with his great eyes! Temperamentally, I dare say, he was vicious enough; but, as you know, it costs money to be vicious, and he spent no money. His expenses were twopence a day for food and fourpence for his bed in a café full of other birds of his feather—sixpence a day, three shillings and sixpence a week. No other sort of human creature can keep this up long. My minimum is tenpence, which is not a bed of roses, but, then, I can't do without tobacco (to a man in extreme poverty a single vice is indispensable). But these "Italians" do without even that. Tchuk-Tchuk sold; not very hard work, you say? Try it for half an hour; try and sell something good—and Tchuk-Tchuk's things were rubbish—flash coral jewellery, Italian enamels made up into pins and brooches, celluloid gimcracks. In the evenings I've often seen him doze off from sheer fatigue, but always with his eyes half-open, like a cat. His soul was in his stall; he watched everything—but only to sell his precious goods, for nothing interested him; he despised all the world around him—the people, the sea, the amusements; they were ridiculous and foreign. He had his stall, and lived to sell. He was like a man shut up in a box—with not a pleasure, not a sympathy, nothing wherewith to touch this strange world in which he found himself.

"I'm of the South," he would say to me, jerking his head at the sea; "it's hard there. Over there I got a girl. She wouldn't be sorry to see me again; not too sorry! Over there one starves; name of a Saint" (he chose this form of oath, no doubt, because it sounded Christian), "it's hard there!"

I am not sentimental about Tchuk-Tchuk; he was an egoist to the bottom of his soul, but that did not in the least prevent his suffering for the want of his South, for the want of his sunshine, and his girl—the greater the egoism the greater the suffering. He craved like a dumb animal; but, as he remarked, "Over there one starves!" Naturally he had not waited for that. He had his hopes. "Wait a bit!" he used to say. "Last year I was in Brussels. Bad business! At the end they take away all my money for the Society, and give me this stall. This is all right—I make some money this season."

He had many clients among "women of morals", who had an eye for his beautiful head of hair, who know, too, that life is not all roses, and there was something pathetic in the persistency of Tchuck-Tchuck and the way his clothes hung about him like sacks, nor was he bad-looking, with his great black eyes and his slim, dirty hands.

One wet day I came on the Estacade when hardly a soul was there. Tchuck-Tchuck had covered his stall with a piece of old tarpaulin. He was smoking a long cigar.

"Aha! Tchuck-Tchuck," I said, "smoking?"

"Yes," says he, "it's good!"

"Why not smoke every day, you miser? It would comfort you when you're hungry."

He shook his head. "Costs money," says he. "This one cost me nothing. A kind of an individual gave it me—a red-faced Englishman—said he couldn't smoke it. He knew nothing, the idiot—this is good, I tell you!"

But it was Tchuck-Tchuck who knew nothing—he had been too long without the means of knowledge. It was interesting to see the way he ate, drank, inhaled, and soaked up that rank cigar—a true revel of sensuality.

The end of the season came, and all of us birds who prey on the visitors were getting ready to fly, but I stayed on, because I liked the place—the gay-coloured houses, the smell of fish in the port, the good air, the long green seas, the dunes; there's something of it all in my blood, and I'm always sorry to leave. But after the season is over—as Tchuck-Tchuck would say—"Name of a saint—one starves over there!"

One evening, at the very end, when there were scarcely twenty visitors in the place, I went as usual to a certain café, with two compartments, where everybody comes whose way of living is dubious—bullies, comedians, off-colour actresses, women of morals, "Turks," "Italians," "Greeks"—all such, in fact, as play the game of stealing—a regular rag-shop of cheats and gentlemen of industry—very interesting people, with whom I am well acquainted. Nearly everyone had gone; so that evening there were but few of us in the restaurant, and in the inner room three Italians only. I passed into that.

Presently in came Tchuk-Tchuk, the first time I had ever seen him in a place where one could spend a little money. How thin he was, with his little body and his great head! One would have said he hadn't eaten for a week. A week? A year! Down he sat, and called for a bottle of wine; and at once he began to chatter and snap his fingers.

"Ha, ha!" says one of the Italians; "look at Tchuk-Tchuk. What a nightingale he has become all of a sudden. Come, Tchuk-Tchuk, give us some of your wine, seeing you're in luck!"

Tchuk-Tchuk gave us of his wine, and ordered another bottle.

"Ho, ho!" says another Italian, "must have buried his family, this companion!" We drank—Tchuk-Tchuk faster than all. Do you know that sort of thirst, when you drink just to give you the feeling of having blood in the veins at all? Most people in that state can't stop—they drink themselves dead drunk. Tchuk-Tchuk was not like that. He was careful, as always, looking to his future. Oh! he kept his heart in hand, but in such cases a little goes a long way, he became cheerful—it doesn't take much to make an Italian cheerful who has been living for months on water and half-rations of bread and macaroni. It was evident, too, that he had reason to feel gay. He sang and laughed, and the other Italians sang and laughed with him. One of them said: "It seems our Tchuk-Tchuk has been doing good business. Come, Tchuk-Tchuk, tell us what you have made this season!"

But Tchuk-Tchuk only shook his head.

"Eh!" said the Italian, "the shy bird. It ought to be something good. As for me, comrades, honestly, five hundred francs is all I've made—not a centime more—and the half of that goes to the patron."

And each of them began talking of his gains, except Tchuk-Tchuk, who showed his teeth, and kept silence.

"Come, Tchuk-Tchuk," said one, "don't be a bandit—a little frankness!"

"He won't beat my sixteen hundred!" said another.

"Name of a Saint!" said Tchuk-Tchuk suddenly, "what do you say to four thousand?"

But we all laughed.

"La la!" said one, "he mocks us!"

Tchuk-Tchuk opened the front of his old frock coat.

"Look!" he cried, and he pulled out four bills—each for a thousand francs. How we stared!

"See," said he, "what it is to be careful—I spend nothing—every cent is here! Now I go home—I get my girl; wish me good journey!" He set to work again to snap his fingers.

We stayed some time and drank another bottle, Tchuk-Tchuk paying. When we parted nobody was helpless, only, as I say, Tchuk-Tchuk on the road to the stars, as one is after a six months' fast. The next morning I was drinking a "bock" in the same café, for there was nothing else to do, when all of a sudden who should come running in but this same Tchuk-Tchuk. Ah! but he was no longer on the road to the stars. He flung himself down at the table, with his head between his hands, and the tears rolled down his cheeks.

"They've robbed me," he cried, "robbed me of every sou; robbed me while I slept. I had it here, under my pillow; I slept on it; it's gone—every sou!" He beat his breast.

"Come, Tchuk-Tchuk," said I, "from under your pillow? That's not possible!"

"How do I know?" he groaned; "it's gone I tell you—all my money, all my money. I was heavy with the wine—" All he could do was to repeat again and again: "All my money, all my money!"

"Have you been to the police?"

He had been to the police. I tried to console him, but without much effect, as you may imagine. The boy was beside himself.

The police did nothing—why should they? If he had been a Rothschild it would have been different, but seeing he was only a poor devil of an Italian who had lost his all—!

Tchuk-Tchuk had sold his stall, his stock, everything he had, the day before, so he had not even the money for a ticket to Brussels. He was obliged to walk. He started—and to this day I see him starting, with his little hard hat on his beautiful black hair, and the unsewn ends of his tie. His face was like the face of the Devil thrown out of Eden!

What became of him I cannot say, but I do not see too clearly in all this the compensation of which you have been speaking.

And Ferrand was silent.

Questions

1. What is your first impression of Tchuk-Tchuk?
2. What happened to Tchuk-Tchuk in the story?
3. What is your last impression of Tchuk-Tchuk?
4. What is the meaning of "compensation" in your view?
5. What do you learn from this story?

约翰·高尔斯华绥
（1867—1933）

约翰·高尔斯华绥是英国小说家、剧作家，1932年诺贝尔文学奖获得者。他以描写英国中上阶层和社会讽刺而著名。他的最著名作品是小说三部曲《福尔赛世家》（1906—1928）。高尔斯华绥所代表的文学传统把小说看作是社会宣传的合法工具。他认为艺术家的责任是指出问题、解释问题，而并非提供解决办法。

高尔斯华绥出生于萨里郡金斯敦一个中上阶层家庭。他就读哈罗公学，后在牛津大学新学院学习法律。但他最喜欢的作家是萨克雷、狄更斯和麦尔维尔，最喜欢的作曲家是贝多芬。1893年，他在南海航海期间与约瑟夫·康拉德相会。这使得他放弃法律决定当作家。1905年他与艾达·帕森·库珀结婚。艾达成为高尔斯华绥创作许多女性人物的灵感。《有产者》（1906）奠定了高尔斯华绥作为重要作家的地位。他在戏剧方面也获得了名声，其剧作如《银盒子》（1906）、《斗争》（1909）以及《正义》（1910），直接揭露了财富分配的不平等和对待穷人的不公。

补 偿

下面的故事讲述了一个叫朱克-朱克的年轻人。他小心翼翼认真赚钱，为的是回国找回自己的女朋友。不幸的是，就在他启程回家的前一天晚上，他所有的钱都在自己醉酒酣睡之际被盗。故事揭露了社会的不公、贪婪、不择手段等丑恶现象。

像你说的（费兰德说），如果今世的每件事都有补偿，那么请告诉我以下这件事是如何补偿的。

两年前，我曾在奥斯坦德一家旅社做翻译，在那儿的海滨等着温顺如羔羊的游客下船叫我宰。有一年来了一个年轻人，他有一货摊不值钱的珠宝。我不知道他叫什么，但我们都叫他朱克-朱克。我认识他——我们做翻译的谁都认识。他来自意大利南部，虽称自己是意大利人，但出身大概是阿尔及利亚犹太人。他是个聪明的男孩，知道这年头做一个犹太人不是一件什么有利可图之事，当然在英国除外。看了他的鼻子和漂亮的卷曲的头发，就知道他差不多是个犹太人了。

他的衣服是一个英国游客给的——一条法兰绒裤子，一件旧双排扣礼服，一顶硬礼帽。不协调吗？是啊，但仔细想想，多便宜！他唯一一件看起来自然的东西就是领带。他系着毛边的领带，却没穿带衣领的衬衣。他又瘦又小，这并不奇怪，因为他一天只吃半磅面包或半磅通心面加一点奶酪，开荤的那天外加一点香肠。穿上那些为胖人制作的衣服，他看起来就像一个有着细长大头的稻草人。底层的生活条件令人难以忍受，他们就像是飞蝗或中亚的土著一样被赶来赶去——一种司空见惯的入侵。每个国家都有那么个同乡会能帮助他们做点事。一旦有了风琴、珠宝，或无论什么职业，他们就可以一无所有地过活，不喝酒、不花钱。抽烟吗？是的，他们抽，但你得给他们烟丝。有时他们会带女人来，但更多时候他会独自来——不带女人他们赚钱更快。他们的目的是要赚二三百英镑后回意大利，成为有钱人。如果你熟悉意大利人在本国的生活方式，你会惊奇地发现他们在国外是如何工作的，真是深谋远虑啊——朱克-朱克就是只身一人，他像个奴隶拼命干活。他日复一日地干活，不管烈日炎炎还是狂风暴雨。他经常浑身湿透，却咧嘴面带微笑，手里拿着廉价纪念品或其他什么东西，从不放过一位游客。他总是试图讨好女人，东西主要卖给她们——尤其是妓女。啊！他睁着大眼睛盯着这些妓女！我敢说他禀性淫秽，但你知道那可是要花钱的，可他不花。他的开销是每天吃东西花两便士，租一张廉价床位花四便士，他和自己的同胞挤在一家小餐馆里——一天六便士，三先令六便士一周。其他任何人这么样都不能坚持长久。我最少要花十便士，这点钱当然不舒服，但我不能不抽烟（即便再穷，抽烟这一项恶习还是允许的）。但这些意大利人甚至连烟都不抽。朱克-朱克卖东西。你可能会问，工作不太辛苦吧？你去试试卖半个钟头，卖些好东西——朱克-朱克卖的可都是破烂——闪光的珊瑚珠宝，意大利搪瓷制成的钉子、胸针，赛璐珞小玩意儿。晚上我常看见他累得打盹儿，但眼睛总是像猫似的半睁着。他的整个魂儿都在货摊上，他哪儿都瞧——但目的都是要卖掉他的宝贝东西，对其他一概无兴趣。他瞧不起周围的一切——人、大海、娱乐设施对他都既滑稽又陌生。他看着货摊，活着就是卖货。他像个关在盒子里的人——没有快乐，没有同情，没有什么东西用以对付这个他生活其中的奇怪世界。

"我是南方来的，"他常用头指向大海对我说，"那里的生活很艰辛。那儿我有个女朋友。她再见到我就不会失望了，不会太失望吧！那儿的人挨饿，我以圣徒的名义起誓。"（他选择这种方式发誓，无疑是因为这听起来像个基督徒）"的确很难！"

我对朱克-朱克并非感情用事，在灵魂深处他是个十足的自私鬼，但这丝毫也没有阻止他对南方的思念，对阳光和他心爱的姑娘的渴求——他越是自大，这种渴求导致的痛苦也就越厉害。他像个愚蠢的动物一样傻傻地渴求着，但他说："那儿的人挨饿！"很自然，他不会干等着挨饿。他有自己的希望。"等一等吧！"他总这么说。"去年我在布鲁塞尔。生意很差！最后他们为了同乡会拿走了我所有的钱，给了我这个货摊。不过没关系——这季度我挣了些钱。"

在"问题女人"中他有很多顾客，这些女人总要瞟一眼他那一头漂亮的头发，她们也知道生活是不尽如人意的。朱克-朱克的韧性和他所穿着的麻布袋一样肥大的衣服博得她们的同情。他有一双大眼睛，双手纤细、肮脏，但人并不难看。

我去爱斯达柯德那天天气潮湿，那儿几乎连人影都没有。朱克-朱克用一张旧防水帆布盖着他的货摊。他正抽着一支长雪茄。

"哈，哈！朱克-朱克，"我说，"抽烟啦？"

"是啊，"他说，"不错！"

"干嘛不每天抽一根，真是个财迷？饿了能使你好受些。"

他摇头说，"浪费钱，这根不是我买的，一个好心人给我的——一个面色红润的英国人——他说他抽不了。他知道个啥儿，这个傻瓜——我跟你说，这可是好货！"

但事实上是朱克-朱克一无所知——他太长时间不知烟是啥味了。看他吃、喝、抽这等劣质烟的样子十分有趣——一种真正的感官享受。

旺季过了，我们这些靠游客赚钱过活的人也该回家了，但我还是待下来了，因为我喜欢这个地方——色彩明快的房子、码头的鱼味、新鲜的空气、宽宽的绿色海洋，还有沙丘。我天生就喜欢这些东西，我总是舍不得离开这里。但旺季过后——就像是朱克-朱克所说——"以圣徒的名义——那儿的人挨饿！"

一天晚上，很晚，这个地方就剩下20个游客，我像往常一样去了一个有两个房间的小餐馆。去那里的人们，他们的生活方式不可告人——有恃强凌弱之人、喜剧演员、粗俗的女演员、"问题女人""土耳其人""意大利人""希腊人"——尽是这类人，实际人是干着尔虞我诈的勾当——一个十足是骗子和小偷聚合的场所——一帮很有趣的人，我都很熟悉。那天晚上几乎所有的人都走了，饭店里只剩下我们几个，在里屋只有三个意大利人。我走了进去。

不一会儿朱克-朱克就进来了，我平生第一次看见他来这个能花点儿钱的地方。他骨瘦如柴，小个子，大脑袋！人们看了他一定会说他一周没吃饭了。一周？应该是一年！他坐下要了一瓶葡萄酒，便开始边捻手指边唠叨开了。

"哈，哈，"其中一个意大利人说，"看看朱克-朱克，一下子变成夜莺啦。来，朱克-朱克，看你最近走运了吧，把你的酒拿来分享吧！"

朱克-朱克把酒给了我们，自己又要了一瓶。

"哦，哦！"另一个意大利人说，"这家伙，想必是把他的全家都埋掉了吧！" 我们喝着——朱克-朱克的酒比我们喝得都快。你知道那种渴的感觉吗？当你喝酒时就像是酒在你全身的血液中流淌。大多数人在这种状态下会喝个不停——他们会喝得酩酊大醉。而朱克-朱克并不那样。他如以往一样很小心，为他的将来打算。啊！他能控制住自己，然而，在这种情况下，喝一点就能使他高兴得控制不住自己，他变得兴奋起来——对于一个几个月每天只喝水和吃半份面包和通心面的意大利人，要他兴奋起来并不难。他很显然有开心的理由。他又唱又笑，其他意大利人也和他一起又唱又笑。其中一个人说，"看来，我们的朱克-朱克最近生意不错，来，朱克-朱克，说说你这个季度赚了多少！"

但朱克-朱克只是摇头。

"唉！"这个意大利人说，"真不爽快。一定有好事，像我，朋友们，老实说，我挣了500法郎——不超过一生丁——一半的钱交给赞助人啦。"

其他的人开始谈论他们的所得，但朱克-朱克只是咧了咧嘴，保持沉默。

"来，朱克-朱克，"一个人说，"不要鬼头鬼脑的，爽快些！"

"他绝不会超过我的一千六百法郎？"另一个人说。

"以圣徒的名誉！"朱克-朱克突然开口，"四千法郎你们信吗？"

我们都大笑起来。

"看哪！"一个人说，"他在愚弄我们！"

朱克-朱克敞开他的旧双排扣礼服。

"看！"他大叫一声，抽出了四张钞票——每张一千法郎。我们都目瞪口呆！

"看，"他说道，"这就是我兢兢业业的结果——我一点都没花——每一生丁都在这儿！现在我要回家了——找我的女朋友去喽，祝我一路顺风吧！"他又开始捻起手指。

我们待了一会儿，又喝了一瓶酒，朱克-朱克请客。分手时没有一个人喝醉，只有朱克-朱克有些轻飘飘的，就像一个人饿了半年似的。第二天早晨，我没事可做，正在同一家小餐馆喝"波客"黑啤酒，突然跑进来一个人，不是别人，正是这个朱克-朱克。啊！他不再轻飘飘的了。他伏倒在桌子上，双手抱着头，泪流满面。

"他们把我给抢了，"他大哭道，"在我睡着时，抢了我所有的钱，一个苏都没留。我把钱放在枕头底下，我枕着它睡的，一个苏都没啦！"他拍打着自己的胸口。

"嗨，朱克-朱克，"我说，"从你枕头底下？怎么可能！"

"我怎么知道？"他大吼道，"就是没啦。我告诉你——我所有的钱都没啦，所有的钱，我喝得昏沉沉的——"他所能做的就是不断重复："我所有的钱，所有的钱？"

"你去找警察了吗？"

他去找警察了。我试图安慰他，但可想而知，没多大用，这个男孩疯了。

警察什么也没做——他们凭什么帮他？如果朱克-朱克是个犹太银行家，事情将会大不一样，但他只是一个丢了所有的钱的意大利穷小子！

朱克-朱克在前一天卖了他的货摊、他的存货和一切可以卖的，现在他连买张去布鲁塞尔的车票的钱都不够。他只得走着去。他就这么起程了。到今天我还记得他启程时的情形——戴着破帽子，一头漂亮的黑发，系着毛边的领带。他脸上的表情就像是被赶出伊甸园魔鬼的表情！

后来他怎么样我不清楚，但我实在看不清，在整个这件事上，你所谓的补偿会是什么。

费兰德只是沉默无语。

Hector Hugh Munro (Saki)
(1870—1916)

Hector Hugh Munro with the pen name Saki is a Scottish writer whose witty and sometimes macabre stories satirize the Edwardian society and culture. He is considered a master of the short story and is often compared to O. Henry and Dorothy Parker. However, his tales feature his own unique delicately drawn characters and finely judged narratives.

Saki was born the son of an inspector-general for the Burma police. At the age of two, he was sent to live with his aunts in England, who gave him bitter experience with their restrictions and mistreatment. When he grew up, he joined the Burma police. After his invalidity out of the Burma police, he turned to journalism, writing political satires for the *Westminster Gazette*, and then published his historical work. In 1908, he settled down in London after acting as foreign correspondent for *The Morning Post* in the Balkans, Russia, and Paris. He was killed in action in World War I. His major stories and sketches are included in the collections *Reginald* (1904), *Reginald in Russia* (1910), *The Chronicles of Clovis* (1911), and *Beasts and Super-Beasts* (1914). His best known short stories are "Tobermory", "The Open Window", "Laura", and the following "Sredni Vashtar". In addition, he wrote two novels and five plays. His short stories are written in a style often studded with epigrams and well-contrived plots of practical jokes and surprise endings, and they reveal a vein of cruelty and self-identification with the enfant terrible.

Sredni Vashtar

The following story narrates the experience of a sickly boy who lives with his strict and nasty cousin and guardian. The boy rebels against her and invents his own religion which centres around idolising a polecat-ferret, a vengeful, merciless god he calls Sredni Vashtar. The boy keeps the polecat hidden in a hutch in the garden shed, and worships the idol in secret. Then comes the climax when his cousin takes action to discover his god. The story seems to release some repression and hatred against certain authorities due to the lack of understanding and affection.

Conradin was ten years old, and the doctor had pronounced his professional opinion that the boy would not live another five years. The doctor was silky and effete, and counted for little, but his opinion was endorsed by Mrs. De Ropp, who counted for nearly everything. Mrs. De Ropp was Conradin's cousin and guardian, and in his eyes she represented those three-fifths of the world that are necessary and disagreeable and real; the other two-fifths, in perpetual antagonism to the foregoing, were summed up in himself and his imagination. One of these days Conradin supposed he would succumb to the mastering pressure of wearisome necessary things—such as illnesses and coddling restrictions and drawn-out dullness. Without his imagination, which was rampant under the spur of loneliness, he would have succumbed long ago.

Mrs. De Ropp would never, in her honestest moments, have confessed to herself that she disliked Conradin, though she might have been dimly aware that thwarting him 'for his good' was a duty which she did not find particularly irksome. Conradin hated her with a desperate sincerity which he was perfectly able to mask. Such few pleasures as he could contrive for himself gained an added relish from the likelihood that they would be displeasing to his guardian, and from the realm of his imagination she was locked out—an unclean thing, which should find no entrance.

In the dull, cheerless garden, overlooked by so many windows that were ready to open with a message not to do this or that, or a reminder that medicines were due, he found little attraction. The few fruit-trees that it contained were set jealously apart from his plucking, as though they were rare specimens of their kind blooming in an arid waste; it would probably have been difficult to find a market-gardener who would have offered ten shillings for their entire yearly produce. In a forgotten corner, however, almost hidden behind a dismal shrubbery, was a disused tool-shed of respectable proportions, and within its walls Conradin found a haven, something that took on the varying aspects of a playroom and a cathedral. He had peopled it with a legion of familiar phantoms, evoked partly from fragments of history and partly from his own brain, but it also boasted two inmates of flesh and blood. In one corner lived a ragged-plumaged Houdan hen, on which the boy lavished an affection that had scarcely another outlet. Further back in the gloom stood a large hutch, divided into two compartments, one of which was fronted with close iron bars. This was the abode of a large polecat-ferret, which a friendly butcher-boy had once smuggled, cage and all, into its present quarters, in exchange for a long-secreted hoard of small silver. Conradin was dreadfully afraid of the lithe, sharp-fanged beast, but it was his most treasured possession. Its very presence in the tool-shed was a secret and fearful joy, to be kept scrupulously from the knowledge of the Woman, as he privately dubbed his cousin. And one day, out of Heaven knows what material, he spun the beast a wonderful name, and from that moment it grew into a god and a religion. The Woman indulged in religion once a week at a church near by, and took Conradin with her, but to him the church service was an alien rite in the House of Rimmon. Every Thursday, in the dim and musty silence of the tool-shed, he worshipped with mystic and elaborate ceremonial before the wooden hutch where dwelt Sredni Vashtar, the great ferret. Red flowers in their season and scarlet berries in the winter-time were offered at his shrine, for he was a god who laid some special stress on the fierce impatient side of things, as opposed to the Woman's religion, which, as far as Conradin could observe, went to great lengths in the contrary direction. And on great festivals powdered nutmeg was strewn in front of his hutch, an important feature of the offering being that the nutmeg had to be stolen. These festivals were of irregular occurrence, and were chiefly appointed to celebrate some passing event. On one occasion, when Mrs. De Ropp suffered from acute toothache for three days, Conradin kept up the festival during the entire three days, and almost succeeded in persuading himself that Sredni Vashtar was personally responsible for the toothache. If the malady had lasted for another day the supply of nutmeg would have given out.

The Houdan hen was never drawn into the cult of Sredni Vashtar. Conradin had long ago settled that she was an Anabaptist. He did not pretend to have the remotest knowledge as to what an Anabaptist was, but he privately hoped that it was dashing and not very respectable. Mrs. De Ropp was the ground plan on which he based and detested all respectability.

After a while Conradin's absorption in the tool-shed began to attract the notice of his guardian. "It is not good for him to be pottering down there in all weathers," she promptly decided, and at breakfast one morning she announced that the Houdan hen had been sold and taken away overnight. With her short-sighted eyes she peered at Conradin, waiting for an outbreak of rage and sorrow, which she was ready to rebuke with a flow of excellent precepts and reasoning. But Conradin said nothing: there was nothing to be said. Something perhaps in his white set face gave her a momentary qualm, for at tea that afternoon there was toast on the table, a delicacy which she usually banned on the ground that it was bad for him; also because the making of it "gave trouble," a deadly offence in the middle-class feminine eye.

Hector Hugh Munro (Saki)

"I thought you liked toast," she exclaimed, with an injured air, observing that he did not touch it.

"Sometimes," said Conradin.

In the shed that evening there was an innovation in the worship of the hutch-god. Conradin had been wont to chant his praises, tonight he asked a boon.

"Do one thing for me, Sredni Vashtar."

The thing was not specified. As Sredni Vashtar was a god he must be supposed to know. And choking back a sob as he looked at that other empty corner, Conradin went back to the world he so hated.

And every night, in the welcome darkness of his bedroom, and every evening in the dusk of the tool-shed, Conradin's bitter litany went up: "Do one thing for me, Sredni Vashtar."

Mrs. De Ropp noticed that the visits to the shed did not cease, and one day she made a further journey of inspection.

"What are you keeping in that locked hutch?" she asked. "I believe it's guinea-pigs. I'll have them all cleared away."

Conradin shut his lips tight, but the Woman ransacked his bedroom till she found the carefully hidden key, and forthwith marched down to the shed to complete her discovery. It was a cold afternoon, and Conradin had been bidden to keep to the house. From the furthest window of the dining-room the door of the shed could just be seen beyond the corner of the shrubbery, and there Conradin stationed himself. He saw the Woman enter, and then he imagined her opening the door of the sacred hutch and peering down with her short-sighted eyes into the thick straw bed where his god lay hidden. Perhaps she would prod at the straw in her clumsy impatience. And Conradin fervently breathed his prayer for the last time. But he knew as he prayed that he did not believe. He knew that the Woman would come out presently with that pursed smile he loathed so well on her face, and that in an hour or two the gardener would carry away his wonderful god, a god no longer, but a simple brown ferret in a hutch. And he knew that the Woman would triumph always as she triumphed now, and that he would grow ever more sickly under her pestering and domineering and superior wisdom, till one day nothing would matter much more with him, and the doctor would be proved right. And in the sting and misery of his defeat, he began to chant loudly and defiantly the hymn of his threatened idol:

Sredni Vashtar went forth,
His thoughts were red thoughts and his teeth were white.
His enemies called for peace, but he brought them death.
Sredni Vashtar the Beautiful.

And then of a sudden he stopped his chanting and drew closer to the window-pane. The door of the shed still stood ajar as it had been left, and the minutes were slipping by. They were long minutes, but they slipped by nevertheless. He watched the starlings running and flying in little parties across the lawn; he counted them over and over again, with one eye always on that swinging door. A sour-faced maid came in to lay the table for tea, and still Conradin stood and waited and watched. Hope had crept by inches into his heart, and now a look of triumph began to blaze in his eyes that had only known the wistful patience of defeat. Under his breath, with a furtive exultation, he began once again the paean of victory and devastation. And presently his eyes were rewarded: out through that doorway came a long, low, yellow-and-brown beast, with eyes a-blink at the waning daylight, and dark wet stains around the fur of jaws and throat. Conradin dropped on his knees. The great polecat-ferret made its way down to a small brook at the foot of the garden, drank for a moment, then crossed a little plank bridge and was lost to sight in the bushes. Such was the passing of Sredni Vashtar.

"Tea is ready," said the sour-faced maid; "where is the mistress?"

"She went down to the shed some time ago," said Conradin. And while the maid went to summon her mistress to tea, Conradin fished a toasting-fork out of the sideboard drawer and proceeded to toast himself a piece of bread. And during the toasting of it and the buttering of it with much butter and the slow enjoyment of eating it, Conradin listened to the noises and silences which fell in quick spasms beyond the dining-room door. The loud foolish screaming of the maid, the answering chorus of wondering ejaculations from the kitchen region, the scuttering footsteps and hurried embassies for outside help, and then, after a lull, the scared sobbings and the shuffling tread of those who bore a heavy burden into the house.

"Whoever will break it to the poor child? I couldn't for the life of me!" exclaimed a shrill voice. And while they debated the matter among themselves, Conradin made himself another piece of toast.

Questions

1. What kind of boy was Conradin?
2. What did he think of his cousin and guardian Mrs. De Ropp, and she of him?
3. Where did Conradin find a haven for himself? And why?
4. What significant role did Sredni Vashtar play in Conradin's life?
5. What happened to Sredni Vashitar in the end? And what was Conradin's response?

赫克托·休·芒罗(萨基)
(1870—1916)

　　赫克托·休·芒罗,笔名萨基,是苏格兰作家,他的短篇小说机巧、怪诞,讽刺了爱德华时代的社会和文化。他被称为短篇小说大师,与欧·亨利和多萝西·帕克齐名,但他的故事风格迥异,人物性格刻画独特、叙事技巧精湛。

　　萨基生于缅甸,父亲是缅甸警察局的总督察。他两岁就被送回英国同姑母一起生活,姑母的严厉和虐待给了他痛苦的经历。长大后他也加入了缅甸警局,后来他由于疾患离开警局,转向记者生涯,开始为《威斯敏斯特报》撰写政治讽刺文章,还出版了历史学著作。他曾在俄国、巴尔干以及巴黎为《晨邮报》当驻外记者,1908年后定居伦敦。他于第一次世界大战期间阵亡。萨基的大多数短篇小说与速写收在《雷金纳德》(1904)、《雷金纳德在俄罗斯》(1910)、《克劳维斯编年史》(1911)、《野兽与超级野兽》(1914)等集子中。其中最著名的短篇有《托伯莫里》《敞开的窗户》《劳拉》以及下面的《斯莱德尼·瓦什塔》。除此之外,他还写了两部长篇小说、五部剧本。萨基的短篇小说以警句和巧妙的情节著称,诙谐幽默,令人惊叹,透漏出些许尖刻和早熟儿童的自我认同。

斯莱德尼·瓦什塔

　　下面的故事叙述了一个病弱男孩与其严厉、讨厌的表姐兼监护人生活在一起的体验。男孩反叛监护人,创造出自己的宗教,而这一宗教的核心则是崇拜一只北美雪貂。他称这只复仇心切、残酷无情的神貂为斯莱德尼·瓦什塔。男孩将雪貂藏于院子里工具屋的箱子里,秘密崇拜这一偶像。当男孩的监护人开始行动去寻找这一神物之时,故事情节达到了高潮。这一故事似乎向人们宣泄了反对某种权威所受的压抑和所怀的仇恨,原因是缺乏理解和情感交流。

　　康拉丁才十岁,而医生则从专业的角度断言,这个孩子再活不过五年。这位医生油腔滑调、一副媚态,很难让人信服,但他的专业诊断却被德·洛普夫人这个无所不能的人所接受。德·洛普太太是康拉丁的表姐,也是他的监护人。在康拉丁眼里,洛普太太代表了世上那五分之三的人,他们在这真实的世界中不可或缺却令人厌恶;而剩下的五分之二则与之前五分之三永远截然对立,由他自己和他的想象世界所囊括。这些日子里,康拉丁在想,他可能不得不屈服于那些令人厌恶却必须去屈从的事情——疾病、出于溺爱的约束以及持续的沉闷。如果没有那孤独中蔓延滋生的想象，他恐怕早就放弃抵抗了。

德·洛普太太绝不会向任何人坦白她并不喜欢康拉丁，尽管她内心暗暗发觉打着"为他好"的幌子管教康拉丁并不是特别令人讨厌的事。对康拉丁来说，他对表姐打心底厌恶，而他却掩饰得完美无缺。他几乎没有什么乐趣，就这一点点他为自己创造的乐趣，却因为这位监护人可能的厌恶而使他快感大增；在他想象的王国里她是被完全排除在外的，就好像是一件不干净的东西，永远被拒之门外。

在这个沉闷的院子里，上方四周所有的窗子都会随时打开，从里面传出不许做这个不许做那个的管教，要么则是该吃药了的命令，这一切都令他厌恶。他眼巴巴地看着院子里几颗伶仃的果树却不能采摘，仿佛它们是在贫瘠的荒地上生长茂盛的稀有品种；其实要想找到一个肯花十先令买下这些果树一年收成的果农都很难。在一个被遗忘的角落里，几乎被阴暗的灌木遮盖的地方，有一个废弃的工具房，面积还不小，而就在那里面康拉丁找到了自己的天堂——一个可兼作游戏室和天主教堂性质的地方。他让里面住满了各色各样熟悉的幽灵，有的来自零星历史，有的则来自他的想象，而让这个屋子感到骄傲的是里面有两个有血有肉的室友。在一个角落居住着一只羽毛杂乱的乌当鸡，这个男孩把他在别处很难流露出的关爱倾注在这只鸡身上。而在阴暗的工具室里面放着一只大箱子，箱子分成两格，其中一个正面是密密的铁条。那是装有一只硕大的北美雪貂的箱子。这只雪貂是由一个够意思的屠夫小子连箱子一起偷运到此地来的，是康拉丁用一小块秘藏的银子换来的。尽管康拉丁极其害怕这个柔软又利齿的野兽，但这家伙是他最宝贵的财产。把雪貂放在工具室里是一个秘密，这让他极度兴奋，他要小心翼翼地保护好这个秘密，不让"那个女人"知道，他私下里叫他表姐"那个女人"。有一天，天知道什么缘故，他突发奇想地给这只野兽取了个绝妙的名字，从那一刻起这只野兽变成了一个神、一种宗教信仰。"那个女人"每周去一次旁边的教堂，沉溺于宗教，她带着康拉丁，然而对康拉丁来说，那些教堂的礼拜只是"临门"教中的异教仪式而已。每个礼拜四，在那个阴暗发霉的工具房里，康拉丁在那个装着他的大雪貂"斯莱德尼·瓦什塔"的木箱前举行秘密而庄严的膜拜。他把应季的红色鲜花和冬季绯红色的浆果献在那个神龛前。在康拉丁看来，雪貂是神灵，着力代表着急迫、狂躁的一面，而与"那个女人"的宗教截然相反。在盛大的节日里他会把粉状的肉豆蔻撒在那个箱子前，那是因为那些肉豆蔻是他偷出来的。那些节日并不是什么常规性的，而主要是为了庆祝发生的一些事情。有一次，德·洛普太太持续三天剧烈牙痛，康拉丁就庆祝了三天。他对自己说，这全都是他的斯莱德尼·瓦什塔的功劳。其实假使他再多庆祝一天，那些粉状肉豆蔻就会用没了。

那只乌当鸡从不被允许斯莱德尼·瓦什塔靠近。康拉丁很久以前就认定那只乌当鸡是再浸礼派教徒。他并不想假装知道到底什么是再浸礼派教徒,但他私下里希望那只不过是些胆大之徒,不值得敬畏。德·洛普太太是他评价一切的标准,他憎恶她所尊敬的一切。

过了一阵子,康拉丁沉溺于工具房的事情引起了监护人的注意。"无论晴雨,他到那里转悠对他都不好,"她突然毅然决然地说,之后一天早饭时候,她宣布已经在晚上把乌当鸡卖了、送走了。她用近视的眼睛窥视着康拉丁的举动,期待他勃然大怒、黯然神伤,她早已准备好了一系列无懈可击的告诫和理由。结果康拉丁什么也没说,没什么可说的。康拉丁那苍白的脸上有某种东西让她感到霎时的疑惑,为此,在当天下午的茶时桌上多了吐司,那是她常常以"对他有害"为借口而禁止给他吃的点心;也正因为烤吐司"带来麻烦",这个麻烦在一个中产阶级女性眼里,可是一个致命的过错。

"我原本以为你喜欢吃吐司,"看到康拉丁对吐司一口没动,她这么说,话里带着点儿被伤害的味道。

"只是偶尔喜欢,"康拉丁说。

那天晚上,对于工具房箱子里的神明,康拉丁变换了祈祷方式。他习惯于唱赞美歌,但今晚他请神施恩。

"为我做一件事,斯莱德尼·瓦什塔。"

康拉丁并没有指明那件事是什么。因为在他看来斯莱德尼·瓦什塔是神,它一定知道自己的愿望。他抑制着哭泣看着那个已经空了的角落,之后,康拉丁又回到了那个他憎恶的世界。

之后,每天夜里在他所期待的卧室的黑暗之中,每天傍晚在工具房的暮色之下,康拉丁一直狠狠地祈祷着:"为我做一件事,斯莱德尼·瓦什塔。"

德·洛普太太发现了康拉丁对那小屋的拜访并没有停止,于是有一天,她对那个屋子进行了更深入的检查。

"你在那个锁了的箱子里藏了什么?"她问道。"我觉得应该是豚鼠吧。我得把它们都清理掉。"

康拉丁紧紧合着两片嘴唇,但是"那个女人"并没马上到那个小屋完成她的发现之旅,而是先彻底搜查了康拉丁的卧室,找到了他精心藏起来的钥匙。那是一个寒冷的下午,康拉丁被命令待在屋子里。在厨房一个最远的窗子里,康拉丁独自站着,从那里顺着灌木的一个角落可以看到那个小屋的门。他看到"那个女人"走了进去,然后想象着她打开了神圣的箱子,用她近视的眼睛看着箱子里厚厚的稻草,草下面便藏着他的神明。可能她会笨拙、不耐烦地戳那些稻草。康拉丁最后一次虔诚地祈祷着。但是他知道连他自己都不相信自己的祈祷。他知道"那个女人"不久就会抿着嘴，带着可恶的笑容走出那个屋子，再过一两个小时园丁会过来把那个属于他的不再是神明的神明——而是箱子里的棕色雪貂带走。他知道，"那个女人"会像现在取得胜利一样，以胜利者的姿态出现在他面前。之后，在她那喋喋不休、飞扬跋扈、深不可测的精明之下，他会更加病病怏怏，直到有一天，一切对他来说都不再重要，证明医生是对的。在那刺痛的失败中，他大声地、挑衅性地为他受到威胁的神明唱起了赞歌：

斯莱德尼·瓦什塔啊，他出来了，
他的想法是红色，他的牙齿是白色。
他的敌人想讲和，可他带来的是死亡。
斯莱德尼·瓦什塔啊，他真了不起！

突然，他停止了赞美歌，靠近窗户。小屋的门一直半开着，和被开启时一样，时间一分一秒地流逝。那时间真漫长，但还是流逝过去。他看着燕八哥成群结队地从草坪上跑来飞去；他一遍遍数着它们，并不时地盯着那扇摇摆的门。一个酸着脸的仆人走过来放桌子准备茶点，而康拉丁依然站在那儿等着、看着。希望一丝一丝在他心里涌起，在他的眼中燃起了胜利的火焰，而那双眼刚才还在耐心地体验着失败的痛苦。在狂喜中，他控制着呼吸的节奏，又一次为自己的胜利而唱起了劫后余生的赞歌。而不久他眼前出现的景象更让他欢欣鼓舞：从那个屋子的门道，一个很长很矮的黄棕色动物溜了出来，暗光下闪烁着眼睛，下颚和喉咙处的毛有多处湿漉漉的暗色污点。康拉丁跪了下来。那个神圣的北美雪貂跑到了园子边的小溪旁，喝了一会儿水，穿过木板桥消失在了灌木丛中。斯莱德尼·瓦什塔就这样消失了。

"茶点准备好了，"那个酸着脸的仆人说，"女主人呢？"

"她去那个屋子好一会儿了，"康拉丁说。佣人去唤女主人回来用茶点，这时康拉丁从餐具抽屉里拿出一个长柄烤面包叉，接着给自己烤了一片面包。他烤着面包，上面放了很多奶油，慢慢地享受着那片面包的美味，此时，康拉丁听到了那来自餐厅外的阵阵喧哗，接着又是阵阵寂静。那是来自愚蠢佣人的尖叫，接着又突然从厨房传出惊讶的应答声，还有过去帮忙的急促脚步声，然后一阵安静，接下来是受到惊吓的哭声和拖着步子抬重东西进屋的声音。

"有谁会将这事儿透漏给这可怜的孩子？我是死都不会的！"这时突然转来尖利的叫喊声。当她们还在为此事纠缠不休之时，康拉丁又为自己烤好了一片吐司。

Walter de la Mare
(1873—1956)

Walter de la Mare, British novelist and poet, is well known for his power to depict the ghostly and fleeting moments in life. He was brought up in an affluent family in Kent. He attended St Paul's School in London and then worked for an oil company, where, however, he began to write and continued to do so throughout his life. He was much influenced by the English Romantic writers such as Wordsworth and Coleridge. He wrote poems, short stories, novels, a fairy play, essays and literary criticism.

His distinctive prose works include the prose romance *Henry Brocken* (1904) where his hero encounters writers from the past, and the ghostly story *The Return* (1910). His successful children's stories include *The Three Royal Monkeys* (1910). *Memoirs of a Midget* (1921) is a novel of the greatest poetic fantasy. His anthology *Come Hither* (1923) is often considered as one of the best and most original in the English language. He is remembered as a versatile and technically skilled writer whose use of the fantastic and imaginative has transformed the ordinary and entertained readers of all ages.

The Creatures

The author in the following, through a fellow traveller's voice, tells us a fantastic story, half-real and half-supernatural. The narrator, tired of modern urban life, wanders into an unknown country as if in a dream. He is intoxicated by the power and beauty of Nature, and is further affected by his encounter with the local inhabitants who are called "queer creatures" and are yet in much harmony with their natural environment. However, awakened back in reality and much to his surprise, he finds that the old woman he encounters has been dead for a long time. This Eden-like place is much like the Chinese Peach-Blossom Springs where people escape from human affliction and evil, and they enjoy simple life and spiritual fulfillment.

It was the ebbing light of evening that recalled me out of my story to a consciousness of my whereabouts. I dropped the squat little red book to my knee and glanced out of the narrow and begrimed oblong window. We were skirting the eastern coast of cliffs, to the very edge of which a ploughman, stumbling along behind his two great horses, was driving the last of his dark furrows. In a cleft far down between the rocks a cold and idle sea was soundlessly laying its frigid garlands of foam. I stared over the flat stretch of waters, then turned my head, and looked with a kind of suddenness into the face of my one fellow-traveller.

He had entered the carriage, all but unheeded, yet not altogether unresented, at the last country station. His features were a little obscure in the fading daylight that hung between our four narrow walls, but apparently his eyes had been fixed on my face for some little time.

He narrowed his lids at this unexpected confrontation, jerked back his head, and cast a glance out of his mirky glass at the bit of greenish-bright moon that was struggling into its full brilliance above the dun, swelling uplands.

"It's a queer experience, railway-travelling," he began abruptly, in a low, almost deprecating voice, drawing his hand across his eyes. "One is cast into a passing privacy with a fellow-stranger and then is gone." It was as if he had been patiently awaiting the attention of a chosen listener.

I nodded, looking at him. "*That* privacy, too," he ejaculated, "all that!" My eyes turned towards the window again: bare, thorned, black January hedge, inhospitable salt coast, flat waste of northern water. Our engine-driver promptly shut off his steam, and we slid almost noiselessly out of sight of sky and sea into a cutting.

"It's a desolate country," I ventured to remark.

"Oh, yes, 'desolate'!" he echoed a little wearily. "But what always frets me is the way we have of arrogating to ourselves the offices of judge, jury, and counsel all in one. For my part, I never forget it—the futility, the presumption. It leads nowhere. We drive in—into all this silence, this—this 'forsakenness,' this dream of a world between her lights of day and night time. Consciousness! … What restless monkeys men are!" He recovered himself, swallowed his indignation with an obvious gulp. "As if," he continued, in more chastened tones—"as if that other gate were not for ever ajar, into God knows what of peace and mystery." He stooped forward, lean, darkened, objurgatory. "Don't we *make* our world? Isn't *that* our blessed, our betrayed responsibility?"

I nodded, and ensconced myself, like a dog in straw, in the basest of all responses to a rare, even if eccentric, candour—caution.

"Well," he continued, a little weariedly, "that's the indictment. Small wonder if it will need a trumpet to blare us into that last 'Family Prayers.' Then perhaps a few solitaries—just a few—will creep out of their holes and fastnesses, and draw mercy from the merciful on the cities of the plain. The buried talent will shine none the worse for the long, long looming of its napery spun from dream and desire.

"Years ago—ten, fifteen, perhaps—I chanced on the queerest specimen of this order of the 'talented.' Much the same country, too. This" —he swept his glance out towards the now invisible sea— "this is a kind of dwarf replica of it. More naked, smoother, more sudden and precipitous, more 'forsaken,' moody. Alone! The trees are shorn there, as if with monstrous shears, by the winter gales. The air's salt. It is a country of stones and emerald meadows, of green, meandering, aimless lanes, of farms set in their clifts and valleys like rough time-bedimmed jewels, as if by some angel of humanity, wandering between dark and daybreak.

"I was younger then—in body: the youth of the mind is for men of an age—yours, maybe, and mine. Even then, even at that, I was sickened of crowds, of that unimaginable London—swarming wilderness of mankind in which a poor lost thirsty dog from Otherwhere tastes first the full meaning of that idle word 'forsaken.' 'Forsaken by whom?' is the question I ask myself now. Visitors to my particular paradise were few then—as if, my dear sir, we are not all of us visitors, visitants, revenants, on earth, panting for time in which to tell and share our secrets, roving in search of the marks that shall prove our quest not vain, not unprecedented, not a treachery. But let that be.

"I would start off morning after morning, bread and cheese in pocket, from the bare old house I lodged in, bound for that unforeseen nowhere for which the heart, the fantasy aches. Lingering hot noondays would find me stretched in a state half-comatose, yet vigilant, on the close-flowered turf of the fields or cliffs, on the sun-baked sands and rocks, soaking in the scene and life around me like some pilgrim chameleon. It was in hope to lose my way that I would set out. How shall a man find his way unless he lose it? Now and then I succeeded. That country is large, and its land and sea marks easily cheat the stranger. I was still of an age, you see, when my 'small door' was ajar, and I planted a solid foot to keep it from shutting. But how could I know what I was after? One just shakes the tree of life, and the rare fruits come tumbling down, to rot for the most part in the lush grasses.

"What was most haunting and provocative in that far-away country was its fleeting resemblance to the country of dream. You stand, you sit, or lie prone on its bud-starred heights, and look down; the green, dispersed, treeless landscape spreads beneath you, with its hollows and mounded slopes, clustering farmstead, and scatter of village, all motionless under the vast wash of sun and blue, like the drop-scene of some enchanted playhouse centuries old. So, too, the visionary bird-haunted headlands, veiled faintly in a mist of unreality above their broken stones and the enormous saucer of the sea.

"You cannot guess there what you may not chance upon, or whom. Bells clash, boom, and quarrel hollowly on the edge of darkness in those breakers. Voices waver across the fainter winds. The birds cry in a tongue unknown yet not unfamiliar. The sky is the hawks' and the stars'. There one is on the edge of life, of the unforeseen, whereas our cities—are not our desiccated jaded minds ever continually pressing and edging further and further away from freedom, the vast unknown, the infinite presence, picking a fool's journey from sensual fact to fact at the tail of that he-ass called Reason? I suggest that in that solitude the spirit within us realises that it treads the outskirts of a region long since called the Imagination. I assert we have strayed, and in our blindness abandoned —"

My stranger paused in his frenzy, glanced out at me from his obscure corner as if he had intended to stun, to astonish me with some violent heresy. We puffed out slowly, laboriously, from a "Halt" at which in the gathering dark and moonshine we had for some while been at a standstill. Never was wedding-guest more desperately at the mercy of ancient mariner.

"Well, one day," he went on, lifting his voice a little to master the resounding heart-beats of our steam-engine — "one late afternoon, in my goal-less wanderings, I had climbed to the summit of a steep grass-grown cart-track, winding up dustily between dense, untended hedges. Even then I might have missed the house to which it led, for, hair-pin fashion, the track here abruptly turned back on itself, and only a far fainter foot-path led on over the hill-crest. I might, I say, have missed the house and — and its inmates, if I had not heard the musical sound of what seemed like the twangling of a harp. This thin-drawn, sweet, tuneless warbling welled over the close green grass of the height as if out of space. Truth cannot say whether it was of that air or of my own fantasy. Nor did I ever discover what instrument, whether of man or Ariel, had released a strain so pure and yet so bodiless.

"I pushed on and found myself in command of a gorse-strewn height, a stretch of country that lay a few hundred paces across the steep and sudden valley in between. In a V-shaped entry to the left, and sunwards, lay an azure and lazy tongue of the sea. And as my eye slid softly thence and upwards and along the sharp, green horizon line against the glass-clear turquoise of space, it caught the flinty glitter of a square chimney. I pushed on, and presently found myself at the gate of a farmyard.

"There was but one straw-mow upon its staddles. A few fowls were sunning themselves in their dust-baths. White and pied doves preened and cooed on the roof of an outbuilding as golden with its lichens as if the western sun had scattered its dust for centuries upon the large slate slabs. Just that life and the whispering of the wind, nothing more. Yet even at one swift glimpse I seemed to have trespassed upon a peace that had endured for ages; to have crossed the viewless border that divides time from eternity. I leaned, resting, over the gate, and could have remained there for hours, lapsing ever more profoundly into the blessed quietude that had stolen over my thoughts.

"A bent-up woman appeared at the dark entry of a stone shed opposite to me, and, shading her eyes, paused in prolonged scrutiny of the stranger. At that I entered the gate and, explaining that I had lost my way and was tired and thirsty, asked for some milk. She made no reply, but after peering up at me, with something between suspicion and apprehension on her weather-beaten old face, led me towards the house which lay to the left on the slope of the valley, hidden from me till then by plumy bushes of tamarisk.

"It was a low grave house, grey-chimneyed, its stone walls traversed by a deep shadow cast by the declining sun, its dark windows rounded and uncurtained, its door wide open to the porch. She entered the house, and I paused upon the threshold. A deep unmoving quiet lay within, like that of water in a cave renewed by the tide. Above a table hung a wreath of wild flowers. To the right was a heavy oak settle upon the flags. A beam of sunlight pierced the air of the staircase from an upper window.

"Presently a dark long-faced gaunt man appeared from within, contemplating me, as he advanced, out of eyes that seemed not so much to fix the intruder as to encircle his image, as the sea contains the distant speck of a ship on its wide blue bosom of water. They might have been the eyes of the blind; the windows of a house in dream to which the inmate must make something of a pilgrimage to look out upon actuality. Then he smiled, and the long, dark features, melancholy yet serene, took light upon them, as might a bluff of rock beneath a thin passing wash of sunshine. With a gesture he welcomed me into the large dark-flagged kitchen, cool as a cellar, airy as a belfry, its sweet air traversed by a long oblong of light out of the west.

"The wide shelves of the painted dresser were laden with crockery. A wreath of freshly-gathered flowers hung over the chimney-piece. As we entered, a twittering cloud of small birds, robins, hedge-sparrows, chaffinches fluttered up a few inches from floor and sill and window-seat, and once more, with tiny starry-dark eyes observing me, soundlessly alighted.

"I could hear the infinitesimal tic-tac of their tiny claws upon the slate. My gaze drifted out of the window into the garden beyond, a cavern of clearer crystal and colour than that which astounded the eyes of young Aladdin. Apart from the twisted garland of wild flowers, the shining metal of range and copper candlestick, and the bright-scoured crockery, there was no adornment in the room except a rough frame, hanging from a nail in the wall, and enclosing what appeared to be a faint patterned fragment of blue silk or fine linen. The chairs and table were old and heavy. A low light warbling, an occasional skirr of wing, a haze-like drone of bee and fly—these were the only sounds that edged a quiet intensified in its profundity by the remote stirrings of the sea.

"The house was stilled as by a charm, yet thought within me asked no questions; speculation was asleep in its kennel. I sat down to the milk and bread, the honey and fruit which the old woman laid out upon the table, and her master seated himself opposite to me, now in a low sibilant whisper—a tongue which they seemed to understand—addressing himself to the birds, and now, as if with an effort, raising those strange grey-green eyes of his to bestow a quiet remark upon me. He asked, rather in courtesy than with any active interest, a few questions, referring to the world, its business and transports—our beautiful world—as an astronomer in the small hours might murmur a few words to the chance-sent guest of his solitude concerning the secrets of Uranus or Saturn. There is another, an inexplorable side to the moon. Yet he said enough for me to gather that he, too, was of that small tribe of the aloof and wild to which our cracked old word 'forsaken' might be applied, hermits, clay-matted fakirs, and such-like, the snowy birds that play and cry amid mid-oceanic surges, the living of an oasis of the wilderness, which share a reality only distantly dreamed of by the time-driven thought-corroded congregations of man.

"Yet so narrow and hazardous I somehow realised was the brink of fellow-being (shall I call it?) which we shared, he and I, that again and again fantasy within me seemed to hover over that precipice Night knows as fear. It was he, it seemed, with that still embracive contemplation of his, with that far-away yet reassuring smile, that kept my poise, my balance. 'No,' some voice within him seemed to utter, 'you are safe; the bounds are fixed; though hallucination chaunt its decoy, you shall not irretrievably pass over. Eat and drink, and presently return to "life."' And I listened, and, like that of a drowsy child in its cradle, my consciousness sank deeper and deeper, stilled, pacified, into the dream amid which, as it seemed, this soundless house of stone now reared its walls.

"I had all but finished my meal when I heard footsteps approaching on the flags without. The murmur of other voices, distinguishably shrill yet guttural, even at a distance, and in spite of the dense stones and beams of the house which had blunted their timbre, had already reached me. Now the feet halted. I turned my head—cautiously, even perhaps apprehensively—and confronted two figures in the doorway.

"I cannot now guess the age of my entertainer. These children—for children they were in face and gesture and effect, though as to form and stature apparently in their last teens—these children were far more problematical. I say 'form and stature,' yet obviously they were dwarfish. Their heads were sunken between their shoulders, their hair thick, their eyes disconcertingly deep-set. They were ungainly, their features peculiarly irregular, as if two races from the ends of the earth had in them intermingled their blood and strangeness; as if, rather, animal and angel had connived in their creation.

"But if some inward light lay on the still eyes, on the gaunt, sorrowful, quixotic countenance that now was fully and intensely bent on mine, emphatically that light was theirs also. He spoke to them; they answered—in English, my own language, without a doubt: but an English slurred, broken, and unintelligible to me, yet clear as bell, haunting, penetrating, pining as voice of nix or siren. My ears drank in the sound as an Arab parched with desert sand falls on his dried belly and gulps in mouthfuls of crystal water. The birds hopped nearer, as if beneath the rod of an enchanter. A sweet continuous clamour arose from their small throats. The exquisite colours of plume and bosom burned, greened, melted in the level sun-ray, in the darker air beyond.

"A kind of mournful gaiety, a lamentable felicity, such as rings in the cadences of an old folk-song, welled into my heart. I was come back to the borders of Eden, bowed and outwearied, gazing from out of dream into dream, homesick, 'forsaken.'

"Well, years have gone by," muttered my fellow-traveller deprecatingly, "but I have not forgotten that Eden's primeval trees and shade.

"They led me out, these bizarre companions, a he and a she, if I may put it as crudely as my apprehension of them put it to me then. Through a broad door they conducted me—if one who leads may be said to be conducted—into their garden. Garden! A full mile long, between undiscerned walls, it sloped and narrowed towards a sea at whose dark unfoamed blue, even at this distance, my eyes dazzled. Yet how can one call that a garden which reveals no ghost of a sign of human arrangement, of human slavery, of spade or hoe?

"Great boulders shouldered up, tessellated, embossed, powdered with a thousand various mosses and lichens, between a flowering greenery of weeds. Wind-stunted, clear-emerald, lichen-tufted trees smoothed and crisped the inflowing airs of the ocean with their leaves and spines, sibilating a thin scarce-audible music. Scanty, rank, and uncultivated fruits hung close their vivid-coloured cheeks to the gnarled branches. It was the harbourage of birds, the small embowering parlour of their house of life, under an evening sky, pure and lustrous as a waterdrop. It cried 'Hospital' to the wanderers of the universe.

"As I look back in ever-thinning nebulous remembrance on my two companions, hear their voices gutturally sweet and shrill, catch again their being, so to speak, I realise that there was a kind of Orientalism in their effect. Their instant courtesy was not Western, the smiles that greeted me, whenever I turned my head to look back at them, were infinitely friendly, yet infinitely remote. So ungainly, so far from our notions of beauty and symmetry were their bodies and faces, those heads thrust heavily between their shoulders, their disproportioned yet graceful arms and hands, that the children in some of our English villages might be moved to stone them, while their elders looked on and laughed.

"Dusk was drawing near; soon night would come. The colours of the sunset, sucking its extremest dye from every leaf and blade and petal, touched my consciousness even then with a vague fleeting alarm.

"I remember I asked these strange and happy beings, repeating my question twice or thrice, as we neared the surfy entry of the valley upon whose sands a tiny stream emptied its fresh waters—I asked them if it was they who had planted this multitude of flowers, many of a kind utterly unknown to me and alien to a country inexhaustibly rich. 'We wait; we wait!' I think they cried. And it was as if their cry woke echo from the green-waned valleys of the mind into which I had strayed. Shall I confess that tears came into my eyes as I gazed hungrily around me on the harvest of their patience?

"Never was actuality so close to dream. It was not only an unknown country, slipped in between these placid hills, on which I had chanced in my ramblings. I had entered for a few brief moments a strange region of consciousness. I was treading, thus accompanied, amid a world of welcoming and fearless life—oh, friendly to me!—

the paths of man's imagination, the kingdom from which thought and curiosity, vexed scrutiny and lust—a lust it may be for nothing more impious than the actual—had prehistorically proved the insensate means of his banishment. 'Reality,' 'Consciousness': had he for 'the time being' unwittingly, unhappily missed his way? Would he be led back at length to that garden wherein cockatrice and basilisk bask, harmlessly, at peace?

"I speculate now. In that queer, yes, and possibly sinister, company, sinister only because it was alien to me, I did not speculate. In their garden, the familiar was become the strange—'the strange' that lurks in the inmost heart, unburdens its riches in trance, flings its light and gilding upon love, gives heavenly savour to the intemperate bowl of passion, and is the secret of our incommunicable pity. What is yet queerer, these beings were evidently glad of my company. They stumped after me (as might yellow men after some Occidental quadruped never before seen) in merry collusion of nods and wreathed smiles at this perhaps unprecedented intrusion.

"I stood for a moment looking out over the placid surface of the sea. A ship in sail hung phantom-like on the horizon. I pined to call my discovery to its seamen. The tide gushed, broke, spent itself on the bare boulders, I was suddenly cold and alone, and gladly turned back into the garden, my companions instinctively separating to let me pass between them. I breathed in the rare, almost exotic heat, the tenuous, honeyed, almond-laden air of its flowers and birds—gull, sheldrake, plover, wag-tail, finch, robin, which as I half-angrily, half-sadly realised fluttered up in momentary dismay only at my presence—the embodied spectre of their enemy, man. Man? Then who were these? ...

"I lost again a way lost early that morning, as I trudged inland at night. The dark came, warm and starry. I was tired, dejected, exhausted beyond words. That night I slept in a barn and was awakened soon after daybreak by the crowing of cocks. I went out, dazed and blinking into the sunlight, bathed face and hands in a brook near by, and came to a village before a soul was stirring. So I sat under a thrift-cushioned, thorn-crowned wall in a meadow, and once more drowsed off and fell asleep. When again I awoke, it was ten o'clock. The church clock in its tower knelled out the strokes, and I went into an inn for food.

"A corpulent, blonde woman, kindly and hospitable, with a face comfortably resembling her own sow's, that puffed and nosed in at the open door as I sat on my stool served me with what I called for. I described—not without some vanishing shame, as if it were a treachery—my farm, its whereabouts.

"Her small blue eyes 'pigged' at me with a fleeting expression which I failed to translate. The name of the farm, it appeared, was Trevarras. 'And did you see any of the Creatures?' she asked me in a voice not entirely her own. 'The Creatures'! I sat back for an instant and stared at her; then realised that Creature was the name of my host, and Mafia and Christus (though here her dialect may have deceived me) the names of my two gardeners. She spun an absurd story, so far as I could tack it together and make it coherent. Superstitious stuff about this man who had wandered in upon the shocked and curious inhabitants of the district and made his home at Trevarras—a stranger and pilgrim, a 'foreigner,' it seemed, of few words, dubious manners, and both uninformative.

"Then there was something (she placed her two fat hands, one of them wedding-ringed, on the zinc of the bar-counter, and peered over at me, as if I were a delectable 'wash'), then there was something about a woman 'from the sea.' In a 'blue gown,' and either dumb, inarticulate, or mistress of only a foreign tongue. She must have lived in sin, moreover, those pig's eyes seemed to yearn, since the children were 'simple,' 'naturals'—as God intends in such matters. It was useless. One's stomach may sometimes reject the cold sanative aerated water of 'the next morning,' and my ridiculous intoxication had left me dry but not yet quite sober.

"Anyhow, this she told me, that my blue woman, as fair as flax, had died and was buried in the neighbouring churchyard (the nearest to, though miles distant from, Trevarras). She repeatedly assured me, as if I might otherwise doubt so sophisticated a fact, that I should find her grave there, her 'stone.'

"So indeed I did—far away from the elect, and in a shade-ridden North-west corner of the sleepy, cropless acre: a slab, scarcely rounded, of granite, with but a name bitten out of the dark rough surface, 'Femina Creature.'"

Questions

1. Why does the traveller say "It's a queer experience, railway-traveling" at the beginning of this story? And from what perspective is the story really told?
2. What are the traveller's attitudes towards modern urban life in contrast with rural life?
3. What is the impact on the traveller in terms of the natural environment at Trevarras? And how does he feel about the family members there?
4. Why are the family members called Creatures? And how are they associated with the title "The Creatures"?
5. What do you learn from this story?

瓦尔特·德·拉·梅尔
(1873—1956)

英国小说家、诗人瓦尔特·德·拉·梅尔以擅长描写生活中光怪陆离、转瞬即逝的体验著称。他出生于肯特郡的一个富裕家庭。他曾在伦敦的圣保罗学校读书,后来在一家石油公司工作,期间开始写作并保持终身。他深受英国浪漫主义作家如华兹华斯和柯尔律治的影响。他的创作有诗歌、小说、童话剧、散文和文学评论。

德·拉·梅尔特色鲜明的作品包括:浪漫传奇《亨利·布罗肯》(1904),讲述的是与过去作家的奇遇;鬼怪故事《重现》(1910)。其成功的儿童故事有《三只高贵的猴子》(1910)。《侏儒回忆录》(1921)是一部超乎寻常的充满诗意幻想的小说。他编撰的文选《来这里》(1923)被认为是最好、最有创意的英语文选之一。德·拉·梅尔创作的多样性和高超技巧令人难忘,他充满幻想和想象力的故事化普通为神奇,古往今来受到读者的欢迎。

精 灵

作者在以下故事中,通过一个旅伴的口吻,讲述了一个半真实半虚幻的神奇经历。讲述者厌倦了现代都市生活,恍如在梦中浪迹于一个不知名的乡下。他陶醉于那里大自然的力与美,进而受到在那儿巧遇的居民的感染。这些人被称为"怪精灵",但他们与那里的自然环境和谐统一。然而,醒来回到现实,他大吃一惊地发现,他所巧遇的老妇人已去世许久。这个伊甸园般的地方很像中国的"桃花源",在那里人们躲避世间的痛苦和邪恶,享受淳朴的生活和精神的满足。

夜幕降临,光线渐暗,这时我才停止阅读手中的故事,恍然意识到自己的所在。我把厚厚的小红书放在膝上,然后透过那狭窄、肮脏的长方形车窗向外看去。我们沿东海岸行驶,一边是悬崖峭壁。在峭壁的尽头,一位农夫跟在两匹高头大马之后蹒跚而行,他在冥冥之中耕作自己最后一垄地。从悬崖裂缝中往下,在远处岩石间,冰冷的海水懒懒、静静地泛起花环般的泡沫。我望着伸向远处的海水,然后转过头来,有点儿突然地径直瞧向唯一与我同行的旅者。

他是在最后一个乡村车站上的车,几乎没人注意,但也并非无人反感。车厢

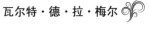

内照在四壁的自然光线渐暗,他的五官有一些模糊,但很显然,他的双眼盯着我的脸有一阵子了。

面对这突如其来的对视,他眯缝起眼睛,往后仰了仰头,目光透过幽暗的单片眼镜,投向那明亮中微微带绿的月亮。此时的月亮正挣扎着爬上暗褐色隆起的山丘,尽显其光彩。

"铁路旅行真是不同寻常的经历,"他突然用手捂着眼睛,声音很低,几乎是不以为然地说道。"一个人被临时地安排与另一位陌生伙伴独处,然后就出发了。"他似乎一直在耐心地等待一位好听众,引起他的注意。

我点点头,看着他。"那也是一种独处啊!"他突然说道,"的确是啊!"我的眼睛又一次朝窗外看去:光秃秃的,满是荆棘,一月份黑黢黢的篱笆,冷漠的盐海岸,平缓荒凉的北部水域。火车司机很快熄了火,我们几乎是悄无声息地滑离了天空和大海进入一段路堑。

"真是个荒凉之地,"我冒昧地说。

"哦,是啊,'真荒凉'!"他有些疲倦地回应道。"不过一直使我烦恼的是:我们为何要将法官、陪审团、辩护律师强加于一身。对于我来说,我从没有忘记——其中的徒劳、专横。出不了什么好结果。我们行驶在——驶入一片寂静,一片寂静——这种"被遗弃"之中,在白昼与夜晚明暗交替的梦幻之中。意识是什么!……人类是多么不安分的猴子啊!"他回过神儿来,明显地咽了一下,压抑着愤怒。"就好像,"他继续说道,语气更压抑——"就好像另一扇大门永远也不会半开一样,在那里只有上帝知道什么是和平、什么是神秘。"他向前俯身,倾斜着,阴沉着脸,责骂着。"难道不是我们创造自己的世界吗?难道那不是我们被赐予的责任,同时也是被我们所背叛的责任么?"

我点点头,安顿好自己,就像是一只躲在麦秆堆里的小狗,对这个不寻常的、虽然有些古怪但很坦诚的问题,做出了最基本的反应——小心谨慎。

"唉,"他略显疲惫地继续说,"那就是症结所在。这也就不足为奇,我们需要喇叭来告诫自己去做最后的'家庭祷告'。这样也许个别隐士——只是个别一些人——会爬出他们的洞穴和堡垒,然后向那些平原之城中的仁慈者博得宽恕。被埋没的天赋仍将会闪光,呈现出由梦想和热望所编织成的长长的幻影。"

"几年前——也许十年,十五年前——我偶然发现了这类'天赋'最奇异的标本。也是在这样的乡下。这儿,——"他向外面望去,可现在大海已模糊不见——"这儿就像是那儿的小型复制品。只是那儿更加裸露、平坦,继而又更突兀、险峻,更有'被遗弃'的感觉,更阴郁。孤零零的!那儿的树木就像被魔鬼的剪子借助冬天的暴风剪过一样。空气是咸的。那儿是石头、绿草之地,有蜿蜒曲折的绿色小路,有悬崖、峡谷中的农田,就像是粗糙、天成的宝石,由天使下凡摆布于此,她们游走于黑夜和拂晓之间。

"我那时还年轻——身体上年轻,但思想上并不太成熟,也许你我都一样。即使那时,即使在那个年龄,我就很讨厌拥挤的人群,讨厌难以想象的伦敦——那儿是挤满了人的荒野,其中有一只可怜、饥渴的、来自异乡的迷途之犬第一次尝到了'被遗弃'这个空泛之词的完整含义。'被谁遗弃了?'这是我现在问自己的问题。当时光顾我这个特殊乐园的来访者寥寥无几——就好像,我亲爱的先生,我们不都是这世上的过客、香客、归来的亡灵,渴望能有机会去诉说和分享我们的秘密,浪迹天涯去寻找证据来证明我们的求索绝非徒劳、并非首创,也不是背信弃义。这些先说到这儿。

"我那时常常天天早上启程,把面包和奶酪放在口袋里,从我住的那幢又旧又空的房子里出发;我的心、我的梦想向往着那无法预测的无名之地。炎热的正午迟迟不肯离去,我躺在开满花儿的田野里或悬崖上的草皮上,或躺在太阳烘烤的沙地和岩石上,像是朝圣者,融入周围的景色和生命之中;我昏昏欲睡,但我的内心是警醒的。每次启程我都希望迷路。不迷路怎么能找到路呢?时而我做到了。那片乡下很大,其土地和海洋给人的印象很容易使生人上当受骗。你知道,我那时的年龄还半开着'小门',我坚实地踏上一只脚不让它关上。不过我怎么知道自己想要什么呢!人只是摇动生命之树,那些珍贵的果实就会掉下来,而大部分果实都会腐烂在茂盛的草地上。

"在那个遥远的乡下,最让人魂牵梦萦的也是最刺激的是它与梦乡多么相似,但却转眼即逝。无论你是站着,坐着,抑或是面朝下地趴在布满蓓蕾的高地上,然后向下看;那绿色的、绵延的、毫无树木遮挡的风景尽收眼底;那儿有山谷和斜坡,片片农田和散落的村庄,这一切在太阳的光芒下和蓝天的映衬下安然不动,就像是几百年的老剧院里令人着迷的最后一场戏。同样,还有那梦想中鸟儿徘徊的海角,那儿风化的石头和巨大的海平面被蒙上了一层微弱虚幻的薄雾。

"在那里你猜不到可能会遇到什么事或是什么人。在黎明破晓前的黑暗之中,钟与钟相碰撞,发出低沉空旷的响声和争吵声。说话声在微弱的风中颤动。鸟儿在鸣叫,曲调不为人知但也并非陌生。天空是鹰隼和星星的世界。那里人们处于生命的边缘,一切不可预知,然而在城市——我们被烘干、疲惫不堪的大脑,难道不是被永远不断地挤向边缘,越来越远离自由,远离那浩瀚的未知世界,远离那无限的存在,而是跟随着被称作'理性'这头公驴的尾巴上,选择了愚人的旅途,从一桩感官的事实走向另一桩事实。但我要提醒大家,在那种独处的环境下,我们内在的精神会意识到它踏足于某个区域的边缘,这个区域长久以来就被称作'想象力'。我敢断言我们迷失了方向,在盲目中抛弃了它——"

陌生人在激动中暂停了下来,从昏暗的角落向外瞥了我一眼,就好像打算用他的暴力邪说让我头脑发昏、目瞪口呆。夜色渐浓，月色渐朗，机车停了好一阵子，这时又从'静止'慢腾腾、吃力地噗噗地喷出烟来。此时的我们就像赴婚礼的宾客牢牢地被攥在载我们的老水手的掌心。

"后来，有一天，"他继续道，提了提嗓音来压倒机车隆隆的节奏声——"在一个下午的晚些时候，在漫无目标的徜徉中，我爬上了一个陡峭的杂草丛生的运材路的顶端。路径在稠密、弃管的篱笆之间蜿蜒穿行，满是尘土。就在这时我也很可能错过这条路所通向的一幢房子，因为路是发卡形的，在这儿就突然回转了，只有一条非常模糊不清的小道继续直通向山顶。我说了，也许我就错过那幢房子了，也见不着里面的住户，可这时我听到音乐声，似竖琴发出的嘣嘣声。这微弱、甜美、不成调子的颤音溢过高处繁茂的青草地，像是来自天外。事实上，也说不清这音乐是源自这里的天空，还是源自我的幻想。我也并没发现是什么乐器，是人还是精灵阿里尔演奏的，可它却散发着一种如此纯净然而又无形的气息。

"我继续往前走，发现自己身处满是金雀花的山顶，这个地方向陡峭险峻的山谷之间延伸几百步。在一个左边呈V字形的入口处，向阳的方向是一片蔚蓝、慵懒的舌型海湾。随着我的眼睛轻轻地向上看，那尖尖的绿色地平线与玻璃般透明的青石色的空间形成对比，我突然发现一个方形烟囱里冒出如燧石摩擦般的闪光。我继续往前走，转眼间就到了一个农场的大门边。

"只有一堆麦草在堆草平台上。几只家禽正在他们的泥土浴里晒太阳。白色和其他色彩斑驳的鸽子正在外屋的屋顶上用喙整理着羽毛、咕咕地叫，金黄色的房舍与青苔交相辉映，就像是西下的太阳在这片宽大的板岩石上播撒了几个世纪的余晖。这儿只有如此的生活和风的窃窃私语，再没有别的什么。然而只要飞快地一瞥，我似乎就已经侵犯了那保持多年的平静，就已经越过了把时间与永恒隔开的无形的藩篱。我斜靠在大门上休息，本来可以待上几个小时，深深地陷入袭上心头神圣的宁静之中。

"一个驼背女人出现在正对着我的石棚入口处。她用手挡着光，停下来审视我这个陌生人。这时我进入大门，解释我迷路了，现在又累又渴，想要点儿牛奶。她没应声，凝视了我一会儿，那张饱经风霜的脸上充满了怀疑与担忧，然后她领我前往坐落在左方峡谷斜坡上的房子，那房子掩藏在撑柳羽毛般的灌木丛中，直到这时我才瞥见。

"那是一幢低矮阴暗的房子，灰色的烟囱，房子的石墙被西下的斜阳所映出的长长的影子所横贯，漆黑的窗户很圆，没有窗帘，房门大开着冲着门廊。她走进房子，我在门槛处停住。屋里寂静无声，就像是洞穴里的水被潮汐所更新一样。桌子上方挂着一个野花编成的花环。右边有一个重重的橡木长凳放在地面的石板上。一束阳光从上窗穿透空气射到楼梯上。

"很快,一个黑长脸、面容憔悴的男子从里面出来,他边往前走边注视着我,那眼神似乎并没有盯在入侵者身上,而是将他的形象团团围住,就像海洋用它宽阔的胸襟容纳远方船只的一点儿影子。那双眼睛就像是盲人的。对着梦一般房子的窗户,主人向外观望现实生活,他一定会把这当作朝圣之事。随后他笑了笑,黝黑的长脸忧郁而宁静,闪烁发亮,就好像断崖石壁上掠过一抹阳光。他用手势欢迎我到一间黑石板铺地的大厨房,室内像地下室一样凉爽,像钟塔楼内一样通风,清新的空气被西下的一缕长长的椭圆形阳光所穿透。

"漆过的碗柜上宽宽的架子上满是陶器。炉壁上方悬挂着一个鲜花编成的花环。当我进屋时,许多小鸟儿叽叽喳喳地叫个不停,有知更鸟、篱雀、花鸟;它们拍打着翅膀从地板上、窗台上、窗座上飞起几英寸高,闪烁着黑黑的小眼睛注视我,又悄无声息地落下。

"我能听到鸟儿的小爪子在石板上发出极微小的嗒嗒声。我的目光飘出窗户转到了远处的花园,那儿是更震撼年轻阿拉丁的一个晶莹透彻、色彩斑斓的深处。除了野花编织的花环、一系列闪闪发光的金属器皿和铜烛扦、擦亮的陶器外,房间里没有什么装饰,只有一个粗糙的框架,用一个钉子在墙上挂着,里面看起来镶着蓝色丝绸或是亚麻的已经褪色的带有图案的残片。椅子和桌子既旧又重。一阵又低又轻的颤音,偶尔有翅膀掠过时的飕飕声,蜜蜂和苍蝇含混的嗡嗡声——这些仅有的声音更衬托出室内的寂静,而远处海洋的起伏声更加剧了寂静的深度。

"这幢房子似乎受魔力寂静下来,然而我的内心没有任何问题要问;任何思索都已经沉睡。我坐下来享用牛奶和面包,还有蜂蜜和水果,这些都是那位老妇人放在桌子上的;男主人坐在我对面,一会儿以低沉的嘶嘶声向鸟儿说话——鸟儿似乎明白他的这种语言,一会儿又似乎吃力地抬起他奇异的灰绿色眼睛静静地向我发问。他只是出于礼貌而非特别有兴趣地问了几个问题,涉及我们的社会,其运作情况和交通问题——我们美好的社会——就像一位天文学家,在凌晨时分的孤独之时,也许会对某个不速之客说几句有关天王星或土星的秘密。另外,还有月球有不可探知的一面。然而他对我说的足以让我去明白他也属于一个远离尘世、尚未开化的小部落里的一员,'被遗弃'这个被喊破了的、老掉牙的词也许在这儿能用得上——隐士,以地为席的苦行僧和诸如此类的人,嬉戏高唱于澎湃的海洋之中的雪鸟,荒野绿洲中的生灵。这一切都分享着同一个现实,而这个现实却是被时间催促、被思想腐蚀的一类人所抱有的遥远的梦想。

"然而不知为何,我意识到我们,他和我,所分享的共存边缘(我是否可以这样说?)是如此狭窄和险要,一次又一次我内心的幻想似乎盘旋在夜晚所熟知的恐惧悬崖之上。似乎是他用那安宁而无所不包的凝望,朦胧却充满鼓励的微笑,使我镇定下来、平和下来。'没事了,'他似乎发出某种声音,'你安全了;界限划定了;虽然幻想在吟诵诱人的曲调引你入网,但你不应该义无反顾地回避。吃点儿、喝点儿,不久便重返'生活'。'我听着,像是摇篮里昏昏欲睡的孩子,我的意识越来越沉、越来越静,悄悄地进入梦乡,似乎这个无声无息的石房子正在构筑四壁,包容这梦想。

"我快要吃完饭了,这时忽然听见外面石板上有脚步声靠近。其他人不断的说话声,尖细而带有喉音,清晰可辨;这些声音虽然从远处传来,而且还有房子厚厚的石头和横梁阻挡,还是传到了我的耳朵里。现在脚步声停了下来。我转过头去——小心翼翼地,甚至还或许有些担心地——面对着在门口的两个人。

"我至今也猜不出款待我之人的年龄。而这些孩子——论表情、姿态和外表给人的印象,他们的确是孩子,但从体型和身高来看,显然他们已快二十岁了——这些孩子则更令人费解。我提到'体型和身高',但很明显他们像侏儒。他们的头陷在两肩之间,头发很粗,眼睛也深陷得令人吃惊。他们相貌难看,五官奇特,就像是来自地球末端的两个种族把他们的血统和奇异之处混合在他们的身上;就像是动物和天使在造物时放纵之举的结果。

"但是如果有某种内在之光注目于那静默的眼睛和憔悴、悲伤、狂想的面容,而现在这面容正全心全意地关注于我,很显然,那目光也同样是属于他们的。他对他们讲话,他们应答——毫无疑问是用英语,我自己的母语,但那英语却含糊不清、支离破碎,我无法听懂,然而却又像铃儿般清亮,像女妖或汽笛的声音那样萦绕于怀,力透寰宇,带着渴望和憔悴。我沉醉在这声音之中,就像是被大漠之沙烘烤的阿拉伯人用干瘪的肚皮扑倒在地,大口喝着晶莹清澈的水一样。鸟儿好像受了魔棍的作用,跳得更近。它们小小的喉咙里发出一阵甜美的喧闹声。羽翼和胸前羽毛精美的颜色忽而发亮,忽而变绿,融化在平射的太阳光里,在远处渐暗的天空中。

"一种悲哀的愉悦,一种可悲的幸福,就像是一曲传统民间音乐的曲调,涌入我的心底。我被召回到伊甸园的边界,卑躬屈膝,筋疲力尽,从一个梦境凝望另一个梦境,饱受思乡之苦,'被遗弃'。

"嗨,几年过去了,"我的旅伴不以为然地嘀咕着,"但是我没有忘记那伊甸园原始的树林和树荫。"

"他们领我出去,这对古怪的伴侣,一'公'一'母',请恕我按当初对他们的看法这么粗鲁地称呼。透过一扇宽敞的门他们引导我到花园——如果一个人在前走也可以被叫作'引导'的话。瞧这花园!足足有一英里长,在两道辨别不清的墙之间,它倾斜着变窄通向大海;那边的大海暗蓝无沫,远远地使我眼晕。

然而这怎么能叫花园呢？这儿连人工雕琢的鬼影儿都没有，没人的苦力，也没有铲子或锄头。

"在野草、花朵和绿叶之间，巨石凸起，镶嵌成花纹，镌刻出浮雕，被一千种不同的苔藓与地衣点缀的斑斑点点。这儿树木的生长受海风阻碍，但树木却仍清亮翠绿，爬满绿苔，叶子和枝干舒缓、减弱了海风的灌入，发出几乎听不见的咝咝音乐。稀疏、倔强、未经管理的水果，把颜色鲜艳的脸颊紧紧地贴向多节的树枝。这里是鸟儿的停泊处，是他们隐匿林中生存之地的小小庇护所，在夜空下，纯净光亮宛如雨滴。它对着浪迹天涯者大声疾呼'到收养院来吧！'

"当我回想起对这两个同伴越来越模糊的记忆时，听到他们甜美而尖锐的喉音，可谓再次捕捉到了他们的秉性时，我意识到他们给人的印象是某种东方的特质。他们瞬间的礼貌举止不是西方式的，无论我什么时候回头看他们，他们向我问候时的微笑都是相当的友好，但却又那么疏远。他们的身体和脸，那重重地插在肩膀里的脑袋，还有那不均衡却优雅的胳膊和手，这些都那么难看，那么与我们对美和匀称的概念大相径庭，英国乡村里的孩子们见了这样的人可能会向他们扔石头，而长辈们也会围观、嘲笑。

"黄昏渐近，不久夜幕就会降临。五彩缤纷的落日从每一片叶子的叶面、叶片上和花瓣上都尽可能地汲取染料。尽管这样，此时此景还是触动了我模糊短暂的惊恐意识。

"我记得我们走近一条浪花翻滚的山谷的入口处，在山谷里的沙地上冒出一小股溪流，吐出淡水；这时，我问这些奇异而幸福的人，两三次地重复我的问题——我问他们这些种类繁多的花是不是他们种的，其中很多种花我完全不认识，甚至对一个植被异常丰富的地区也是陌生的。'我们等待，我们只是等待！'我想他们是在祈求。他们的祈求声就好像唤醒了我迷失于日渐减绿的心灵之谷中的回声。我该坦诚相告，当我用渴望的眼神凝视着周围由于他们的耐心而取得的收获时，我的眼里充满泪水。

"现实从未离梦想如此之近。这儿不仅仅是一个不为人知的乡下，滑落于宁静的丘陵之间，我有幸在此徜徉。而且在此，有几段短暂的时刻，我进入了一个奇异的自觉之地。我在一个好客、充满无畏生活的世界中行进，如此陪伴着我——噢，对我是多么友好！——行进在人类的想象之途，从这个王国里产生的想法和好奇心，令人焦虑的审慎和欲望——这个欲望可能也算不上比现实更不虔诚——这些早在史前就已被人类毫无知觉的流放所证明。'现实'，'意识'：在当下，他是否在不知不觉中，在毫不情愿中就迷失了方向呢？他是否最终还会被带回到那个连毒蛇和蛇妖都能和平相处、舒适愉快的花园么？

"现在我有时间深入思考这件事。可在当时那种奇异的境遇中，是啊，也可能是险恶的境遇中，称之为险恶只不过是因为那儿的一切对我都很陌生，我并没有机会深入思考。在他们的花园里，熟悉的事物变成陌生之物——这'陌生之物'藏在内心深处，在恍惚中表白它的富有，用光芒给爱镀上金色，给放纵的欢宴之激情以神圣的品味，它是我们不可言传的怜悯之秘密。更奇异的是，这些人显然乐意与我为伍。他们磕磕绊绊地跟着我（就像黄种人跟在从未见过的西方四足动物后面一样），对这也许是空前的造访不时报以愉悦、会心地点头和微笑。

"我站了一会儿，向外远望那平静的海面。一只正在航行的船幽灵般地悬在地平线上。我渴望将自己的发现通报给那儿的水手。潮水涌上岸，浪花飞溅，打在光秃的巨石上；我突然感到寒冷、孤独，于是欣然地返回，向花园走，陪我的人本能地让我从他们之间穿过。我呼吸着珍稀、几乎是异域的浓香，还有花鸟儿独享的稀薄、甜蜜、充满杏仁味的空气——海鸥、雄麻鸭、鸧、鹡鸰、燕雀、知更鸟，这些鸟儿见到我都振翅高飞，我既生气又悲伤地意识到，鸟儿刹那间的惊恐都是由于我的出现——他们的敌人，魔鬼的化身就是人类。人类？那么这些又是谁呢？……

"由于夜晚我在内陆长途跋涉，我那天清晨迷了路，现在又迷了路。夜幕降临了，温暖而多星。我很疲倦，情绪低落，精疲力竭，难以形容。那晚我睡在一个谷仓里，第二天破晓就被公鸡的报晓声给惊醒了。我走出去，太阳光刺得我眼睛晕眩，我在附近的小河里洗了脸和手，然后来到一个还在沉睡中的村庄。草地上的墙底长满海石竹，墙上冠有荆棘，我就在墙根坐下，又一次打着瞌睡，睡着了。当我再次醒来，已经是十点了。教堂里钟楼敲响了报时的钟声，于是我进了一家小饭店去吃饭。

"店里有一个肥胖、白肤金发碧眼的女人，善良而好客，她的脸长得就像她家的猪；当我坐下来吃我点的饭时，她家的猪喘着粗气用鼻子顶开了门。我向她描述了——当时不无带有某种渐消的惭愧，好像那是一件大逆不道之事——我去过的农场，农场的位置。

"她用小蓝眼睛'猪猡似地'扫了我一眼，脸部表情一闪而过，我破译不出其中的奥妙。农场的名字好像是特拉瓦勒斯。'你看到什么怪精灵了吗？'她用不完全属于她自己的嗓音问我。'怪精灵！'我仰坐了一会儿，盯着她，随后意识到"怪精灵"就是我造访过的农场主人的名字，马菲亚和克里斯特斯（虽然店主的口音也可能使我弄不准他们的名字）是那两个园丁的名字。她编造了一个荒谬的故事，我还能把它们凑在一起使故事连贯。对于那个男人有一段迷信传说，当他行游到此地时，本地的居民都感到吃惊和好奇，之后他就在特拉瓦勒斯安了家——一个陌生客兼朝圣客，就像一个'外国人'，话很少，举止可疑，二者的原委都不得而知。

"然后还有一些（她摊开胖胖的手放在锌面的吧台上，其中一只手上戴着结婚戒指，并且凝视着我，好像我是一个爽口的什么'淡饮料'），还有一些关于'来自于海洋'的那个女人的故事。她穿一件"蓝色长袍"，不是哑巴、口齿不清，就是只能讲外语的主妇。此外，那女人一定生活在负罪感里，此时述说者猪猡般贪婪的眼睛似乎在渴望着什么，因为她的孩子们都很'单纯'，'缺心眼儿'——这一般都是天意。不多说了，再说也没用。有时候人的胃口对有益健康的'第二天一早'的凉汽水也会拒绝，而我这荒唐的自我陶醉型的述说已经使我口干舌燥了，但并没有完全让我冷静下来。

"不管怎么样，店主告诉我说，我见到的蓝袍主妇，头发像亚麻一样淡黄，她已经死了，被埋在附近教堂的墓园里（离特拉瓦勒斯最近，但也有几英里远）。店主反复向我保证，我会在那儿找到她的坟墓，她的'石碑'，就好像否则的话我会怀疑这一复杂事实的真实性。

"所以，我的确这样做了——她埋在离上帝选民的墓地很远处，在那沉睡寂静、不长农作物的教堂墓地荫凉的西北角上：那里有一块不太圆的花岗岩石板，黑色粗糙的表面上刻着一个名字，'精灵菲尔娜'。"

William Somerset Maugham
(1874—1965)

William Somerset Maugham, English novelist and playwright, was born in a lawyer's family. His parents died when he was still very young. His miserable childhood became the root for the morose, sensitive and introversive aspects of his character, and it had profound influence on his worldview as well as literary production. Maugham spent five years studying medicine and later worked as a doctor. This early period enabled him to look into the suffering and pain of the low class. He also learned to analyze the society and life with a severe and incisive attitude. He gained brilliant literary achievements in the early 1930's and became the highest paid author of his era.

Maugham wrote lots of works in almost all literary genres except poetry, including 20 novels, over 100 short stories, 32 plays, some travelogues, reminiscences, and literary criticism. His works display a simple style with clear threads, distinctive characters, and complicated plots. They represent a calm, objective and critical observation of life. *Of Human Bondage* (1915) is often considered as his masterpiece. The novel is a semi-autobiography telling the story of how Philip Carey is devastated by the unreasonable education system, bound by the religious thought, and stricken by the loss of love. Another novel *The Moon and Sixpence* (1919) tells how the main character, Charles Strickland, abandons his home, wife, and children to devote himself slavishly to painting. *The Razor's Edge* (1944) is about a young American in search of the absolute in the progress of his spiritual odyssey ending in the Indian religion.

The Luncheon

This story is from Maugham's collection Here and There (1948), in which he depicted three vivid characters with elegant and simple words and undemonstrative scorn, and thus a greedy and hypocritical woman, an unsophisticated young writer and a wily and mercenary waiter all came to life.

I caught sight of her at the play, and in answer to her beckoning I went over during the interval and sat down beside her. It was long since I had last seen her, and if someone had not mentioned her name I hardly think I would have recognised her. She addressed me brightly.

"Well, it's many years since we first met. How time does fly! We're none of us getting any younger. Do you remember the first time I saw you? You asked me to luncheon."

Did I remember?

It was twenty years ago and I was living in Paris. I had a tiny apartment in the Latin Quarter overlooking a cemetery, and I was earning barely enough money to keep body and soul together. She had read a book of mine and had written to me about it. I answered, thanking her, and presently I received from her another letter saying that she was passing through Paris and would like to have a chat with me; but her time was limited, and the only free moment she had was on the following Thursday; she was spending the morning at the Luxembourg and would I give her a little luncheon at Foyot's afterwards? Foyot's is a restaurant at which the French senators eat, and it was so far beyond my means that I had never even thought of going there. But I was flattered, and I was too young to have learned to say no to a woman. (Few men, I may add, learn this until they are too old to make it of any consequence to a woman what they say.) I had eighty francs (gold francs) to last me the rest of the month, and a modest luncheon should not cost more than fifteen. If I cut out coffee for the next two weeks I could manage well enough.

I answered that I would meet my friend—by correspondence—at Foyot's on Thursday at half past twelve. She was not so young as I expected and in appearance imposing rather than attractive, she was, in fact, a woman of forty (a charming age, but not one that excites a sudden and devastating passion at first sight), and she gave me the impression of having more teeth, white and large and even, than were necessary for any practical purpose. She was talkative, but since she seemed inclined to talk about me I was prepared to be an attentive listener.

I was startled when the bill of fare was brought, for the prices were a great deal higher than I had anticipated. But she reassured me.

"I never eat anything for luncheon," She said.

"Oh, don't say that!" I answered generously.

"I never eat more than one thing. I think people eat far too much nowadays. A little fish, perhaps. I wonder if they have any salmon."

Well, it was early in the year for salmon and it was not on the bill of fare, but I asked the waiter if there was any. Yes, a beautiful salmon had just come in, it was the first they had had. I ordered it for my guest. The waiter asked her if she would have something while it was being cooked.

"No," she answered, "I never eat more than one thing. Unless you have a little caviare. I never mind caviare."

My heart sank a little. I knew I could not afford caviare, but I could not very well tell her that. I told the waiter by all means to bring caviare. For myself I chose the cheapest dish on the menu and that was a mutton chop.

"I think you are unwise to eat meat," she said. "I don't know how you can expect to work after eating heavy things like chops. I don't believe in overloading my stomach."

Then came the question of drink.

"I never drink anything for luncheon," she said.

"Neither do I," I answered promptly.

"Except whiter wine," she proceeded as though I had not spoken. "These French white wines are so light. They're wonderful for the digestion."

"What would you like?" I asked, hospitable still, but not exactly effusive.

She gave me a bright and amicable flash of her white teeth.

"My doctor won't let me drink anything but champagne."

I fancy I turned a trifle pale. I ordered half a bottle. I mentioned casually that my doctor had absolutely forbidden me to drink champagne.

"What are you going to drink, then?"

"Water."

She ate the caviare and she ate the salmon. She talked gaily of art and literature and music. But I wondered what the bill would come to. When my mutton chop arrived she took me quite seriously to task.

"I see that you're in the habit of eating a heavy luncheon. I'm sure it's a mistake. Why don't you follow my example and just eat one thing? I'm sure you'd feel ever so much better for it."

"I am only going to eat one thing." I said, as the waiter came again with the bill of fare.

She waved him aside with an airy gesture.

"No, no, I never eat anything for luncheon. Just a bite, I never want more than that, and I eat that more as an excuse for conversation than anything else. I couldn't possibly eat anything more unless they had some of those giant asparagus. I should be sorry to leave Paris without having some of them."

My heart sank. I had seen them in the shops, and I knew that they were horribly expensive. My mouth had often watered at the sight of them.

"Madame wants to know if you have any of those giant asparagus," I asked the waiter.

I tried with all my might too will him to say no. A happy smile spread over his broad, priest-like face, and he assured me that they had some so large, so splendid, so tender, that it was a marvel.

"I'm not in the least hungry," my guest sighed, "but if you insist I don't mind having some asparagus."

I ordered them.

"Aren't you going to have any?"

"No, I never eat asparagus."

"I know there are people who don't like them. The fact is, you ruin your taste by all the meat you eat."

We waited for the asparagus to be cooked. Panic seized me. It was not a question now how much money I should have left over for the rest of the month, but whether I had enough to pay the bill. It would be embarrassing to find myself ten francs short and be obliged to borrow from my guest. I could not bring myself to do that. I knew exactly how much I had, and if the bill came to more I made up my mind that I would put my hand in my pocket and with a dramatic cry start up and say it had been picked. Of course, it would be awkward if she had not money enough either to pay the bill. Then the only thing would be to leave my watch and say I would come back and pay later.

The asparagus appeared. They were enormous, succulent, and appetizing. The smell of the melted butter tickled my nostrils as the nostrils of Jehovah were tickled by the burned offerings of the virtuous Semites. I watched the abandoned woman thrust them down her throat in large voluptuous mouthfuls and in my polite way I discoursed on the condition of the drama in the Balkans. At last, she finished.

"Coffee?" I said.

"Yes, just an ice-cream and coffee," she answered.

I was past caring now, so I ordered coffee for myself and an ice-cream and coffee for her.

"You know, there's one thing I thoroughly believe in," she said, as she ate the ice-cream. "One should always get up from a meal feeling one could eat a little more."

"Are you still hungry?" I asked faintly.

"Oh, no, I'm not hungry; you see, I don't eat luncheon. I have a cup of coffee in the morning and then dinner, but I never eat more than one thing for luncheon. I was speaking for you."

"Oh, I see!"

Then a terrible thing happened. While we were waiting for the coffee the head waiter, with an ingratiating smile on his false face, came up to us bearing a large basket full of huge peaches. They had the blush of an innocent girl; they had the rich tone of an Italian landscape. But surely peaches were not in season then. Lord knew what they cost. I knew too—a little later, for my guest, going on with her conversation, absentmindedly took one.

"You see, you've filled your stomach with a lot of meat"—my one miserable little chop—"and you can't eat any more. But I've just had a snack and I shall enjoy a peach."

The bill came, and when I paid it I found that I had only enough for a quite inadequate tip. Her eyes rested for an instant on the three francs I left for the waiter, and I knew that she thought me mean. But when I walked out of the restaurant I had the whole month before me and not a penny in my pocket.

"Follow my example," she said as we shook hands, "and never eat more than one thing for luncheon."

"I'll do better than that," I retorted. "I'll eat nothing for dinner tonight."

"Humorist!" she cried gaily, jumping into a cab. "You're quite a humorist!"

But I have had my revenge at last. I do not believe that I am a vindictive man, but when the immortal gods take a hand in matter it is pardonable to observe the result with complacency. Today she weighs twenty-one stone.

Questions

1. Why did the protagonist of the story care so much about the woman's teeth and give such a clear description of them? What does the sentence "She gave me a bright and amicable flash of her white teeth" imply?
2. How did the protagonist have his revenge?

3. What were the characteristics of the woman, the young writer and the waiter? How did Maugham reveal such characteristics?
4. There are many rhetorical devices employed in this story. Demonstrate such devices. Do you think the ending is dramatic enough to catch the reader's attention?
5. Sum up the stylistic features of the story.

威廉·萨默塞特·毛姆
(1874—1965)

英国小说家、戏剧家威廉·萨默塞特·毛姆生于律师之家，因父母早亡，童年孤寂凄清，形成了孤僻、敏感、内向的性格。这些对其世界观和文学创作影响深远。毛姆早年学医，行医五年间他认识到底层人民的艰辛，也学会用冷峻、犀利的视角来剖析社会和人生。20世纪30年代初，毛姆迎来人生的辉煌，他成为该时期稿酬最高的作家。

毛姆著作颇丰，除诗歌以外，他在其他文学领域都有所建树。其作品包括长篇小说20部，短篇小说一百多篇，剧本32部，此外还著有游记、回忆录、文艺评论等。他的作品文笔质朴，脉络清晰，人物性格鲜明，情节跌宕有致，时常用一种冷静、客观乃至挑剔的态度审视人生。其代表著作长篇小说《人生的枷锁》（1915）带有自传成分，描写了青年菲利普被不合理教育制度摧残，受宗教思想束缚，并且在爱情上遭到打击。《月亮和六便士》（1919）叙述了主人公查尔斯·斯特克里兰放弃妻儿，追求艺术的故事。《刀锋》（1944）讲述了一位美国青年执著探索人生的道路，历尽艰险后终于在印度宗教中找到了人生归宿。

午　餐

本篇选自毛姆的短篇小说集《这里和那里》（1948）。他用优雅简约的笔触，不露声色的冷峻讥诮，刻画了三个生动的人物形象，令一个贪婪虚伪的中年女人、一个抹不开情面的青年作家、一个唯利是图的狡猾侍者跃然纸上。

我看戏的时候瞧见她向我招手示意，于是我便在演出间隙走过去在她身边坐了下来。上一次见到她已经是很久以前的事了，如果不是有人提起她的名字，我可不一定能认出她来。她快活地同我打招呼。

"哎呀，离我们上次见面有好多年啦。真是时光飞逝啊！我们都不再年轻了。你还记得我第一次见你的情形吗？你还邀请我共进午餐了呢！"

我能不记得吗？

二十年前，当时我住在巴黎，在拉丁区有一小间屋子，从窗子望出去，正好俯瞰公墓。我那时一点可怜巴巴的收入只够糊口度日。她看过我写的一本书，并就那本书写信给我。我回了信，表示感谢，接着又收到她的来信，说她不久要路经巴黎,很想和我当面聊聊。她说自己时间有限,只有下星期四才有点空闲。她上午参观卢森堡公园,问我是否愿意随后中午请她在福伊约吃点午餐?福伊约那个地方是法国参议员吃饭的餐厅,那里的消费远远超出我的收入,我从没想过要去那里。被人捧着,又年轻脸薄,我还没学会对女人说不。(让我补充一句,大部分男人只有到上了年纪以后,说什么对女人已经无关紧要了,才学会拒绝女人。)我有八十法郎(金法郎)来维持到月底,一顿还说得过去的午餐最多也就十五法郎。如果接下来的两个星期不喝咖啡的话,我还能度日。

我回信说愿意见我这位朋友——并在信中约定——星期四12点半在福伊约餐厅见。她并不像我想象得那么年轻,相貌也说不上妩媚动人,倒是气度不凡。她其实四十多岁了(这是一个很有魅力的年纪,但第一眼看到她却不会让人产生一种突如其来、汹涌澎湃的激情),给我的印象是牙齿长得过多,又白,又大,又整齐,这么多牙齿实在是无用武之地。她很健谈,好像很喜欢谈论我,因此我打算做一位聚精会神的听众。

菜单拿来后,我吃了一惊,因为上面的价格远远超出我的预期。不过她的一番话打消了我的顾虑。

"我午餐从来不吃什么,"她说。

"噢,别客气!"我慷慨地回应。

"要吃也只吃一样。我觉得现在的人吃得太多了。就来一条小鱼如何,也不知道他们有没有鲑鱼。"

哦,现在离吃鲑鱼的时节还有点早,况且菜单上也没有,不过我还是问侍者是否有这道菜。真巧,刚到了一条肥美的鲑鱼,也是该店今年第一条。我为客人点了这条鱼。侍者问她是否在鲑鱼烹饪好之前吃点什么别的。

"不了,"她回答说,"我从不多吃一样,除非你这儿有鱼子酱。鱼子酱倒是可以考虑。"

我的心一沉,因为我清楚自己吃不起鱼子酱,但对她又不能直说。我叮嘱侍者务必要上鱼子酱。我为自己挑选了菜单上最便宜的一道菜,一份羊排而已。

"我觉得你点肉食有点不太明智,"她说,"真不明白,你吃完像羊排这种油腻的食物后,还指望能做事吗?我可不赞成把自己的肚子撑得太饱。"

接下来是喝什么的问题。

"午餐时我什么也不喝,"她说。

"我也是,"我赶紧回答。

"除非是白葡萄酒,"她接着说,就当我什么也没说一样,"法国白葡萄酒口味清淡,用来促消化再好不过了。"

"你喝点什么呢?"我问道,虽然好客依旧,但不再热情洋溢。

她回报我以灿烂友好的微笑，那白森森的牙齿闪闪发亮。

"医生告诫我除了香槟其他的都别喝。"

我猜想自己的脸色都变得有点儿白了。我要了半瓶，装作漫不经心地说医生严禁我沾染香槟。

"那你自己喝什么？"

"水。"

她吃了鱼子酱，又吃鲑鱼，兴高采烈地谈论着艺术、文学和音乐。而我在想账单的金额会是多少。羊排上来后，她又开始教训起我来。

"看得出你习惯午餐吃得油腻。这可是陋习。难道你不可以学学我，只吃一样吗？我保证你这样做感觉会好得多。"

"我是准备只吃一样，"我回答说，这时侍者再次拿着菜单过来了。

她手轻轻一挥，将侍者指到一边。

"不用，不用，我午餐从不吃什么。要吃也就一小口，从不超量，吃了那么多，也只是为了谈话方便，不为别的。我再也吃不下别的东西了，不过他们有那种大芦笋的话倒是可以试一试。没吃到大芦笋就离开巴黎，那会让我觉得太遗憾了。"

我的心又一沉。我在商店里见过芦笋，知道价格高得吓人。每每见到芦笋我都会满口生津。

"这位女士想知道你们有没有大芦笋？"我问侍者。我竭尽全力地祈祷，希望他能回答说没有。侍者宽大如神父般的脸上洋溢出开心的微笑，他向我保证他们的芦笋足够大，足够好，足够嫩，简直就是稀世珍宝！

"我一点都不饿，"客人叹了口气，"不过你要坚持的话，来点芦笋我也不介意。"

我点了芦笋。

"你自己不吃点吗？"

"不用了，我从来不吃芦笋。"

"我知道有人不喜欢吃。其实是你刚吃下的肉坏了你的胃口。"

我们等着芦笋上桌。此时我一阵心慌。现在的问题不是还能剩下多少钱来打发这个月剩余的日子，而是我是否有足够的钱来支付账单。假如付账还差十法郎，不得不向客人借的话，那就太难堪了。我绝不能让自己陷于这样的窘境。我很清楚自己有多少钱，如果账单超出我的支付能力，我想定主意，就把手伸进口袋，然后夸张地大叫着站起来，惊呼被偷了。当然，如果她也没有钱来付账的话，那会很尴尬。接下来唯一可行的就是留下我的手表，然后说之后再回来付账。

芦笋端上来了，看上去丰美多汁，让人垂涎欲滴。融化后的黄油散发扑鼻香味，挑逗着我的鼻孔，正如善良的闪米特人敬献的燔祭让耶和华的鼻腔痒痒一样。我注视着这个寡廉鲜耻的女人，她正心满意足地含着一嘴的芦笋，然后猛地咽下。出于礼貌，我和她谈论着巴尔干地区的戏剧。最后，她全吃光了。

"来杯咖啡？"我问她，

"好吧，只要冰淇淋和咖啡，"她回答道。

我已无所顾忌了，为自己要了咖啡，为她点了冰淇淋和咖啡。

"你看，有一件事我坚信不疑，"她边吃冰淇淋边说，"吃饭的时候应该不时地站起来一下，这样可以感觉自己还可以再吃一点。"

"你还饿啊？"我小声地问她。

"哦，不，我不饿。你瞧，我不吃午餐。我早上喝杯咖啡然后就吃晚餐，我午餐只吃一样。我是在说你呢。"

"哦，我明白了！"

接下来发生了一件糟糕的事。等咖啡时，领班拎着满满一篮子大个儿桃子走到我们跟前，他那面具般的脸上带着谄媚的笑容。桃子色如天真少女两颊的红晕，有着意大利风景画的华美格调。毫无疑问，这些桃子并不当季，天知道它们有多贵。我会知道的——只要稍等一小会儿，因为我的客人在和我聊天时顺手拿了一个。

"你看，你塞太多肉到肚子里了。"——我只吃了一块小小羊排而已——"你都吃不下其他东西了。我只吃了点儿小食，所以还可以再享用桃子。"

该结账了，我付完款后，发现自己所剩的钱只能给一次微不足道的小费。客人的眼睛在留给侍者作小费的三个法郎上停了停，我知道她一定觉得我很吝啬。走出餐厅后，我的面前还有一个月要捱，口袋里却没剩一个便士。

"跟我学学吧，"我们边握手她边说，"午餐时别多吃一样。"

"我能做得更好，"我回敬她说，"晚餐我什么都不吃了。"

"真幽默！"她快乐地叫嚷着，跳进一辆出租车，"你真是个幽默家！"

但我终于还是出了口气。我觉得自己不是一个坏心眼的人，可是一旦诸神干预了此事，看到干预的结果后自己有点儿得意，这也是情有可原的。现今她体重168磅。

Theodore Francis Powys
(1875—1953)

Theodore Francis Powys is a British novelist, short story writer and modern allegorist. Powys was born in Derbyshire and his father was a clergyman of Welsh origin. The Powys family consisted of several talented members. The three Powys brothers were just like the three Brontë sisters. The eldest brother John Cowper Powys and the youngest brother Llewelyn Powys also achieved remarkable literary fame. After running his White House Farm for several years in Suffolk, Powys settled down in Dorset in 1901, whose local landscape was to become the setting for most of his works. Powys spent most of his hermit-like life in rural Dorset, far removed from the literary world. Due to the war, in 1940 he moved to Mappowder, where he spent his days reading and meditating until his death in 1953.

Powys was deeply religious and his works belonged to the tradition of fictional meditation rather than the mainstream of modern fiction. The allegorical gloomy stories of rural England often deal with the conflict of good and evil and reflect his dark vision of humanity. His major works include the novels *The Soliloquy of a Hermit* (1918) and *Mr. Weston's Good Wine* (1927), and the short story collections *The House with the Echo* (1928) and *The White Paternoster* (1930). His *Fables* (1929) is also much admired. Its style is relatively simple, traditional, and full of biblical echoes and cadences. In almost all of them inanimate objects such as a withered leaf, a clout, a pan, a stone, a bucket, a rope, a clock, or animals like the ass, the rabbit, a dog, a worm, and a flea, act as instructors of erring man, or as keen-sighted commentators on the vicissitudes of mortal life.

The Bucket and the Rope

The following fable is an effective meditation by the two innocent household implements on the death of their master. The bucket and the rope are too simple-minded and straightforward to comprehend the personal tragedy played out behind the scenes. Powys employs his artfulness here by the dramatic omission of obvious knowledge.

A bucket once lay upon its side in a little shed, that was a short way down a by-lane, near to the village of Shelton.

This bucket, a large one, had been kicked over by a man who had hanged himself up by the neck, by means of an odd piece of rope that he had tied to a strong beam.

The man's name who had hanged himself was Mr Dendy, who rented a few pleasant fields that he used to plough happily, and, besides keeping a few good cows, he fattened some nice pigs.

Every servant, be he never so humble, is interested in his master, whose habits of life, goings and comings, loves and hates, are watched and commented upon. Mr Dendy's movements as well as his behaviour had always been of great interest to the bucket and to the rope; who, when together, which was often the case, for they lived in the same shed, would speak of all that Mr Dendy did, and endeavour to find out as best they might a reason for his actions.

Both were interested in any kind of life that was not like themselves, such as mankind, because both were humble and did not consider, as so many do, that they or their own kind deserved the most notice.

In order to study men, both the bucket and the rope decided to take Mr Dendy as an example of humanity, believing, as they well might, that the ways and notions of a simple countryman ought to be easier to understand than those of one more sly and cunning. They wished to study Mr Dendy in order to find out from his behaviour what other men were like; to learn from his doings how they did, to find out the causes of their sorrows and joys, so as to journey a little nearer to the Truth that is always so hard to discover.

Now and again the two friends had been a little puzzled by Mr Dendy, who did not often act as they would have expected him to, for sometimes he would seem to be troubled, when, according to the bucket's ideas of cause and effect, there was no reason for him to be so.

And now that Mr Dendy had hanged himself, pressing both of them into this last service, to forward his self-destruction, the bucket and the rope thought they would review the man's life, in the hope of finding one true reason at least for his final act.

"Is it not a little curious, if not altogether surprising," observed the bucket, "that we should have been put to so sad a use in helping our good master to die? Perhaps you can remember as well as I the joyful day when we were first purchased, which happened to be the very day before Mr Dendy was married.

"He married, as you know, a woman, a creature created to ease a man of the heavy burden of desire, a burden as troublesome to carry as a kicking ass."

"And who also," observed the rope, "was intended to cook and prepare a man's food, to rear his children and to clean his house."

"That should certainly be so," said the other.

"The day we were purchased," continued the rope, "happened to be one of those delightful May days when all things, animate and inanimate, that exist under the sun, are entirely happy.

"I was coiled up in the shop window of Mr Johnson, the ropemaker, a man whose shirt-sleeves were always turned up, so that his hairy arms made the children stare. The sun shone upon me, and in its pleasant warmth I soon fell asleep. I dreamed of my happy childhood, when I grew up in a large field, beside a million brothers and sisters who were all beautiful flowers. But I did not sleep long, for as soon as the sun rose too high to shine into the window I awoke and looked out into the street.

"Anyone with a proper desire for knowledge, if he has eyes, can always see something of interest in what goes in a street. He has only to look and something will be sure to come near.

"I began to watch the folk who moved along the pavement in front of the shop, and a few of them particularly attracted my notice. Two old women came by, whose feet seemed to stick to the stones at every step, while their tongues cackled and gabbled about the ill-conduct of their neighbours.

"A grand military gentleman sauntered past, who saw his own reflection in every window that he went by, and became prouder than ever. A lady who followed him at a little distance wished to see herself too, but did not dare to look, because she feared that a servant girl who walked behind might notice what she did.

"Presently there was a fine clatter of running feet; some schoolboys came by, pulling the caps from one another's heads, and then an alderman passed, who looked about him as if the town were all his own.

"After him came two young and pleasing girls, who were ready for love; they watched coyly every young man in the street, and laughed in order to show what they longed for. The clock in the church tower at the top of the town struck three, but no one seemed to give any heed to it, except a poor debtor, whose examination was to be at that very hour in the town hall, and who wished he had taken his wife's advice earlier and drowned himself.

"The clock had hardly finished striking when a young man, who had the joyful looks of a would-be bridegroom, together with a young girl entered the shop. I looked at her with admiration, and at him with pleasure. They seemed made for one another. Anyone could see that she had the sweetest of natures, that would be unlikely, for fear of being cruel, to refuse anything a man might ask of her. The man was Mr Dendy, and she was to be his wife."

"Her arms had been opened to another before him," murmured the bucket.

"Only a grave could have prevented that," answered the rope; "but allow me to continue:

"Mr Dendy came forward to the window and looked at me, together with Mr Johnson. The girl looked elsewhere. Mr Johnson's hands, that were as hairy as his arms, took me up, uncoiled me, and stretched me out. Our master examined me for a little, satisfied himself that I was what he needed, and made the purchase."

"Mr Dendy was about twenty-nine years old then, and the young girl about eighteen," remarked the bucket.

"So she was," said the rope, "but it is curious to think now what she did next. While Mr Johnson and Mr Dendy were talking, she coiled and uncoiled me, and then, in her girlish amusement, for she looked at him lovingly, she made a running noose of me, slipped it over our master's head, and pulled it tight."

"Mr Johnson laughed, I suppose?"

"Yes, but a little uneasily. While she toyed with me," said the rope, "I had the chance to look at her the more narrowly. She seemed just the creature to delight any man with her sweetness and eagerness for love. She had a yielding kindness, but no wickedness in her. She showed her good nature to a young man, the son of the lawyer, who happened to pass her in a by-street when Mr Dendy slipped into a small inn. The lawyer's son looked unhappy and she allowed him to kiss her, while Mr Dendy was out of the way."

"She had a little foot," observed the bucket, "and a winning gait, and had Mr Dendy peeped through the dingy bar-window, when he was having a merry jest with Farmer Pardy, he should have been glad to see that the lawyer's son thought her as nice as he did."

"A rope would have fancied so," said the other dryly.

"Mr Dendy had no sooner bought you," said the bucket, "than he went to the ironmonger's and purchased me. We were carried off together, and so we became acquainted, and that very evening I was made use of to collect the swill for the pigs; I remember even now the unpleasant smell of the rotten potatoes."

"It was not the stink of the sour garbage that made our master hang himself," observed the rope thoughtfully, "for he would be often whistling when he brought you in, full of the nastiest stuff. Neither could it have been the weight of you that troubled him, for he would ever carry you jauntily, as if the burden of a few gallons of swill was nothing to so powerful an arm as his."

"Oh no, he never minded carrying me," said the bucket, "for whatever the time of year was, whether the summer sun shone or whether a dreary autumn rain fell, Mr Dendy would bear me along with the same sprightliness. He would perhaps tarry at a cottage gate, and have a merry word with the occupants, telling a droll story of country matters for the young girls to smile at, and bidding them to ask of his kind Betty what the fancies were that she had found the most useful in the getting of a husband."

"We could watch nearly all that he did," remarked the rope, "and he certainly appeared to be living a very happy life: the sweet country air, the plain and wholesome food that he ate, as well as his constant though not too tedious toil, gave him health and joy, and he was never in want of a shilling to spend when he needed one."

"Only once," observed the bucket sadly, "did I notice Mr Dendy act in a way that was not usual for a village man. He was bearing me, full, along a path from a small cottage where he bought swill. On each side of the path there were flowers, both white and yellow. Mr Dendy set me down, a rotten orange bobbed up on my surface. Mr Dendy rested by the path, plucked some of the flowers, and seemed to take delight in holding them in his hand."

"What did he do next?" asked the rope.

"He carried the flowers home to his wife," replied the bucket…

"The summer pleased Mr Dendy, and so did the winter," said the rope.

"In the winter we saw more of him, for we were used the more. During the winter the horses lay in, and straw had to be carried to them, and in the winter there were more pigs to be fattened. In the winter, too, a strong man feels his strength and his happiness more than in the summer. He learns to brave the keenest wind without a shudder, and cares nothing when the rain soaks him to the skin. No weather daunted Mr Dendy, and the more he bore with the storms outside the pleasanter was his parlour, with its cheerful light, and the warm presence of a wife who loved him."

"Why, then, did he hang himself?" asked the bucket.

"The winter weather was certainly not to blame," answered the rope, "for I cannot think of those happy days without being sure that he enjoyed them. I was stouter then, and yet I think not, for I appear to be strong enough now to hold a pretty fair burden. Mr Dendy, who is carried by me, could carry a bundle then, he thought nothing of carrying as much straw with me as was enough for three men to bear. However large the bundle was, he would somehow get it upon his back, so that the straw upon either side of him would sweep the hedges in the lane, almost as though a whole stack was out a-walking."

"Yes, there was Mr Dendy!" exclaimed the bucket, "a true and joyful countryman, doing his proper tasks. What could harm him? What could prevent him from living out his life contentedly and going down, as a good man should, gently into the grave? Surely never was a poor man created who meant so well."

"Look at him now," said the rope quietly; "at first when he kicked you over I wondered if I should be strong enough to hold him. He struggled horribly, and I fancy that when he first felt me tighten round his throat he would have changed his mind. He tried to catch me to lessen the dreadful feeling of suffocation."

"You must have hurt him very much," observed the bucket, "for his face became quite black, and his eyes bulged out of his head. I wonder you did not let him fall, for in his death agony he kicked his legs and swung round, but you held him fast. Why did he do it?"

"I believe the reason was," replied the rope, "that Mr Dendy did not like to see others happy."

"That is not easy to believe," remarked the bucket, "when one considers how happy he was himself."

"His wife made him so," said the rope, "and feeling her success with him she naturally wished to make another happy too."

"What could be more proper?" said the bucket.

"It was this summer," continued the rope, "and the master, having saved a few guineas, bought for himself a new Sunday suit. 'You look so well in it,' his wife told him, 'that you should go to church more often, for people will know how well you are getting on when they see you in your new clothes.' Now, it was the time when Mr Dendy began to go to church of an evening that I noticed passing this shed the same young man who had given Betty a kiss in the by-street when Mr Dendy was drinking a glass in the little tavern. He still looked unhappy."

"A chance for Betty to turn his sorrow into joy!" laughed the bucket.

"She wished to do so, and they met in this very shed, on a Sunday evening, when Mr Dendy was supposed to be gone to church."

"But had he gone?" asked the bucket.

"No," replied the rope. "He had only put on his best clothes and walked out, as if to go. Instead of going to church, he came to this shed, took me up, and bound me round a large bundle of straw. The bundle he placed against the wall of the shed, where there was a little chink, and, creeping under the straw to hide himself, he waited."

"For the pleasure of witnessing the kindness of his wife, I suppose," said the bucket.

"One would have thought so," replied the rope, "but the look upon Mr Dendy's face when he saw what was going on did not warrant such a supposition."

"Perhaps he thought," reasoned the bucket, "that Betty should have remained at home and warmed the rabbit pie for his supper; for the sermon preached by Mr Hayball always made him extremely hungry, and Betty was not to be expected to know that he was not at church. I have seen the pigs fed so often, and I know how hungry animals are, and, as food keeps a man alive and prevents him from becoming a dead carcass, it is natural that a man should wish the woman that he keeps to prepare food for him, even though she may prefer to be loving and kind to another man."

"You should have heard Mr Dendy," said the rope; "he gnashed his teeth and moaned horribly, and when his wife's friend seemed to be altogether forgetting his sorrow, being come, as the lyric poet says, 'Where comfort is —' Mr Dendy crept out of the bundle and hid in the lane, snarling like a bitten dog."

"His hunger, I suppose, had gone beyond the proper bounds," suggested the bucket.

"It is difficult," said the rope, after a few minutes' silence, as the body swung to and fro, "for us to decide what could have troubled this good man. No one had robbed him. No one had beaten or hurt him, and never once since they had been married had Betty refused his embraces."

"It must have been that nosegay," exclaimed the bucket.

Questions

1. Why did Mr Dendy hang himself? Did the bucket and the rope find out the real reason at last? Why or why not?

2. What kind of person is Mr Dendy? What about Betty? What do they represent respectively?
3. Identify the figures of speech used in the following sentences: "She had a yielding kindness…" and "What could be more proper?" Can you find more examples of rhetorical devices in this story?
4. What are the stylistic features of this story? What kind of words and sentences are used here? Discuss their appropriateness.
5. What is the author's view on humanity? How does the story reveal it?

西奥多·弗朗西斯·波伊斯
（1875—1953）

英国作家西奥多·弗朗西斯·波伊斯写长、短篇小说俱佳，同时还是一位现代寓言作家。波伊斯出生于德贝郡，父亲是一位具有威尔士血统的牧师。波伊斯家人才辈出。波伊斯三兄弟可与勃朗特三姐妹相媲美，其哥哥约翰·考珀·波伊斯和弟弟卢埃林·波伊斯在文坛上也颇有建树。在萨克福经营了几年自己的白宫农场之后，波伊斯于1901年在多塞特定居下来，这里也成为他大多数作品的背景。波伊斯一生大部分时间在多塞特乡村过着隐居生活，远离文坛。由于战争原因，波伊斯在1940年迁往马鲍德，在那里他终日读书冥想，直到1953年辞世。

波伊斯是虔诚的基督徒，其作品属于传统的冥想式小说而非现代小说主流。那些寓言式的阴郁的英国农村故事揭示了善与恶的冲突，反映出他对人性的悲观看法。波伊斯的主要作品有长篇小说《隐士独白》（1918）和《韦斯顿先生的佳酿》（1927），以及短篇小说集《带回音的房屋》（1928）和《白色咒文》（1930）。他的《寓言故事》（1929）也深受人们的喜爱。其风格仿效《圣经》，相对简单、传统。几乎在所有的寓言故事中，无论是没有生命的物体，诸如枯萎的树叶、破布、平底锅、石头、桶、绳、时钟等，还是像驴、兔子、狗、虫、跳蚤这样的动物，要么指导着误入歧途的人类，要么敏锐地观察、评述凡夫俗子的人生浮沉。

桶与绳

下面的寓言故事描述了两件头脑简单的家用工具对它们的主人之死的沉思冥想。桶与绳的头脑是如此简单，以至于无法理解在幕后上演的人类悲剧。波伊斯在这个寓言故事中戏剧般地省略了一些显而易见的信息，展示了其巧妙的写作技巧。

从前，有一只桶倒在一个小棚子里，从那里沿着一条乡间小路走不远就到了谢尔顿村。

这只大桶是被一个上吊自杀的人给踢倒的。那人用一根孤零零的绳子悬在粗梁上自尽了。

上吊自杀的是邓迪先生。他曾租了几块好地，过去一直快乐地耕耘。此外，他还养了几头好奶牛和几头肥猪。

每个奴仆，无论多么卑微，都对主人感兴趣，观察、评论主人的生活习惯，来来往往和爱恨情仇。邓迪先生的一举一动总是令桶和绳感兴趣。由于同住在一个棚子里，它们常常在一起，它们一到一起就会谈论邓迪先生的所作所为，并竭尽全力为他的行为找出理由。

它俩都对不同于自己的生命形式感兴趣，比如人类，因为它俩都很谦卑，跟很多人一样，认为自己或同类不值得密切关注。

为了研究人类，桶和绳决定以邓迪先生为例，这很可能是因为它们相信一个纯朴的乡下人的作风和想法要比一个更狡猾的人更容易理解。它们希望通过研究邓迪先生的行为弄清楚其他人是什么样的。通过他的所作所为学习人类的行为，找出人类悲喜的原因，以便向难求的真理更靠近一些。

两个朋友偶尔会对邓迪先生感到迷惑不解：他并不总像它们预想的那样行动，因为他有时看起来好像很烦恼，而从桶的因果观念来看，没什么理由值得他那样。

既然邓迪先生已经上吊了，迫使它俩完成了最终任务，助其自我毁灭，桶和绳认为它俩应该重温此人的一生，希望借此至少为他最后的行为找到一个真正的原因。

"我们被派上如此可悲的用场，帮助我们的好主人自尽，"桶评论道，"即使这一切不令人惊讶，难道一点儿也不令人好奇吗？也许你能跟我一样记得主人买我们回来的那个大喜日子，那天正好是邓迪先生结婚的前一天。

"如你所知，他娶了一个女人，一个天生就是为了减轻男人欲望重负的女人，背负那重担就像对付一头尥蹶子的毛驴一样麻烦。"

"这女人也应该为男人烧菜做饭，生儿育女，打扫房屋。"绳评论道。

"那当然。"另一个说。

"主人买咱俩那天，"绳继续说，"恰巧是令人愉快的五月的一天，天下万物，无论是有生命的还是无生命的，都兴致勃勃。

"我被卷起来挂在约翰逊先生的商店橱窗里。约翰逊先生是做绳子的，他的衬衫袖子总是卷得老高，毛乎乎的胳膊让孩子们目瞪口呆。太阳照在我的身上，暖洋洋的，很快我就进入梦乡。我梦见了自己快乐的童年，那时我和无数的鲜花兄弟姐妹生长在一大片田野上。但我没睡多久，因为太阳一升到高处照不进橱窗，我就醒来了，向大街上张望。

"任何有正常求知欲的人，只要他长眼睛，就能看见街上发生的趣事。他只要看，一定会有事发生。

"我开始观察商店前人行道上来来往往的人们，有些人引起了我的特别关注。两个老太太走了过来，她们迈着沉重的步伐，嘴里却叽里咕噜地数落着邻居们的不端品行。

"一个傲慢的军人闲逛过来，每路过一个橱窗，他都要朝里面张望一下自己的身影，越看越骄傲。他后面不远处的一位女士也想看看自己，却又不敢看，唯恐身后的女仆会注意到她的所作所为。

"不一会儿，伴随着一阵啪嗒啪嗒的跑步声，跑过来一群学生，他们互相抢着对方的帽子，然后一个高级市政官走了过来，他环顾四周的样子仿佛整个小镇都是他的。

"他后面来了两个年轻可爱的姑娘，正值情窦初开。她们羞涩地观看着街上的每一个小伙子，笑着展露出自己的渴望。镇上最高的教堂钟楼里的钟敲了三下，但除了一个可怜的欠债人，好像没人理会，此时正是欠债人应该在市政厅里接受审查的时候。他后悔当初没听妻子的劝告，溺死算了。

"钟刚敲完，一个面带准新郎倌喜色的小伙子和一个姑娘走进店里。我充满羡慕地看着那个姑娘，兴高采烈地望着那个小伙子。他们真是天造地设的一对儿。谁都能看出她温柔至极，不会拒绝男人的任何要求，因为那样太残酷。那人就是邓迪先生，而她即将成为他的妻子。"

"在他之前，她曾对另一个男人敞开过怀抱，"桶嘟囔着。

"只有死亡才能阻止那种事儿发生，"绳答道，"但让我把话说完：

"邓迪先生和约翰逊先生走到橱窗前看着我，那姑娘看着别处。约翰逊先生用他那跟胳膊一样毛乎乎的手把我拿起来，展开拉长。咱们的主人把我检查了一番，确认我正是他所需要的，就把我买下了。"

"邓迪先生那时二十九岁左右，那姑娘大约十八岁。"桶评论道。

"是的，"绳说，"但现在想起来她接下来做的事情很稀奇古怪。当约翰逊先生和邓迪先生谈话时，她把我卷起来又打开，然后就像小女孩闹着玩似的，因为她充满爱意地望着他，她把我打了个活套，套在咱们主人头上，拉紧。

"我猜约翰逊先生笑了吧？"

"是的，但有一点不安。当她摆弄我玩的时候，"绳说，"我有机会更仔细地看她。她好似那种能用自己的甜美和对爱的渴望来愉悦任何一个男人的女人。她温婉亲切，毫无恶意。当邓迪先生溜进一家小酒馆时，她对一个碰巧在胡同里邂逅的律师的儿子祖露了自己的温柔。那律师的儿子看起来郁郁寡欢，于是她就趁邓迪先生不在让他吻了自己。"

"她脚步轻盈，步态动人，"桶评论道，"如果邓迪先生一边和帕迪农夫打趣，一边透过昏暗的酒馆窗户向外看，他就会很高兴地看见那律师的儿子跟他一样喜爱她。"

"连绳子都会这么想，"另一个冷淡地说。

"邓迪先生刚买完你，"桶说，"他就进了五金店买了我。咱们被一起带走了，就这样咱们相识了。当晚我就被用来装喂猪的泔水，至今我仍记得烂土豆的那股恶心味儿。"

"并不是那馊泔水味儿使咱们的主人上吊的，"绳若有所思地说，"因为他经常一边吹着口哨，一边把装满恶心东西的你提进来。也不可能是你的重量令他不堪重负，因为他总是神气活现地提着你，仿佛几加仑泔水的负重对他那强健的胳膊来说微不足道。"

"噢，是的，他从不在乎提着我，"桶说，"因为一年四季，无论是夏日炎炎还是秋雨凄凄，邓迪先生都会轻快地提着我。他也许会在某个农舍门前逗留，跟住在那儿的人愉快地攀谈，讲讲村里的趣闻轶事、逗年轻姑娘们笑笑，叫她们去问问他的好贝蒂，要把丈夫弄到手，什么主意最有用。"

"他的所有行为，我们几乎都可以观察到，"绳说，"他看起来无疑过得相当快活：清新的乡间空气，清淡且有益健康的食物，持续不断却不枯燥乏味的劳作，所有这些使他健康快活，而且他从不缺钱花。"

"只有一次，"桶悲伤地评论说，"我注意到邓迪先生的行为对于一个乡下人来说有点儿反常。他买泔水回来提着满满的我沿着一条小路走着。小路两旁盛开着白色和黄色的野花。邓迪先生把我放下，一个烂桔子迅速浮上表面。邓迪先生在路边休息，摘了一些花儿，他把花儿捧在手里，看起来喜滋滋的。"

"接下来他做了什么？"绳问。

"他把那些花儿捧回家送给了他的妻子，"桶答道……

"夏天邓迪先生很快活，冬天他也是如此，"绳说。

"冬天咱们看见他的次数就更多了，因为他使用咱们的次数更多了。冬天马儿待产，他得把草料给它们送去，而且在冬天有更多的肥猪要养。也是在冬天，身体强健的人比在夏天感到更强壮更快活。他学会顶风冒雪也毫不颤抖，即使被冬雨浇得浑身湿透也毫不在意。没有什么天气让邓迪先生气馁，他在外面经受的暴风雪越多，就越发觉得自己的家温暖舒适，那里有其乐融融的灯光，爱妻守候的温暖。"

"那他为什么还上吊？"桶问。

"肯定不怪冬天的天气，"绳说，"因为我敢肯定地说我想不出哪天他过得不快活。我那时比现在更结实，现在我只是看起来很结实，好像能承受相当重的负荷，但实际上我并不这样认为。我身上现在悬着的邓迪先生，那时他能背一大捆麦秆，对于邓迪先生来说，用我背起足有三个人才能背得动的麦秆是很平常的事情。不论草捆有多大，他都能设法把它背在背上，以至于他左右的麦秆都擦到了小路两旁的树篱，就好像是一整堆麦秆自己在——在走路。"

"是的，这就是邓迪先生！"桶感叹道，"一个真正的快活的乡下人，本本分分。是什么伤害了他？是什么阻止他心满意足地过活，不让他这个好人善始善终呢？肯定从来没有哪个可怜人心肠像他这么好。"

"看看他现在，"绳静静地说，"他刚踢倒你时，我还不知道自己是否经得住他。他拼命地挣扎，我以为当他一感觉到我勒紧他喉咙时，他就已经改变了主意。他试图抓住我来缓解可怕的窒息感。"

"你一定让他很痛苦，"桶说，"因为他的脸都变黑了，眼睛也突出来。我很奇怪为什么你没有把他放下，因为他在死亡的痛苦中蹬腿摇晃，而你却紧紧地勒住他。他为什么那样做呢？"

"我想原因是，"绳说，"邓迪先生不喜欢看见别人高兴。"

"这令人难以置信，"桶谈论说，"想想那时他自己是多么快活啊。"

"是他妻子使得他这般快活，"绳说，"感到自己在他身上的成功，她自然而然地希望让另一个人也快活。"

"还有什么比这更恰当的呢？"桶说。

"就在今年夏天，"绳接着说，"主人攒了点儿钱，给自己买了套新礼服。'你穿上礼服帅极了，'妻子告诉他，'所以你应该多去教堂，因为人们看见你穿新衣服就会知道你过得有多好。'于是邓迪先生开始晚上去教堂。一天晚上，我注意到上回趁着邓迪先生在小酒馆里喝酒时在胡同里偷吻贝蒂的那个年轻人路过这个小棚子。他仍旧郁郁寡欢。"

"这正是贝蒂让他化悲痛为喜悦的机会！"桶笑道。

"她正想这么做呢，于是在一个星期日的晚上，他们在这个小棚子里幽会。那晚邓迪先生本该去教堂做礼拜的。"

"可是他去了吗？"桶问。

"没有，"绳答道，"他只是穿上最好的衣服，走出家门，好像要去。他没有去教堂，而是来到这个小棚子，拿起我捆在一大捆麦秆上。他把麦秆靠在小棚子的墙上，挡住墙上的裂缝。然后，他爬到麦秆下藏起来，等着。"

"我猜他这么做是为了满心欢喜地亲眼看见妻子的爱意吧。"桶说。

"谁都会这么想，"绳答道，"但当邓迪先生看到接下来发生的事时，他脸上的表情并没有证明这种推测。"

"也许他认为，"桶推理说，"贝蒂应该待在家里，为他晚饭准备兔肉馅饼吧。因为黑鲍先生的布道总是让他饥肠辘辘，而贝蒂没料到他不在教堂。我曾看过人们喂猪，知道动物们饿起来是什么样。既然食物能使人维持生命而不会饿死，那么一个男人希望他的女人为他烧菜做饭也是很自然而然的了，即使她可能更愿意对另一个男人示爱。"

"你当时一定听到邓迪先生的声音了，"绳说，"他咬牙切齿，呜咽呻吟。当他妻子的朋友看起来完全忘记了自己的忧伤时，就如同抒情诗人所吟诵的，'陷入温柔乡——'，邓迪先生爬出草捆，躲在小路上，像一条被咬伤的狗一样咆哮。"

"我猜他已经饿得不行了，"桶说。

尸体前后晃动，几分钟的沉寂过后，绳才说，"对于咱们来说，很难认定是什么让这个好人烦恼不堪。没人打劫他，没人打他伤他，而且婚后贝蒂从来没有拒绝过他的拥抱。"

"一定是因为那束花儿，"桶喊到。

Alfred Edgar Coppard
(1878—1957)

Alfred Edgar Coppard was born the son of a tailor and a housemaid. He lived a life of semi-obscurity for many years in a small cottage in Essex. He had his first story collection *Adam and Eve and Pinch Me* (1921) published when he was forty-three. His rare talent was soon recognized, that of a true tale teller with no large statements to make. However, he remained outside the English literary society, receiving no honors and very little money up to his death at seventy-nine. "My Hundredth Tale" tells about his life story.

He preferred the story being spoken at you to being read at you. He achieved his reputation by depicting the English rural scene and its characters. Another story collection *Fishmonger's Fiddle* (1925) contains his best story "The Higgler." He uncovered the queerly pied quality of human life in quite unimportant people such as shop girls, gypsies, higglers, sailors, tailors, tramps, and country folk. He filled the countryside with his poetic feeling and his rustic characters with amusing and dramatic presentation. Coppard was an oddity as well as an artist.

Dusky Ruth

This is a sad and enchanting poetic love story and yet rendered in prose. Its magic perhaps lies in the fact that it tells of one of those erotic adventurers, beautiful yet incomplete, that everyman in his hidden heart would like to have had and to be able, many years afterward, to remember.

At the close of an April day, chilly and wet, the traveler came to a country town. In the Cotswolds, though the towns are small and sweet and the inns snug, the general habit of the land is bleak and bare. He had newly come upon upland roads so void of human affairs, so lonely, that they might have been made for some forgotten uses by departed men, and left to the unwitting passage of such strangers as himself. Even the unending walls, built of old rough laminated rock, that detailed the far-spreading fields, had grown very old again in their courses; there were dabs of darkness, buttons of moss, and fossils on every stone. He had passed a few neighborhoods, sometimes at the crook of a stream, or at the cross of debouching roads, where old habitations, their gangrenated thatch riddled with birds holes, had been not so much erected as just spattered about the places. Beyond these signs an odd lark or blackbird, the ruckle of partridges, or the nifty gallop of a hare had been the only mitigation of the living loneliness that was almost as profound by day as by night. But the traveler had a care for such times and places. There are men who love to gaze with the mind at things that can never be seen, feel at least the throb of a beauty that will never be known, and hear over immense bleak reaches the echo of that which is no celestial music, but only their own hearts' vain cries; and though his garments clung to him like clay it was with deliberate questing step that the traveler trod the single street of the town, and at last entered the inn, shuffling his shoes in the doorway for a moment and striking the raindrops from his hat. Then he turned into a small smoking-room. Leather-lined benches, much worn, were fixed to the wall under the window and in other odd corners and nooks behind mahogany tables. One wall was furnished with all the congenial gear of a bar, but without any intervening counter. Opposite, a bright fire was burning, and a neatly dressed young woman sat before it in a Windsor chair, staring at the flames. There was no other inmate of the room, and as he entered, the girl rose up and greeted him. He found that he could be accommodated for the night, and in a few moments his hat and scarf were removed and placed inside the fender, his wet overcoat was taken to the kitchen, the landlord, an old fellow, was lending him a roomy pair of slippers, and a maid was setting supper in an adjoining room.

He sat while this was doing and talked to the barmaid. She had a beautiful but rather mournful face as it was lit by the firelight, and when her glance was turned away from it her eyes had a piercing brightness. Friendly and well spoken as she was, the melancholy in her aspect was noticeable—perhaps it was the dim room, or the wet day, or the long hours ministering a multitude of cocktails to thirsty gallantry.

When he went to his supper he found cheering food and drink, with pleasant garniture of silver and mahogany. There were no other visitors, he was to be alone; blinds were drawn, lamps lit, and the fire at his back was comforting. So he sat long about his meal until a white-faced maid came to clear the table, discoursing to him about country things as she busied about the room. It was a long, narrow room, with a sideboard and the door at one end and the fireplace at the other. A bookshelf, almost devoid of books, contained a number of plates; the long wall that faced the windows was almost destitute of pictures, but there were hung upon it, for some inscrutable but doubtless sufficient reason, many dish-covers, solidly shaped, of the kind held in such mysterious regard and known as "willow pattern"; one was even hung upon the face of a map. Two musty prints were mixed with them, presentments of horses having a stilted extravagant physique and bestridden by images of inhuman and incommunicable dignity, clothed in whiskers, coloured jackets, and tight white breeches.

He took down the books from the shelf, but his interest was speedily exhausted, and the almanacs, the county directory, and various guidebooks were exchanged for the *Cotswold Chronicle*. With this, having drawn the deep chair to the hearth, he whiled away the time. The newspaper amused him with its advertisements of stock shows, farm auctions, traveling quacks and conjurers, and there was a lengthy account of the execution of a local felon, one Timothy Bridger, who had murdered an infant in some shameful circumstances. This dazzling crescendo proved rather trying to the traveler; he threw down the paper.

The town was all as quiet as the hills, and he could hear no sounds in the house. He got up and went across the hall to the smoke-room. The door was shut, but there was light within, and he entered. The girl sat there much as he had seen her on his arrival, still alone, with feet on fender. He shut the door behind him, sat down, and crossing his legs puffed at his pipe, admired the snug little room and the pretty figure of the girl, which he could do without embarrassment, as her meditative head, slightly bowed, was turned away from him. He could see something of her, too, in the mirror at the bar, which repeated also the agreeable contours of bottles of coloured wines and rich liqueurs—so entrancing in form and aspect that they seemed destined to charming histories, even in disuse—and those of familiar outline containing mere spirits or small beer, for which are reserved the harsher destinies of base oils, horse medicines, disinfectants, and cold tea. There were coloured glasses for bitter wines, white glasses for sweet, a tiny leaden sink beneath them, and the four black handles of the beer engines.

The girl wore a light blouse of silk, a short skirt of black velvet, and a pair of very thin silk stockings that showed the flesh of instep and shin so plainly that he could see they were reddened by the warmth of the fire. She had on a pair of dainty cloth shoes with high heels, but what was wonderful about her was the heap of rich black hair piled at the back of her head and shadowing the dusky neck. He sat puffing his pipe and letting the loud tick of the clock fill the quiet room. She did not stir and he could move no muscle. It was as if he had been willed to come there and wait silently. That, he felt now, had been his desire all the evening; and here, in her presence, he was more strangely stirred in a few short minutes than by any event he could remember.

In youth he had viewed women as futile, pitiable things that grew long hair, wore stays and garters, and prayed incomprehensible prayers. Viewing them in the stalls of the theatre from his vantage-point in the gallery, he always disliked the articulation of their naked shoulders. But still, there was a god in the sky, a god with flowing hair and exquisite eyes, whose one stride with an ardour grandly rendered, took him across the whole round hemisphere to which his buoyant limbs were bound like spokes to the eternal rim and axle, his bright hair burning in the pity of the sunsets and tossing in the anger of the dawns.

Master traveler had indeed come into this room to be with this woman, and she as surely desired him, and for all its accidental occasion it was as if he, walking the ways of the world, had suddenly come upon what, what so imaginable with all permitted reverence as, well, just a shrine; and he, admirably humble, bowed the instant head.

Were there no other people within? The clock indicated a few minutes to nine. He sat on, still as stone, and the woman might haven been of wax for all the movement or sound she made. There was allurement in the air between them; he had forborne his smoking, the pipe grew cold between his teeth. He waited for a look from her, a movement to break the trance of silence. No footfall in street or house, no voice in the inn but the clock, beating away as if pronouncing a doom. Suddenly it rasped out nine large notes; a bell in the town repeated them dolefully, and a cuckoo no farther than the kitchen mocked them with three times three. After that came the weak steps of the old landlord along the hall, the slam of doors, the clatter of lock and bolt, and then the silence returning unendurably upon them.

He rose and stood behind her; he touched the black hair. She made no movement or sign. He pulled out two or three combs and, dropping them into her lap, let the whole mass tumble about his hands. It had a curious harsh touch in the unraveling, but was so full and shining; black as a rook's wings it was. He slid his palms through it. His fingers searched it and fought with its fine strangeness; into his mind there traveled a serious thought, stilling his wayward fancy—this was no wayward fancy, but a rite accomplishing itself! (*Run, run, silly man, y'are lost!*) But having got so far, he burnt his boats, leaned over, and drew her face back to him. And at that, seizing his wrist, she gave him back ardour for ardour, pressing his hands to her bosom, while the kiss was sealed and sealed again. Then she sprang up and picking his scarf and hat from the fender said:

"I have been drying them for you, but the hat has shrunk a bit, I'm sure—I tried it on."

He took them from her and put them behind him; he leaned lightly back upon the table, holding it with both his hands behind him; he could not speak.

"Aren't you going to thank me for drying them?" she asked, picking her combs from the rug and repining her hair.

"I wonder why we did that?" he asked, shamedly.

"It is what I'm thinking too," she said.

"You were so beautiful about—about it, you know."

She made no rejoinder, but continued to bind her hair, looking brightly at him under her brows. When she had finished she went close to him.

"Will that do?'

"I'll take it down again."

"No, no, the old man or the old woman will be coming in."

"What of that?" he said, taking her into his arms. "Tell me your name."

She shook her head, but she returned his kisses and stroked his hair and shoulders with beautifully melting gestures.

"What is your name? I want to call you by your name," he said. "I can't keep calling you Lovely Woman, Lovely Woman."

Again she shook her head and was dumb.

"I'll call you Ruth, then, Dusky Ruth, Ruth of the black, beautiful hair."

"That is a nice-sounding name—I knew a deaf and dumb girl named Ruth; she went to Nottingham and married an organ-grinder—but I should like it for my name."

"Then I give it to you."

"Mine is so ugly."

"What is it?"

Again the shaken head and the burning caress.

"Then you shall be Ruth; will you keep that name?"

"Yes, if you give me the name I will keep it for you."

Time had indeed taken them by the forelock, and they looked upon a ruddled world.

"I stake my one talent," he said jestingly, "and behold it returns me fortyfold; I feel like the boy who catches three mice with one piece of cheese."

At ten o'clock the girl said:

"I must go and see how *they* are going on," and she went to the door.

"Are we keeping them up?"

She nodded.

"Are you tired?"

"No, I am not tired." She looked at him doubtfully.

"We ought not to stay in here; go into the coffee room and I'll come there in a few minutes."

"Right," he whispered gaily, "we'll sit up all night."

She stood at the door for him to pass out, and he crossed the hall to the other room. It was in darkness except for the flash of the fire. Standing at the hearth he lit a match for the lamp, but paused at the globe; then he extinguished the match.

"No, it's better to sit in the firelight."

He heard voices at the other end of the house that seemed to have a chiding note in them.

"Lord," he thought, "is she getting into a row?"

Then her steps came echoing over the stone floor of the hall; she opened the door and stood there with a lighted candle in her hand; he stood at the other end of the room, smiling.

"Good night," she said.

"Oh no, no! come along," he protested, but not moving from the hearth.

"Got to go to bed," she answered.

"Are they angry with you?"

"No."

"Well, then, come over here and sit down."

"Got to go to bed," she said again, but she had meanwhile put her candlestick upon the little sideboard and was trimming the wick with a burnt match.

"Oh, come along, just half an hour," he protested. She did not answer, but went on prodding the wick of the candle.

"Ten minutes, then," he said, still not going towards her.

"Five minutes," he begged.

She shook her head and, picking up the candlestick, turned to the door. He did not move, he just called her name: "Ruth!"

She came back then, put down the candlestick, and tiptoed across the room until he met her. The bliss of the embrace was so poignant that he was almost glad when she stood up again and said with affected steadiness, though he heard the tremor in her voice:

"I must get you your candle."

She brought one from the hall, set it on the table in front of him, and struck the match.

"What is my number?" he asked.

"Number-six room," she answered, prodding the wick vaguely with her match, while a slip of white was dropped over the shoulder of the new candle. "Number six… next to mine."

The match burnt out; she said abruptly: "Good night," took up her own candle, and left him there.

In a few moments he ascended the stairs and went into his room. He fastened the door, removed his coat, collar, and slippers, but the rack of passion had seized him and he moved about with no inclination to sleep. He sat down, but there was no medium of distraction. He tried to read the newspapers that he had carried up with him, and without realizing a single phrase. He forced himself to read again the whole account of the execution of the miscreant Bridger. When he had finished this he carefully folded the paper and stood up, listening. He went to the parting wall and tapped thereon with his fingertips. He waited half a minutes, one minute, two minutes; there was no answering sign. He tapped again, more loudly, with his knuckle, but there was no response, and he tapped many times. He opened his door as noiselessly as possible; along the dark passage there were slips of light under the other doors, the one next his own, and the one beyond that. He stood in the corridor listening to the rumble of old voices in the farther room, the old man and his wife going to their rest. Holding his breath fearfully, he stepped to her door and tapped gently upon it. There was no answer, but he could somehow divine her awareness of him; he tapped again; she moved to the door and whispered: "No, no, go away." He turned the handle, the door was locked.

"Let me in," he pleaded. He knew she was standing there an inch or two beyond him.

"Hush," she called softly. "Go away, the old woman has ears like a fox."

He stood silent for a moment.

"Unlock it," he urged; but he got no further reply, and feeling foolish and baffled he moved back to his own room, cast his clothes from him, doused the candle and crept into the bed with soul as wild as a storm-swept forest, his heart beating a vagrant summons. The room filled with strange heat, there was no composure for mind or limb, nothing but flaming visions and furious embraces.

"Morality…what is it but agreement with your own soul?"

So he lay for two hours—the clocks chimed twelve—listening with foolish persistency for her step along the corridor, fancying every light sound—and the night was full of them—was her hand upon the door.

Suddenly, then—and it seemed as if his very heart would abash the house with its thunder—he could hear distinctly someone knocking on the wall. He got quickly from his bed and stood at his door, listening. Again the knocking was heard, and having half-clothed himself he crept into the passage, which was now in utter darkness, trailing his hand along the wall until he felt her door; it was standing open. He entered her room and closed the door behind him. There was not the faintest gleam of light, he could see nothing. He whispered: "Ruth!" and she was standing there. She touched him, but not speaking. He put out his hands, and they met around her neck; her hair was flowing in its great wave about her; he put his lips to her face and found her eyes were streaming with tears, salt and strange and disturbing. In the close darkness he put his arms about her with no thought but to comfort her; one hand had plunged through the long harsh tresses and the other across her hips before he realized that she was ungowned; then he was aware of the softness of her breasts and the cold naked sleekness of her shoulders. But she was crying there, crying silently with great tears, her strange sorrow stifling his desire.

"Ruth, Ruth, my beautiful dear!" he murmured soothingly. He felt for the bed with one hand, and turning back the quilt and sheets, he lifted her in as easily as a mother does her child, replaced the bedding, and, in his clothes, he lay stretched beside her, comforting her. They lay so, innocent as children, for an hour, when she seemed to have gone to sleep. He rose then and went silently to his room, full of weariness.

In the morning he breakfasted without seeing her, but as he had business in the world that gave him just an hour longer at the inn before he left it for good and all, he went into the smoke-room and found her. She greeted him with curious gaze but merrily enough, for there were other men there now—farmers, a butcher, a registrar, an old, old man. The hour passed, but not these men, and at length he donned his coat, took up his stick, and said good-bye. Her shining glances followed him to the door, and from the window as far as they could view him.

Questions

1. The small countrytown the traveler passed by seemed a forlorn and desolate place. Then did he like the place or not, and why?
2. Why were the dish-covers that hung upon the wall of the dinner room arranged in the way known as the "willow pattern"? What may it signify?
3. Why did the narrator say that "the contours of bottles of coloured wines and rich liqueurs seemed destined to charming histories"? How do you understand "charming histories"?
4. How did the traveler regard his encountering with the beautiful black-haired woman in the desolate small town? What was his feeling towards her?
5. A. E. Coppard is a true tale-teller. In this erotic adventurous story he is very economical and colloquial with the language in the dialogue part. However, this story is also an "enchanting love lyric". Then with what language style is the lyrical aspect of the story successfully rendered?

阿尔弗雷德·埃德加·柯帕德
(1878—1957)

阿尔弗雷德·埃德加·柯帕德出生在一个裁缝之家，母亲曾做过女佣。一生大部分时间他都默默无闻地在埃塞克斯乡间的一个农舍度过。当他的第一部短篇小说集《亚当、夏娃和苦恼的我》发表时，他已经43岁了。他的杰出才能很快就被发现，他是那种真正会讲故事的人，没有任何夸大其词。然而，他一直徘徊在英国文学界之外，没有得到任何荣誉，到他79岁去世时，也没赚多少钱。《我的第一百个故事》讲述了他的生平。

他更喜欢故事讲出来而不是读出来。他通过描写英格兰乡村风土人情赢得了自己的声誉。另一部短篇小说集《鱼贩子的琴》（1925）中包括他的代表作《小贩》。他刻画了许许多多小人物，在他们身上揭示了人类生活的复杂而奇妙的本质，例如：女店员、吉卜赛人、小贩、水手、裁缝、流浪汉，以及乡下人。他对乡间的描写充满诗情画意，对乡下人的描写有趣而生动。柯帕德是个怪才艺术家。

黑发露丝

这是一首忧伤而迷人的爱情抒情诗，但却用散文写就。它的魅力或许就在于故事叙述了一个美丽而并不完满的、每个男人内心都渴望邂逅并在多年以后仍难释怀的爱情奇遇。

四月末的一天，春寒料峭，空气潮湿，旅行者来到了一座乡镇。在科滋沃丘陵一带，虽然镇子都小而温馨，旅店也舒适，但那一带的土地总的来说比较阴郁而荒芜。他刚刚踏上丘陵地区的道路，那里是如此空旷寥落、偏僻荒凉，这也许是离乡的游子们修造的，但现在已不知何用，仅仅使得像他这样的陌生人在不经意间打此经过。甚至那原野上向远方伸展的无限绵亘的墙垣、那粗砺的沉积岩的壁垒，也再度显示了岁月的沧桑，每块石头都已风化，颜色微黑，长满了蘑菇状的苔藓。他经过了几个居民区，它们或位于河流的转弯处，或位于开阔的街道的十字路口，那些屋顶茅草已朽的老房子像筛子一样布满了鸟巢，那些房子不是立在那儿，而是散落地堆在那里。远处，偶尔一只云雀或一只黑鹂掠过，惊起一群松鸡，或者一只伶俐的野兔疾驰而过，才使得那不论白天和夜晚都同样令人感到铭心刻骨的寂寥得到一些缓和。但是，这位旅人却格外留意这样的时间和这样的地点。有些人喜欢用心去体会那些眼睛永远也无法看到的事物，至少去感受那种人类永远也无法理解的美的律动，并且去聆听那巨大的、凄凉的回响：那并非是天籁的音乐，而是他们内心徒劳的呼喊。尽管他的衣服像黏土一样粘在身上，旅行者还是从容不迫地以探寻的脚步笃笃地走在小镇的唯一一条街道上，最后走进了旅店，在门口把鞋子蹭了蹭，并且把雨水从帽子上掸下去。接着，他转身进入一间小吸烟室。屋子里有几张桃花心木的桌子，桌子后面、窗子底下以及其他几个角落里固定了几个皮革边的长椅，已经很破旧了。靠一面墙陈设的是同样材质的吧台，不带柜台。对面，明亮的炉火在燃烧着，一位衣着整洁的年轻女人坐在炉前的温莎椅上，盯着火焰。屋内没有其他人，看他进来，女孩站起来迎接他。他了解到可以在此留宿一夜，不一会儿，他的帽子和围巾就摘下来，被放到壁炉架的内侧，他的湿外套被拿到厨房；房东，一位老者，借给了他一双宽松的拖鞋，女佣在隔壁房间摆放晚餐。

他坐着等候时，和酒吧女郎聊了起来。她有一张美丽的面庞，在火光的映衬下却显得十分忧伤；当她的目光从火上移开时，一双明眸熠熠生辉，好像能穿透一切。尽管她友好而又善谈，但面容仍旧有一种明显的忧郁——或许因为屋内光线晦暗，或许是因为天气潮湿，也可能是由于长时间服侍饥渴的客人们喝鸡尾酒的缘故。

当他去吃晚饭时，发现饭菜很合口味，而且还有银色餐具的装点和桃花心木餐桌的衬托，令人胃口大开。没有其他客人，他自己独斟独酌；百叶窗已经放下，灯也点上了，背后的炉火暖烘烘的，很惬意。他在桌边悠然享用，过了好久，一位肤色白皙的女仆过来收拾桌子，一边忙碌着，一边和他闲聊乡下的事儿。这是一个狭长的房间，一端是餐具架和门，另一端是壁炉。有一个书架，上面几乎没有什么书，却放着许多盘子；那面对着窗户的墙很长，空落落的，几乎没挂什么画，却令人不可思议地挂着许多盘盖子，这无疑是有充分理由的；但不知出于什么用意，这些盘盖儿一律被摆成"柳景图案"的形状。有一只甚至扣在地图上面。两幅旧版画陈列其间，上面画的是体态健硕、奋蹄腾奔的骏马，骑在马上的人，长着络腮胡子，穿着彩色的夹克上衣、白色的紧身骑马裤，脸上带着一种冷峻而又无法言传的尊严。

他从架上拿了本书，但很快就没了兴致；他又翻了翻年鉴、当地的电话簿以及各种旅游指南等，最后，换成了手中的《科滋沃纪事》。拿着它，他把椅子拖到壁炉旁，打发时间。报纸上吸引他的是一些广告：剧院上演的剧目、农庄的拍卖会、江湖郎中和魔术师等等，还有一个关于处决当地一个重罪犯的较长篇幅的报道：一个叫提摩西·布里格的在某种可耻的情形下杀了一个婴儿。报纸的内容令人眼花缭乱，对旅行者来说更觉疲倦。于是他放下报纸。

整个镇子像周围的群山一样岑寂，他听不到房子里有一点声音。他起身穿过大厅走到吸烟室。门关着，但里面有灯光，他走了进去。那姑娘依旧独自坐在那里，脚放到壁炉架上，像他刚到时一样。他随手把门带上，坐了下来，盘腿吸着烟斗，欣赏着这个舒适的小房间和姑娘漂亮的身材，他可以毫无窘迫地这样做，因为她陷入了沉思，微微低垂的头扭向另一边。他从吧台的镜子里也能看到她，镜子里还反射出色彩斑斓的酒瓶，里面装着葡萄酒、利口酒等，看起来令人愉悦——这些形态各异的酒瓶如此令人赏心悦目，以致它们似乎注定与令人销魂的故事有关，即使搁置在那儿不用——而那些装着烈酒或啤酒的瓶子，还有装着劣质油、牲口药、消毒剂和凉茶等的比较眼熟的瓶子，则只能与命运较为严酷的故事有关了。此外，还有玻璃杯：彩色的是用来喝苦葡萄酒的；白色的是喝甜葡萄酒的；下面还有一个铅质的洗涤槽和啤酒机的四个手柄。

那姑娘穿一件丝绸的宽松上衣，一条黑色天鹅绒短裙，一双薄如蝉翼的长筒丝袜，把脚背和胫部的肌肉清楚地显露出来，他甚至能看到它们在温暖的炉火的辉映下变得很红润。她脚上穿了一双精致的棉布高跟鞋，但是她身上最令人注目的是那一头浓密的黑发，披垂在脑后，覆盖了她微黑的颈项。他坐在那儿默默地吸着烟斗，钟表的响亮的滴嗒声充满整个安静的房间。她一动也不动，而他也纹丝不动。仿佛他是身不由己地被驱使着到了那里，沉默地等待着。他感到那才是整个晚上他真正想要做的。而在这儿，在她面前，有那么短短几分钟，他感觉到一种奇怪的骚动，是他以前从不曾有过的。

年轻时，他认为女人都是轻浮而可怜的。她们梳长发，穿紧身内衣和吊袜带，做着令人无法理解的祷告。他在剧院楼上的座席间的有利位置向下注视，她们坐在贵宾席上，裸露的肩膀一目了然，他很反感。但是，天上依然有一位神灵，一位长发飘拂、美目流盼的神灵，以极大的热情，跨着巨步，带着他穿越整个地球，他的轻快灵活的四肢依附于这个星球，就像车轮的轮辐永远被缚于外轮和轮轴而转动；他闪闪的金发在如血的残阳中仿佛在燃烧，在喷薄的朝霞中随风飘扬。

这位大旅行家走进这个房间的确是为了和这个女人在一起，而她肯定也在期待着他，因为这一偶然的机缘对他来说，仿佛是穿越了整个世界的漫漫人生路而突然邂逅，就好像遇到了一座神殿，他带着可以想象到的敬畏和值得赞赏的谦恭，立刻俯下了头。

屋内没有其他人吗？时钟指示还差几分九点。他继续坐着，依旧如石雕，而这女人也一声不响、一动不动地像蜡像一样。空气中仿佛有什么在诱惑他们；他已停止吸烟，齿间的烟斗已经变冷了。他等待她的一瞥，或一个动作，好打破这种沉默状态。街道上和房子里都没有脚步声，旅店里没有别的声音，除了时间在钟表的滴嗒声中流逝，似乎在宣告世界末日。突然，时钟以刺耳的声音连续敲了九响，镇上的一个钟也悲哀地重复着，而离厨房不远的一只布谷鸟好像嘲讽一般地唱了三三得九声。之后，传来房东穿过大厅的微弱的脚步声、关门声、上锁和上门闩的咔哒声，然后，静默又一次令人无法忍受地笼罩了房间。

他起来站到她身后，抚摸她的黑发。她既没动，也没有表示。他拿掉二三个小发梳，把头发垂到她的膝上，并让满捧的头发在他手中翻卷。解开她的头发时他感觉到一种奇妙的粗糙，但那黑发却如此稠密而光泽，黑亮如山乌的羽翅。他让手掌在发间滑动。他的手指在探寻，并努力地感觉着这种奇怪的愉悦；他的脑海中闪现出一个严肃的念头——遏制了他的恣意的想象——这不是恣意的想象，而是一个正在完成的庄严的仪式！（跑，快跑，蠢货，你已经迷失了！）但是，到了这会儿，他已经没有退路了，他靠过去，把她的脸转向自己。她就势抓紧他的手腕，热烈地回报他的热情，她把他的手按到她的胸上，两个人以吻封唇。之后，她跳开，从壁炉架上拾起他的围巾和帽子说：

"我已经把围巾和帽子烘干了，但是帽子肯定是缩了一点——我试戴过。"

他把围巾和帽子从她手中接过放到身后，稍微靠回到桌边，两手背到身后拿着围巾和帽子，感到说不出话来。

"你不想谢谢我把它们烘干了吗？"她问，把她的发梳从地毯上拾起来重新别到头发上。

"我在想我们为什么那么做？"他问，很难为情。

"我也在想同样的问题，"她说。

"你知道吗，你那样真的——真的很美？"

她没作声，继续绑她的头发，眼睛从睫毛下愉快地望着他。绑好头发后，她走近他。

"这样好看吗？"

"我会把它再放下来。"

"不，不，房东老头或老太太会随时进来的。"

"那又怎样？"他说，把她揽到怀里。"告诉我你的名字。"

她摇了摇头，但是用吻回应着他的亲吻，同时轻抚着他的头发和肩膀，姿势温柔而优美，他感到自己要融化了。

"你叫什么名字？我想叫你的名字，"他问道，"我不能总叫你可爱的女人，可爱的女人吧？"

她又一次沉默地摇摇头。

"我要叫你露丝，好吧，黑发露丝，美丽的黑发露丝。"

"这名字很好听——我知道有一个聋哑女孩儿叫露丝;她去了诺丁汉并和一个流浪的手风琴手结了婚——但我也喜欢把它作为我的名字。"

"那我就这样称呼你了。"

"我的名字不好听。"

"叫什么?"

还是摇头和热烈的爱抚。

"那你就叫露丝,你会一直叫这个名字吗?"

"是的,如果你给我这个名字,我就为你保留它。"

时间过得飞快,他们眼中的世界变得意乱情迷。

"我拿自己的一个才能打赌,"他开玩笑地说,"你看它给我以四十倍的回报。我感到自己就像那个用一块奶酪捉到三只老鼠的小男孩儿。"

十点钟女孩说:

"我得去看看他们怎样了,"于是她朝门口走去。

"我们打扰他们睡觉了吗?"

她点点头。

"你累了吗?"

"不,我不累。"她犹疑地看着他。

"我们不该待在这儿。到咖啡室去,我随后就到。"

"好,"他快活地耳语,"我们要坐到天亮。"

她站在门边让他过去,他穿过大厅到另一个房间。房间里除了火光的闪烁,一片漆黑。站在炉床前,他擦着了一根火柴,点亮灯,在灯罩前停顿了一下,然后他熄灭火柴。

"不,最好还是坐在火光前。"

他听到房子的另一头传来说话声,听起来有点责备的意思。

"天啊,"他想,"她和人吵架了吗?"

接着,她的脚步声沿着大厅的石头地板传来;她打开门站在那儿,手里拿着一支点燃的蜡烛;他站在房间另一端,微笑着。

"晚安,"她说。

"哦不,不!来吧,"他抗议道,但并没有从炉床边移开。

"应该去睡觉了,"她答道。

"他们对你生气了吗?"

"没有。"

"那好,那么,过来到这儿坐吧。"

"该去睡觉了,"她又说,但边说边把手中的烛台放到小餐具架上,并用一根点着的火柴修剪烛芯。

"哦，来吧，就半个小时，"他抗议着。她没作答，但继续拨弄着蜡烛的烛芯。

"那么，十分钟，"他说，仍旧没有朝她走去。

"五分钟，"他恳求道。

她摇摇头，端起烛台，转向门口。他没有动，他只是叫了她的名字："露丝！"

她走回来，放下烛台，踮着脚尖儿走过房间，直到他们面对面。拥抱带来的巨大幸福强烈到使他感到刺痛，以至于当她再次起身，故作镇静地对他说话时，他几乎感到高兴，尽管他能听到她声音中的颤抖。

"我得去给你拿蜡烛。"

她从厅里拿来一支，把它放到他面前的桌上，划着火柴。

"我的房间号是多少？"他问。

"六号房间，"她答，漫不经心地用火柴杆拨弄烛芯，一滴烛泪滴落到新的蜡烛上。"六号……在我隔壁。"

火柴燃尽了；她突然说："晚安。"拿起她的蜡烛，把他留在那儿了。

过了一会儿，他上楼进入自己的房间。他锁好门，脱掉外套、衣领和拖鞋，但感情的折磨攫住了他，他走来走去，丝毫没有睡意。他坐下来，但没有什么可以分散他的注意力的。他试着读从楼下带上来的报纸，他强迫自己再读一遍关于那个恶棍布里格的详细报道，却一个字也读不进去。当他做完这事，就小心把报纸折好，站起来倾听。他走近分隔两个房间的墙壁，用指尖轻敲。他等了半分钟，一分钟，两分钟；没有回应。他再敲，声音更大一些，用指关节，但仍没有回应，他敲了许多遍。他尽可能不出声地打开房门；沿着黑暗的过道，在其他房门底下透出一线线灯光，他的隔壁，隔壁的隔壁，都有灯光泻出。他站在走廊上，倾听远端那间房里的苍老而低沉的声音，老头和他的妻子即将就寝。他紧张地屏住了呼吸，迈步到她的房门前，在门上轻叩。没有应答。但不知为何他感到她知道自己在门外；他又敲，她走到门边悄悄说："不，不行，走开。"他转了一下门把手，门是锁着的。

"让我进去吧，"他请求到。他知道她就站在门那边离他一二英寸的地方。

"嘘，"她柔声唤道。"走吧，老太太的耳朵像狐狸的那样灵呢。"

他沉默地站了一会儿。

"打开门，"他催促着，但没得到进一步回应。感到自己又可笑又困惑，他走回自己的房间，抛掉衣服，熄灭蜡烛，爬到床上，一颗狂野的灵魂像暴风雨扫过的森林，他的心狂跳，发出任性的呼唤。房间内弥漫着奇怪的热浪，他身心都不得安宁,眼前全都是热烈的场景和激情的拥抱。

"道德……是什么?不就是和灵魂的契约吗?"

于是他躺在那儿有两个小时——钟响了十二下——傻傻地、执著地倾听她的脚步会沿着走廊过来,想象着每一个微小的声响——黑夜充满了这种微小的声响——都是她的手在敲门。

突然,此刻——仿佛他自己的心跳会像响雷一样,使整座房子都为他脸红——他能清楚地听到有人在敲墙。他迅速从床上起来站到门边倾听。又一次听到敲墙声,他半披着衣服,闪进过道,这会儿已经漆黑一片,他用手在墙上摸索着,直到触到她的房门,房门敞开着。他进入她的房间,随手在身后把门关上。没有一丝光线,他什么也看不见。他低语道:"露丝!"她就站在那儿。她抚摸他,没有说话。他伸出双手,环住她的脖颈;她的秀发像巨浪一样在她身体上起伏流动;他用唇触碰她的面颊,发现她泪水盈盈,咸咸的,怪怪的,令人不安。在令人窒息的黑暗中,他用双臂环抱她,只想抚慰她;他一只手探入那粗硬而又浓密的长发中,另一只手滑落到她的腰部,这才意识到她没有穿衣服;他感触到她柔软的胸部和冰凉赤裸而又光滑的肩膀。但是她在哭泣,默默地哭泣,流出大滴的眼泪,她那令人奇怪的悲伤抑制了他的欲望。

"露丝,露丝,我漂亮的宝贝!"他呢喃着安抚道。他一只手向床上摸索,掀开被子和被单,把她轻轻抱起,就像母亲抱着孩子一样,把被子盖好,然后他合衣躺在她身边,抚慰她。他们就这样躺着,像儿童那样单纯,这样过了一个小时,直到她看起来像是睡着了。他起身,默默地走回房间,充满疲惫。

早餐时,他没有见着她,但他还有事,要继续在滚滚红尘中奔波,在他永久地离开这家旅店前仅有的一小时时光,他走进吸烟室找到她。她凝视着他,算做招呼,目光难以捉摸,但却很愉快,房间里还有其他人——几个农民、一个屠夫、一位户籍员、一个很老的老头。一小时就这样流逝了,这些人仍在那儿。最后,他穿上外衣,拿起手杖,说了声再见。她烁烁的目光追随着他到了门口,然后又移到窗户,目送着他渐渐远去。